MODERN HUMANITIES RESEARCH ASSOCIATION
CRITICAL TEXTS
VOLUME 39

EDITOR
JUSTIN D. EDWARDS
(ENGLISH)

JEWELLED TORTOISE
VOLUME 2

EDITORS
STEFANO EVANGELISTA
CATHERINE MAXWELL

SPIRITUAL ADVENTURES

ARTHUR SYMONS

EDITED BY
NICHOLAS FREEMAN

Spiritual Adventures

by
Arthur Symons

Edited with an Introduction and Notes by
Nicholas Freeman

Modern Humanities Research Association
2017

Published by

The Modern Humanities Research Association
Salisbury House
Station Road
Cambridge CB1 2LA
United Kingdom

First published 2017

ISBN 978-1-78188-010-4 (paperback)
ISBN 978-1-78188-613-7 (hardback)

Copies may be ordered from www.tortoise.mhra.org.uk

CONTENTS

ACKNOWLEDGEMENTS

'In what modern editor,' asks George Gissing's Henry Ryecroft, 'shall I find such love and enthusiasm as glows in the annotations of old scholars? Even the best editions of our day have so much of the mere schoolbook; you feel so often that the man does not regard his author as literature, but simply as text. Pedant for pedant, the old is better than the new.' I hope this edition of *Spiritual Adventures* will prove an exception, and that my pedantry would meet with Ryecroft's approval!

I have incurred a great many debts of gratitude while working on this book, and should like to thank the following people and institutions for their help and support. Catherine Maxwell and Stefano Evangelista must have wondered whether this jewelled tortoise would ever crawl across the carpet, and their patience, and that of Gerard Lowe at the MHRA, has been much appreciated. The librarians at the Firestone Collection, Princeton University, were unremittingly helpful, especially when assisting me in navigating my way through Symons's unpublished writings. I should also like to thank the staff of Loughborough University Library, the John Rylands Library, Manchester, the Victoria and Albert Museum (especially Sally Williams), Janet Walwyn at the Bodleian Library, the British Library, the National Library of Scotland, Reading University Library, Bristol University Library, Bristol Public Library, the Harry Ransom Research Center, and the proprietors of numerous antiquarian bookshops, most notably 'Recto and Verso'.

Loughborough University granted me a semester's research leave to work on this project. My colleagues and students at Loughborough have been extremely supportive throughout the process, and if they were ever weary of the name 'Arthur Symons', they did not show it. I extend particular gratitude to Anne-Marie Beller, Carol Bolton, Robert Brocklehurst, Ruth Broughton-Salt, Deborah Burton, Jennifer Cooke, Lucy Dawkins, Merlin Elliot, Kerry Featherstone, Beth Hartshorne, Olivia Hayton, Lina Minou, Isabelle Morgan, Jennifer Nicol, Sarah Parker, Helen Relf, Oliver Tearle, Daniel Watt, and Nigel Wood. Gillian Spraggs answers recondite and stupid questions alike with unblushing good humour.

In the wider world, I am grateful to Kostas Boyiopoulos, Matthew Bradley, Joseph Bristow, Matthew Creasy, William Greenslade, Simon Eliot, Isabella Gaetani, Jason Hall, Ben Hawes, Matthew Ingleby, Stephen James, Alex Murray, Patricia Pulham, John Stokes, Timothy Webb, and Sarah Young. I should also like to thank the members of MIVSS (the Midlands Interdisciplinary Victorian Studies Seminar), and organisers and delegates of the following conferences for widening my knowledge and understanding of the *fin de siècle*: 'Decadent Poetics'

(Exeter University, 2011), 'Victorian Value' (Sheffield University, 2012), 'Decadence and the Senses' (Goldsmiths, 2014), 'Aestheticism and Decadence in the Age of Modernism' (Senate House, 2015), 'Arthur Symons: Writing Across Arts and Cultures' (Venice, September 2015).

Brian Read kindly granted permission to reprint Symons's work. Thank you.

My most heartfelt thanks go to Jan Elliot, my mother Anne, and my sister, Liz. The book is dedicated to the memory of my father, Norman.

INTRODUCTION

~

I

Reviewing Walter Pater's *Imaginary Portraits* in August 1887, the twenty-two-year-old Arthur Symons responded warmly to the book's ambitions and stylistic execution.[1] He had at this point published no fiction of his own, but even at this early stage of his career, he was strongly sceptical of received wisdom. Reading Pater, he suggested, required a different set of expectations from those prompted by conventional narratives, for Pater's idea of characterization was far removed from the narrow constraints of contemporary realist art. '[I]t is quite obvious that neither Watteau, nor Denys, nor Sebastian, nor Duke Carl really lives, in so much as a finger-tip, with actual imaginative life,' Symons announced, audaciously translating what some saw as shortcomings into artistic virtues. '[T]hey are all ghosts, names, puppets of an artist and a philosopher who has constructed them for his purpose, but has not been able, or has not wished, to endow them with flesh and blood, with the breath of life.' Such figures were a world away from those found in the novels of Eliot, Trollope, or Oliphant. They existed instead, 'to give a concrete form to abstract ideas; to represent certain types of character, to trace certain developments, in the picturesque and attractive way of narrative.'

Furthermore, each portrait was 'the study of a soul, or rather of a consciousness', and the book itself was to be regarded as a series of 'studies in narrative form' rather than simply a collection of short stories about historical figures.[2] The language of criticism and pedagogy joined with the very different 'studies' of painters and musicians in formulating a series of practices, intentions, and expectations quite distinct from the main currents of Victorian storytelling. The 'study' would soon become central to Symons's critical method, and even appeared in the subtitle of his account of his madness, *Confessions: A Study in Pathology* (1930). Tellingly, there was nothing in either Pater's portraits or Symons's appraisal of them to encourage readers to identify or even sympathize

---

[1] Arthur Symons, 'Walter Pater, "Imaginary Portraits"', *Time*, 6, n.s. (August 1887), pp. 157–62. The review is reprinted in *Walter Pater: The Critical Heritage*, ed. by R. M. Seiler (London: Routledge, 1980), pp. 175–82.

[2] Symons's terminology and thinking were equally radical here. After all, these comments were made fourteen years before Henry James refers to the figure who would become May Bartram as 'a second consciousness' in his notes for 'The Beast in the Jungle'. See entry for 27 August 1901 in James's *The Complete Notebooks*, ed. by Leon Edel and Lyall H. Powers (Oxford: Oxford University Press, 1987), p. 199.

with their subjects, much less come to a moral assessment of their behaviour. Symons already committed to the idea of art for art's sake which he would champion for the rest of his life, and was quite frank in pointing out that Pater 'feels called upon to draw no moral, to deduce no consequences, from the failures or successes he has chronicled to a certain cumulating point.' Earlier Victorian writers, most famously Dickens, had been celebrated for their skill in the creation of entertaining and realisable (if not always wholly believable) characters who seemed to possess a vital essence wholly distinct from their creator's personality. They also had openly didactic aims, typically through satirical treatments of folly or the extolling of virtue. Pater, by contrast, offered only 'looking within [...] projecting now this now that side of himself on an exterior plane.' The diversity applauded in a painting such as Robert William Buss's *Dickens' Dream* (c. 1875), where the novelist is depicted sitting in his study surrounded by his various creations, was replaced by ever more elaborate variations on a single figure:

> The picture [is always] of a delicate, subtle, aspiring, unsatisfied personality, open to all impressions, living chiefly by sensations [...] a personality withdrawn from action, which it despises or dreads, solitary with its ideals, in the circle of its 'exquisite moments', in the Palace of Art, where it is never quite at rest.[3]

Symons's review of *Imaginary Portraits* revealed an obvious admiration for Pater, but the young critic was no mere idolator. Original and incisive, he was clearly at odds with many Victorian conventions and indeed, keen to supplant them. His search for a new aesthetic would, in time, produce a remarkable body of work which, in its daring engagement with continental literature and art, its disdain for accepted moral standards, and its abiding concern with the subtleties of creative subjectivity, would prove highly influential.

II

Symons's review of *Imaginary Portraits* was an early indication of the sensitivity and insight applauded by W. B. Yeats, who felt that, 'more than any man I have ever known, [Symons] could slip as it were into the mind of another'.[4] He delighted in his friend and fellow poet's subtle appreciation and understanding of creativity, which made him an excellent sounding board for his own ideas, but this intellectual malleability was to prove a mixed blessing. T. S. Eliot would in due course theorize the choosing of one's contemporaries in 'Tradition and the

---

[3] The 'exquisite moments' are, of course, those of the 'Conclusion' to Pater's *The Renaissance* (1873). 'The Palace of Art' is a poem by Tennyson, originally published in 1832 (revised 1842).
[4] W. B. Yeats, 'The Trembling of the Veil, Book IV: The Tragic Generation' (1922), in *Autobiographies*, ed. by William H. O'Donnell and Douglas N. Archibald (New York: Scribner, 1999), p. 246.

Individual Talent' (1919), but Symons's choices were more intuitive than
systematic, deriving from his tastes and temperament rather than a consistent
schema. He certainly responded most warmly and insightfully to those writers
and artists for whom he felt some personal or artistic affinity, and the versions
he fashioned of them at once influenced and reflected his own concerns. Pater,
Verlaine, Baudelaire, and Whistler quickly became central to his thinking about
art, and their influence on his fiction is very clear. From Pater, who presided over
Spiritual Adventures and his critical essays, he took a fascination with interdisciplinary aesthetic relationships and a preoccupation with the 'delicate, subtle,
aspiring, unsatisfied personality, open to all impressions, living chiefly by
sensations' which became his literary trademark. He also thoroughly absorbed
Pater's gospel of momentariness and 'the destructive power of living as the sort
of seeker after beauty which Pater appears to counsel.'[5] Verlaine and Whistler
imbued him with a sensitivity to nuance, and the power of the implied over the
starkly stated, qualities which manifested themselves in his lyrical and descriptive
writing. Finally Baudelaire, the most enduring of the four and the one who would
become dominant in the years following Symons's breakdown, supplied a
fascination with cities and modern life, not to mention forms of sexuality Symons
saw as perverse, morbid, Satanic, and wholly fascinating. Perhaps most
significantly, reading Baudelaire encouraged him to believe that 'rules are made
for normal people by normal people, and the man of genius is fundamentally
abnormal.'[6] 'The artist, it cannot be too clearly understood, has no more part in
society than a monk in domestic life: he cannot be judged by its rules, he can
neither be praised nor blamed for his acceptance or rejection of its conventions,'
he wrote in a later essay.[7] Such a thesis shapes the characters of Christian
Trevalga, Peter Waydelin, and, in the last analysis, Symons himself.

III

The 1890s were a tumultuous decade for Symons. He had arrived in London in
1891, the son of a Methodist minister whose provincial upbringing had left him
eager to experience all the capital could offer. Renting rooms in Fountain Court
in the Temple, he swiftly metamorphosed from the young man who signed
himself 'Arthur W. Symons of Yeovil' into 'Silhouette', the dramatic critic of the

---

[5] Wendell V. Harris, *British Short Fiction in the Nineteenth Century: A Literary and
Bibliographic Guide* (Detroit: Wayne State University Press, 1979), p. 79.
[6] Symons, 'Paul Verlaine', *The Symbolist Movement in Literature*, ed. Matthew Creasy (1900;
Manchester: Carcanet, 2014), p. 43. He was still reiterating this claim forty years later. See his
Confessions: A Study in Pathology (London: Jonathan Cape, 1930), p. 5.
[7] Symons, 'Unspiritual Adventures in Paris' (1913), in *Wanderings* (London: Dent, 1931),
p. 77.

Star.[8] He stressed always the inspiration of Pater's *Marius the Epicurean: His Sensations and Ideas* (1885), but he was perhaps more influenced by the version of Pater's ideas propounded by Oscar Wilde, one which vulgarized them on some levels but made them extremely appealing to would-be young writers and men-about-town. Like Dorian Gray, Symons heard only too clearly the seductive exhortations of Lord Henry to 'Live the wonderful life that is in you! Let nothing be lost upon you. Be always searching for new sensations'.[9] He belonged to the Rhymers' Club, contributed to the *Yellow Book*, wrote for most of London's major reviews, produced a definitive account of Anglo-French literary relations in his essay, 'The Decadent Movement in Literature' (1893), gamely carried the banner for avant-garde art in the post-Wilde climate by founding *The Savoy* in the summer of 1895, and travelled from Constantinople to Seville, from Naples to Prague, always restless, always seeking to capture his evanescent impressions in poetry and prose. His poetry, particularly his second and third collections, *Silhouettes* (1892) and *London Nights* (1895) caused controversy with its frank portrayals of sexual commerce, but it also broke new ground in its experiments with impressionism and indeed, in its willingness to tackle subject matter many deemed unsavoury and attempt its transmutation into art. He had a gift for forging influential friendships, and to judge by his self-estimation, a powerful appeal for women, though as Yeats told James Joyce, 'Symons had always a longing to commit a great sin,' but was never 'able to get beyond ballet girls.'[10] One of these, 'Lydia', renamed 'Bianca' in a number of poems, was his lover between late 1893 and early 1896, and haunted him ever after.[11] Others meant

---

[8] This was how Symons signed himself in his first published article, 'Robert Browning as Religious Poet', *Wesleyan-Methodist Magazine*, 6 (December 1882), pp. 943–47. The Temple is an area of central London associated with English legal system; it houses many barristers' and solicitors' offices. It takes its name from the Knights Templar, who owned the land during the medieval period. Symons moved into rooms in Fountain Court in January 1891, describing his residence as 'the realization of a dream' (Beckson, *Arthur Symons: A Life*, p. 65). Sharing that at times with the Irish novelist, George Moore, the sexologist and critic, Havelock Ellis, and W. B. Yeats, Symons kept the rooms until January 1901, finally moving out in preparation for his marriage. It was at Fountain Court that he wrote much of his best poetry and criticism, and also enjoyed many sexual adventures, notably those involving the mysterious Lydia. His poems 'In the Temple' (2 March 1891) and 'In Fountain Court' (11 June 1891) from *Silhouettes* record his early delight in living there. See too 'In the Temple' (1 January 1893) from *London Nights*. Alvin Langdon Coburn's photogravure, 'The Temple' in his *London* (1909) records the view from Symons's window.

[9] Oscar Wilde, *The Picture of Dorian Gray*, ed. by Joseph Bristow (1891; Oxford: World's Classics, 2006), p. 22.

[10] Stanislaus Joyce, *My Brother's Keeper* (New York: Viking, 1958), p. 197.

[11] Lydia was a London ballet dancer, apparently the illegitimate daughter of a Spaniard (with gypsy blood) and an Englishwoman. Symons kept photographs of her for the rest of his life, but he never records her full name. See Beckson, *Arthur Symons: A Life*, pp. 100–03. She is 'Bianca' in *London Nights*, and the unnamed lover throughout *Amoris Victima* (1897).

far less. They included Violet Pigott, a dancer who appears as 'Lilian' in early poems and 'The Extra Lady' (1895), and Josephine 'Cassie' Casaboni, with whom Symons was involved in the summer of 1893, before she rose to become principal dancer at London's Alhambra.[12] Symons was a stage-door Don Juan, and a steady stream of dancers, ingénues, and prostitutes, muses of a sort, made their patchouli and peau d'espagne-scented way through his rooms, his transient passions for them celebrated in his lyrics and unpublished reminiscences.[13]

During this exciting and extremely busy period of Symons's life, he was active as a reviewer (of everything from contortionists to George Meredith), a notable poet, an editor (*The Savoy* ran from January to December 1896), and a literary theorist. In his major work, *The Symbolist Movement in Literature* (1900), he made a determined attempt to move away from the 'decadence' with which he had been strongly associated in the mid-1890s by reading contemporary French fiction with an eye to its mystical properties, hoping to 'spiritualise literature, to evade the old bondage of rhetoric, the old bondage to exteriority' and re-fashioning literary art as 'a kind of religion, with all the duties and responsibilities of the sacred ritual'.[14] Kelsey Thornton has suggested that the doctrine of the symbol allowed Symons to fuse the world of lived experience with the transcendental and imaginative, so that 'the ideal and the real' were, through the symbol, 'at once life and art, real and ideal, timeless and in time'.[15] This aesthetic underpinned some of Symons's lyric poetry, and the epiphanic perceptions of his essays on cities, musicians, and artists, but his deployment of it was erratic, and his ability to develop and refine the idea handicapped by his burgeoning literary and journalistic commitments.

Symons's career can be divided into several phases. Born in Milford Haven, Pembrokeshire, in February 1865, he belonged to a generation which would come to prominence during the 1890s, the era with which he remains most closely associated.[16] His father's ministerial work meant regular changes of parish; the Symons family moved with him from Wales to the Channel Islands, Cornwall, Devon, Somerset, Northumberland, Warwickshire, and finally to Buckingham. Perennial upheavals meant that Symons's schooling was often irregular (he did not learn to read 'properly', as he put it, until he was nine) and also instilled a

---

[12] Their relationship is documented in 'Notes on the Sensations of a Lady of the Ballet' (1914).
[13] See his boastful treatment of these encounters in 'The Confessions of Arthur Symons: Part One', *Two Worlds* (New York) 2 (September 1926), pp. 27–34, repr. as 'Bohemian Years in London', in *The Memoirs of Arthur Symons: Life and Art in the 1890s*, ed. by Karl Beckson (University Park: Pennsylvania State University Press, 1977), pp. 70–74.
[14] Symons, *The Symbolist Movement in Literature*, p. 8.
[15] R. K. R. Thornton, *The Decadent Dilemma* (London: Edward Arnold, 1983), p. 164.
[16] His contemporaries included Arthur Machen (1863–1947), Rudyard Kipling (1865–1936), W. B. Yeats (1865–1939), H. G. Wells (1866–1946), Beatrix Potter (1866–1943), Lionel Johnson (1867–1902), and Ernest Dowson (1867–1900).

sense of detachment regarding place and nation. Bookish and artistically-inclined (the influence of his mother rather than his father), Symons read widely (if idiosyncratically), wrote verse imitations of Byron, Swinburne, and Scott, taught himself the piano, and developed a remarkable gift for languages which would see him in time add French, Italian, Spanish, German, and Romany to the typical bourgeois Englishman's Latin and Greek.[17] He soon began to practise criticism as well as creative composition, making his debut with 'Robert Browning as Religious Poet', a contribution to the December 1882 number of the *Wesleyan-Methodist Magazine*, for which he was paid 21 shillings.

Between 1882 and the appearance of his first collection of poetry, *Days and Nights*, in 1889, Symons developed into a hard-working textual editor and reviewer-critic, attempting to become established in the literary world despite lacking the inestimable advantages of a university education, a private income, and metropolitan residence. From 1889 until the collapse of *The Savoy* at the end of 1896, he was closely associated with first impressionism (notably in *Silhouettes*) and then, more controversially, decadence, becoming the movement's historian, theoretician, and sponsor as well as one of its leading poets. After this, his close friendship with Yeats drew him further into the investigation of symbolist doctrines, something he had first discussed in 'The Decadent Movement in Literature' but to which he now returned in the aftermath of Wilde's downfall and long conversations with the Irish poet in Fountain Court. It was here that Emily Burbank, an American acquaintance, heard him discuss Christina Rossetti's poetry:

> I can see him now, big, blond and very English, his hands deep in the pockets of his gray tweeds; an old, brown velveteen jacket, faded blue socks, and soft tan slippers, harmonizing with his 'stage-setting' — well mellowed by time. Books lined the walls, and a spinnet [*sic*], on which Symons played when alone, stood in one corner.[18]

This period ended with his marriage to Rhoda Bowser in January 1901 and his moving out of the Temple. Although he remained friends with Yeats until his breakdown at the end of 1908, his working and social life changed quite markedly, largely because of a rash determination that the newlyweds would live on his income despite Rhoda being the daughter of a wealthy shipbuilder. The unwise purchase of a seventeenth-century Kent cottage, and the requirement for the maintenance of a London *pied-à-terre* as a base from which Rhoda could pursue her largely forlorn theatrical ambitions combined with Symons's desire for regular foreign travel and apparent refusal to pursue employment which would

---

[17] He claimed to struggle with German, though it did not prevent him from travelling around the country, translating Heine and von Hofmannsthal, and studying Wagner's libretti.
[18] Emily M. Burbank, 'Josiah Flynt — An Impression', in Flynt's *My Life* (New York: Outing Publishing Co., 1908), p. 345.

comfortably underwrite such a lifestyle, such as the editorship of one of the prestigious reviews.[19] The consequence was a steady increase in the amount of journalistic commissions he accepted, a decline in the quality of his verse, and the growing incompatibility between his ambition to produce a coherent aesthetic philosophy and the piecemeal methods by which it was pursued.

IV

Symons's bibliography reveals that the years in which he was writing *Spiritual Adventures* saw him publish at least one review, essay, or other critical piece every week, in addition to pursuing his increasingly side-lined creative work. Some of these contributions to periodicals were lengthy and complex, their author judging them worthy of collection in books such as *Plays, Acting and Music* or *Cities* (both 1903). Others were briefer notices of music hall or theatrical entertainments, reviews of recitals, exhibitions, or now-forgotten plays. Few were seriously remunerative, and such a volume of commitments surely retarded his progress as a poet: Roger Lhombreaud points out that his collected works contain 125 poems from between 1896 and 1898, but only thirty between 1901 and the end of 1903.[20] Despite believing that the newspaper was 'the plague, or black death, of the modern world', Symons could never escape its clutches or cure himself of the vain pleasures of seeing his name before the public.[21] He may have posed as a worldly bohemian, a man who, like Byron's Childe Harold, 'vexed with mirth the drowsy ear of night', giving himself over to 'concubines and carnal companie', but his louche persona only partially disguised how well suited he was to the rigours of Fleet Street. He rarely if ever missed deadlines, and his copy typically required very little by way of editorial intervention. He could be direct and accessible when writing for a general readership in the *Star*, or offer sophisticated erudition in *The Weekly Critical Review*; his assessments of poetry in *The Athenæum* were perceptive, judicious, even, on occasion, witty, and he had a flair for generating debate and controversy which his editors often appreciated. He was also a gifted diplomat, who seems to have been able to work alongside such powerful personalities as Charles Lewis Hind, editor of *The Academy*, or Frank Harris of the *Saturday Review*.

These attributes, together with an initially robust constitution — his friend Havelock Ellis recalled, until his breakdown 'he had no serious illness and seemed

---

[19] Island Cottage in Wittersham's Swan Street still stands, and was made a listed building in 1979. It may have been ruinously expensive for Symons and Rhoda, but it is a desirable property today, selling for £497,000 in February 2006 and now worth substantially more.

[20] Roger Lhombreaud, *Arthur Symons: A Critical Biography* (London: Unicorn Press, 1963), p. 187.

[21] Symons, 'A New Guide to Journalism', *Saturday Review* 96 (8 August 1903), p. 165.

never to know fatigue' — conspired to lead Symons away from his creative work, even if he ostensibly regarded critical writing as merely another form of artistic expression.[22] They also won his contributions to newspapers and periodicals a far wider readership than he ever gained from his poetry, travel essays, editing, or reviews. *The Symbolist Movement in Literature*, issued by Heinemann in March 1900 and swiftly recognized as Symons's most important work, had an initial run of only 750 copies. Symons's stock rose a little when it was well-received, but the types of critical study he offered had little appeal to a general audience — many of the texts discussed in *The Symbolist Movement* were then unavailable in English translation — and those who appreciated his essays may already have read them in periodicals. *Plays, Acting and Music*, published by Duckworth in September 1903, received an initial run of 1250 copies, *Cities* (J. M. Dent, October 1903), ostensibly more appealing because it showcased travel writing rather than aesthetic criticism, 1600, and *Studies in Prose and Verse*, also issued by Dent in November 1904, 1650. None of these had a rapid or prolonged sale: *The Symbolist Movement* apparently sold a third of its run in less than a month, but was not reprinted for eight years.

In short, Symons's voice was a significant one in London's literary media, but did not carry far beyond it. He moved from publisher to publisher, remaining on good terms with most but never finding one willing to provide the level of support and indulgence support Hardy received from Osgood, McIlvaine or James from Macmillan: his titles only rarely appear in block capitals at the head of advertisements of forthcoming attractions. Symons wrote about places few of his readers had visited for themselves, but they were not genuinely exotic (or fashionable) enough to inspire sustained interest, and his temperamental reconstruction of the British Isles as essentially London, Cornwall, and the Irish west coast meant he had only limited followers in either the provinces or the principalities. His wanderings never took him as far north as Scotland and despite persistently hymning the joys of urban life, he had little interest in what they might constitute for the denizens of Birmingham or Leeds. Unlike contemporaries such as Richard Le Gallienne, he gave no public lectures and did not possess an especially marketable public image. 'I am only known to a limited number, and only a limited number (though I hope a much larger one) will ever buy my books to any great extent,' he told Rhoda in March 1900. 'My books have so far brought me almost nothing,' he added, pointing out that it was 'the magazine articles, translations, that pay.'[23] Pater addressed 'a public within the

---

[22] Havelock Ellis to Louis J. Bragman, 13 August 1933, in *Arthur Symons: Selected Letters, 1880–1935*, ed. by Karl Beckson and John M. Munro (Basingstoke: Macmillan, 1989), p. 269. Ellis was responding to Bragman's 'The Case of Arthur Symons: The Psychopathology of a Man of Letters', *British Journal of Medical Psychology* 12 (1932), pp. 346–62.

[23] Symons to Rhoda Bowser, 6 March 1900, in Lhombreaud, *Arthur Symons*, p. 176.

public; those fine students of what is fine in art, who take their artistic pleasures consciously, deliberately, critically, with the learned love of the amateur.'[24] This may have been Symons's ideal, but his personal circumstances and lifestyle were far removed from those of the retiring Oxford don. Like Peter de Vries in a later day, or perhaps James's Ralph Limbert in 'The Next Time' (1895), Symons would have liked 'a mass audience large enough for his elite audience to despise.'[25] 'I have never understood what a compromise was,' he wrote in 1913, 'or, indeed, any concession to circumstances.'[26]

Unfortunately, despite his best efforts, he remained tainted by the scandals of the 1890s, and those antipathetic to his outlook tended to regard him as a relic of that decade. In 1910, Edward Thomas remarked that 'in this critic's composition the literary aesthete is too predominant still, as at one time it was supreme', a view reinforced by many subsequent commentators, notably Eliot in *The Sacred Wood* (1920).[27] A change in national mood prompted by the growing seriousness of war in South Africa left his art-for-art's-sake credo at odds with what the *Times Literary Supplement* later termed 'fighting-for-fighting's sake',[28] and he had only limited success in the growing American periodicals market, despite (or perhaps because of) 'The Decadent Movement in Literature' having appeared in *Harper's New Monthly Magazine*.

In 'Pachmann and the Piano' (1902), Symons noted that the reappraisal of Chopin's music had occurred 'not because the taste of any public has improved, but because a few people who knew have whispered the truth to one another, and at last it has leaked out like a secret.' This might be a summation of Symons's approach to writing on art, in that he sought to influence the discerning who might then shape wider opinion, rather than attempting to educate a mass audience. Such a project required diligent labour and membership of differing networks of influence, and by the early years of the twentieth century, working extremely hard as a literary journalist, Symons was unable to give it his complete attention. He was writing dramatic criticism for the *Star* almost daily (and being paid £4 a week), commenting on painting and sculpture for *The Outlook*, and

---

[24] Symons, 'Walter Pater', in *Strangeness and Beauty: An Anthology of Aesthetic Criticism 1840–1910, Volume II*, ed. by Eric Warner and Graham Hough (Cambridge: Cambridge University Press, 1983), p. 216. Originally published as 'Walter Pater: Some Characteristics', *The Savoy*, No. 8 (December 1896), pp. 33–41. The essay was reprinted as the introduction to Georges Khnopff's translation of *Imaginary Portraits, Portraits imaginaires* (1899).
[25] Christopher Hichens, 'Tragicomic Clive James', *TLS* (17 November 2006), p. 12.
[26] Symons, *For Api*, XV, *Collected Works: Poems III* (London: Martin Secker, 1924), p. 322.
[27] Edward Thomas, review of Symons's *The Romantic Movement in English Literature*, *Morning Post*, 20 January 1910, p. 5. For Eliot's views on Symons, see his *Inventions of the March Hare: Poems 1909–1917*, ed. by Christopher Ricks (London: Faber, 1996), pp. 394–409.
[28] Anon. [Francis Gribble], 'The Yellow 'Nineties', [Review of Holbrook Jackson's *The 1890s*], *TLS* (4 December 1913), p. 587.

producing regular pieces for the *Monthly Review* on theatre, music, and musicians. Symons had pressing financial reasons to turn to fiction in the early twentieth century, but despite the expenses associated with his married life, there seems to have been no suggestion that *Spiritual Adventures* represented a determinedly commercial project. Whether or not he and Rhoda had conversations akin to those between Edwin and Amy Reardon in Gissing's *New Grub Street* (1891), Symons had no intention of writing a pot-boiler.[29] Had he been prepared to make an artistic compromise in pursuit of financial reward, he would surely have attempted a novel or a fashionable play, something which drew either on his bohemian days in London's theatres, his travels, or else tailored his short stories more determinedly for publication in magazines such as *Pearson's* or *The Strand* instead of *The Dome* or *The Senate*. Even the most elite-minded of artists rarely return their royalty cheques, but though Symons would have appreciated a bestseller's boost to his income, he remained a purist. His primary motivation was to extend the artistic theorizing of *Plays, Acting and Music* and other works to the creative sphere, applying the same critical intelligence found in his essays to the evocation of subjectivity.

V

In his preface to *Plays, Acting and Music*, Symons outlined his ambitious critical agenda in 'gradually working my way towards the concrete expression of a theory, or system of aesthetics, of all the arts.'[30] His quest had begun with the literary analyses of *The Symbolist Movement*, had moved into music and drama, and would, he said, expand in *Studies in Seven Arts* (1906) to considerations of painting, sculpture, architecture, handicrafts, dance, and acting. 'Each art has its own laws,' he concluded, 'its own capacities, its own limits; these it is the business of the critic to jealously distinguish.' He would make a similar point to Rhoda in the acknowledgements of *Studies in Seven Arts*, via a lengthy quotation from 'The School of Giorgione' in which Pater rebuked a tendency 'of popular criticism' to assume that all art was merely a 'translation into different languages' of 'the same fixed quantity of imaginative thought'. Pater insisted that poetry, painting, and music each had their specific 'sensuous material' and 'a special phase or quality of beauty untranslatable into the forms of any other'.[31] While Symons agreed with this, he claimed too that a critic's 'study of art as art' compelled him 'to

---

[29] 'I don't write (as Conrad for one has to) pot-boilers, and am even now not anything like as popular as I ought to be,' Symons told John Quinn in January 1921. *Selected Letters*, p. 247.
[30] Symons, 'Preface' to *Plays, Acting and Music: A Book of Theory* (London: Duckworth, 1903), p. vii.
[31] Walter Pater, *The Renaissance: Studies in Art and Poetry* quoted in Symons, 'To Rhoda', *Studies in Seven Arts* (London: Archibald Constable, 1906), p. v.

endeavour to master the universal science of beauty', an insistence which in his case would in time lead to 'tempting and easy conclusions', particularly when deadlines were pressing and he was thrown back on personal perceptions rather than scholarly discipline and research.[32] It was one thing to be a critic of catholic tastes and interests who could comment intelligently on a Wagnerian music-drama or the paintings of G. F. Watts, but quite another to address these and many other aesthetic productions through a single, unifying lens, particularly when one's preferred critical medium was the discrete essay. What tended to link Symons's perceptions was less a consciously worked 'system of aesthetics' than a series of personal judgements and affiliations, or, as Derek Stanford puts it, 'Behind his "appreciations" there is no firm structure of ideas, social, religious, or philosophical. His criticism of literature takes place within a cultural context consisting almost solely of travel, languages, and the arts.'[33]

Symons saw almost everything from the same viewpoint, and gave successive essays a patina of interconnectedness by using particular touchstones, quotations, and allusions reinforced on occasion by self-plagiarism, the latter a consequence of his hectic schedule but also a mark of his commitment to particular opinions and ideas. The more essays, causeries, and reviews he wrote, the harder it would be to imply their overall coherence when they were harvested in volume form, but he seemed not to perceive this difficulty, or, if he did, failed to resist it forcefully enough. Worse still, rather than consolidating his empire, he sought instead new worlds to conquer. 'And, as life too is a form of art, and the visible world the chief storehouse of beauty,' he argued in *Studies in Seven Arts*, 'I try to indulge my curiosity by the study of places and people.' This would involve first, the urban evocations of *Cities*, in which Symons confessed:

> It is part of my constant challenge to myself, in everything I write, to be content with nothing short of that *vraie vérité* which one imagines to exist somewhere on this side of ultimate attainment. It is so much easier to put oneself into things than to persuade things to give up their own secrets; and I like to aim at this difficult kind of truth.[34]

It would then lead on to 'a book of "imaginary portraits"' to be called *Spiritual Adventures*. Not content with seeking a critical language or method that could encompass with equal facility puppet theatre and the paintings of Degas, Symons now moved into using fiction as a tool for the exploration of consciousness and doing exactly what he had assured the Comtesse de la Tour, the dedicatee of *Cities*, he had tried to avoid. *Cities* is often beautifully written, but it is at heart a

---

[32] Symons, *Plays, Acting and Music*, p. ix; *Studies in Seven Arts*, p. v. Christian Trevalga believes that 'there is but one art, but many languages through which men speak it.'
[33] Derek Stanford, 'Arthur Symons' in his *Critics of the 'Nineties* (London: John Baker, 1970), p. 115.
[34] Symons, 'Dedication', *Cities* (London: J. M. Dent, 1903), pp. vi–vii.

series of impressionistic colonizations in which the perceptions of the author appropriate Venice or Prague or Budapest, relegating their actual inhabitants to the status of imaginative stimuli or local colour. The *TLS* observed that 'these pictures of many places leave in our mind a garish and unnatural impression, as of people in a ballet rather than of men who must work to live and bury their dead.'[35] As someone who frequently remarked that he saw the world in exactly these terms, Symons could scarcely contest the justice of the comment, but it did reveal how his exquisite perceptions were somewhat out of step with those of Edwardian England.

In a consideration of Pater's *Imaginary Portraits*, Elisa Bizzotto points out how the form, at least in Pater's hands, 'resulted from a combination of narrative writing and critical writing on figurative arts', one galvanized by a late nineteenth-century interest in 'artistic hybridization.' Pater's 1878 letter to George Grove concerning 'The Child in the House' explained that the story was meant to prompt the same thoughts in a reader that might occur to a viewer of a painted portrait, namely, 'what came of him?' This, Bizzotto explains, emphasizes not only the 'contiguity' of literary and artistic portraiture, but also 'the reader's active and sympathetic involvement' with the work's 'central personality.' The process 'requires a co-participation, or even an identification, of the reader and, implicitly, the author of the literary work with its subject in order to both communicate and grasp its essence.'[36] Pater's experiments took place at a historical moment when autobiography and biography were increasingly popular and artistically defensible modes of writing, yet as Bizzotto observes, prefixing a work with 'imaginary' automatically complicates any presumed relationship between the portraitist and their creation. Pater went to significant lengths to do this, adopting, for example, the character of a female diarist to observe the progress of Antoine Watteau in 'A Prince of Court Painters', or opening 'Duke Carl of Rosenmold' at the turn of the nineteenth century before almost immediately pushing the narrative back another hundred years. In Pater's hands, therefore, or indeed, in those of Vernon Lee, the imaginary portrait could conceal and reveal while at the same time blurring any clear distinction between those terms. It could be read as a 'short story', but only if the reader accepted that it would also contain elements of history (both verifiable and invented), criticism, mythography, and plentiful allusion, the whole operating in texts whose

---

[35] Anon. [Mrs William Wyamer Vaughan], 'Venice and Other Cities' [Review of Symons's *Cities*], *TLS* (20 November 1903), p. 336. The critic also pointed out that 'All Mr Symons's female population is "animal"; he discovers the fact afresh in each city', identifying a recurrent motif in his travel journalism.

[36] Elisa Bizzotto, 'The Imaginary Portrait: Pater's Contribution to a Literary Genre', in *Walter Pater: Transparencies of Desire*, ed. by Laurel Brake, Lesley Higgins, and Carolyn Williams (Greensboro, NC: ELT Press, 2002), pp. 214–15.

wide-ranging, multi-disciplinary and often obscure references could be recognized only by the most educated, intelligent, and observant readers.[37] Reticent and evasive as Pater was, the extent to which his 'portraits' are vehicles for self-exploration and analysis must remain wholly speculative.

If Pater used his imaginary portraits to scrutinize and critique himself, then he did so through the smoked glass of historical and geographical distance. Symons however set his stories very much in the present, at times giving his self-portraiture (and concomitant self-absorption) only cursory disguise. His first excursions into fiction, such as 'The Extra Lady' were strongly autobiographical, allowing him to explore the types of encounter recorded in the poems of *Silhouettes* and *London Nights* in more detail than was allowed in a fugitive lyric, and letting him practise the impressionist effects that would become characteristic of his later essays on travel and art. 'The first thing is to see,' he wrote later, 'and then to write, from a selecting memory'.[38] The stories of *Spiritual Adventures* were less transparent, but even those in which his avatars did not play a leading role were shaped by his experiences, friendships, and perceptions, as for instance, when evoking Methodist revivalism on the Cornish coast, or somewhat unscrupulously borrowing details of his mistress's life in order to replay them as French naturalist-inflected art. In his critical essays, Symons seems to have differentiated between creative artists, Wagner, Verlaine, and Whistler, for example, and interpretative ones such as the dancer, Jane Avril, or the cabaret singer, Yvette Guilbert. This distinction, which is generally implicit in his critical writing, is less a matter of sex than of temperament: the 'feminine' temperament, which is traditionally regarded as passive, is less creative than its assertively 'masculine' counterpart. Such a binary model has significant implications for Symons's own practice, caught as he is between 'creative' writer and 'interpretative' critic or editor, and it is played out in many of his short stories, notably 'Esther Kahn', 'Christian Trevalga', and 'The Death of Peter Waydelin', all of which interrogate the relationship between the production of art *ex nihilo* (if such is possible) and the refashioning of a script or score by a gifted performer, a creative act which continually threatens to destabilize convenient polarities. In these fictions, 'the disappearance of the self is a necessary antecedent for the conversion to art.'[39]

---

[37] Lene Østermark-Johansen begins her edition of the stories with the frank admission, 'Editing Walter Pater is no small task, and one inevitably ends up in academic areas far beyond one's own field of expertise.' *Imaginary Portraits* (London: MHRA, 2014), p. x.

[38] Symons, 'Impressionistic Writing', from *Dramatis Personae* (1923). Reprinted in his *Selected Poetry and Prose*, ed. by R. V. Holdsworth (Cheadle Hulme: Carcanet, 1974), p. 93.

[39] Jan B. Gordon, 'The Dialogue of Life and Art in Arthur Symons's *Spiritual Adventures*', *English Literature in Transition* 12.3 (1969), p. 112.

The relationship between the Symons who wrote *Spiritual Adventures* and the semi-fictionalized author surrogates depicted within it is often rather more obvious than any corresponding relationship in Pater, though his unpublished essay, 'The Genesis of Spiritual Adventures', probably written in the late 1920s, reveals nothing of consequence where his general intentions for the book are concerned.[40] Symons was undeniably interested in theatricality, masks, make-up, and performance, but while some of his contemporaries, Henry Harland for example, fashioned various alter-egos and alternative identities, he showed little intention to follow suit.[41] Symons's authorial persona was neither the flamboyant 'Yellow Dwarf' (Harland's waspish guise when editor of the *Yellow Book*) nor a radical departure from personal experience, but a polishing and idealisation of actuality. Like Wordsworth, Symons invariably gave the impression of being solitary when he was actually accompanied (often by Havelock Ellis before his marriage, and Rhoda after it), and portrayed himself as untroubled by such vulgar obligations as money, deadlines, or train timetables even though they must have intruded frequently upon his contemplative detachment. The Daniel Roserra who makes his melancholy way along the rain-lashed Allée des Tombeaux in 'An Autumn City' is essentially Symons as he might have been; his perceptions of Arles are Symons's own (as can be seen from his essays on the town), and even the story's overtly fictional element, the character of Livia, is a result of transplanting feelings, desires, and realizations from one context into another. However much Symons felt the erotic allure of Lydia, his one-time mistress, he must have suspected that as an uneducated dancer, she would probably have struggled to participate in his imaginative and creative life to the same degree as she did his sexual one.[42] Only the first story, 'A Prelude to Life' was ostensibly autobiographical, but Symons's travels, tastes, outlook, and attitudes surfaced throughout the collection, and even the title's initials are the mirror image of his own.[43] There is also little attempt to find different styles of expression: Symons's

---

[40] 'The Genesis of Spiritual Adventures' is an unpublished, undated, and unpaginated forty-three page typescript held at Princeton University (C0182, Arthur Symons Papers, Box 9, Folder 7). Obviously typed by the elderly Symons rather than a professional typist, it is filled with typographical errors and hand-written corrections and additions, as well as material cut and pasted from Symons's other essays.

[41] 'Silhouette' was, initially, the generic name of whoever was reviewing theatre and music hall performances for the *Star*. As Symons became well known in London's theatres, his identity as 'Silhouette' became common knowledge, and is even alluded to in the title of his second collection of verse. Eventually, the newspaper dispensed with the name entirely, and granted Symons his own by-line.

[42] Symons brooded obsessively over this relationship, even before his breakdown. See 'Lydia', in *The Memoirs of Arthur Symons*, pp. 157–69.

[43] The obituarist of the *Times* remarked that it was 'very difficult to regard ['A Prelude to Life'] as a piece of pure fiction.' 'Mr Arthur Symons, Poet and Critic' (25 January 1945), p. 7. Perhaps the reversing of the initials for an exercise in quasi-autobiography came from a similar mirroring between Charles Dickens and his alter-ego, David Copperfield.

chosen register is very much that of his travel and critical essays. Henry Luxulyan confesses that the best way to 'quiet' himself is 'by writing down all these fears and scruples of mine, as coldly as I can, as if they belonged to somebody else, in whose psychology I am interested.' It was a troubling approach, which drew Symons ever more into himself. 'Mr Symons lives luxuriously on his sensations,' remarked *The Athenæum*. 'He treats life as the fuel of mood, not caring so much for what things are to each other as for what they are to him.' The consequence of this was a 'voracious egoism of the soul' which the reviewer found 'curiously affrighting' and 'the subtlest form of that cruel decadence which is eating into our life.' It was, s/he concluded, 'the disease of civilization uttering itself in art. It is the soul flying from its own satiety, and, seeking to renew its sensations, like a spiritual vampire, by devouring the souls of others.' Symons was 'afflicted with super-consciousness of life' and 'turn[ed] away from exteriority towards its own organization, playing with itself, exasperating itself, torturing itself.' Such an outlook was 'spiritual suicide', for all that Symons's evocations were 'fresh, sharp, tingling, trembling, like the vivid hues of the mackerel flopping in the net.'[44] Those more conservative than Symons considered his methods to be extremely dangerous. Attributing his thoughts, feats, and longings to Henry Luxulyan or Daniel Roserra would not necessarily guard against their destructive energies.

VI

Pater's stylistic and technical influence is immediately obvious in *Spiritual Adventures*, though less so in Symons's more obviously autobiographical productions. The central aspects of Pater's fiction are well summed up by Lene Østermark-Johansen, who notes how:

> Pater does not create character through voice. He makes very little use of direct speech, and descriptive passages tend to relate to landscape background, architecture or the evocation of historical atmosphere, rather than to the painting of character. He thus also distinguishes himself from the nineteenth-century novel where lengthy descriptions of dress, posture and faces enabled social or physiognomical readings of fictional characters, with outer form as the key to inner qualities [...] the absence of direct speech leaves many of the figures strangely silent and two-dimensional.[45]

This is very much the case in a story such as 'A Prelude to Life', where one might expect an (auto)biographer to recall conversations which have lodged in the memory or to have described the people he knew best, or 'Esther Kahn', where the reader is not vouchsafed the details of what passes between the actress and her lover. Dialogue was an ever more visible feature in fiction of the *fin de siècle*,

---

[44] *'Cities*. By Arthur Symons', *The Athenæum*, 14 November 1903, pp. 641–42.
[45] Pater, *Imaginary Portraits*, ed. by Lene Østermark-Johansen, pp. 6–7.

not least because it allowed a hard-pressed writer to fill a page of type more quickly, but Symons rejected such short-cuts. There is little suggestion in his work that he had an ear for the well-observed and convincing speech associated with Gissing, the matching of idiom to character so often found in Wells or Somerset Maugham, or the dialogue that sparkles despite its independence from its speakers which is so characteristic of Wilde. This was however of little concern, for by avoiding lengthy conversation, which forces a writer to animate more than one consciousness, Symons could instead hover over details of experience and subjectivity, communicating a sense of what it might be like to live as Seaward Lackland or Christian Trevalga, rather than expressing such knowledge through speech. This was perhaps his greatest strength as a writer, and a defining characteristic of the stories collected here.

Symons remarked on several occasions that he wished to become a literary version of Edgar Degas. He was of course far from the only writer of his time to experiment with literary impressionism, though his application of it to all areas of his work was certainly unusual. His general approach was remarkably like the one which Henry Harland outlined in an 1897 article on the writing of short stories. As a novelist, short story writer, and magazine editor, Harland had an intimate knowledge of literary trends, but as a high-minded aesthete and follower of Henry James, he was unsympathetic towards their more popular incarnations. Distinguishing between an 'artist' and a 'normal man', he argued that short fiction arose not from an idea or incident but 'by taking an impression'. '[Y]ou look at the universe,' he wrote, 'and you see something; and the thing you see produces within you a certain state of mind and a certain state of emotion. That state of mind and that state of emotion between them constitute an impression.' 'Normal' people take this no further, but artists 'are constantly possessed by a desire to give [their] expression'. This desire was, almost inevitably, a torment, for 'an impression is never a simple thing'. Neither is it 'obvious'. 'It is always a complex thing,' Harland concluded. 'It is always elusive. It is a thing of shades and niceties and fine distinctions.'[46] This language recalled Symons's discussions of Verlaine, and indicated the difficulties of combining endlessly subtle perceptions within a conventional, plot-driven structure. Symons's portraits would therefore concern themselves with the inner essence of personality rather than placing that personality within a more dynamic narrative environment. In an unpublished essay dealing with his failed attempt to write his 'Lucy Newcome' novel, he observed that 'To represent life by a series of moments, and to choose these moments for a certain subtlety and rarity in them, is to challenge grave perils.' Again, had he been driven by more obviously commercial ambitions, it is unlikely that he would have pursued such a course.[47]

---

[46] Henry Harland, 'Concerning the Short Story', *The Academy*, 5 June 1897, pp. 6–7.
[47] Symons, 'Original Preface' to 'Pages from the Life of Muriel Broadbent', unpublished typescript, Arthur Symons Papers, Princeton University, Co182, Box 14, Folder 7, p. 2.

What did Symons mean by 'spiritual adventures'? 'Spiritual' was clearly not a straightforward synonym for 'religious'; only 'Seaward Lackland' explores such ideas in any detail. Symons turned instead to the consideration of the soul and the essence of personality, the spirit. Nearly twenty years earlier, he had recognized this emphasis as a central component of Pater's psychological portraiture, and however his own aesthetic had developed during this time, it remained the dominant aspect of his own.

The sense of a word or term being given a personal and particular meaning slightly different from its popular usage was characteristically Paterian. In an essay published shortly after Pater's death in the autumn of 1894, Symons's fellow Rhymer, Lionel Johnson, argued that rather than showcasing a '*bizarre vocabulary*' writers should instead develop:

> a sensitiveness to the value, the precise value, of common words in their precise signification. *Mystery, economy, pagan, gracious, cordial, mortified* — to use such words with just a hint of their first meanings, is, for the scholarly writer and reader a delicate pleasure, heightening the vivid interest of a phrase.[48]

Symons and Johnson certainly differed in their poetic practice, Johnson deploring the sexual content of Symons's verse (and life) and finding his impressionism descriptive rather than revelatory, but they responded to Pater's influence where prose was concerned. It was 'the scholarly writer and reader' whom Symons addressed in his fiction, for his understanding of 'adventure' was obviously not the hazardous and risky undertaking of uncertain outcome characterized by swashbuckling and feats of derring-do found in Stevenson or Rider Haggard, let alone the prolific novelist G. A. Henty, 'the boys' Dumas'. As Joseph Bristow demonstrates, the debates concerning the respective virtues of realism and romance during the 1880s left the adventure story in the intellectual wilderness. It was entertaining and diverting, but escapist and hardly fit reading for the serious-minded. Its enormous popularity — popularity of a kind Symons never remotely approached at any point of his career — similarly rendered it beyond the critical pale where those of sophisticated tastes were concerned. Often regarded as aimed at the juvenile of all ages, and staunchly supportive of the imperial project, the adventure stories of the *fin de siècle* were rarely treated with respect, even when written by Kipling or Conrad.[49] Adventure was a genre in which Symons had no interest whatsoever; his later enthusiasm for Conrad was founded upon his mastery of form and his view of humanity rather than the compelling narrative energy of his fiction. The pairing of spirituality and

---

[48] Lionel Johnson, 'The Work of Mr Pater', first published in the *Fortnightly Review* (September 1894) and collected in *Post Liminium: Essays and Critical Papers by Lionel Johnson*, ed. by Thomas Whittemore (London: Elkin Mathews, 1911), p. 31.

[49] Joseph Bristow (ed.), *The Oxford Book of Adventure Stories* (Oxford: Oxford University Press, 1996), pp. xiv–xv.

adventure was therefore a bold and potentially puzzling one for readers, particularly when offered by a writer who had, until the appearance of *The Symbolist Movement*, largely prioritized the sensual and external, particularly the visible, over inner concerns.

Symons used 'adventure' in two ways. In his travel and autobiographical writings, it referred to curious journeys and encounters with unusual people; it need hardly be added that particularly after his breakdown, almost all of Symons's activities fell into this category. More important is the secondary meaning of the term, which implied a Baudelairean *voyage à l'intérieur*. Symons rarely described the external appearance of his subjects, but he dwelled at length on their thoughts, feelings, and responses to the world. Whether he was depicting Esther Kahn's ambitions to become a great actress despite the emotional cost of her theatrical success, or the unbridgeable distance between Christian Trevalga and his fellow human beings, Symons asked provocative and unsettling existential questions. In posing them, he interrogated himself while wearing only notional disguises, and he may not have wholly enjoyed the answers he received.

VII

In 1976, Kerry Powell suggested that *Spiritual Adventures* was 'a stage' on which Symons could 'reconstitute his life as art and act out various roles to achieve the equilibrium which evades him in what he refers to as the "real world".'[50] Few Edwardian critics however seem to have appreciated the stories' interconnectedness, or to have grasped what was at stake in Symons's attempt to develop a unified critical aesthetic. He remained, for many, either a 'personality' from the previous decade who, turning forty, could no longer be thought of as anything approaching an *enfant terrible*, or a superior literary journalist whose work had a dedicated core of admirers but which offered little to the more general or casual reader. To evolve a critical practice which extended to travel essays and short fiction was too ambitious to be widely understood, while at the same time those better-versed in the development of the late-nineteenth-century *avant garde* saw a perhaps overly significant debt to Pater, notably the inspiration offered by 'The School of Giorgione' which Symons acknowledged in *Studies in Seven Arts*. A century later, when neologisms such as 'autobiografiction' find a place in the critical lexicon, Symons's ability to navigate between observation, invention, reminiscence, and reflection seems perhaps more 'modern' than it did in 1905. Certainly, neither Constable's publicists nor the reviewers of the day were able to properly appreciate what

---

[50] Kerry Powell, 'Arthur Symons' *Spiritual Adventures* and the Art of Illusion', *Studies in the Humanities* 5.2 (1976), p. 44.

Symons attempted. '[T]he range of the book's forms of auto/biography is striking,' Max Saunders concludes. 'It includes not only autobiography (or autobiografiction) and pseudo-journal, but varieties of pseudo-autobiography as well, some more autobiographical than others.'[51]

The Constable archives at the National Library of Scotland reveal nothing of Symons's original proposal or his contract for the book. In the early twentieth century, he had published his critical works with Heinemann and Dent; perhaps his move to Constable was prompted by the firm's long history of publishing commercially successful fiction: it had issued Stoker's *Dracula* (1897) among other works, though its expertise was very much in novels rather than story collections, and had Symons been on better terms with John Lane, he would have been well advised to pursue publication with The Bodley Head. Certainly Constable did not seem overly confident about the likely sales of Symons's collection, for the print run of the first edition was only 750 copies, 250 of which were shipped off to the United States.[52] Such was Symons's standing as a critic that the firm issued significantly larger (though by no means extravagant) runs of *Studies in Seven Arts* and *William Blake*, and in time would publish his book on the Romantic movement (1909) and *Figures of Several Centuries* (1916). As a writer of fiction, however, he was a largely unknown quantity. He had published a handful of stories before *Spiritual Adventures*, but only the two 'Lucy Newcombe' stories, fictional renderings of the life of his lover, Muriel Broadbent, which appeared in *The Savoy* in 1896, could be adjudged significant contributions to the literature of their time. Symons's other works from the 1890s are vignettes of chiefly biographical interest; significantly, he made no effort to reprint them until after his illness. Following his self-inclusion in *The Savoy*, he published no further fiction until October 1902, when 'Esther Kahn' appeared in *Smart Set*. It was followed by 'An Autumn City' in *The Weekly Critical Review* (June–July 1903), and the soon-retitled 'Peter Waydelin's Experiment' (*Lippincott's Monthly Magazine*, February 1904), but publishers were wary of a collection comprised entirely of previously issued material, and the remaining five 'adventures' did not appear in advance of the volume.

Nobody could accuse Constable of enthusiasm in marketing Symons's book. Advertisements were muted, and served largely to show the unlikely company he was keeping as a writer of short stories and the erratic quality of the Constable list. *The Times* announced that 'MR. SYMONS'S NEW BOOK, *Spiritual Adventures: A Series of Studies in Temperament*' was now available for 7s. 6d.,

---

[51] Max Saunders, *Self Impressions: Life-Writing, Autobiografiction, and the Forms of Modern Literature* (Oxford: Oxford University Press, 2010), pp. 254–55.
[52] They also produced the book in exactly the same style as *Studies in Seven Arts*, making a work of fiction strongly resemble a more academic text. While this strategy probably reassured Symons's admirers, it is unlikely to have appealed to the reading public *per se*.

along with George Bernard Shaw's *The Irrational Knot*,[53] Robert Chambers's *The Reckoning* (part of a series of historical novels set during the American War of Independence), John Fox's American adventure, *A Cumberland Vendetta*, published in the States in 1896, and Kate Douglas Wiggin's *Rose o' the River*, a 'homespun tale' by the author of *Rebecca of Sunnybrook Farm* (1903). A full page, three-column advertisement in *The Athenæum* throughout October 1905 marooned *Spiritual Adventures* almost at the bottom of its central column, a tiny snippet of text with no accompanying critical endorsements dwarfed by Walter Sichel's *Emma, Lady Hamilton* and Alexander Innes Shand's *Days of the Past*. Constable's fiction list struggled to compete against more appealing fare: Rider Haggard's *Ayesha*, Bram Stoker's gothic romance, *The Man*, H. G. Wells's *Kipps* and *The Food of the Gods*, Arthur Morrison's *Divers Vanities*, and Kipling's *Traffics and Discoveries*, the collection containing 'They', 'Wireless', and 'Mrs Bathurst'. Faced with such seductive alternatives, Symons's stories received little commercial or critical attention. He may have been adept and dogged where 'placing' his articles and reviews was concerned, but he was far less skilled when it came to promoting his fiction, and did not employ a literary agent until 1907.[54] This inability or unwillingness to adapt to the financial imperatives of early twentieth-century publishing certainly had significant consequences for Symons, particularly in his failure to consider long-term and strategic projects. His reputation and contacts assured him of regular work, but he was now on a treadmill, albeit a genteel one.

Inevitably, the critical response to *Spiritual Adventures* was mixed. The *Manchester Guardian* felt Symons asked readers to make a choice between art and 'social obligations' in presenting his 'melancholy and lonely people'; it praised 'The Death of Peter Waydelin' and felt the book was 'one of the most suggestive of recent works of fiction.'[55] The *Sunday Times* barely ventured beyond summary and generalization in examining 'such characters as seem separated from "the general" by a touch of inchoate genius', 'individualities' who are 'not yet ranged by public assent or critical acknowledgement with successful talent'.[56] There was little here to appeal to the diversion-seeking 'common reader', but more specialist reviews recognized that Symons was attempting to go beyond the slice-of-life stories that had been so characteristic of the previous decade.

---

[53] Shaw finished his novel on 1 December 1880, but in the world before Ibsen, the new woman and the 'sex fiction' of the 1890s, found it impossible to publish. It was serialized by a Socialist magazine between 1885 and 1887; the Constable edition was its first appearance in volume form, but hardly constituted an impressive scoop for the firm.

[54] Symons was represented by James B. Pinker (1863–1922), who also represented (among many others) Henry James, H. G. Wells, Arnold Bennett, Joseph Conrad, and James Joyce. Had he enlisted Pinker's services earlier in his career, *Spiritual Adventures* would surely have been more financially successful.

[55] *Manchester Guardian* (27 October 1905), p. 5. The reviewer was 'A. N. W.'

[56] *Sunday Times* (1 October 1905), p. 9.

Symons was well-connected in the journalistic world as well as the literary one, but he had always been too principled to endorse his friends' work on purely personal grounds and there seems to have been precious little log-rolling on his behalf. *The Academy*, which had at one time often featured his articles and reviews, and which he had edited for a short period, felt that his stories 'are surprisingly well told' but marred by excessive exposition, a lack of emotional variety (chiefly humour), and failures in characterization. Failing to recognize (or indulge) Symons's Paterian aims, the paper remarked that figures such as Esther Kahn did not exist 'as individuals'. Instead, 'they embody points of view, but they are not of flesh and blood.'[57] Ten years on from *London Nights*, *The Academy* again highlighted Symons's past in its headline, 'The Soul of a Decadent'.

The Athenæum was more perceptive in some respects, but it too saw the stories as 'studies of decadence' and the narrator of 'A Prelude to Life' as 'an adolescent decadent beginning the pursuit of life as a sensation.' It also discerned a surely unintentional didacticism in its discussion of 'Christian Trevalga', where 'The moral is plain — to wit, that morbid absorption in even a purely imaginative sensation imperils the equilibrium of personality.'[58] *Spiritual Adventures* had been published in early October, but *The Athenæum* review did not appear until the following year, suggesting that a new book by Symons was hardly its most urgent concern.

There was a similar delay in responding to the book in the United States, though an anonymous reviewer went further than their English counterparts in assessing a work which required 'a strong taste for analysis, for intricate psychological problems.' Such 'self-revelation' was 'decidedly foreign to the Anglo-Saxon temper,' said the reviewer, following in the footsteps of the editor and humorist E. V. Lucas, who had brusquely pointed out to Symons that 'to be of one's own country is essentially a more genuine and more poetical thing than to masquerade as a Frenchman.'[59] Unlike the other reviews, *The Dial*'s recognized the formal qualities of Symons's fiction, though in its reference to the 'thoroughly subjective and tantalizingly incomplete' episodes which comprised the 'adventures', it wondered 'whether it is by intention or chance that Mr Symons always keeps back the salient point of the story.' *Spiritual Adventures* had 'charm', it admitted, but it was poetic rather than dramatic in character.

---

[57] 'The Soul of a Decadent,' *The Academy* 69 (1905), pp. 1148–49 excerpted in C. Jay Fox, Carol Simpson Stern, Robert S. Means, *Arthur Symons, Critic Among Critics: An Annotated Bibliography* (Greensboro, NC: ELT Press, 2007), p. 285.
[58] '*Spiritual Adventures*. By Arthur Symons', *The Athenæum* 4085 (1906), pp. 161–62, in Fox et al., *Arthur Symons*, p. 285.
[59] Anon. [E. V. Lucas], *TLS*, 2 June 1905, p. 177.

The Dial's review concluded that '[H]is very cleverness and facility make it more to be regretted that he has wasted his time in portraiture, brilliant but without significance, of subjects that are hardly worthy of such distinction.'[60] Such a comment would never have occurred to a Paterian, or indeed, to the radical writers and artists of nascent modernism, who hailed technical innovation and prowess over the worth or novelty of subject matter. Whereas his realist rivals such as Wells, Bennett, and Galsworthy 'laid an enormous stress upon the fabric of things', Symons used the openly subjective modes of letters, journals, and diaries to explore the inner lives of his characters, as well as to examine himself.[61] The novelist and music critic, James Gibbons Huneker, who beat the drum for the book in the *New York Times*, acknowledged this, arguing that Symons had developed ideas found in Pater rather than merely deploying them. The 'hauntingly strange' stories of *Spiritual Adventures*, Huneker maintained, 'adhered to the low-toned harmonies' associated with Pater but unlike that sage, whom he compared to the Lady of Shalott weaving a tapestry of words, Symons had been out into the modern world and filled himself with its sensations. In his view, the stories were a riposte to 'commerce' and would be welcomed by those 'to whom English fiction has become too material, too much a thing of bricks and mortar,' a remark that anticipating the arguments of Woolf's 'Mr Bennett and Mrs Brown' (1923) by almost twenty years.[62]

Another American critic, Elia W. Peattie of the *Chicago Daily Tribune*, was equally impressed, arguing that all Symons's work showed 'a marked distinction' because of its beautiful style. Nevertheless, she added, 'whenever you start a journey with Symons, you must expect to be taken in subterranean passages.' His stories were less stories than 'excursions of human souls into strange relationships, into curious houses of life, into obsessions, and into regions of doubt.' As such, they were 'never anything but interesting', even if, as in the case of 'Peter Waydelin' they were visits to 'human crypts'.[63] Considering *Spiritual Adventures* in the light of *Imaginary Portraits*, *The Symbolist Movement in Literature*, and *Plays, Acting and Music* showed that some critics at least understood what Symons was attempting to achieve. Unfortunately, there was little in such encomia to win over the wavering reader or those deterred by words such as 'melancholy' or 'strange', let alone 'human crypts'. It was ironic that while Symons had sought to take criticism into the realm of fiction, his readers had

---

[60] *Dial* 40 (1906), pp. 201–02, in Fox et al., *Arthur Symons*, p. 285.

[61] Virginia Woolf, 'Mr Bennett and Mrs Brown' (1924), in her *Collected Essays* I (London: Hogarth Press, 1966), p. 332.

[62] James Huneker, 'Ideas and Fancies of Arthur Symons', *New York Times Saturday Review of Books*, 7 April 1906. The review renames Seaward Lackland 'Steward Lackland' throughout.

[63] Elia W. Peattie, 'Brilliant Lot of New Fiction for the Holidays', *Chicago Daily Tribune* (16 December 1905), p. 9.

read his stories largely as fictionalized critical works, that is, his usual display of 'impressions and sensations' embodied in unsympathetic and distant characters instead of being seen as effusions of his own.

There was, however, one very significant reader of Symons's book whose views of it were personal rather than public. This was Thomas Hardy, the collection's dedicatee and one of the few contemporary British or Irish novelists — the three Georges of Gissing (with some reservations), Moore, and Meredith being the others — whom Symons admired as much as their French counterparts. Hardy's comments to Symons, in a letter of 20 October 1905, show that he had read the book with 'deep interest' and 'fascination', drawn to 'its contents without regard for the author' and thus offering the compliment of dispassionate observation and 'frankness'. Disregarding the text's various engagements with autobiography, Hardy saw each as a 'mental study' which was either 'a rounded story' (like 'Seaward Lackland') or an example of 'the slice-of-life school or impressionist' (as was the case with 'An Autumn City'). He favoured those which offered some form of resolution (hence his praise for 'Seaward Lackland', 'Peter Waydelin', and 'Henry Luxulyan'), finding 'An Autumn City' insufficiently conclusive. Henry James may have claimed that 'art is all discrimination and selection', but Hardy saw his influence as lacking the 'selecting reason' which motivated events. Readers, Hardy said, liked 'a tale with an ending': having served up many dramatic finales in his work, he knew precisely what could be done with a situation such as Tess's flight to Stonehenge. Symons however was at once a 'of the more modern school' or 'advanced set', sympathetic to inconclusiveness and a writer less thoroughly divorced from tradition than many might assume. He was therefore poised between two different narrative styles, and, as the book contained examples of both, unable to decide which was superior. As the author of stories such as 'The Withered Arm' (1888), it was perhaps unsurprising to see Hardy respond with enthusiasm to Symons's 'unusual power in the *weird*', as evidenced by the smoke music in 'Christian Trevalga' and the fate of the Baroness in 'Henry Luxulyan'. There was certainly a market for strange and horrible tales in the years before the First World War, but here as elsewhere, the impetus for Symons's work came not from the popular but from the rarefied and avant-garde, chiefly the *Contes cruels* of Villiers de l'Isle-Adam to which he would return after his illness, notably 'The Sinister Guest' (1919).

The 'studies' were, Hardy finished, 'miles above what we get in that kind year by year', a remark which admitted their distinctiveness but also the level of competition that characterized the Edwardian literary marketplace.[64] The edition

[64] Hardy to Symons, 20 October 1905. *The Collected Letters of Thomas Hardy, Volume Three: 1902–1908*, ed. by Richard Little Purdy and Michael Millgate (Oxford: Clarendon Press, 1982), pp. 185–86. Symons obviously respected Hardy's plain speaking. He remained friends with the older novelist for the rest of his life, asked his advice on his plans for a novel about Lucy

sold slowly, and it was three years before Constable produced a reprint. In the aftermath of Symons's illness, the book was largely forgotten, and was not back in print until 1924, when Martin Secker made it the fifth volume of his projected edition of Symons's complete works. Constable reprinted it once again in 1928, but with Symons's reputation in decline until the tentative revival initiated by Frank Kermode's *Romantic Image* (1957), it was almost forty years before his short stories attracted the attention of anthologists such as Stanley Weintraub, who included 'The Childhood of Lucy Newcome' in his *The Savoy: Nineties Experiment* (1966), Helmut E. Gerber, whose *The English Short Story in Transition 1880–1920* (1967) features 'Christian Trevalga', and Derek Stanford, who reprinted 'Esther Kahn' in *Short Stories of the 'Nineties* (1968) and 'An Autumn City' in *Writing of the 'Nineties* (1971). Since then, Symons has received steadily increasing recognition for his work as one of modernism's midwives, though his fiction is still under-appreciated beside his early poetry and critical essays.[65]

Whether or not Symons would have continued to develop as a short story writer, or even as a novelist, had he not suffered his calamitous breakdown is difficult to say. *Spiritual Adventures* was, after all, part of a much larger artistic project, and once he had completed the book, he immediately started work on others. He seems to have written no further fiction until he was hospitalized, when he produced a mass of poetry, drama, and miscellaneous writing, most of which was destroyed either by himself or by Rhoda. If he did have ambitions outside the spheres of poetry and criticism, then he was probably more keen to become a playwright than a novelist. Rhoda's continued attempts to have a career on the stage reinforced this longing.

Nevertheless, Symons did continue to write fiction after 1908. The archives at Princeton contain typescripts of a number of unpublished pieces, notably the substantial novella, 'The Tragedians'. Undated, these stories were probably written after the First World War, though their literary and cultural reference points are very much those of the *fin de siècle*. The fair copies are obviously the work of a professional typist, as the contrast between them and the chaos of 'The Genesis of Spiritual Adventures' is quite marked, but their uniformity of presentation conceals their widely variable quality. In surveying this material, the series editors and I have decided to reprint only the two stories from the 1890s that Alan Johnson edited for publication in *English Literature in Transition* during the 1980s: 'An Episode in the Life of Jenny Lane' and 'The Life and

---

Newcome in 1915, and published a short study of him shortly after Hardy's death early in 1928. He was also among the mourners at Hardy's funeral.

[65] A notable exception is *The Decadent Short Story: An Annotated Anthology*, ed. by Kostas Boyiopoulos, Yoonjoung Choi, and Matthew Brinton Tildesley (Edinburgh: Edinburgh University Press, 2015), which reprints 'Pages from the Life of Lucy Newcome' and 'The Death of Peter Waydelin'.

Adventures of Lucy Newcome'. We have opted not to include the later stories, partly for reasons of space, and partly because they add little to either our understanding of Symons's fiction or to his artistic reputation.[66] They are not without interest, but they do not fit with the aims of the current project.

It would be wrong to claim too much for the early stories collected here, written when Symons was still finding his way as a writer of fiction. *Spiritual Adventures* however, is a far more significant work, one which Ezra Pound felt '[a]s culture' to be 'worth all the Freudian tosh in existence' and which deserves to stand alongside Symons's poetry of the 1890s, *The Symbolist Movement in Literature*, and his editorship of *The Savoy*.[67] Symons's fiction now seems an intriguing example of early modernism, providing further evidence of that movement's evolutionary development rather than implying a clean break from earlier conventions. A marked French influence reconfigures plot devices from Victorian melodrama and realist fiction alike, while the rejection of didacticism is no longer a shock tactic, as it was so often in the 1890s, but a more mature and considered means of depicting psychological dissidence without the distractions of moral judgement. '[O]bessed, diseased, but never shallow,' Symons's portraits of melancholy, socially dislocated individuals made uncomfortable reading for his Edwardian audience, and they remain haunting and troubling today.[68]

---

[66] The two published stories not included in this edition are 'Notes on the Sensations of a Lady of the Ballet', first published in *International* 8 (April 1914), and reprinted in the *English Review* (February 1920), pp. 104–20, and 'The Sinister Guest', a free adaptation of Villiers de l'Isle Adam's *Le Convive des dernières fêtes* ('The Unknown Guest') (1874), which appeared in *The English Review* (August 1919), pp. 105–19.

[67] Ezra Pound, *Guide to Kulchur* (Norfolk, CT: James Laughlin, 1952), p. 71.

[68] Alan Johnson, '"An Episode in the Life of Jenny Lane" by Arthur Symons with an Afterword by Alan Johnson', *English Literature in Transition* 29.4 (1986), p. 358.

SELECT BIBLIOGRAPHY

~

Editions

Spiritual Adventures (London: Archibald Constable, 1905)

Life and Letters

BECKSON, KARL, 'Symons, Arthur William (1865–1945)', *Oxford Dictionary of National Biography* (Oxford: Oxford University Press, 2004)
—— *Arthur Symons: A Life* (Oxford: Clarendon Press, 1987)
—— 'Arthur Symons', in *Victorian Prose Writers After 1867*, ed. by William B. Thesing (*Dictionary of Literary Biography*, Vol. 57) (Detroit: Gale, 1986), pp. 330–41
—— and JOHN M. MUNRO, *Arthur Symons: Selected Letters, 1880–1935* (Basingstoke: Macmillan, 1989)
LHOMBREAUD, ROGER, *Arthur Symons: A Critical Biography* (London: The Unicorn Press, 1963)
SYMONS, ARTHUR, *The Memoirs of Arthur Symons: Art and Life in the 1890s*, ed. by Karl Beckson (University Park and London: Pennsylvania University Press, 1977)

Bibliographies

BECKSON, KARL, IAN FLETCHER, LAWRENCE W. MARKERT, and JOHN STOKES, *Arthur Symons: A Bibliography* (Greensboro, NC: ELT Press, 1990)
FOX, C. JAY, CAROL SIMPSON STERN, and ROBERT S. MEANS, *Arthur Symons, Critic Among Critics: An Annotated Bibliography* (Greensboro: ELT Press, 2007)

Secondary Material

ALFORD, NORMAN, *The Rhymers' Club: Poets of the Tragic Generation* (Basingstoke: Macmillan, 1994)
BALAKIAN, ANNA, *The Symbolist Movement* (New York: Random House, 1967)
BECKSON, KARL, *London in the 1890s: A Cultural History* (New York: Norton, 1992)
BIZZOTTO, ELISA, 'The Imaginary Portrait: Pater's Contribution to a Literary Genre', in *Walter Pater: Transparencies of Desire*, ed. by Laurel Brake, Lesley Higgins, and Carolyn Williams (Greensboro, NC: ELT Press, 2002), pp. 213–23
BLOCK, EDWIN F. JR, *Rituals of Dis-Integration: Romance and Madness in the Victorian Psychomythic Tale* (New York: Garland, 1993)
—— 'Walter Pater, Arthur Symons, W. B. Yeats and the Fortunes of the Literary Portrait', *Studies in English Literature 1500–1900* 26.4 (1986), pp. 759–76

BRADBURY, MALCOLM, 'London 1890–1920', in *Modernism 1890–1930*, ed. by Malcolm Bradbury and James MacFarlane (Harmondsworth: Penguin, 1976), pp. 172–90

CEVASCO, G. A., 'Delineating Decadence: The Influence of J.-K. Huysmans on Arthur Symons', *Nineteenth Century Prose* 23.1 (1996), pp. 74–86

CHAMBERLIN, J. E., *Ripe was the Drowsy Hour: The Age of Oscar Wilde* (New York: Seabury, 1977)

CHARLESWORTH, BARBARA, *Dark Passages: The Decadent Consciousness in Victorian Literature* (Madison: Wisconsin University Press, 1965)

CLAYTON, ANTONY, *Decadent London* (London: Historical Publications, 2005)

CLEMENTS, PATRICIA, *Baudelaire and the English Tradition* (Princeton: Princeton University Press, 1985)

CONSTABLE, LIZ, DENNIS DENISOFF, and MATTHEW POTOLSKY (eds), *Perennial Decay: On the Aesthetics and Politics of Decadence* (Philadelphia: University of Pennsylvania Press, 1999)

DANIEL, ANNE MARGARET, 'Arthur Symons and *The Savoy*', *Literary Imagination* 7.2 (2005), pp. 165–93

DIERKES-THRUN, PETRA, 'Arthur Symons' Decadent Aesthetics: Stéphane Mallarmé and the Dancer Revisited', in *Decadences: Morality and Aesthetics in British Literature*, ed. by Paul Fox (Stuttgart: Ibidem-Verlag, 2006), pp. 33–65

DONOHUE, JOSEPH, *Fantasies of Empire: The Empire Theatre of Varieties and the Licensing Controversy of 1894* (Iowa City: University of Iowa Press, 2005)

DOWLING, LINDA, *Language and Decadence in the Victorian Fin de Siècle* (Princeton: Princeton University Press, 1986)

ELIOT, T. S., *The Sacred Wood: Essays on Poetry and Criticism* (London: Methuen, 1920)

—— *Inventions of the March Hare: Poems 1909–1917*, ed. by Christopher Ricks (London: Faber, 1996)

FAULK, BARRY J., *Music Hall and Modernity: The Late-Victorian Discovery of Popular Culture* (Athens, OH: Ohio University Press, 2004)

FREEMAN, NICHOLAS, *Conceiving the City: London, Literature and Art, 1870–1914* (Oxford: Oxford University Press, 2007)

—— '"Mad music rising": Chopin, Sex, and Secret Language in Arthur Symons' "Christian Trevalga"', *Victoriographies* 1.2 (2011), pp. 157–76

—— 'The Harem of Words: Attenuation and Excess in Decadent Poetry', in *Decadent Poetics*, ed. by Alex Murray and Jason Hall (Basingstoke: Palgrave Macmillan, 2013), pp. 83–99

—— 'Symons, Whistler, and the Art of Seeing', in *Decadence and the Senses*, ed. by Jane Desmarais (Oxford: Legenda, 2017), pp. 15–31

GARDNER, JOANN, *Yeats and the Rhymers' Club: A Nineties Perspective* (New York: Peter Lang, 1989)

GERBER, HELMUT E. (ed.), *The English Short Story in Transition 1880–1920* (New York: Pegasus, 1967)

GIBBONS, TOM, *Rooms in the Darwin Hotel: Studies in English Literary Criticism and Ideas 1880–1920* (Nedlands: University of Western Australia Press, 1973)

GORDON, JAN B., 'The Dialogue of Life and Art in Arthur Symons's *Spiritual Adventures*', *English Literature in Transition* 12.3 (1969), pp. 105–17

—— 'The Imaginary Portrait: Fin-de-Siècle Icon', *University of Windsor Review*, Fall 1969, pp. 81–104

GRIBBLE, FRANCIS, 'The Pose of Mr Arthur Symons', *Fortnightly Review*, July 1908, pp. 127–36

GUEST, IVOR, *Ballet in Leicester Square: The Alhambra and the Empire, 1860–1915* (London: Dance Books, 1992)

HALL, JASON DAVID, and ALEX MURRAY (eds), *Decadent Poetics: Literature and Form at the British Fin de Siècle* (Basingstoke: Palgrave Macmillan, 2013)

HARRIS, WENDELL V., *British Short Fiction in the Nineteenth Century: A Literary and Bibliographic Guide* (Detroit: Wayne State University Press, 1979)

HUNEKER, JAMES, 'A Critic of the Seven Arts', *North American Review* 185 (1907), pp. 75–9

HUNT, JOHN DIXON, *The Pre-Raphaelite Imagination, 1848–1900* (London: Routledge, 1968)

JACKSON, HOLBROOK, *The Eighteen Nineties* (London: Grant Richards, 1913)

JEPSON, EDGAR, *Memoirs of a Victorian* (London: Victor Gollancz, 1933)

JOHNSON, ALAN, 'Arthur Symons' "Novel à la Goncourt"', *Journal of Modern Literature* 9.1 (1981), pp. 50–64

—— 'Arthur Symons' "The Life and Adventures of Lucy Newcome": Preface and Text', *English Literature in Transition* 28.4 (1985), pp. 332–45

—— '"An Episode in the Life of Jenny Lane" by Arthur Symons with an Afterword by Alan Johnson', *English Literature in Transition* 29.4 (1986), pp. 351–59

KERMODE, FRANK, *Romantic Image* (London: Routledge and Kegan Paul, 1957)

MARKERT, LAWRENCE W., *Arthur Symons: Critic of the Seven Arts* (Ann Arbor: UMI, 1988)

MIX, KATHERINE LYON, *A Study in Yellow: The Yellow Book and its Contributors* (London: Constable, 1960)

MUNRO, JOHN M., *Arthur Symons* (New York: Twayne, 1969)

O'NEAL, MICHAEL, 'The Syntactic Style of Arthur Symons', *Language and Style* XV, 3 (1982), pp. 208–18

PITTOCK, MURRAY G. H., *Spectrum of Decadence: The Literature of the 1890s* (London: Routledge, 1993)

PORTERFIELD, SUSAN AZAR, 'Arthur Symons as Critic of the Visual Arts', *English Literature in Transition* 44.3 (2001), pp. 260–74

POWELL, KERRY, 'Arthur Symons' *Spiritual Adventures* and the Art of Illusion,' *Studies in the Humanities* 5.2 (1976), pp. 44–49

REED, JOHN R., 'Decadent Style and the Short Story', *Victorians Institute Journal* 11 (1982), pp. 1–12

—— *Decadent Style* (Athens, OH: Ohio University Press, 1985)

ROBINSON, ALAN, *Poetry, Painting and Ideas, 1885–1914* (Basingstoke: Macmillan, 1985)

STANFORD, DEREK, *Introduction to the 'Nineties*, Salzburg Studies in English Literature 78.1 (Salzburg: Institut für Anglistik unt Amerikanistik Universität Salzburg, 1987)

STANGE, G. ROBERT, 'The Frightened Poets', in *The Victorian City: Images and Realities*, Vol. 2, ed. by H. J. Dyos and Michael Wolff (London: Routledge, 1973), pp. 475–94

STETZ, MARGARET D., *Gender and the London Theatre, 1880–1920* (Buckingham: Rivendale Press, 2004)

STOKES, JOHN, 'The Legend of Duse', in *Decadence and the 1890s*, ed. by Ian Fletcher (London: Arnold, 1979), pp. 151–72

—— (ed.), *Fin du Siècle/Fin du Globe: Fears and Fantasies of the Late Nineteenth Century* (Basingstoke: Macmillan, 1992)

SYMONS, ARTHUR, *Selected Writings*, ed. by R. V. Holdsworth (Cheadle Hulme: Carcanet, 1974)

TEMPLE, RUTH Z., *The Critic's Alchemy: A Study of the Introduction of French Symbolism into England* (New York: Twayne, 1953)

THORNTON, R. K. R., *The Decadent Dilemma* (London: Arnold, 1983)

WOODCOCK, GEORGE, 'Arthur Symons: Mediator of Modernism', in *Julian Symons at 80: A Tribute*, ed. by Patricia Craig (Helsinki: Eurographica, 1992), pp. 133–41

YEATS, W. B., 'The Tragic Generation', in *The Autobiography of William Butler Yeats* (New York: Macmillan, 1938)

NOTE ON THE TEXT

This edition reprints the 1905 edition of *Spiritual Adventures*. Other stories are reproduced as per original publication. The texts unpublished during Symons's lifetime are reproduced as edited by Alan Johnson in *English Literature in Transition* during the 1980s.

I have modernized Symons's hyphenation of words such as 'to-day', 'good-bye' and 'some-one' throughout, and italicized titles of novels and plays.

All Biblical references are to the King James Version.

Details of original publication are given in the introductions to the stories.

A SYMONS CHRONOLOGY

~

1865   Arthur William Symons, second child of Reverend Mark (1824–98), a Methodist minister, and Lydia Symons (*née* Pascoe, 1828–96), born, Milford Haven, Wales, 28 February. He has an older sister, Anna (1864–1933).

1866–73   The family leave Wales and move to Guernsey. Family legend claims the baby Arthur is kissed by Victor Hugo, living in exile there. Mark Symons moves parishes regularly, going from Alnwick in Northumberland to St Ives in Cornwall and Tavistock in Devon.

1874   Starts school and learns to read 'properly' ('A Prelude to Life'). Early experiment with narrative verse. Composes pious lyric, 'The Lord is Good' which his mother keeps for the rest of her life.

1876   Family moves to Tiverton, Devon.

1878   Begins an unfinished verse tragedy, *Almansor*. Other pieces include 'A Dream of the Garden of God', 'Cain', 'Judas', 'A Ballad of the Vanity of All Things', All Things Pass By', and 'Everything is Vain'. Also writes 39 stanzas of 'Don Ismaeli', an *ottava rima* epic modelled on Byron's *Don Juan*.

1879   Family moves to Bideford in Devon.

1880   Continues poetic apprenticeship, imitating Swinburne, Tennyson, Browning, and Longfellow. Writes, on his fifteenth birthday, a dramatic monologue, 'Mad', and also works on a blank verse tragedy, *Cassandra,* influenced by *Atalanta in Calydon*. Attends The High Street Classical and Mathematical School, Bideford. Befriended by American schoolmaster, Charles Churchill Osborne, who lends him books and broadens his cultural outlook.

1881   Comes first in school examinations in Latin and English. Studies Greek and Latin alongside candidates for matriculation at London University, but does not apply there. Joins Browning Society.

1882   Receives first volume of Browning Society papers and begins correspondence with Society's founder, F. J. Furnivall. Leaves school and begins rigorous course of self-education. Moves to Yeovil,

Somerset. December — 'Robert Browning as Religious Poet' by Arthur W. Symons appears in the *Wesleyan-Methodist Magazine*. It is his first publication; he is paid 21 shillings.

1883   Publishes first review, the anonymous *Bone et Fidelis: A Poem*, the versified life of a Wesleyan minister, in the *London Quarterly Review*. Begins translating Heine.

1884   Furnivall accepts 'Is Browning Dramatic?' for the Browning Society, and asks him to write the introduction to an edition of Shakespeare's *Venus and Adonis* for his Shakespeare Quartos Facsimile series. Publishes Browning homage, 'A Fancy of Ferishtah', *Academy* (13 December). Translating poems from Gautier.

1885   Furnivall reads 'Is Browning Dramatic?' at the Browning Society (30 January), though Symons is not present. *Venus and Adonis* published with 19 page introduction by 'Arthur Symons of Yeovil'. Begins study of Pater. Meets the blind poet, Philip Bourke Marston. Writes an introduction for Furnivall's edition of *Titus Andronicus*. Moves to Nuneaton with family. Corresponds with John Addington Symonds. Reviews work by Meredith and Michael Field.

1886   Begins correspondence with Havelock Ellis, who invites him to edit Elizabethan texts for his 'Mermaids' series. Writes introduction to Furnivall's edition of *Henry V*. Edits the essays of Leigh Hunt for Ernest Rhys's 'Camelot Classics'. Publishes his first book, *An Introduction to the Study of Browning* (October).

1887   Hunt edition published, plus a selection from Massinger. Meets Furnivall. Offered further editing work on the 'Henry Irving Shakespeare' series. Reviews Pater's *Imaginary Portraits* (*Time*, August). The review impresses Oscar Wilde, who solicits contributions to the *Woman's World*. Begins correspondence with Herbert Horne. Reading Villiers de l'Isle-Adam's *Contes cruels*. Contributes six poems to Gleeson White's *Ballades and Rondeaus*.

1888   Corresponds with Pater, whom he meets in Oxford (7 August). Family moves to Buckingham. Acquires Reader's Ticket for the British Museum (September). First poetry collection, *Days and Nights*, accepted by Macmillan's. Meets Havelock Ellis (October) who introduces him to Michael Field (November).

1889   *Days and Nights* published (March), dedicated to Pater. Spending more time in London. Sees performance of Ibsen's *A Doll's House*. Has his first love affair with 'Gladys Vane or Fane', a fifteen-year-old music hall performer whom he meets in a London rooming-house, later detailing the event in an unpublished manuscript headed 'This is one of my Unspiritual Adventures, Gladys Vane, Savoy Buildings, July 24, 1889'. Attends dinner in honour of Whistler (1 May). Meets Olive Schreiner, Ford Madox Brown, Mathilde Blind, Holman Hunt, William Michael Rossetti, Amy Levy, Alice Meynell, Edmund Gosse, and Browning (25 August). Goes to Paris with Ellis for eight days (September), his first foreign visit. Publishes essay on Villiers de l'Isle-Adam (the first in English) in *Woman's World* (October). Attends Browning's funeral at Westminster Abbey (December).

1890 Joins Rhymers' Club at invitation of Ernest Rhys. Goes to Paris with Ellis (17 March until mid-June). Meets Rodin, Verlaine, Mallarmé, Maeterlinck, Redon, Rémy de Gourmont, and J.-K. Huysmans. Back in London meets Coventry Patmore, Cardinal Manning, Madame Blavatsky, Wilde. Leaves family home and moves into shared house in Hampstead with Rhys (summer). Begins friendship with George Moore. Stands in for the holidaying editor of *The Academy* (August).

1891 Moves to rooms in Fountain Court, The Temple. Regular contributor to *The Athenæum*. Meets W. B. Yeats, Ernest Dowson, John Gray. Visits Provence and Spain with Ellis (April–May). Goes to Germany with the American writer Frank Willard (who publishes as 'Josiah Flynt', July-September). Frequenting music halls and theatres. Mark Symons retires and moves to Willesden.

1892 Contributes four poems to *The Book of the Rhymers' Club* (February). Becomes music hall reviewer for the *Star* under pseudonym 'Silhouette' and meets many stars of the stage. Adapts Frank Harris's story, 'A Modern Idyll' for a one act play, *The Minister's Call*, staged by Independent Theatre Society (4 March). Audience includes Wilde (plus young male friends wearing green carnations), Moore, J. M. Barrie, John Lane, and Henry James. Reviews discouraging. Visits Paris (May) and sees Jane Avril perform. Second collection of poetry, *Silhouettes* published (June). Consumes hashish with Dowson, Symonds, and ballet girls at Fountain Court (July). Visits Rhys in Wales (August–September). Begins relationship with Muriel Broadbent, a prostitute he has met at the Alhambra music hall, about whom he writes the 'Lucy Newcome' stories.

1893 Despite publishing nearly 60 articles and reviews in the previous year, is short of money and bailed out by his father. Meets William Rothenstein, Aubrey Beardsley, Hubert Crackanthorpe, and Arnold Dolmetsch. 'The Decadent Movement in Literature' published

(*Harper's New Monthly Magazine*, November). Helps with organization of Verlaine's visit to England (November–December); Verlaine stays at Fountain Court and commemorates the occasion in a poem of that title (1896). Meets 'Lydia', a dancer at the Empire, and begins passionate affair with her.

1894   Ellis moves into Fountain Court. Visits Milan and Venice with Herbert Horne (March–April), meets Henry James. Studies Casanova's archives in Venice. Contributes 'Stella Maris' to the first *Yellow Boo* (April), and four poems to the Rhymers' second collection (June). Translates Zola's *L'Assommoir*. Caught up in the controversy surrounding prostitution in music halls (October–November). Watches Yvette Guilbert perform at the Empire (December).

1895   Meets Leonard Smithers who publishes Symons's third collection, *London Nights*, dedicated to Verlaine (June). Widely condemned in moral backlash following Wilde's trials. Breaks with Lydia and goes to Dieppe (August–early October) where he spends time with Beardsley, Smithers, Charles Conder, Crackanthorpe, and others. Has portrait painted by J.-E. Blanche. Plans *The Savoy* as rival to the *Yellow Book*. Ellis sub-lets his rooms in Fountain Court to Yeats and he and Symons become increasingly close.

1896   First issue of *Savoy* (11 January). Lydia marries (early February). Lydia Symons dies (16 March). Second edition of *Silhouettes* and second number of *Savoy* (April). Third number published in July. From then on, the magazine is monthly until it folds following the December issue. Visits Ireland with Yeats (July). Visits Paris with Yeats (November), then goes on to Rome. Meets D'Annunzio. Attends mass at St Peter's on Christmas Day.

1897   Remains in Italy until June. *Amoris Victima* published by Smithers (March). Travels widely with Ellis that summer, visiting Bayreuth, Moscow, St Petersburg, Prague, Budapest, and Vienna. *Studies in Two Literatures* published (August). Returns to London (20 September). Second edition of *London Nights* published, with preface responding to earlier criticisms. Writes introduction to edition of Mathilde Blind's poems.

1898   Wins 100 guineas for *Studies in Two Literatures* in the *Academy's* annual awards to authors. Reviews *The Ballad of Reading Gaol* (*Saturday Review*, 12 March). Meets Rhoda Bowser (b. 1874) (May). Mark Symons dies (27 May). Visits France (mid-August onwards) staying with Comtesse de la Tour, before journeying to Spain, visiting

Valencia, Madrid, and Seville and staying at the Benedictine monastery at Monserrat. *Aubrey Beardsley* published (December). Translates the poems in D'Annunzio's *Il Piacere* for Georgina Harding's English edition (*The Child of Pleasure*). Also translates Émile Verhaeren's play, *Les Aubes* (*The Dawn*).

1899   Visits Paris (April). Appears in Walter Crane's *Beauty's Awakening: A Masque of Winter and Spring* (Guildhall, 28 May). Growing friendliness with Rhoda, who nicknames him 'Mimos'. He calls her 'Dodo'. Visits Swinburne and Watts-Dunton in Putney. Visits Bayreuth (August), then on to Bohemia and Leipzeig to study unpublished Casanova manuscripts. Discovers the missing fourth and fifth chapters of Book Twelve of his memoirs, publishing his account of their discovery in the *North American Review* (September 1902). They will be published by the Casanova Society in 1922. Returns to London (24 September). Translates D'Annunzio's play, *La Città Morta* (*The Dead City*). Writes introduction to the French translation of *Imaginary Portraits*.

1900   *The Symbolist Movement in Literature* published (5 March, but dated 1899). Also publishes new collection of poems, *Images of Good and Evil* (May). Writes Dowson's obituary in *The Athenæum* (3 March) and a lengthy essay on him in the *Fortnightly Review* (June). Reviews a number of performances by Eleonora Duse. Visits Hardy at Max Gate. In preparation for marriage to Rhoda, destroys many old papers and manuscripts. Tells her 'I have lived all my live evading responsibility [...] Shall we join two discontents and see if they make one happiness?' (Letter, 6 May).

1901   Marries Rhoda in Newcastle (19 January) and the couple move to 134 Lauderdale Mansions, Maida Vale. From April, his *Star* reviews appear under his own name instead of his 'Silhouette' pseudonym. He is paid £4 a week. *The Loom of Dreams* privately printed in an edition of twelve copies. December, publishes the two-volume edition of his *Poems* containing 'all that I care to preserve of those five volumes of verse which I have published.' Only nine poems from *Days and Nights* are retained. The edition is reprinted in 1906, 1907, 1909, 1919, and 1921. Translates D'Annunzio's *La Gioconda*.

1902   Sees Vladimir de Pachmann perform for the first time (February). Spends a fortnight in Paris with Rhoda (April). Leaves the *Star* and becomes drama and music critic for *The Academy*: his final review is of a play by John Oliver Hobbes and Murray Carson, *The Bishop's Move* (31 July) . Begins work on *Spiritual Adventures*. Between August and October, he and Rhoda visit Cologne, Munich, Bayreuth, Salzburg, Vienna, Budapest, Belgrade, Sofia, and Constantinople, though she is unacknowledged in his accounts of these cities. Meets James Joyce (December). Contributes articles on Hardy and the Goncourt Brothers to *Encyclopaedia Britannica*. Translates Dumas, *The Lady of the Camelias* and D'Annunzio's *Francesca da Rimini*.

1903   Meets J. M. Synge and Augustus John. Publishes lengthy essay on Whistler in *Weekly Critical Review* (July–August) plus many reviews and essays. *Plays, Acting and Music* appears (September) as well as *Cities* (October), the latter largely an account of his travels the previous year. Visits Switzerland and Italy in October–November, and writes the Venice sections of 'Henry Luxulyan' while staying in the city. Also journeys to Ravenna and Rome. *Lyrics* published (October).

1904   Returns to London after an absence of nine months (Spring). Meets Irish-American lawyer, John Quinn, later an important patron (November). *Studies in Prose and Verse* issued (November). Fails to find publisher for his play, *Tristan and Iseult*.

1905   John Lane's edition of Dowson's poems, with memoir by Symons, appears (May) and does much to establish the 'Dowson Legend'. Spends summer in Cornwall writing unperformed verse play, *The Harvesters*. *Spiritual Adventures* published (October), dedicated to Hardy. Translates Baudelaire's *Poems in Prose*. *A Book of Twenty Songs* published (December).

1906   Often in the British Museum working on Blake. Morality play, *The Fool of the World* produced by New Stage Club (Victoria Hall, Bayswater, 5 April). Translates a Sanskrit play, *Mrichchukati* by Sudraka he re-titles *The Toy Cart*. Publishes *The Fool of the World and Other Poems* (October), which includes all the poems from *A Book of Twenty Songs*. Buys seventeenth-century Island Cottage in Wittersham, Kent, and moves there in July. The property will prove ruinously expensive. Photographed by Alvin Langdon Coburn (22 September) — the portrait appears in his collection, *Men of Mark* (1913). Spends winter collaborating with Coburn on a book about London. *Studies in Seven Arts* published (November).

1907   Acquires pet dog, Api (February). *William Blake* (September) and *Cities of Italy* (October) published. Poems and some essays translated into French as *Poésies* and *Portraits Anglais*. Fails to find publisher for London book. Coburn publishes his photogravures of the city as *London* (1909). Death of Api (25 December) plunges the Symons into grief.

1908   Growing financial difficulties. Translates von Hofmannsthal's *Electra*. Co-edits the *Poésies fugitives* of Laclos. Visits France and Italy with Rhoda during autumn. Relations between them are poor. Symons leaves his wife in Venice and heads off to Bologna (26 September). She follows him there, but he leaves her again and heads to Ferrara where he has a serious psychotic episode and is imprisoned in Castello Vecchio. Rhoda gets the Italian ambassador to London to intervene, and Symons is returned to England in early October accompanied by two male nurses and placed in an institution in Crowborough, East Sussex. The *Saturday Review* publishes 'Music in Venice' (17 October), the 'document', Symons later says, 'in which my madness is most evident'. Certified insane (2 November) and committed to Brooke House, Upper Clapton Road, East London (now demolished). Prose section of the Coburn collaboration published privately for copyright purposes as *London: A Book of Aspects* (November). Visited by Yeats (December).

1909   Writes obsessively while in Brooke House, though much of this work is later lost or destroyed. Doctors predict Symons has only 12–18 months to live, but recovery begins, helped by friends such as the American poet and translator, Agnes Tobin, Ezra Pound, and Augustus John (who does a drawing, now lost, of Symons in Brooke House). Begins to revisit old haunts such as Empire Theatre with friends and Brooke House attendants. *The Romantic Movement in English Poetry* published (September). Awarded a lifelong Royal Literary Fund grant.

1910   Moves to Hampstead under medical care before returning to Island Cottage (7 April). Meets Joseph Conrad.

1911   Attempts to rebuild career with a few reprinted articles and short pieces in the *Journal of the Gypsy Lore Society*. Visited by André Gide.

1912   Publishes his first poem since his breakdown, 'Hymn of Thanksgiving to Our Lady' (*English Review*, June). Writing poetic and prose elegies for Api. Four poems by Symons included by Arthur Quiller-Couch in *The Oxford Book of Victorian Verse*.

1913   Awarded Civil List pension of £120. Publishes *Knave of Hearts*, poems and translations 1894–1908 (November). *For Api* and *Songs for Api* privately printed. They are reprinted in the third volume of his *Collected Works* (1924).

1914   Receives copy of *Dubliners* from Joyce. 'Notes on the Sensations of a Lady of the Ballet' appears in *International* (April).

1915 Tentative recovery continues with around a dozen new articles published. Considers publishing his 'Lucy Newcome' stories as a novel, but is advised against it by Hardy. Holidaying in Cornwall, is briefly detained by police who fear he may be a spy.

1916 *The Toy Cart: An Oriental Melodrama* receives two matinée performances at The Queen's Theatre with Rhoda in the lead role. Reviews are poor, with *The Times* calling it 'a mild, slightly soporific entertainment' (11 July). Contributing to *Vanity Fair* and other journals. Publishes *Tragedies* (September) and *Figures of Several Centuries* (December), the latter dedicated to Conrad. Burns all unpublished poems written during childhood and adolescence except for 'A Dream of the Garden of God'.

1917 Has portrait painted by Augustus John. *Tristan and Iseult* published (December), dedicated to Duse.

1918 *The Toy Cart* enjoys a three week run in Dublin. *The Dead City* performed in London by the Incorporated Stage Society. *Cities and Sea-Coasts and Islands* published (October), reproducing John's recent portrait as the frontispiece and incorporating *London: A Book of Aspects*. The *Times Literary Supplement* calls it a relic of 'yellow bookery' (3 October). *Colour Studies in Paris* published (November).

1919 New edition of radically revised *The Symbolist Movement in Literature* published in US by E. P. Dutton, along with *Studies in the Elizabethan Drama* (published in Britain in 1920). *The Toy Cart* published in London. Writes introduction to an American edition of Pater's *The Renaissance*.

1920 Visits Paris. Begins writing memoirs, visits Café Royal regularly. *Lesbia and Other Poems* and *Charles Baudelaire* published.

1921 Visits Paris again. Spends summer in Cornwall with Ellis. Translating Villiers de l'Isle-Adam. Contributes to the music journal, *The Sackbut*, edited by the composer Philip Heseltine ('Peter Warlock').

1922 Meets W. H. Davies and Heseltine, who will compose settings of some of his lyrics. Richard Le Gallienne includes three poems from *Silhouettes* in his American anthology, *The Le Gallienne Book of English Verse*.

1923 Martin Secker agrees to print sixteen-volume edition *Collected Works*. Visits Paris with Ellis, meets Nancy Cunard, to whom he dedicates *The Café Royal and Other Essays* (December). *Dramatis Personae* published in US (British edition 1925).

1924   Nine volumes of *Collected Works* published: three of poetry, *William Blake, Spiritual Adventures, Tragedies* (two volumes), *Studies in Two Literatures, Studies in Seven Arts*. Also publishes volume of translations, *From Catullus*.

1925   Secker abandons the collected edition after disappointing sales. Travels to Paris alone. *Studies on Modern Painters* and *Notes on Joseph Conrad* published, along with controversial selection of translations from Baudelaire.

1926   His last prolific year, with thirteen articles published along with *Eleonora Duse* and *Parisian Nights*. Visits Hardy on his 86th birthday. Publishes translations of Villiers de l'Isle-Adam's *Claire Lenoir*.

1927   Publishes *A Study of Thomas Hardy* and translation of Villiers de l'Isle-Adam's *Queen Ysabeau*. Meets Arnold Bennett.

1928   Attends Hardy's funeral (January). Contributes introduction to Alistair's illustrated edition of Poe's 'The Fall of the House of Usher'. A. J. A. Symons (no relation) includes ten Symons poems in *An Anthology of 'Nineties Verse*. Publishes translation of Baudelaire's letters to his mother. Increasingly frail, writes to *Times* about the noise of traffic and motor horns, 'a positive peril and devastating menace to the more sensitive of us' (27 August).

1929   The first year since 1882 in which Symons does not publish in periodicals. He does however publish *Studies in Strange Souls, From Toulouse-Lautrec to Rodin* and *Mes Souvenirs*, brief memoirs of Verlaine and others.

1930   *Confessions: A Study of Pathology* and *A Study of Oscar Wilde* published. *The Toy Cart* revived in London.

1931   Publishes *Wanderings*, a mixture of old and new travel essays, plus *Jezebel Mort and Other Poems* and a translation of *The Adventures of Giuseppe Pignata*.

1932   *A Study of Walter Pater* published. Attempts to find publisher for memoirs, but refuses to compromise on their contents and organization and is unable to issue them.

1935   Rhoda diagnosed with leukaemia. She has pursued a theatrical career without success and has often lived at their London flat while Symons remains at Island Cottage. Their marriage has frequently been unhappy. Publishes translation of Pierre Louÿs's *The Woman and the Puppet*.

1936   Death of Rhoda (3 November). Her estate is in excess of £43,000, throwing into relief the couple's money problems during their marriage. Henceforth, Symons is cared for by Bessie Seymour, who has been his housekeeper since 1921. Yeats includes two of the Verlaine translations from *Knave of Hearts* in his *Oxford Book of Modern Verse, 1892–1935* but no original poems.

1938   Sees Yvette Guilbert perform for the last time.

1940   Private publication of *Amoris Victimia* (*sic*), his final account of his relationship with Lydia. John Betjeman publishes his poetic account of seeing Symons alone in a London restaurant, 'On Seeing an Old Poet in the Café Royal', in *Old Lights for New Chancels: Verses Topographical and Amatory*.

1945   Dies from pneumonia at Island Cottage (22 January). Library and effects auctioned at Sotheby's (25–26 June). His wealth at death is a mere £486.

Early Stories and Essays

~

An Episode in the Life of Jenny Lane

Probably the earliest of Symons's extant stories, 'Jenny Lane' was unpublished until it appeared in *English Literature in Transition* (29.4) with an afterword by Alan Johnson in 1986. Johnson suggested the story was written around 1892, a reasonable supposition which might be supported by its plethora of Tennysonian references: the Laureate died in October that year. He reads the story as gently ironic at the expense of the young Symons of *Silhouettes*, noting its oppositions of town and country and the contrast between Jenny's Tennysonian affiliations and the Paterian ones of Herbert Travers, the Symons-surrogate. Symons spent most of August 1888 in Bodmin, Cornwall, where he had plentiful relatives. His letters paint a picture of 'drives & excursions & picnics'; his visit was 'a delightful change' from his usual life[1] The fourth section of 'A Prelude to Life' reflects on that summer's events, and Travers's trip to the fictitious country town of Deresham (probably Liskeard) is probably inspired by them. 'Prelude's' daughter 'with a touch of rebellious refinement' may also allude to Jenny's real-life inspiration, though neither fiction should be taken at face value.

Symons's title employed another of his favourite words. The 'episode' was central to his plans for 'Lucy Newcome', and it appeared in early poems such as 'An Episode under the Nihilists' and 'Episode of a Night in May', the most accomplished piece in *Days and Nights*. The episode was a brief, self-contained, and intensely realized experience which lingered in the memory and shaped the future. Seven years after Travers's departure, Jenny still keeps the proofs of his poems in a locked drawer, and cannot bring herself to burn them, even though she has chosen to reject a life of 'renunciation for an ideal.'

Johnson sees elements of self-parody in this story, which he feels mocks Symons's affectations and the defence of urban subject matter that forms the preface to the second edition of *Silhouettes* in 1896. However, for all that Travers is presented as self-centred and somewhat patronising, it is difficult to miss the cruel exposure of Jenny's romantic longings as she seeks 'somebody who should

---

[1] Beckson, *Arthur Symons: A Life*, p. 42.

complete the promise of the moonlight'. 'She realised quite well the fate she was preparing for herself — that she would never care for anyone again.' Will her brief taste of honey turn her into Emma Bovary once she marries a humble farmer? Dorian Gray abandons the innocent country girl, Hetty, in chapter nineteen of Wilde's novel, believing that he is sparing her from tragedy. 'The fact of having met you, and loved you, will teach her to despise her husband, and she will be wretched,' Lord Henry drawls, noting how she can now never be happy with 'a rough carter or a grinning ploughman.'[2] Symons may indeed be looking wryly at his pursuit of sensation, but even in this early story, he implies literature's incompatibility with life. At its conclusion, an emotionally inexperienced young woman is about to be sacrificed on the altar of Travers's art, as he seeks 'the rhythm that would render her charm in verse.' What produces poetry in him sentences his muse to a life of drudgery and compromise. Symons's own experience of marriage would, in due course, make 'An Episode' still more ironic.

* * *

Jenny Lane rose every morning at seven o'clock, and found, every morning, the same pile of socks to darn. Every morning, after the maid had done her dusting, she took down the seven cups and saucers, which a grandfather had brought in his ship from India, and carefully dusted them; then she dusted the harp which had belonged to her mother, and which stood, recalling her memory, in a corner of the parlour. The younger children had to be in school by nine; at nine Onslow had to start on his bicycle, so as to reach the office in town by ten o'clock. Her father was no longer anxious to be afield early, and he would sometimes call to her to help him in finding one of those curious old books which he took such pride in possessing, and which he liked to bring home from sales, and range in rows, one above the other, where he could see them and handle them. It was Onslow who read them, and Mr Lane was sometimes a little put out at finding a volume of Ben Jonson or Pope missing from his book-case: of course Jenny did not read Pope or Ben Jonson, but there was a Tennyson which no one else cared for, in which she used to read some poems over and over again.[3] She generally

---

[2] Wilde, *The Picture of Dorian Gray*, p. 177.

[3] Ben Jonson (1572–1637), English poet and dramatist, author of *Volpone* (1605) and *The Alchemist* (1610) amongst other plays. Alexander Pope (1688–1744), English poet, translator, and satirist; master of the heroic couplet. Alfred, Lord Tennyson (1809–1892), English poet and dramatist, Poet Laureate from 1850 until his death. Tennyson was a dominant presence in Victorian poetry, but by the time Symons wrote this story, there had been a notable reaction against him. Symons himself paid his work little attention, though he was clearly familiar with it. Though he always preferred Browning and Swinburne, he had been influenced by Tennyson in his juvenile verses, and sent him a presentation copy of *Days and Nights*.

had time in the evening; indeed, her life was not over-filled with occupation, though such tasks as she had were the same every day.

She was not expected to see to anything on the farm; her duties were all indoors. She had made so many antimacassars in her time, that at twenty-seven it seemed to her that it was time to adopt a new kind of fancy-work; her younger sister Emily, too, before she was married, had made antimacassars,[4] and there were not enough chairs for them in the house. She could not think of anything else to do, and she was rather glad on the whole, when young Jones, and the farmer from the neighbouring village, came over to Hilldene to see her. She knew why he came, and she had not absolutely said No, as she had done to all who had come before; not that she liked him better, but because it seemed, after all, the only thing to do. There was no reason why Jones should not make a good husband, as husbands went; she had extravagant ideas on the subject.

One day she unlocked a certain drawer in her room, took out a small bundle, and sat down by the fire with the bundle on her knees. It was a packet of printer's proofs, the proofs were a volume of poems. She turned over the pages: there were corrections here and there in a picturesque handwriting of a man who wrote for effect. When she had turned over several pages she took up the packet in her hands and held it towards the fire, hesitated, drew it back, and sat for a long time looking into the fire and holding the packet on the edge of her knees. Finally, she drew it towards her, tied it up again, and put it back in the drawer. Next day she accepted young Jones.

Seven years before, Jenny had said to herself that she would never marry, and that it had seemed to her a splendid sentiment — a renunciation for an ideal. In seven years a sentiment gets worn out. She had not forgotten her ideal, but it seemed useless living up to it any longer. She felt that the time for being romantic had passed. It was difficult even to remember how she had been affected by the episode which was the romance of Jenny Lane's existence. She had been twenty then, and now she was twenty-seven. That was the difference.

One day (this was when she was twenty) Onslow had come home full of excitement, to tell them that Herbert Travers, the poet, was really coming to see them. All the children clapped their hands, for they had heard of Onslow's wonderful new friend. Jenny said nothing; turning her head, it was doubtless by accident that she caught sight of her own face in the glass.

Onslow Lane, Jenny's younger brother, was an odd youth, whom his father's library had made a reader, and whom his reading had driven into verse. He had read the English poets steadily through Chaucer down to Wordsworth, learning whole scenes from the Elizabethan dramatists and whole cantos of the *Faerie*

---

[4] Macassar hair oil was extremely popular throughout the nineteenth century. An antimacassar is a small piece of cloth, often embroidered or decorated, that prevents furniture from being damaged by it.

Queene by heart.[5] How much he understood of what he read it was difficult to determine. He cared, at all events, for nothing else, and his desk, at the office where he dreamed away his time, always contained one or two volumes of poetry, which he took out as soon as his master's back was turned. From learning poetry by heart, he naturally went on to writing in imitation of what he had read; and he would make love to all the girls within walking distance of his home in Spenserian stanzas, which they could not in the least understand. If they were discouraging, he lampooned them in the same measure; and then they usually found the poetry quite clear.

Onslow's acquaintance with modern poetry was very limited. He had not come to it in his reading, which was chronological. But the young man at the bookseller's shop in town had told him that a young poet, whose first book had been very well received by the critics, was there on a visit to friends; and the news filled him with excitement. He had never seen a poet in his life, and here was one, actually walking about the lazy streets of Deresham. He knew in a minute that the elegant young man who generally came over the bridge about midday — he had seen him from the office door — was Herbert Travers. He was tall and slender, with light brown hair that curled about his ears; he walked lightly, with a certain spring; and seemed to take a pleasant note of things and people, as he passed, carelessly enough, about them. Every day Onslow watched him, wishing he could summon up courage to speak to him; and at home he was constantly talking of Herbert Travers. At last he happened to meet him in the bookseller's shop, and with a tremendous effort he went up to him, as Travers stood by the counter, looking whimsically at a photograph he had just discovered — a portrait of a great friend of his, an actress, which it amused him to find so unexpectedly under his hand. Travers turned, hearing himself addressed, and still holding the photograph he considered with some curiosity the fresh-faced, boyish-looking young man at his side. It amused him to be considered a personage, in this little country town, and when the young man begged that he would lend him his poems to read, he promised readily enough. Some days afterwards Travers called at the office with a copy of the proofs of his book, which was all he had with him. Onslow was reading 'Hero and Leander,' which he was learning by heart.[6] He began to recite the splendid verses, correctly, though with a mechanical delivery. It all seemed very strange to Herbert Travers, and the more he questioned the

---

[5] Onslow's survey of the English canon highlights Geoffrey Chaucer (*c.* 1343–1400), author of *The Canterbury Tales* and other works. William Wordsworth (1770–1850), English Romantic poet and Tennyson's predecessor as Laureate (1843–50). *The Faerie Queene* is a lengthy but unfinished allegory by the Elizabethan poet, Edmund Spenser (1552 or 1553–99) published initially in 1590 and extended in 1596. It is renowned for its consciously archaic and richly decorative style, making it a poor model for Onslow's immature poetic experiments.

[6] An unfinished classical mock epic by Christopher Marlowe (1564–93), later completed by George Chapman (*c.* 1559–1634) and published in 1598.

youth the more did the youth surprise him. He went to see him again, and in a casual fashion, became friendly with him, for Travers liked people who amused him.

Onslow took home the book with him, and told all about the poet. It was Jenny who appropriated the sheets, which seemed so specially wonderful to her in their unbound form, with a few corrections here and there. She carried them away to her bedroom, and read them over and over again. The poems were of a kind she hardly understood, some of them frightening her a little: it seemed wicked to have written them. Herbert Travers had written *Fate's Disguises* rather under the influence of Baudelaire and Heine.[7] There was a certain perversity about the work (partly natural, partly assumed) which seemed to the girl dreadfully dangerous and fascinating. And then there were pieces which charmed her by their melancholy sweetness. He had loved, this young poet, but he had never (so the pieces said) found the ideal love.

And Jenny, too, felt that she had an ideal, which had certainly never been satisfied. How often she had read Tennyson, and dreamed vague dreams under the moonlight! The dreams had been very vague, but she had fancied somebody, some day, coming shiningly into the dullness of her life, somebody who would complete the promise of the moonlight. Onslow and his verses, his recitations, his talk about all these things, had intensified in her a queer sentimental, half unconscious craving for the romantic in life; and she had never, never so long as she could remember, had the least satisfaction of her desires. She had always lived at Hilldene, nobody had ever come to Hilldene, it seemed ridiculous to expect anyone to come to Hilldene.

And now, with a new kind of delight, she was reading these poems of the new poet, in the copy that was so peculiarly his; and the new poet was good to her brother, and came to see him. If he would only — she checked herself at the thought; and yet, why not? — if he would only come and see them! It always seemed to Onslow that he had been the first to suggest that they should invite Mr Travers out some fine Sunday. The suggestion, anyway, once made, seemed delightful to everybody: none of them had ever seen a poet! But would the poet come?

'My sister would like to see you,' Onslow said, with great simplicity, when he ventured, rather timidly, to suggest a drive into the country. And Travers, who had been on the point of refusing, changed his mind, and agreed to come.

---

[7] Charles Baudelaire (1821–67), French poet much admired by Symons. His influential first collection, *Les Fleurs du mal* (*The Flowers of Evil*, 1857), was successfully prosecuted for offending public morals. Heinrich Heine (1797–1856), German poet whose *Buch der Leider* (*Book of Songs*, 1827) was enormously popular. Many of its lyrics were set to music by the likes of Schubert, Mendelssohn, and Schumann. *Fate's Disguises* perhaps fuses the German's fondness for lyricism, irony, and disillusionment with the Frenchman's more transgressive subject matter.

It was with a certain anxiety that Travers got out of the trap that Sunday afternoon, and followed Onslow up the path to the porch. Was he going to be bored? he wondered, as he stooped under the trails of clematis; and the silence of the house made him vaguely uneasy. Probably he was going to be bored.

He had not talked ten minutes with Mr Lane, who rose to greet him, with a cheery welcome, from a leisurely arm-chair in the parlour, before he was quite sure he was not going to be bored. The farmer seemed to him to talk like nobody he had ever met before: all his phrases had a quaint, rustic wit (with an odd touch of book-learning) that quite enchanted the town-bred man of letters, always on the look-out for new sensations.[8] And presently the village school-master came in, and it was indeed a comedy to hear the young man, with his country accent, allude in every other sentence to 'when I was at college' — some training school apparently. But where were those sisters? thought Travers. At last there was a sound of voices, and one after another the sisters crowded into the room, carrying hymn-books in their hands. They had just returned from Sunday-school.

Travers shook hands with the five, one after another, pleased most of all, at the first glance, with one of the smaller ones, whose brown hair tumbled in curls about her face, and who looked at him with such friendly and delighted wonderment. It was only when he went into the kitchen to tea that it occurred to him to take any notice of Jenny.

To Jenny the moment was the most wonderful moment of her life. The poet of whom she had heard so much, whose book she had upstairs in her bedroom, the poet about whom she had dreamed so many dreams, was here; she had shaken hands with him; he was sitting opposite to her, and she was asking him if he took sugar in his tea. Oh! This was not how she had fancied him: she had imagined a more remote creature, handsome in quite a different kind of way. That other person of her imagination, she would have looked up to him from a distance, she would have admired him from afar off. But Herbert Travers was not in the least remote; here he was sitting at their tea-table as if he were but taking his natural place, eating their country bread and butter with an evident relish, and chatting very gaily about nothing at all, as if he had known them all his life. And she too felt — how could she explain it to herself? — strangely at home, a great contentment swallowing up all the strangeness, as the clear blue eyes that seemed to take things so for granted, in their kindly and confident smile, rested steadily upon her.

---

[8] Perhaps a gentle caricature of John Lane (1854–1925), the Devon-born book dealer and publisher who co-founded The Bodley Head and published the radical magazine, the *Yellow Book* (1894–97). The Wildean 'gospel of sensation' was regularly alluded to in fiction and journalism of the early 1890s. '[N]ew sensations are the only things worth living for,' says Lightmark, the bohemian artist in Ernest Dowson and Arthur Moore's *A Comedy of Masks* (New York: D. Appleton, 1893), p. 64.

After tea, there was some talk of church, and Travers, finding that the young people, as a matter of course, were going, declared he would go too. Jenny had hardly ventured to hope for this, and it was with immense pride that the girls marched up the aisle, escorting their distinguished guest. Travers had not been in church for so long that the service was itself a new sensation. He thought that he could often go to church, if it were with these bright young people, the friendly Maggie sitting next to him, her brown curls sitting next to him. And afterwards, walking back with them to the farm-house, the girls told him stories about their neighbours — all the little gossip of the village, with delightful touches of natural wit. Jenny did not say much, and Travers found himself considering the pretty profile of the girl, as she walked quietly by his side, with a pensive look on her face. She was thinking that after all he could not be really wicked and unbelieving, since he had come with them to Church, and had behaved so reverently there. She was well aware, too, that he had looked at her once or twice, rather intently, and she felt that now, at the moment, he was thinking about her. A sudden wave of crimson flooded her cheeks, and seemed to burn there; at which an overwhelming self-consciousness took possession of her. She was glad when they reached the door; for now there was supper to attend to.

By the time supper was over, everyone was talking to Herbert Travers as if he were an old friend, and there was a joyous proposal that they should all sit around the fire and be merry. It seemed to Travers the most odd, the most delightful position, as he found himself at the end of a long semi-circle, in what was almost a chimney-corner. The stories which had amused him on the way home from church were resumed, and all the comedy of the countryside seemed to pass before him, as father and children told tale after tale, with a humorous appreciation of every comic possibility. At the time, entering into the situation with his usual absorption in the moment, he declared to himself that here, after all, among these people who were not too educated to be natural, was the true wit. And he tried to remember when he had been so genuinely amused in London.

The family did not spare one another, and many a story was told at the expense of Onslow and his verse-makings. At this Jenny grew a little indignant, and she suggested that he should read one of his poems to Mr Travers and get the benefit of his criticism. Travers was conscious, during the reading, that the eyes of all the family were upon him, and he found it quite easy, at the conclusion of the ordeal, to say a sympathetic word about the astonishing production to which he had listened — it was one of those lampoons against some village Mary written in the loftiest Spenserian language, with which Onslow generally concluded his transitory passages of love. Jenny was really proud of her brother, she was full of gratitude to the poet for his serious reception of the verses, and Travers seemed to her every moment more adorable. She would have turned the clock, had she dared, with its face to the wall, so acutely did she dread the moment which came only too soon, when he rose suddenly, and declared he must be going.

Again it seemed to Onslow that it was from him the suggestion had come, that Jenny should drive into town with them, and so be company for him in coming back. Meanwhile, Jenny was upstairs, feeling horribly, as she adjusted it before the glass, that her prettiest hat would seem countrified to the poet who had sung, in one of the lighter pieces of *Fate's Disguises*, of the delights of dainty dress, the town elegance. When she came downstairs, Travers realised that she was prettier than he had fancied, and he wondered vaguely what rhythm would fit the country charm of her aspect.

It was a long goodbye, and everyone wanted to say the last word. 'Come and see us again,' they begged, 'if you should ever again visit Deresham,' for Travers, they knew, was returning to London within two days. The promise given — Travers always gave his promises readily — he followed Onslow and Jenny into the trap, and the drive through the moonlight began.

The road twisted through the village, a green path even before the few houses were left behind, and the hedges pointed the way to Deresham. As they passed into the shadow of the trees, Jenny felt a great longing that the man who, for once, was so near to her, would tell her something about himself; and she turned to him so expectant, so strangely sympathetic a face, that Travers, half deliberately, half instinctively, threw himself into the mood of the hour, and began to talk to her in quite a different way from the gay chatter of that circle round the fireside. In a simple phrase, which to her meant much, she told him how she had read his poems, and he begged her to keep the poor copy, which she seemed to prize so strangely. With the sentimental girl nestling against him in the trap, Travers found it quite natural to tell her about his poems, about some moods of his which the situation seemed to call up, and which she received in a silent ecstasy. He seemed to her to be telling her all his soul; she fancied herself entrusted with great confidences, no one had ever so answered to her vague, unconfessed longings before. Here, at last, was the somebody she had dreamed of, somebody who should complete the promise of the moonlight! She lifted her eyes to the serene brightness of the heavens, as if she saw the stars for the first time. It was with a passionate exultation, with the acutest sense, too, that her joy was born only for the briefest death. In that moment she summoned all her faculties into eager activity — to keep, at all events, the supreme sensation! She would never forget one word, one look, the tone of his voice, the infinite delight of his presence. She realized quite well the fate she was preparing for herself — that she would never care for anyone again. But she abandoned herself to the perilous delight. Herbert Travers, looking down upon her with, himself, a pleasant sense of the situation, saw enough of the feeling he had evoked to quicken in him the artistic instinct.

As the drive came to an end, Jenny said goodbye very briefly, but it was with a look into which she put her soul, all her soul, naked of disguise. She gave him her heart then, with her hand, at the last parting. He did not notice it: he had just found the rhythm that would render her charm in verse.

~

The Extra Lady

'The Extra Lady' is a mixture of the autobiographical and the fashionable. It is far more detailed and precise than later pieces such as 'A Prelude to Life', and both its atmosphere and incidental detail suggest that it is drawn from personal experience. Bitter vignettes, which combined well observed London settings with a dash of Maupassant were very much in vogue in the early to mid 1890s, and this story is surely strongly influenced by Hubert Crackanthorpe, soon to be a contributor to *The Savoy*.[1] Anecdotal, sketchy, and downbeat, the 'new realism' won its practitioners publication in the *English Illustrated Magazine*, where Gissing published a number of stories, *Black and White* and, most famously, the *Yellow Book*: Arnold Bennett's story, 'A Letter Home' (1895), is a good example. Despite occasional infelicities in his first collection, *Wreckage* (1893), Crackanthorpe's stories are, 'strikingly modern in their presentation of such contemporary themes as loneliness, alienation, the inability of human beings to communicate with each other, and the need to be loved,' says William Peden.[2] 'The Extra Lady' similarly offers pathos without sentimentality in picturing Becky's commonplace and joyless life. Symons knew Crackanthorpe reasonably well, and after Crackanthorpe's death, wrote a generous appreciation of him in the *Saturday Review* (8 January 1898).

'The Extra Lady' appeared in the eccentric journal, *The Senate*, 'A Review of Modern and Progressive Thought' in July 1895, and was reprinted in *Everyman* (7 September 1918). As Alex Murray shows, *The Senate* shared a number of its contributors with the *Yellow Book* and *The Savoy*; its openness to 'decadent' writers probably explains why Symons published his story in it rather than elsewhere.[3] 'The Extra Lady' is unexceptionable in itself, but Symons's public

---

[1] Symons's obituary of Maupassant appeared in *The Athenæum*, 15 July 1893, p. 97.
[2] William Peden, 'Introduction' to Hubert Crackanthorpe, *Collected Stories* (Gainesville, FL: Scholars' Facsimiles and Reprints, 1968), p. x.
[3] Alex Murray, 'Decadent Conservatism: Politics and Aesthetics in *The Senate*', *Journal of Victorian Culture* 20.2 (February 2015), pp. 186–211. Between March 1895 and July 1897, Symons contributed regularly to the journal: a story, five poems, two critical essays, and an account of a visit to Arles (later reprinted in *Wanderings*).

association with decadence made it difficult for him to place his work in the summer of 1895. 'We were very unpopular,' he told Katherine Lyon Mix in a discussion of the public reaction against radical young writers. 'There was a great exodus. We all went [to France]; we didn't dare stay.'[4]

The seemingly direct treatment of personal experience in this story lacks the artfulness of later pieces. Read in conjunction with 'At the Alhambra', it forms a valuable account of his adventures in the London theatre world of the early to mid 1890s. It is likely that 'Lilian' is Violet Pigott, a dancer with whom Symons had an affair in 1892 and who appears in *London Nights*. She was, he says, 'stupid, sensual, pretty and not perverse; she was slender and had shapely legs.' The relationship could hardly be described as a meeting of minds, Symons remarking that 'she was no more to me than a thing of the flesh' and there was 'naturally no question' of love between them. Nevertheless, he was hurt by their parting when Violet emigrated to America. Symons attended a horrible leaving party at a public house aptly called The Final. 'The whole scene was so sordid and so mean, so abominable,' he recalled, 'that it reminded me of certain scenes of Zola'.[5]

* * *

At the Folly Theatre of Varieties, Becky had only one friend, and that friend was the prettiest girl at the theatre.[6] Becky was the plainest. She could never understand why Lilian had ever accepted her as a companion, though in reality the reason was quite simple. They both lived in the same direction, and Lilian disliked going home by herself at night.

Becky was the plainest girl at the theatre, so plain that it was a wonder how she could ever have found her way into the position of even an 'extra lady.' She was short and thickset, with a sort of squat face; she had large ears, a large mouth, heavy eyebrows, and eyes that were always wide open in a fixed, unalterably solemn stare. Her expression was uniform; it was one of awkward, eager, painful amiability. She never had anything to say, and, as Lilian put it, if you talked to her for a month you could get nothing out of her. Lilian did not mind her friend being plain: she certainly did not choose her for that reason: she never gave a thought to the matter. She knew that Becky was devoted to her, and she was

---

[4] Katherine Lyon Mix, *A Study in Yellow: The Yellow Book and its Contributors* (London: Constable, 1960), p. 160.

[5] Symons, *The Memoirs of Arthur Symons*, pp. 113–14. Emile Zola (1840-1902), French novelist and pioneer of literary naturalism. He was often criticized for the sordidness and obscenity of his subject matter, even in France. When Henry Vizetelly translated *La Terre* ('The Earth') into English in 1888, he was prosecuted for obscenity and later jailed.

[6] The Folly Theatre in King William IV Street, Strand, began life as the Lowther Rooms in 1840, becoming the Folly in 1876. Renamed Toole's Theatre in 1882, it endured mixed fortunes before being closed in 1896, when its buildings became part of Charing Cross Hospital.

always ready to accept devotion, when it did not become troublesome. Lilian was seventeen (a year older than her friend), tall for her age, slim, almost boyish in figure. The colour came and went in her cheeks with every mood, in variable little waves. Her face was a delicate oval, delicately irregular in profile, the nose like a curved shell, the mouth a little pouting, softly arched. Her eyes, under their long eyelashes, were of a deep, luminous blue, the eyeballs tinged with that beautiful blue mist that one sees so rarely, and that gives the eyes so curious a beauty. She had the queerest little shy air — an air of shy defiance — through which peeped and laughed a little laughing devil of mischief. She always talked on the stage; was down in the fine book every night; and had her fines let off at Treasury on Saturday afternoon. Becky on the other hand, was the best conducted girl in the theatre. She never talked, she was never late, she was never away. It is true she had no provocation to misbehaviour. No one wanted to talk to her on the stage, no one shot smiles to her across the foot-lights from the front row of the stalls, no one asked her to go to a theatre in the evening. It was only Lilian who was good to her, who was her friend; and the whole life of the poor little person was concentrated on the half hour during which she walked down the road with Lilian to the stage-door, before the performance, and the half-hour during which she walked up the road with her, after it.

One night, at the stage-door, Lilian was introduced to a young man who often came round there, vaguely enough, to while away the half-hour before and after midnight, in some pleasant company. He knew a good many of the girls, but he had no special friend there, and he would ask sometimes one, sometimes another, to have a drink with him. He was a young painter, to whom Degas had revealed the charm of the ballet; and he haunted the Folly Theatre, looking for subjects, which he painted impressionistically.[7] His friends at the theatre thought his pictures ugly and unintelligible; but they looked on him with a certain respect, all the same, because he was a painter; and they liked him, because he was nice to be with. Lilian had often noticed him; she had heard pleasant stories of him from the other girls, and she was very proud of making his acquaintance. That first night, he only talked with her for a few minutes, and then he said 'goodbye,' and went off with someone else. Lilian watched him move down the road with a sort of vague, instinctive disappointment. She was rather silent with Becky that night, and the next day, as they were coming down the road together, she said, suddenly 'I wonder if Mr Winter will be round tonight.' As she ran on to the stage, in the first scene of the ballet, in her fisher-boy's dress, she saw him there, in the front

---

[7] Edgar Degas (1834–1917), French artist often associated with Impressionism (a term he disliked). He produced many studies of dancers and ballerinas, and in *London: A Book of Aspects* (written in 1907 but unpublished until 1918), Symons saw himself as having 'tried to do in verse something of what Degas had done in painting' (*Cities and Sea-Coasts and Islands*, p. 208). Winter would seem to be another of Symons's self-portraits.

row of the stalls; their eyes met, and he smiled. She dressed quickly after the performance was over, and was one of the first to be out. He was there, and he looked pleased to see her, and they had a merry little chat before someone else came along to interrupt them. That night Lilian talked to Becky of nothing but Mr Winter, of what he had said, and how he had looked. Becky listened, as she had listened so often before, looking up with her great round eyes, into the face of her beautiful friend, drinking in everything she said, with so entire an absorption, that it never occurred to her to say anything in return. Lilian did not notice the omission.

To Winter, Lilian was only a child, but he had often noticed her on the stage, and her shy grace, her adolescent charm, a quaint lily-like way she had of drooping her head a little on side, had come to him with an exquisite sensation of youth, and the fleeting perfection of its moment. It had amused him to meet her, and he very soon saw that she always looked out for him at the stage door, and that she smiled at him with the frankest welcome whenever he came in front. One night he asked her to have a drink with him, and, rather to his surprise, for he had never seen her with any of the other girls, in the bars that they all frequented, she came at once. Only, she introduced him to her friend Becky, and it was as a matter of course that Becky went with them. Winter thought her hideous, and he did not like to be seen in her company. They all walked up the road together afterwards, and at the corner of Becky's street he put Lilian into her 'bus.

Soon it came to be the recognised thing most evenings, for Winter and Lilian, always with the prim little chaperone Becky, to turn into the private bar of the Chequers, and then to walk up the road together. To Lilian, it was quite a new experience, something altogether different from the boy and girl flirtations, of which she had tripped so lightly through so many. She told Becky all her heart, and Becky, always unselfish, and living more in her friend than in herself, had her part in the little romance, and was quite happy in seeing the happiness of Lilian. She had never come so near to a romance in her life, and it seemed to her the most wonderful of privileges to be allowed to share in it. Winter was scrupulously polite to her, and she too adored him at a distance, in that odd, impersonal way of hers. For the present she seemed to have lost nothing in Lilian, and to have gained a new interest in life.

That was at first, while Lilian still thought a sort of chaperone needful. But gradually Lilian came to wish that Becky sometimes would not accept the invitation which Winter, to humour her, still felt bound to extend to her friend. Once or twice, for one reason or another, Becky did not come with them; and it was a relief to Lilian as well as to Winter. Then, alone with her new friend, her lover, as she could begin to fancy him, how freely, with what ardent abandonment, she would chatter to him, of all the little nothings that made up her life, at home, with her mother, her sister, and the lodgers, and at the theatre, with all the girls, the stage-manager, the vague public in front. To the young man, living so quietly, so very different a life, all this was like news from another planet, and Lilian's confidences, the overflowing chatter of a delightful child, had an exquisite charm for him. He would find himself, during the day, as he stood brush in hand, before a canvas, on which he was trying to fix some wandering mystery of light, thinking suddenly of what Lilian would have to tell him that evening; and he looked forward to half-past eleven, as the most delightful hour of the day. If only Becky could be got rid of! One night, when Becky had had to hurry home, he suggested to Lilian that they should walk on beyond the usual stopping place, and she could take the 'bus higher up. Strolling along side by side, they forgot the distance, and found themselves, almost before they knew it, at the corner of the remote street where Lilian lived. For the first time, Winter saw the house of which he had heard so much; and he stood on the doorstep a long time, with his arm round her, talking in whispers. As he walked down the long road, presently, along the deserted pavement, with the thrill of her soft kiss still in his veins, he said to himself once more, and with greater decision, that Becky must be got rid of, once for all.

Lilian was thinking the same thing, as she slipped upstairs, hoping her mother would be asleep, and so not notice how late she was. She sat in her bedroom a long time, that night, before getting into bed, thinking over the events of the day, and that wonderful evening. Next day she said very little to Becky on the way down, she was cross and frettish, and poor Becky could not make out how she had offended her, or what was the matter. It happened that that evening there were festivities among the extra ballet; it was a club night, and they had some money to spend. Everyone was expected to drink, and Becky, who never took anything stronger than lemonade and a dash, was made to drink some whisky.[8] Of course it flew to her head, she got giddy, almost fell down in the second dance, and had to go off in the last scene. Lilian was really and sincerely disgusted, and she saw, too, just the opportunity she wanted. 'Becky,' she said, 'you're horrid, horrid! I'll never speak to you again. To go and get tipsy! You shall never walk up the road with us again. Now mind: don't you come near me; you go straight home, you horrid thing!'

Becky burst into tears and obeyed. Next day she waited in vain at the usual meeting place; she saw Lilian pass on the top of the 'bus, looking carefully the other way.[9] At the theatre not a word. Becky knew Lilian, and she knew that when

---

[8] Lemonade augmented with a small quantity of an alcoholic beverage. Becky's low tolerance levels suggest that she typically drinks lemonade with a splash of beer, i.e. a very weak shandy. Unlike many of his 'decadent' contemporaries, Symons rarely drank to excess. This may have been the lingering influence of his Methodist upbringing.

[9] At this time, it was considered somewhat 'fast' for women to ride on the top deck of an omnibus or tram, especially if unaccompanied.

she said a thing she meant it, and that there was no moving her when once her mind was made up. She had already felt how much in the way she was, and she knew that she was dismissed now, and for ever. She did not even feel that they were cruel, these lovers, whose life had spoilt her life. She only felt that everything was over for her, that she would never find her friend again, that she would never find another friend; and the little romance that had come so near her, which she had seemed so humbly to share in, was taken away from her, and she was not even to watch it from afar. She accepted her fate meekly, and every night she dressed quickly, came out before Lilian was ready, and walked fast up the road so that she should not seem them or be in their way. If Winter was already at the stage door he always shook hands with her, quite politely, as she came out; that was her only pleasure, and yet she was rather glad when she did not see him.

One night, as Winter and Lilian were walking up the road together, arm in arm, a little earlier than usual, they almost stumbled against a girl who had suddenly bent down, just at the corner of the pavement, to tie her shoe. They had to pass on either side of her, and both walked back, with a momentary annoyance at the interruption. 'Did you notice?' said Winter; 'that was Becky!' 'Still in our way,' said Lilian with a laugh. Becky's shoelace broke in her hands; she went slowly up the road, hobbling a long way behind the gaily marching couple. She had always tried so hard to keep out of their way, and she could not succeed even in that. She nearly cried as she hobbled painfully up the street, now so long and dreary for her. She was afraid they would be angry. But they had already forgotten all about her.

~

'Pages from the Life of Lucy Newcome' and 'The Life and Adventures of Lucy Newcome'

'Pages from the Life of Lucy Newcome' was published in *The Savoy* in April 1896, though its events postdate those of 'The Childhood of Lucy Newcome'. Naturalist fiction frequently involves narratives of decline, so Symons's chosen ordering of the texts allows a kind of flash-back in the later story to his protagonist's more innocent days. The non-chronological relationship between the two may be a consequence of financial pressure, as noted below.

The inspiration for Lucy Newcome was Muriel Broadbent, a prostitute whom the poet and designer Selwyn Image met at the Alhambra during the early 1890s. In his unpublished reminiscence, 'Pages from the Life of Muriel Broadbent', Symons recalled how he met her 'a few nights' after her encounter with Image, finding her shy and ill at ease, entirely unused to London, its theatres and their sexual mores. 'I went home with her that night,' Symons added.[1]

He and Muriel, whom he called 'Mu', and whose actual name was Edith, were friends and occasional lovers for several years afterwards, and he celebrated her in a poem, 'To Muriel: At the Opera', dated 14 November 1892 and collected in *London Nights*, in which she longs 'To live on love and roses!' She was, he said, 'frightfully nice and kind to me, one of those women who are sensual and excitable though not passionate'. There was 'something bright and attractive about her, apart from her erotic nature.' Muriel helped him ready his rooms at Fountain Court in preparation for Verlaine's visit in November 1893 and acted as hostess at a number of other literary gatherings there: the daughter of a doctor,

---

[1] Symons, 'Original Preface' to 'Pages From the Life of Muriel Broadbent', p. 1. The unpublished fragment soon leaves her (and the novel) behind however, drifting into a looser discussion of the representation of prostitutes in late nineteenth-century French novels such as Huysmans's *Marthe* (1876) and Goncourt's *Chérie* (1884). Tellingly, the list does not include Zola's *Nana* (1880).

Muriel seems to have been capable of holding her own in such company. Symons and Image provided character references for her when she was renting rooms, and she often took refuge with them when the many complications of her romantic and commercial lives became overly entwined.[2]

Muriel obviously intrigued Symons on several levels, and he listened with fascination to her tales of her early life, reworking them in his fiction in ways which make it difficult to adjudicate between Muriel's memories and his artistic deployment of them. Their relationship even survived Muriel transferring her allegiance to Symons's sometime friend, the poet and architect Herbert Horne, but she eventually left him for a more respectable life, seemingly with Horne's encouragement, marrying William Llewelyn Hacon, a business partner of the artist and designer, Charles Ricketts.[3]

In some respects, 'Pages from the Life' covers similar ground to another of *The Savoy*'s contributions, Frederick Wedmore's 'To Nancy' (No. 1, January 1896) and 'The Deterioration of Nancy' (No. 2, April). In these pieces, a portrait painter becomes fascinated with a young dancer, fearing that when she turns sixteen, she will be morally 'ruined' and 'besmirched' by her life in the theatre and its sexual consequences. Laurel Brake sees 'the curve of her life determined by the plot of naturalism', and Lucy's follows much the same trajectory.[4] Wedmore's narrative method is however rather different, with the second 'Nancy' story being told through a series of letters. Symons, by contrast, offers a much more established version of naturalist writing, complete with the sociological and financial detail that readers living more privileged lives often found so revelatory. As in 'The Death of Peter Waydelin', there is a strong suggestion of the social explorer at work in the depictions of overcrowded rooms, domestic budgeting and laundry work. Symons may have disliked Zola, whom he criticized in 'A Note on Zola's Method' in *Studies in Two Literatures* (1897), but he had received detailed critical discussion in *The Savoy* and his influence on this story would seem undeniable. The laundry scenes in particular recall *L'Assommoir* (1877), which Symons had translated in 1894.

The early years of Lucy's life are more individual than those documented here, probably because the descent plot is so constricting, particularly for female characters: as Symons says, 'when you are once fallen you go on falling'. Much of

---

[2] Symons, 'A Study in Morbidity: Herbert Horne', in *The Memoirs of Arthur Symons*, pp. 125–29 (p. 127).

[3] 'The actual girl is still alive,' Symons told John Quinn in March 1915. 'Got married about 1899.' She was, he reflected, 'a sensual enough creature — whose favours I shared with her *amant de coeur*.' Symons, *Selected Letters*, p. 102. Edith Caherne Broadbent (1874–1952) married Hacon at the District of Westminster Register Office on Valentine's Day 1895. Hacon died in 1910. Fletcher, *Herbert Horne*, p. 157.

[4] Laurel Brake, *Subjugated Knowledges Journalism, Gender and Literature in the Nineteenth Century* (Basingstoke: Macmillan, 1994), p. 157.

'Pages from the Life' has the feeling of being researched with a diligence that impedes its narrative momentum, with infant mortality, hostile workmates, physical drudgery, and squalid housing the stock ingredients of naturalist writing on both sides of the Channel. Nevertheless, there are moments when Symons's observation is astute and telling, as when Lucy looks at her ring-less finger, or when she appraises the apparently kindly Mr Barfoot. The story's concluding section contains a number of well-worked ironies as the implications of Lucy's predicament become clear.

Unpublished until 1985, 'The Life and Adventures' is a very different work.[5] Less tied to plot and therefore much closer to the ideal of the Goncourts, it presents Lucy through a series of vivid glimpses whose effect is at once individual and cumulative, as when viewing an exhibition of impressionist paintings. Much of the detail is again taken from Muriel Broadbent's conversation, but the story also contains a strong satirical element. Certainly, Symons's evocation of the Rhymers' Club and the self-conscious bohemians who drank in The Crown on Charing Cross Road is very different from Yeats's recollections of 'The Tragic Generation' or the nostalgic accounts of Richard Le Gallienne, Ernest Rhys, or Edgar Jepson. He seems alive to the pretentiousness and affectation of the group, the gulf between their artistic theories and the practice of their lives, and the incestuous nature of their activities. Discussing the media-driven image of the 'Swinging London' of the 1960s in March 1971, Michael Caine remarked that the 'permissive society' was 'a bit of myth [...] kept going by a couple of hundred ravers.'[6] A similar point might be made about the decadent 'movement', which here poses far less of a threat to Victorian orthodoxy than the hysterical newspaper editorials of the time declared. Grant Richards recalled that when Symons turned up at The Crown a few minutes after the Alhambra had closed, it 'was not a dissipation; it was the end of the day's work, a chance of meeting and talking with congenial friends, of exchanging ideas'.[7]

Lucy's activities and the company that she keeps reveal a lot about Symons's preoccupations of the mid-1890s, and the social whirl in which he moved. As Alan Johnson has pointed out, the story takes place 'in the triangle between Trafalgar Square, Leicester Square, and Piccadilly Circus,' an area of the city Symons knew well, and here as elsewhere in his fiction, his familiarity with his chosen setting helps to imbue the story with authenticity.[8] While previous 'Lucy' stories had kept the protagonist at a distance through third person narration, here

---

[5] See Alan Johnson, 'Arthur Symons' "The Life and Adventures of Lucy Newcome": Preface and Text', *English Literature in Transition* 28.4 (1985), pp. 332–45.

[6] Ray Connolly, *Stardust Memories: Talking About My Generation* (London: Pavilion, 1983), p. 131.

[7] Grant Richards, *Memoirs of a Misspent Youth* (London: Heinemann, 1932), p. 342.

[8] Johnson, 'Arthur Symons' "The Life and Adventures of Lucy Newcome"', p. 333.

she is seen through the eyes of Cecil, another of Symons's barely-disguised fictional selves. In his recollections of Muriel Broadbent, he admits 'I am Cecil' — Sebastian, is, by implication, Herbert Horne.[9] Ian Fletcher finds the portrayal of both men to be 'curiously colourless', but this is unfair.[10] Symons may have been known for what Augustus John called his 'high-pitched professions of turpitude', but he was less emotionally distant than many believed, being especially upset when Muriel chose to get involved with Horne, a man whom he was still denigrating in unpublished essays thirty years later.[11] Cecil is hardly the first (or last) man to trust that friendship and shared interests will eventually win out over a stronger sexual attraction towards another, and he clearly demonstrates the 'sympathetic submissiveness to things' Symons so prizes in 'An Autumn City' and elsewhere. The final vivid scene of Lucy in wig and make-up dancing before the mirror is a veritable compendium of Symons's sexual and aesthetic fantasies of the 1890s, but the bourgeois priggishness of its blunt final line signals the distance between Symons's self-presumptions and their underlying realities. It also implies that however determined Symons may have been in his attempts to depict the consciousness of female characters, he could only go so far. He was able to create a believable life story and incidents through careful listening and observation, and dissect various modes of performance with considerable acuity, but for all that he protested about the libidinousness of men such as Horne clouding their ability to engage with women on anything but a physical level, he shared many of these traits.

The 'Lucy Newcome' project indicates how Symons might have developed as a novelist had he not opted to explore other creative avenues. His emotional investment in it was considerable, partly because of his close relationship with Muriel Broadbent but the story was not merely a relic of his mythologized past. Although Symons claimed not to tailor his opinions for the marketplace, he could be dogged in the pursuit of publication (and payment) even before he employed an agent. In that sense, 'Lucy Newcome' became a saleable asset, its potential worth becoming more significant as Symons's ability to provide fresh copy declined after 1908.

In 1915, Symons sent the 'Lucy' stories to Hardy asking for advice, a request Hardy took to mean 'advice in the practical sense: i.e., as to the advisability of printing'. The older writer's pragmatic response allowed him to circumvent 'the goodness or otherwise of the work', but he pulled no punches. 'I do not call the composition quite a story,' he began. '[I]t seems rather a study of a certain class of womankind, & mind.' 'Candidly then,' he went on, 'I should not, if I were you,

---

[9] Symons, 'Pages from the Life of Muriel Broadbent', p. 1.

[10] Fletcher, *Herbert Horne*, p. 13.

[11] Augustus John, 'Fragment of an Autobiography, X' (1943), quoted in Munro, *Arthur Symons*, p. 116.

publish the study. The present time is particularly unsympathetic with such phases of life, & and your reputation might not be advanced in printing this.'[12]

* * *

I

As Lucy Newcome walked down the street, with the baby in her arms, her first sensation was one of thankfulness, to be out of the long, blank, monotonous hospital, where she had suffered obscurely; to be once more free, and in the open air. How refreshing it is to be out of doors again! she said to herself. But she had not walked many steps before the unfamiliar morning air made her feel quite light-headed; for a moment she fancied she was going to faint, and she leant against the wall, closing her eyes, until the feeling had passed. As she walked on again, things still seemed a little dizzy before her eyes, and he had to draw in long breaths, for fear that curious cloudy sensation should come into her brain once more. She held the baby carefully, drawing the edges of the cloak around its face, so that it should not feel cold and wake up. It was the first time she had carried the baby out of doors, and it seemed to her that everyone must be looking at her. She was not much afraid of being recognized, for she knew that she had altered so much since her confinement; and for that reason she was glad to be looking so thin and white and ill. But she felt sure that people would wonder who she was, and why such a young girl was carrying a baby; perhaps they would not think it was hers; she might be only carrying it for some married woman. And she let her left hand, on which there was no wedding-ring, show from under the shawl in which it had been her first instinct to envelope it. Many thoughts came into her mind, but in a dull confused way, as she walked slowly along, feeling the weight of the baby dragging at her arms. At last they began to ache so much that she looked around for somewhere to sit down. She had not noticed where she had been going; why should she? where was there for her to go? and she found herself in one of the side streets, at the end of which, she remembered, was the park. There, at all events, she could sit down; and when she had found a seat, she took the baby on her knees, and lay back in the corner with a sense of relief.

At first she did not try to think of plans for the future. She merely resigned herself, unconsciously enough, to the vague, peaceful, autumn sadness of the place and the hour. The damp smell of the earth, sharp and comforting, came to her nostrils; the leaves, smelling a little musty, dropped now and then past her face on to the shawl in which the baby was wrapt. There was only enough breeze to make a gentle sighing among the branches overhead; and she looked up at the

[12] Hardy to Symons, 31 May 1915, *Collected Letters of Thomas Hardy, Volume Five: 1914–1919*, ed. by Richard Little Purdy and Michael Millgate (Oxford: Clarendon Press, 1985), p. 105.

leafy roof above her, as she had looked up so often when a child, and felt better for being there. Gradually her mind began to concentrate itself: what am I to do, she thought, what am I to do?

Just then the little creature lying on her knees stirred a little, and opened its blue eyes. She caught it to her breast with kiss after kiss, and began to rock it to and fro, with a passionate fondness. 'Mammy's little one,' she said; 'all Mammy's, mammy's own;' and began to croon over it with a sort of fierce insistence. Yes, she must do something, and at once, for the child's sake.

But the more she tried to find some plan for the future, the more hopeless did the task seem to become. There was her aunt, whom she would never go back to, whom she would never see again; never. There was her cousin, who had cast her off; and she said to herself that she hated her cousin. All her aunt's friends were so respectable: they would never look at her; and she could never go to them. Her cousin's friends were like himself, only worse, much worse. No, there was nowhere for her to look for help; and how was she to help herself? She knew nothing of any sort of business, she had no showy accomplishments to put to use; and besides, with a baby, who would give her employment? Oh, why had she ever listened to her cousin, why had she been such a fool as to have a baby? she said to herself, furiously; and then, feeling the bundle stir in her arms, she fell to hugging and kissing it again.

As she lifted up her face, a woman who was passing half paused, looking at her in a puzzled way; and then, after walking on a little distance, turned and came back, hesitatingly. Lucy knew her well: it was Mrs Graham, her aunt's laundress, with whom she had to settle accounts every week. She had never liked the woman, but now she was overjoyed at meeting her and as Mrs Graham said, questioningly, 'Miss Lucy? Lord, now, it isn't you?' she answered, 'Yes, it's me; don't you know me, Mrs Graham?'

'Well,' the woman said, 'I wasn't sure; how you have changed, miss. I asked Mrs Newcome where you was, and she said you was gone abroad.'[13]

The woman stopped and looked curiously at the baby. She had taken in the situation at a glance; and though she was rather surprised, she was not nearly so much surprised as Lucy had expected, and she seemed more interested than shocked.

'Pretty baby, miss,' she said, stooping down to have a closer look.

'Yes,' said Lucy, in a matter of fact way, 'it's my baby. I've been very unhappy.'

'Have you now, miss?' said Mrs Graham, sitting down by her side and looking at her more curiously than ever. 'Well, you do look ill. But where have you been

---

[13] 'Going abroad' or 'recovering in the country' were familiar middle-class euphemisms where (unwanted) pregnancy was concerned. Symons's intended readers would have recognized this, even if Mrs Graham does not.

all this time, and where are you living now?' 'I'm not living anywhere,' said Lucy; 'I only came out of hospital today and I've nowhere to go.'

'You don't mean to say that!' said Mrs Graham; 'but,' she added, looking at the baby, 'his father ...'.

'He has left me,' said Lucy, as quietly as she could.

At this Mrs Graham glanced at her in a somewhat less favourable way. She did not disapprove of people running away from home and getting children as irregularly as they liked; but she very much disapproved of their being left.

'I haven't a penny in the world,' Lucy went on; 'at least, I have only a little more than two shillings; and I don't know what I am going to do.'

'Oh dear now, oh dear!' said Mrs Graham, rather coldly, 'that's very sad, it is. I do say that's hard lines. And so you was left without anything. That's very hard lines.'

'I'm so glad I met you, Mrs Graham,' said Lucy. 'Perhaps you can help me. Oh, do try to help me if you can! I haven't anybody, really, to look to, and I haven't a roof to shelter me. I can't stay in the streets all day. I'm so afraid the baby will take cold, or something. It isn't for myself I mind so much. What shall I do?'

Wile Lucy spoke, Mrs Graham was considering matters. Without being exactly hard-hearted, she was not naturally sympathetic, and, while she felt sorry for the poor girl, she was not at all carried away by her feelings. But she did not like to leave her there as she was, and an idea had occurred to her which made her all the more ready to act kindly towards a creature in distress. So she said, after a moment's pause, 'Well, you'd better come along with me, miss, and have a rest, anyway. Shan't I carry the baby?'

'Oh, you are good!' cried Lucy, seizing her hand, and almost crying as she tried to thank her. 'No, no, I'll carry the baby! And may I really come in with you? You don't mind? You don't mind being seen?'

'Oh no, I don't mind!' said Mrs Graham, a little loftily. 'It's this way, miss.'

And they began to walk across the park. Lucy felt so immensely relieved that she was almost gay. She gave up thinking what was going to happen, and trudged contentedly by the side of the older woman. After they had left the park and had reached the poorer quarter of the town, she suddenly stopped outside a sweet-shop. 'It won't be very extravagant if I get a pennyworth of acid-drops,[14] will it?' she said, with almost her old smile; and Mrs Graham had to wait while she went in and bought them. Then they went on together through street after street, till at last Mrs Graham said, 'It's here, come in.'

As the door opened Lucy heard the barking of a dog; and the next moment she found herself in a room such as she had never been in in her life, but which

---

[14] Boiled sweets with a sharply sour lemon taste. They would not have been an extravagant purchase for Lucy earlier in her life, but in her straitened circumstances a bag of sweets consumes half her remaining money.

seemed to her, at that moment, the most delightful place in the world. It was a kitchen, horribly dirty, with a dog-kennel in one corner, and a rabbit-hutch on the top of the kennel; there was a patchwork rug on the floor, and a deal table[15] in the middle, with a piece of paper on one end of it as a table-cloth, and a loaf of bread, without a plate, standing in the middle of the table.[16] 'Have something to eat, miss,' said Mrs Graham, and Lucy sank into an old stuffed armchair, which stood by the side of the fire-place, the springs broken and protruding, and the flock[17] coming through the horse-hair in great gray handfuls.

The baby was still asleep, and lay quietly on her lap as she munched ravenously at the thick slice of bread and butter which Mrs Graham cut for her. All at once she heard a little cry, and, looking round in the corner behind her, she saw a baby lying in a clothes-basket.

'You'll have to sleep with the children tonight,' said Mrs Graham. 'We've only got two rooms besides this, and the children has one of them. When you've had a bit of a meal, you'd better lie down and rest yourself.'

When Lucy went into the room which was to be her bedroom for the night, she could not at first distinguish the bed. There were no bedclothes, but some old coats and petticoats had been heaped up over a mattress on a little iron bedstead in the corner.

'Now just lie down for a bit,' said Mrs Graham, 'and you give me the baby. I know the ways of them.'

Lucy threw herself on the bed. She could at least rest there; and she put a couple of acid-drops into her mouth, and then, almost before she knew it, she was asleep, in her old baby-fashion, sucking her thumb.

II

Lucy slept at Mrs Graham's two nights. She had been told that she would have to work; and she would do anything, she said, anything. Mrs Graham had a cousin, Mrs Marsh, who had a large laundry; and Mrs Marsh happened to be just then in want of a shirt and collar hand. Lucy knew nothing about ironing, but she was sure she could learn it without the least difficulty. So the two women set out for Mrs Marsh's. It was not very far off, and when they got there Mr and Mrs Marsh were standing at the big side-gate, where the things were brought in and out, watching one of their vans being unloaded. The shop-door was open, and inside, in the midst of the faint steam, rising from piles of white linen, smoking under the crisp hiss of the hot irons, Lucy saw four young women, wearing loose blouses,

---

[15] A table made from cheap softwood such as pine.
[16] This description recalls many similarly sordid interiors in the work of Victorian sociologists such as Charles Booth.
[17] Low-quality wool used for stuffing furniture.

their sleeves rolled up above their elbows, their faces flushed with the heat, bending over their work. Mrs Marsh looked at her amiably enough, and she led the way into the laundry. Beside the four girls, the two short and collar hands, the guaferer[18] and the plain ironer, there was a man ramming clothes into a boiler with a long pole, and a youth, Mrs Marsh's son, turning a queer, new-fangled instrument like a barrel, which dollied[19] the clothes by means of some mechanical contrivance. Clothes were hanging all around on clothes-horses; and overhead, on lines; the shirts were piled up in neat heaps at the end of the ironing-boards; some of the things lay in baskets on the ground. As Lucy looked around, her eye suddenly caught a white embroidered dress which was up to dry; and for the moment she felt quite sick; it was exactly like a dress of her mother's.

And the heat, too, was overpowering; she scarcely knew what was being said, as the two women discussed her to her face, and bargained between themselves as to the price of her labour. She realized that she was to come there next day; that she was to learn to iron cuffs and collars and shirt-fronts like the young woman nearest to her, whom they called Polly; and as a special favour, she was to be paid eight shillings a-week, the full price at once instead of only six shillings, which was generally given to beginners.[20] That she realized, she realized it acutely; for she was already beginning to find out that money means something very definite when you are poor, and that a shilling more or less may mean all the difference between everything and nothing.

That day it was arranged that she should rent a little attic in a house not far from Mrs Graham's, a house where a carpenter and his wife lived: they had no children, and she could have a room to herself. She was to pay five shillings a-week for her room and what they called her keep, that is to say, breakfast and supper, which she soon found out, meant bread and cheese one day, bread and dripping another, and bread and lard a third, always with some very weak tea, water just coloured.[21] Then there was the baby; she could not look after the baby while she was out at work, so the carpenter's wife, who was called Mrs Marsh, like the laundress, though she was no relation, promised to take charge of the baby during the day for half-a-crown extra.[22] Five shillings and half-a-crown made seven-and-six, and that left her only sixpence a-week to live on: could one say to live on? At all events, she had now a roof over head; she would scarcely

---

[18] 'Gauferer' is a corruption of 'gofferer', goffering being a technique for ironing fancy collars and trimmings and for crimping lace and frills.

[19] To 'dolly' is to stir clothes as they are washed.

[20] To put this into context, it is worth noting that an agricultural labourer of the time earned around ten shillings a week, a sum Oscar Wilde was spending on buttonholes each day in 1894–95. Symons had received twenty-one shillings for his first critical article.

[21] Dripping is fat left over from cooking lamb, mutton, or beef. Lard is pork fat. Both were staples of the Victorian working-class diet.

[22] Half-a-crown is two shillings and sixpence.

starve, not quite starve; and she sat in her attic, the first night she found herself there, and wondered what was going to happen: if she would have strength to do the work, strength, to live on, day after day, strength to nurse her baby, whose little life depended on hers. She sat on the edge of the bed, looking out at the clear, starry sky, visible above the roofs, and she sent up a prayer, up into that placid, unresponsive sky, hanging over her like the peace that passeth understanding, and has no comfort in it for mere mortals, a prayer for strength, only for the strength of day by day, one day at a time.[23]

Next morning she took up her place at the ironing-board, next to Polly, between her and the head ironer, whom she was told to watch. They were all Lancashire girls, not bad-hearted, but coarse and ignorant, always swearing and using foul language. Lucy had never heard people who talked like that; it wounded her horribly, and her pale face went crimson at every one of their coarse jokes. They had no sort of ill-will to her, but they knew she had a child, and was not married, and they could not help reminding her of the fact, which indeed seemed to them no less scandalous than their language seemed to her. They really believed that a woman who had been seduced was exactly the same as a prostitute;[24] they talked of people who led a gay life: 'Ah, my wench, it's a gay life, but a short one;' and they were convinced that everyone who led a gay life came to a deplorable end before she was five-and-twenty. To have had a child, without having been married, was the first step, so they held, in an inevitably downward course; indeed, they believed that all kinds of horrible things came of it, and they talked to one another of the ghastly stories they had 'heerd tell.' Lucy had never heard of such things, and she half believed them. 'Can all this really be true?' she said to herself sometimes, in a paroxysm of terror; and she tried not to think of it, as of something that might possibly be true, but must certainly be kept out of sight and out of mind.

One of the girls, Polly, was always very nice to her, and would come round sometimes to her little room and hold the baby for her; but the others called her 'Miss Stuck-Up,' 'Miss Fine-airs,' and when she blushed, cried, even, at the ribaldries which seemed to them so natural and matter-of-course, they would taunt her with her bastard and ask her if she didn't know how a baby was made, she who pretended to be such an innocent. She never tried to answer them; she did her work (after three days she could do it almost as well as the most practised of them), and she got through day after day as best she could. 'It was for baby's sake,' she whispered to herself, 'all for baby's sake.'

---

[23] 'And the peace of God, which passeth all understanding, shall keep your hearts and minds through Christ Jesus.' Philippians 4. 7.
[24] The term 'prostitute' was rarely used in fiction at this point, but in keeping with *The Savoy*'s radical ethos, Symons refuses to employ euphemisms.

In the middle of the day they had a dinner-hour, and the girls brought their dinner with them, which they generally ate out of doors, in the drying-ground at the back, glad to be out of the steam and heat for a few minutes. That hour was Lucy's terror. She had no dinner to bring with her: how could she, out of sixpence a week? and every day she pretended to go out and get her meal at an eating-house, scared lest one of them should come round the corner, and see her walking up and down the road, filling up the time until she could venture to go back again. She knew that if any one of them had guessed the truth, had known that she could never afford even the cheapest price of a dinner, they would one and all have shared with her their sandwiches, and bread and cheese, and meat pies, and apple dumplings. But she would not have let them know for worlds; and the aching suspense, lest she should be found out, was almost as bad to bear as the actual pang of hunger. She grew thinner and paler, and every day it seemed to her that the baby grew thinner and paler too. How could she nourish it, when she had no nourishment herself? She wept over it, and prayed God in agony not to visit her sin on the child. All this while the poor little thing lay and wailed, a feeble, fretful, continual wail, ceasing and going on, ceasing and going on again. It seemed to her that the sound would lodge itself in her brain, and drive her mad, quite mad. She heard it when she was in the laundry, bending over the steaming linen; it pierced through the crisp hiss of the irons as they passed shiningly over the surface; she heard it keeping time to her footsteps as she walked hungrily up and down that road in the dinner-hour; she dreamt of it even, and woke up to hear the little wail break out in the stillness of the night, in her attic bed. And the wail was getting feebler and feebler; the baby was dying, oh! she knew it was dying, and she could not save it; there was no way, absolutely no way to save it.

III

She had now been eight weeks at the laundry, and she seemed to get thinner every day. As she looked at her face in the glass, she was quite frightened at the long hollows she saw in her white cheeks, the dark lines under her eyes: her own face seemed to fade away from her as she looked at it, away into a mist; and through the mist she heard the small persistent crying of the baby, as if from a great way off. 'Am I going to be ill?' she wondered, looking down at her fingers helplessly. Certainly both she and the child were in need f the doctor; but who was to pay for a doctor? It was impossible.

That day, for the first time since she had been at the laundry, she had a half-holiday, and she put on her hat and went out into the streets, merely to walk about, and so think the less. 'I can at least look at the shops,' she said to herself, and she made her way to the more fashionable part of the town, where the milliners' and jewellers' shops were, and as she looked at the rings and bracelets, the smart hats and stylish jackets, it seemed to her worse than ever, to see all these things, and to know that none of them would ever be hers. It was now three o'clock; she had had nothing since her early breakfast, and the long walk, the loitering about, had tired her; it seemed to her, once more, as if a mist came floating up about her, through which the sound of voices was deadened before it reached her ears, and the ground felt a little uncertain under her feet, as if it were slightly elastic as she trod upon it. She turned out of the main street, into the big arcade, where she thought it would be quieter, and she found herself staring at a row of photographs of actresses, quite blankly, hardly seeing them. As she put her hand to her forehead, to press down her eyelids for a moment, she heard someone speaking to her, and looking round she saw a middle-aged gentleman standing by her side, and saying in a very kind voice: 'My child, are you ill?' Was she looking so ill, she wondered, or was she really ill? She did not think so, only hungry and faint. How hungry and faint she was! And as she shook her head, and said 'No, thank you,' she felt that the certain old gentleman, who looked so kind, would not believe her. Evidently he did not believe her, for he continued to look at her, and to say ... what was it? she only knew that he told her, quite decidedly, that she must come and have some tea. 'Thank you,' she said again: how was she to say no? and she walked along beside the gentleman in silence. He did not say anything more, but before she quite knew it, they were sitting at a little table in a tea-shop, and she had a cup of tea before her, real tea (how well she remembered, from what a distance, the taste of real tea!), and she was buttering a huge scone that made her mouth water, only to look at it.

When she had eaten her scone and drunk her tea, she saw that the gentleman was looking at her more kindly than ever, but with a certain expression which she could not help understanding.[25] He was a man of about fifty, somewhat tall, with broad shoulders and a powerful head, on which the iron-gray hair was cut close. His face was bronzed, he had a thick, closely-cut beard, and his eyes were large, gray, luminous, curiously sympathetic eyes, very kind, but a little puzzling in their expression. And he began to talk to her, asking her questions, feeling his way. She blushed furiously: how he had misunderstood her! She was not angry, only frightened and disturbed; and of course such a thing could never be, never. He seemed quite grieved when she told him hurriedly that she must go; and when they were outside the shop he insisted on walking a few steps with her; if not then, would she not come and see him some other day? He would be so glad to do anything he could to help her; that is, if she would come and see him. But she blushed again, and shook her head, and told him how impossible it was; but as he insisted on her taking his card, she took it. What was the harm? He had been kind to her. And of course she would never use it.

[25] The man obviously regards Lucy as sexually available, probably suspecting her of being a prostitute or a so-called 'dolly mop', a woman who supplements her earnings through occasional prostitution. Lucy's walking the streets has been misconstrued as streetwalking.

That night, as she ate her supper of bread and dripping, washing it down with what Mrs Marsh called tea, she thought of the tea-shop and the meal she had had there, the pleasantness of the place, the bright little tables, the waitresses gliding about, the well-dressed people who had been in there. And the life she was living seemed more unbearable than ever. At first she had been so glad to be anywhere, to find any sort of refuge, where there was a roof over her head, and some sort of bed to lie on, that the actual sordidness of her surroundings had seemed of little moment; but now it seemed more and more impossible to go on living among such people, without an educated person to speak to, without a book to read, without any of the little pleasantnesses of comfortable life. No, I cannot go on with this for ever, she said to herself; and she began to muse, thinking vague things, vaguely; thinking of what the girls at the laundry said to her, what they thought o her, and how to them it would be no difference at all, no difference at all; for was she not (they all said it) a fallen creature? When she went upstairs, and heard the feeble wail of her child, she almost wondered that she could have refused to take the man's money, which would have paid for a doctor. Oh yes, she was a fallen creature, no doubt; and when you are once fallen you go on falling. But of course, all the same, it was impossible: she *could* not; and there was an end of it.

But such thoughts as these, once set wandering through her brain, came back, and brought others with them. They came especially when she was very hungry; they seemed to float to her on the steam of that tea which she had drunk in the tea-shop; they whispered to her from the small, prim letters of the card which she still kept, with its sober, respectable-looking name, 'Mr Reginald Barfoot,' and the address of a huge, handsome building which she had often seen, mostly laid out in bachelor's flats, very expensive flats. But of course, all the same, it was impossible.

IV

On the Saturday of that week, while she was working at the laundry, she had a message from Mrs Marsh to say that her child was very ill. She hurried back, and found the little thing in convulsions. The poor little wasted body shook as if every moment would be its last. She held it in her arms, and crooned over it, and cried over it, and with her lips and fingers seemed to soothe the pain out of it. Presently it dropped into a quiet slumber. Lucy sat on the chair by the fireside and thought. She had never seen an attack like that: she was terribly frightened: would it not come on again? and if so, what was to be done? A doctor, certainly a doctor must be called. But she had no money, and doctors (she remembered her aunt's doctor) were so expensive. The money must be got, and at once. She looked at the card, at the address. Was it not a matter of life or death? She would go.

Then she felt that it was impossible; that she could never do it. Was it really a matter of life or death? The baby slept quietly. She would wait till tomorrow.

Through that night, and halfway through Sunday, the child seemed much better; but about three the convulsions came on again. Lucy was frantic with terror, and when the little thing, now growing feebler and feebler, had got over a worse paroxysm than ever, and had quieted down again, she called Mrs Marsh and begged her to look after the child while she went and fetched the doctor. 'I may be a little while,' she said, 'but baby is quiet now; you'll be very careful, won't you?' She gave the child one big kiss on both his little eyes; then she put on her hat and went out.

She went straight to the address on the card, without hesitation now, rang at the door, and a man-servant showed her into a room which seemed to her filled with books and photographs and pretty things. There was a fire in the grate, which shed a warm, comfortable glow on everything. She held out her hands to it; she was shivering a little. How nice it i here, she could not help thinking, or, rather, the sensation of its comfort flashed though her unconsciously, as she stood there looking at the photographs above the mantelpiece, as blankly as she had looked at those photographs, that other day, in the arcade. And then the door opened and Mr Barfoot came in, smiling, as he had smiled at her before. He did not ay anything, only smiled, and as he came quite close, and took her hand, a sudden terror came into her eyes, she drew back violently, and covering her face with her hands, sobbed out, 'I can't, I can't!'

For a moment the man looked at her wonderingly; then the expression of his face changed, he took her hands very gently, saying, 'My poor child!' Something in the voice and touch reassured her; she let him draw away her hands from before her eyes, in which tears were beginning to creep over the lower eyelids. She looked straight into his face; there was no smile there now, and she almost wondered why she had been so frightened a moment before. He led her to a chair. 'Sit down, now,' he said, 'and let us have a talk.' She sat down, already with a sense of relief, and he drew up the chair beside her, and took her hand again, soothingly, as one might take the hand of a timid child. 'Now,' he said, 'tell me all about it. How ill you look, my poor girl. You are in trouble. Tell me all about it.'

At first she was silent, looking into his face with a sort of hesitating confidence. Then, looking down again, she said, 'May I?' 'I want you to,' he said. 'I want you to let me help you.'

'Oh, will you?' she said impulsively, pressing the hand he held. 'I haven't a friend in the world. I am all alone. I have been very unhappy. It was all my fault. Will you really help me? It isn't for myself, it … it's my baby. I am afraid he's dying, he's so very ill, and today he had convulsions, and I thought … I thought he would really have died. And I haven't a penny to get a doctor. And that's why I came.

She broke off, and the hesitation came into her eyes again, She let her hand rest quite still; he felt the fingers turning cold as she waited for what he would say.

'Why didn't you tell me before?' was all he said, but the voice and eyes were kinder than ever. She almost smiled, she was so grateful; and he went on, 'Now we must see about the doctor at once. There's a doctor who lives only three doors from here. If he's in, you must take him back with you. Here, do you see, you'll give him this card; or, no, I'll see him about that. Just get him to come with you. And now I'm going to give you a sovereign,[26] for anything you want, and tomorrow ... but first of all, the doctor. Would you like me to come with you?'

'No, please,' said Lucy.

'Well, you had better go there at once. and mind you get anything you want, and for yourself, too. Why, you don't know how ill you look yourself! And then tomorrow I shall come and see how you are getting on, and then you must tell me all about yourself. Not now. You go straight to the doctor. By the way, what is your address?'

Lucy told him, hardly able to speak; she could not quite understand how it was that things had turned out so differently from what she had expected, or how everything seemed to be coming right without any trouble at all. She was bewildered, grateful, quiescent; and as she got up, and closed her hand mechanically over the sovereign he slipped into it, she was already thinking of the next thing to do, to find the doctor, to take the doctor back with her at once, to save her child.

'Now I shall come in tomorrow at eleven,' she heard him saying, 'and then I'll see if you want anything more. Now goodbye. Dr Hedges, the third door from here, on the same side.'

He opened the door for her himself, and as she went downstairs she felt the sovereign in her hand, pressing into her flesh, in a little round circle. She wrapped up the sovereign in her handkerchief, and thrust it into her bodice. She was repeating, 'Dr Hedges, the third door from here, on the same side' over and over again, without knowing it, so mechanically, that she would have passed the door had she not seen a brougham[27] standing outside. It was the doctor's brougham, and as she went up the steps in front of the house, the door opened and the doctor himself came out. 'I want *you*, please, to come with me at once,' she said, 'my baby ... I'm afraid he'll die if you don't. Can you come at once?'

The doctor looked at her critically; he liked pretty women, and this one was so young too. 'Yes, my dear,' he said, 'I'll come at once, if you like. Where is it? All right, jump in; we'll be there in a minute.'

The doctor talked cheerfully, and without expecting any answer, all the way to the house. 'It's the mother,' he thought to himself, 'who wants the doctor.' Lucy

---

[26] A sovereign was a gold coin worth £1 (i.e. 20 shillings), an impossibly high price for a woman in Lucy's situation.

[27] A light, horse-drawn carriage with four wheels, named after Lord Brougham, the Scottish jurist who had such a vehicle made in the late 1830s.

sat by his side white and motionless, putting up her hand sometimes to her bodice, to feel if the gold was there. 'Heart wrong,' thought the doctor.

When they reached the house, Lucy opened the door. 'Come in,' she said, and began to fly up the stairs; then, suddenly checking herself, 'No, come quietly, perhaps baby is sleeping.' They went up quietly, and Lucy opened the attic door with infinite precaution. As she held open the door for the doctor to come in, she saw Mrs Marsh move towards her, she saw the bed, and on the bed a little body lying motionless, its white face on the pillow; she saw it all at a glance, and, as the doctor came cheerfully into the room, she realized that everything had been in vain, that (she said to herself) she had waited just too long.

She sat down by the side of the bed, and looked straight in front of her, not saying a word, nor crying; she seemed to herself to have been stunned. The doctor examined the child, and then, taking Mrs Marsh into a corner of the room, began to question her. 'Poor little thing,' said Mrs Marsh, 'he just went off like you might have snuffed out a candle. He was always weakly, like; and she, you know, sir, she ain't by no means strong, not fit to have the charge of a baby, sir. I'm that thankful she takes it so quiet like. Did you say, sir, there'll have to be a crowner's quest?[28] Well, I do hope not; it do look so bad.'

At this moment they heard a wild cry behind them; both turned, and saw Lucy fling herself full length upon the bed, clasping the little body in her arms, sobbing convulsively. The tears streamed down her cheeks, the sobs forced themselves out in great bursts, almost in shouts. 'It will do her good to have a good cry,' said the doctor. 'I'll leave you now; rely on me to see after things.' And he went out quietly.

Lucy never remembered quite how she got through the rest of that day. It always seemed to her afterwards like a bad dream, through which she had found her way vaguely, in a thick darkness. Early in the evening she undressed and went to bed, and then, lying awake in the little room where the dead baby lay folded in white things and covered up for its long sleep, her mind seemed to soak in, unconsciously, all the discomfortable impressions that had made up her life since she had been living in that miserable little room. Through all the hopeless sordidness of that life she lived again, enduring the insults of the laundry, the labour of long days, starvation almost, and the loneliness of forced companionship with such people as Mrs Marsh and Polly the ironer. She had borne it for her child's sake, and now there was no longer any reason for bearing it. Her life had come to a full stop; the past was irrevocably past, folded away like the little dead body; her mind had not the courage to look a single step before her into the future; she closed her eyes, and tried to shut down the darkness upon her brain.

---

[28] That is 'a coroner's inquest,' a legal investigation of the circumstances surrounding the baby's death. Such inquests are typically held following sudden or unexpected deaths.

When she awoke in the morning it was nearly nine o'clock. She got up and dressed slowly, carefully, and when she had had her breakfast she went out to an undertaker's, from whom she ordered a baby's coffin. Remembering that she had a sovereign, she asked him to make it very nicely, and chose the particular kind of wood. She stayed in the shop some time, looking at inscriptions on the coffin lids, and asking questions about the ages of the people who were going to be buried. When she got back it was nearly eleven. She had taken off her hat, and was tidying her hair, quite mechanically, in front of the glass, when she heard a clock strike. Then she remembered that Mr Barfoot was coming to see her about eleven. She stood there, lifting the hair back from her forehead with her two thin hands, and her eyes met their reflection in the glass, very seriously and meditatively.

~

The Life And Adventures Of Lucy Newcome

I

The metamorphoses of Mrs Mellish were a constant amusement to Lucy. The great red woman, with her bulging bodice, her eternal apron, her eternal half-emptied glass, who, in the morning, would sit in the kitchen swearing and drinking, had her evening manners, which she put on when she lit the gas; and her very way of talking underwent a transformation as soon as one of her gentlemen made his appearance. She would mince up the words as well as her thick lips could manage, and behave, as she herself declared with great vehemence, like a perfect lady. Mrs Mellish's ideas of the ladylike in manner were so transparently grotesque that Lucy was always on the point of bursting into a roar of laughter; sometimes, when a man was nice, he would make some joke in order to let the girl have her laugh out, and in safety, and she would sometimes hold herself up to the girls as a model of the effective graces. She had phrases which continually came to her lips, and of which she was hugely proud. One of them was the word 'aesthetic'.

In after days, when Lucy looked back to the time at No. 79, she generally saw Mrs Mellish under the 'aesthetic' aspect; and one scene would recur to her mind, a certain day when the house was being done up, and a man from Liberty's[1] had brought his patterns for the drawing-room. In comes Mrs Mellish, dustpan and brush in hand, her hair powdered with the dust she has been sweeping up, her face a shade redder than usual; she surveys the man and the room and the patterns, and smoothing down her apron with a hand all rings and dirt, she proclaims: 'What *I* want, now, is something aesthetic!'

---

[1] Liberty's is a department store in London's Regent Street, founded by Arthur Lazenby Liberty in 1875. It stocked ornaments, fabrics, clothes, and *objets d'art* from around the world, notably Japan, and became a popular hub of Aesthetic fashion. In his memoir of the 1890s, *Wales England Wed* (1940), Ernest Rhys recalls Herbert Horne's impressionable younger brother going to Liberty's to buy fans as presents for the Alhambra's ballet girls.

II

When Lucy woke up suddenly, with a start, the room was quite dark, and she heard, outside, at the church nearby, three strokes of the clock, each stroke frightfully distinct. The sound seemed to thrill through the room, and she held her breath as she counted slowly, one, two, three; and then waited on the pause, which prolonged itself into the oppressive silence. A paroxysm of terror went over her, and she clutched at the bedclothes by her side, still and trembling; all her senses concentrated into an intense, feverish listening. There was not a sound, and as the suspense grew unbearable, she turned over on her side, with a great effort, and buried her face in the pillows, while she dragged the clothes up about her ears. Thoughts which had hardly time to form into thoughts went tumbling through her mind; and while she repeated to herself mechanically that she was alone in the house, she remembered story after story, of ghosts and burglars, and the nameless horrors of the night. Now she dared not move; she heard the veins in her temple ticking louder and louder; and she tried to blot out sight and sound and thought alike in the depths of the pillows. When she ventured to look up she could at first distinguish nothing; then a faint, nebulous light appeared in the square of the window, as she looked at it. She shut her eyes again, trying to find the courage to light a match. At last she put out her hand with a sudden movement, seized the matchbox, and struck a light. There was the familiar room, her things littered all over it; and the terror from which she was still shaking was gone in a moment. She got out of bed, and lit the gas.

'How absurd I am!' she said to herself, as she covered herself up again, and stared at the comforting flame. Still a child! just as when she used to clutch at the nurse's dress, and shriek with fright, at merely a pretence of having to go to sleep in the dark. She smiled at the recollection, and was dropping asleep again, when a noise, like the creak of a door, startled her into a sharp wakefulness. She listened, but heard nothing more. To assure herself, she got out of bed, and turned the key, very softly.

When Lucy woke in the morning, she could not imagine, for a moment, why the gas was alight and flaring.

III

A few days afterwards she had a more serious fright, which left her shaking for days. A man whom she knew, a man whom everyone knew, big Lord Jimmy, who divided his time equally between Ascot[2] and the Continental,[3] had arranged to

---

[2] Ascot Racecourse, in Berkshire, was founded by Queen Anne in 1711. Its close proximity to London made it popular with Victorian race-goers. It has traditionally attracted an aristocratic clientele; though Queen Victoria did not attend, her son, Edward VII, was the inspiration for the Prince of Wales Stakes, a race first held in 1862.

[3] In an unpublished essay written on his birthday in 1924, Symons recalled that the 'infamous Hotel Continental, named after the one in Paris in la rue de Rivoli' stood 'on the right of Regent

come back to her place after a dinner-party, which would not be over till late. It was nearly two o'clock in the morning when he arrived, and he was, not by any means drunk, quite amiable in his heavy way, but, undoubtedly, he had been drinking. He went off to sleep almost at once, and he snored persistently a monstrous snore which rang in Lucy's ears and held her tediously, annoyingly, awake. She kicked the poor man, woke him, and told him not to snore; he promised, and was snoring again the moment after. It was five o'clock before Lucy could close her eyes, and she dropt off into an uneasy slumber, to the accompaniment of this interminable snore. When she awoke, only an hour and a half later, the room was perfectly still. In her confusion she remembered only that when she went to sleep the room had not been quiet; a noise still rang in her ears, a noise which had now absolutely ceased. Then she remembered the persistent, irritating snore. She turned her head, with a vague sensation of fright, she knew not why; and the great head of the man lay there motionless on the pillow by her side; motionless, without a breath, it seemed to her; and in the early morning twilight, coming through the muslin curtains at the window opposite, the face had a livid, bluish look, like the face of a dead man. He was dead! the thought flashed through her brain, and almost simultaneously, the thought: Dead, and in my bed: what will become of me? She remembered a scandal, curiously similar, which had leaked out seven or eight years ago; this would leak out, for the man in this case, too, was a lord; and here there was no one to send the dead man home in his carriage, and lay him out decently in the family bed. A cold wave of horror broke over her, chilling her to the bone. She screamed: 'Oh! Jimmy, wake up!' sure that there would be no answer; but the head turned on the pillow, the dead man's head, and the eyes opened, slowly, placidly, and then, wider still, in consternation, as the girl gave one shriek, and fell back on the pillow in a dead faint. The poor man jumped out of bed, threw cold water over her face, and wondered how it was that women's nerves had such a trick of getting out of gear, without anything whatever to account for it.

IV

Lucy still liked men who had done something artistic, and now and again, by some caprice of chance, a poet or painter would meet her in the promenade at the Pavilion,[4] and, astonished by her odds and ends of book-learning, go home

Street as you go in the direction of Carlton House Terrace.' It was, he added 'mostly frequented by foreigners' and 'the dancing-women, Spanish and Russian.' It was here Symons interviewed the Spanish dancer and courtesan, Otero ('Otero at the Empire', *St James's Gazette*, 21 October 1892). 'The Hotel Continental', Arthur Symons Papers, Princeton University, CO182, Box 10, Folder 9, p. 1.

[4] The Pavilion was a palace of varieties, initially located in Tichbourne Street (now Windmill Street), which opened in 1859. It was extremely popular, and when the original was demolished

with her to her lodging. Then she would talk of Simeon Solomon, whom she had known; of Botticelli[5], whose name she was never quite sure of being able to pronounce; of the young poets and painters who had fluttered round her in the old days.[6] She generally began by quoting the opening stanzas of Austin Dobson's 'Dorothy'[7]; then, after a vague but reverential allusion to Milton[8] (*'of course Milton was the greatest English poet. Shakespeare? I have never read Shakespeare'*), she would tell a naughty story about Nell Gwynne, the only courtesan she admitted into the circle of her famous acquaintants, because Nelly had lived under the second Charles, and had been written about by 'dear Pepys.'[9]

---

in 1885 after the Metropolitan Board of Works bought the site, a new, grander Pavilion was established on the north side of Piccadilly Circus. It became a cinema in 1933, but closed in 1981. Although its interior has been remodelled, its exterior was restored to its former glory during the mid-1980s. The building now houses shops and tourist attractions.

[5] Alessandro di Mariano di Vanni Filipepi, better known as Sandro Botticelli (c. 1445–1510), Florentine painter of such works as 'The Birth of Venus' (1486).

[6] Simeon Solomon (1840–1905) was a Jewish painter associated with Pre-Raphaelitism through close friendship with Swinburne and D. G. Rossetti. He was hailed as a genius, but his career was curtailed when, in 1873, he and another man were arrested in a public lavatory near Oxford Street and found guilty of indecency. Shunned by his famous friends, Solomon spent his final twenty years as an alcoholic 'broken-down artist' in St Giles's Workhouse, Endell Street, London. Nevertheless, he continued to produce exquisite chalk and crayon drawings, many of which were lost because they were done on pavements for passing pennies. Symons saw some of his works at the Manchester Exhibition of 1887, and told Horne that he was so impressed with 'their beauty and originality, and a certain morbid grace they have.' Solomon, he felt, '*had*, at any rate, a remarkable genius; and there is nothing in this world so pitiful as a shipwreck of a genius.' (*Selected Letters*, p. 30.) Symons included an essay on the painter in *Studies on Modern Painters* (1925) and *From Toulouse-Lautrec to Rodin* (1929).

[7] Henry Austin Dobson (1840–1921), civil servant, poet, and literary historian, instrumental in popularising 'antique' French forms such as the rondeau and triolet in English. 'Dorothy: A Reverie Suggested by a Name Upon a Pane' (1873) listed in his *Complete Poetical Works* (1923) as one of his 'Vignettes in Rhyme', includes the following stanza:

What was she like? I picture her
Unmeet for uncouth worshipper; —
Soft, pensive, — far too subtly graced
To suit the blunt bucolic taste,
Whose crude perception could but see
'Ma'am Fine-airs' in 'Miss Dorothy'.

Lucy is nick-named 'Miss Fine-airs' by the laundry girls in the previous story.

[8] Despite his influence on Tennyson, John Milton (1608–74) was very much out of fashion during the 1890s. His stylistic brilliance was respected, but his puritanical politics and Christianity led avant-gardists such as Symons to see him as essentially irrelevant to modern life. Lucy's allusions to Milton, Dryden, Pope, and Bach play up her credentials as educated, thoughtful, and quite distinct from the frivolous young girl she may appear to be.

[9] Eleanor 'Nell' Gwyn (also spelt Gwynn, Gwynne, 1650–87), one of the first English actresses and a long-term mistress of Charles II. Samuel Pepys (1633–1703), English naval administrator and Member of Parliament, famous for the revealing diary he kept from 1660–69. Pepys called Gwyn, 'pretty, witty Nell'.

And she would calmly ask a racing-man who had tried to strum 'Ta-ra-ra'[10] on her piano if he could play Bach; adding that she preferred to hear Bach on the harpsichord.[11] She still, whenever she found herself in that quarter, hunted greedily over the little calf-bound books on the barrow near Farringdon Street Station,[12] in which she had been accustomed to pass so often on her way; and she would carry off odd volumes of Pope and Dryden, for which she had given a penny apiece, and which she never read.[13] And she would stop at the music-shop in Fleet Street, turning over all the 17th and 18th century music, of which she could not play a note, and sometimes buying a Bach or a Corelli, for the sake of the name, and all it meant to her.[14] The landlady generally swore when another piece of dusty music, or a cracked calf binding, was added to the tumbled litter strewed about the floor; but Lucy paid no attention, for a great part of her happiness lay now, dusty and tarnished as those covers, in the little heaps that Mrs Turnbull would have liked to sweep up with a broom, and empty away, once for all, into the dust-bin.

V

A change had already begun to come over Lucy (in her own rooms at last, in a curious cul-de-sac), partly a return to her older self, partly something new which she had absorbed from the new surroundings in which she naturally found

---

[10] 'Ta-ra-ra-boom-de-ay' was a vaudeville song, performed at the Strand's Tivoli music hall by the singer and dancer Lottie Collins (1865–1910) who had heard it in America. Her thrilling rendition of the song involved high-kicks which exposed stockings with diamante garters and bare thighs. The tune was widely played on barrel organs; John Davidson used it as the basis of 'To the Street Piano: A Labourer's Wife' in *Ballads and Songs* (1894). Such was the song's popularity, recalled Holbrook Jackson, that 'it became a veritable song-pest' which, between 1892 and 1896, 'affected the country like an epidemic', *The Eighteen-Nineties* (London: Grant Richards, 1913), p. 35. See too Symons's article, 'The Transformation of "Ta-Ra-Ra"', *Star*, 23 April 1892, p. 4. There is a useful overview of the song's impact in Barry Anthony, *Murder, Mayhem and Music Hall* (London: I. B. Tauris, 2015), pp. 98–114.

[11] The music of Johann Sebastian Bach (1685–1750) became increasingly well known in Victorian England, not least because of the pioneering efforts of the composer and pianist, Felix Mendelssohn (1809–47). However, Lucy is certainly radical in insisting on more 'authentic' performances of his keyboard music, perhaps reflecting the influence of Arnold Dolmetsch, whom Symons and Muriel knew.

[12] Farringdon Street was created in 1737 when the River Fleet was arched over, and by the 1890s was well known for used book market-stalls. Being close to Fleet Street, it was often frequented by journalists.

[13] John Dryden (1631–1700), poet and dramatist, Poet Laureate from 1688 and like Pope, celebrated for his satirical poems in heroic couplets.

[14] Arcangelo Corelli (1653–1713), Italian violinist and composer. During the 1890s, the average Victorian was more likely to think of Marie Corelli (1855–1924), the bestselling novelist who claimed the composer as an ancestor despite not actually being related to him.

herself. For a month after Sebastian went away she lived very quietly, passing whole days in the South Kensington, in the National Gallery,[15] trying to remember everything she was told about the painters.[16] At last one day she declared that she was tired of it all, and she rushed down precipitately to Gladys' flat, where Gladys and Flossie, who were, or pretended to be, very hard up at the moment, welcomed her profusely. They felt, with that intimate cunning in such matters which they possessed, that the visit was serious, a sort of prodigal's return. How often had they lamented over the inconceivable folly of Lucy's seriousness, in which, now that Sebastian was away, they could not even see the excuse of self-interest, or that kind of polite participation in the tastes and pursuits of your 'boy' which was a cardinal point in their sentimental education. This time they had really had their fears: was Lucy's brain, after all, completely turned? her sense of things, irretrievably perverted? A single glance at her flushed face, her shining eyes, the new, fast hat which waved and flapped over her forehead, as she dashed breathlessly into the room, and stood there smiling at them, and tapping the table with her long white feather-fan, reassured them. The two sisters came up and cooed about her, in their prettiest way; they even brought themselves to praise her hat, without so much as a suggestion that they had better ones themselves, which had cost three times as much, though the word was on Flossie's lips when a repressive glance from Gladys checked her in the utterance. That night Lucy paid for both of them at the Empire[17] ('of course, you only *lend* us the money, dear,' said Gladys), and Gladys introduced Lucy to a man who she knew had quite given up herself. They all had one or two liqueurs, and the next morning Lucy woke up, with a headache, in the more bachelor part of Belgravia.[18]

After that she gave up going to the South Kensington, and contented herself with tearing prints out of all the magazines and papers she could get hold of, as a sort of compromise with art. She saw a great deal of Gladys and Flossie, who

[15] An art gallery in London's Trafalgar Square, which was founded in 1824 and houses one of the world's finest collections of old masters.
[16] The South Kensington Museum, in Brompton Road, founded in 1852, specializes in fine and applied arts and has always had strongly educational principles. Outgrowing its original buildings, it was redesigned during the 1890s, with Queen Victoria laying the foundation stone in her final important public act in 1899. It was she who insisted on the change of name to today's Victoria and Albert Museum.
[17] The Empire Theatre in Leicester Square opened in 1884. In 1887, it became a music hall and was renamed the Empire Theatre of Varieties and in March 1896 was the venue for the first commercial screening of a cinematograph film in Britain: the building now houses a cinema. Symons frequently wrote about it: the first poem of the 'Décor de Théâtre' sequence in *London Nights* is 'Behind the Scenes: Empire'. The purity campaigner, Laura Ormiston Chant (1848–1923) regarded the Empire as a sink of depravity because of the number of prostitutes who haunted it. She caused great controversy by opposing the renewal of its license in the autumn of 1894.
[18] Belgravia is a wealthy and fashionable residential district of south-west London.

began to be in easier circumstances. Lucy made a lot of money, and she flung it about with an absolute oblivion of those economies which were to have been practised all that time that Sebastian was away. She still wrote regularly, telling him how much she wanted him to come back; and she added, that she was making heaps of money.

So far, Lucy had merely relapsed into her former self; the new influence came in with the acquaintance, which she now made somewhat intimately, though (as they were friends of Sebastian) quite platonically, of a certain set who professed an elegant and quite literary immorality, with a suspicion of various curious vices, which they supposed it *fin-de-siècle* to profess.[19] They were a group who fringed, obscurely enough, upon the outskirts of Letters; they impressed you that their extraordinary brilliance was invisible merely because it was repressed; like Congreve, it was their own citation, they would be gentlemen first, and the rest, perhaps, if they liked to take the trouble, afterwards.[20] Meanwhile they earned a little money, quite honestly, by contributing humble paragraphs to some of the less known papers; and they gamed, and sometimes won on the races, and drank at the bars of all the music-halls, to which they had free passes, and frequented the night clubs, and really lived up to their principles by going after the less expensive women about town whenever they had the money. They also talked a great deal about what one of them called 'the New Culture,'[21] and one or two of

---

[19] Symons is here parodying the Rhymers' Club, a loosely-organized group of London-based poets who met for readings, discussions, and conviviality at Ye Olde Cheshire Cheese in Fleet Street, the Domino Room of the Café Royal, and in private houses, during the early 1890s. It was founded by Yeats and Ernest Rhys, and members included Dowson, Le Gallienne, John Gray, John Davidson, Victor Plarr, and Selwyn Image. Oscar Wilde came to gatherings in private houses, though he never officially joined the club, while Francis Thompson was a member but did not attend any meetings. Symons did belong, and contributed to its two anthologies, *The Book of the Rhymers' Club* (1892) and the *Second Book of the Rhymers' Club* (1894). The club was much mythologized by its members, notably Yeats in his various autobiographies, but the version here seems rather more daring and outspoken than its real-life equivalent.

[20] William Congreve (1670–1729), dramatist and poet, author of *The Way of the World* (1700). He told the French philosopher, Voltaire, that he would rather be considered as a gentleman than as a famous author. 'I answered that had he been so unfortunate as to have been a mere gentleman, I should never have come to see him,' Voltaire recalled in *Letters Concerning the English Nation* (1733).

[21] The New Culture is a parodic extension of the 'new hedonism' about which Lord Henry holds forth in Chapter Eleven of *Dorian Gray* and which was the title of an essay by Grant Allen in March 1894's *Fortnightly Review*.

[22] The poem Symons is probably thinking of here is 'To A Sicilian Boy' by Theodore Wratislaw (1871–1933), a contributor to the *Yellow Book* and *The Savoy*, which appeared in the *Spirit Lamp*, an Oxford University magazine, in August 1893. The sonnet concludes, 'Ah let me in thy bosom still enjoy | Oblivion of the past, divinest boy, | And the dull ennui of a woman's kiss!'

them wrote rhymes to Sicilian boys, though none of them had ever been in Sicily.[22] But they talked still more about Sappho,[23] and, after reading Martial in a French translation, about the 'new Lucretia of our times,' whom it was their passion to search for, and occasionally their delight to discover.[24] When Lucy came into their midst, they were teased and puzzled by what seemed to them so enigmatic in her, especially by her absolute refusal to allow any of them to come home with her. They found it annoying to their self-esteem; whereupon one of them invented a hypothesis that would satisfactorily explain everything. This, there could be no doubt, was the new Lucretia of our time! Lucy at first thought they were fooling her; then, finding at once an excuse and an amusement in the notion, she pretended that it was true; and she found the same curiosity in talking, with due vagueness, of such very forbidden things (despite her actual antipathy to them, which had never varied since that early experience) as she did in bed reading the Grammont Memoirs,[25] and in turning over *Le Nu au Salon*,[26] in her bedroom, with a man who was merely going to have tea with her. She played with the notion, and gradually it began to really interest her. One night she dressed up in Sebastian's things, and went down to see her new friends. 'I want a woman,' she pretended, in the spirit of the masquerade; and they applauded her with ecstasy. They would have a little comedy; a woman should be brought in, the lights lowered, she should make love, as a man might, and the denouement … should be what she pleased. But Lucy only laughed, a little hysterically, and said, 'No, no, of course I didn't mean it'; and the little comedy was never acted.

---

[23] Female lyric poet in Ancient Greece (*c.* 600 BC). Much of her poetry is now lost, and little is known of her life, though there are numerous stories about her. She was probably a lesbian.
[24] 'The new Lucretia of our times' comes from Charles Sedley's translation of the Roman poet Martial's epigram, 'On Bassa' (Book I, No. 90). Sedley (1639–1701) used the phrase ironically to refer to a lesbian. Sedley's version was included in the Bohn Classical Library's translation of Martial's *Epigrams* (1890); French translations were more salacious. Lucretia (or Lucrece) was a Roman noblewoman who committed suicide *c.* 510 BC after being raped by an Etruscan prince. The event led to a constitutional crisis in Rome. She is the subject of Shakespeare's *The Rape of Lucrece* (1594).
[25] The Grammont memoirs are *The Memoirs of the Count de Gramont* [*sic*]: *Containing the Amorous History of the English Court Under the Reign of Charles II* by Anthony Hamilton (1713). Lucy has probably encountered these in Henry Vizetelly's 1889 edition, the sort of text Beardsley browsed when working on *Venus and Tannhäuser*.
[26] *Le Nu au Salon* was a French journal which ran from 1888 to 1930. During the 1890s, it was edited by the poet and dramatist, Paul Armand Silvestre (1837–1901). It reproduced nude paintings exhibited in Parisian art galleries, and had a quasi-pornographic reputation, especially in England.

VI

Once a month, as regularly as the day came round, Sebastian knew what he had to expect. The poor child was really insupportable, and, sorry as he was to see her suffer, he found the only thing to do was to keep out of the way as much as possible. With the physical pains that came upon her, the fever that heated her blood, and played such odd tricks with her senses, a sort of demon seemed to enter into her; she flew into hysterical rages, developed prodigious jealousies, and between the two paroxysms of tears would smash the furniture and beat on the floor with a poker until she had bent it nearly double. He would beg her to rest quietly in bed, and he would leave her in the morning, promising to stay there till he came back. In the afternoon it would suddenly occur to her that he had been playing her a trick, that he was after some girl: she was sure there was a girl with him in his rooms. She would dress, flinging on the first things that came to hand, and rush down to his rooms, a whirlwind of unreasoning and inexplicable fury. If he came back half an hour later than she had expected, he would find her hanging half out of the window, her eyelids swollen red, her hair hanging about her ears, a dripping handkerchief on the window-sill. Next day, when she returned to her ordinary health, 'How could I have been so foolish!' she would murmur, with a little smile of penitent shame. And she always promised to be better next time, to be at least reasonable; and next time, as regularly as the day came round, the same blind torment would drive her, as it had driven her before, into a sort of actual temporary madness. One day, coming down to Sebastian's rooms, she found he was going out to dine with a friend at a new, interesting restaurant, of which he had heard encouraging things. Lucy declared that she must come too. The little dinner had been a long-standing arrangement, and Sebastian explained, with some annoyance, that it was impossible. Just then Cecil happened to come along, in time to see the wave of fury that broke and sputtered over the three of them, a fury that flung itself on him in turn, when, with his usual good-humour, he proposed to look after her for the evening. She came with him, dashing her handkerchief at her eyes to keep back the tears until she was safely indoors, and on the familiar sofa, where she lay and shook with sobs, murmuring out all sorts of wild charges against Sebastian, who didn't care anything for her anymore, who never had cared for her, who had never given her anything, never, except, indeed, the ring she was wearing, oh yes, and the chain, and of course there was … but he never thought about her, like other men did, he never brought her little things; oh, he was unkind to her, and only wanted to get rid of her. Cecil went without his dinner, but after several hours she quieted down, and at ten they went out and had something to eat. Next day, with her arms round Sebastian's neck, she reminded Cecil of the night before. 'And you believed it all!' she said with a perfectly happy laugh. Cecil, to please her, said that he had believed it all.

VII

The one luxury for which Lucy always longed, was the luxury of a child. 'If a child comes, I go,' Sebastian had said to her, and she had to resign herself to so unsympathetic a necessity, but the instinct for maternity in her was not to be silenced. When Gladys had a baby, a wretched little wizened thing, that never grew, but slid painfully out of a wrinkled infancy into the fortunate relief of death, Lucy would spend whole days at the flat, holding the little creature in her arms, feeding it, acting the mother to it, far more feelingly than the real mother ever did. On the rare occasions, a railway-journey for instance, when she had the chance of seeing anything of small children, she seized upon them with a winning obstinacy, nor was she ever happier, or flushed with a prettier, self-conscious delight, than when she was permitted to nurse one of these casual infants. At home, at the bottom of a large trunk, where she kept some of her evening dresses, she had a little store of baby-clothes, the clothes that her baby had worn, the very violet powder[27] that she had bought for it. When the mood came round she would go to this box, and take out every little garment, shed tears over each in turn, until she had cried out her memories, and then she would put the things back into the box, all of a heap, and the evening dresses on the top. If she was not well at the time, the crying and the thinking generally left her peevish for the rest of the day; and Sebastian dreaded these sentimental excursions in so inconvenient a direction. He never quite believed in their sincerity, sincere as they really were, in their way; and he preferred, too, to avoid the discussion of incompatibilities.

It was no doubt through a fantastic deviation of this desire for maternity that Lucy derived her curious fondness for dolls. There had never been a moment when Lucy had not possessed a doll, to which she was sometimes quite childishly attached, and which at other times she looked on with an almost impersonal amused interest. Now, under the influence of her present surroundings, the dolls were to be works of art; and it amused her particularly to dress them in various appropriate costumes, and give them to her friends by way of friendly satire. Thus, Cecil was one night hurried breathlessly into a room not much frequented, in the general way, the room where the heavy books were, and the terrestrial globe, and a candle was held up to an amazing line of wooden dolls in all kinds of costumes, which almost covered the mantelpiece. There were soldiers and Dutch girls, there were dresses of muslin and of silk; but he was not an instant in seeing the doll that was meant for him. It was a ballet-dancer, in a white muslin skirt trimmed, suggestively, with a 'dash of heliotrope'; she smiled a large, red, wooden smile, and held one little rough, jointed leg in the air, with a triumphant equilibrium. He was not allowed to laugh at the dolls; Lucy looked almost hurt; and he was

---

[27] Talc or farina scented with ground orris-root, which has a violet-like scent, was a toiletry used by women and for infants in the Victorian period.

expected to carry off the danseuse. Lucy dressed dolls till she was tired of dressing them; then, like all her fancies, the fancy evaporated; and the dolls were bundled away among old dresses, in some out of the way corner. But the dolls were not forgotten.

VIII

The night after Sebastian had gone, Cecil came into the Mitre,[28] about midnight, and found Lucy, very pale and sad-eyed, sitting on a chair, not drinking anything, and talking very little. Her face brightened as she saw him, and she called him over, and said in a whisper, 'I haven't had any dinner; take me to have something to eat.' 'Shall we go to Gatti's?'[29] he said, as soon as they were outside; but Lucy hurried him along, towards Leicester Square, crying, 'No, no, not Gatti's, I want some stout and oysters;[30] there's a little shop along here.' He went with her, in some surprise, and she led the way to a tiny place in Coventry Street, a little shop as large as a small bath-room, where there were great strips of paper pasted sideways along the windows, announcing the price of the oysters. Beyond the bar there were three minute tables. Lucy ordered a dozen oysters, and Cecil had to give the boy threepence for the stout, which had to be brought in. 'Have you often been here?' he asked Lucy, as she looked down admiringly at a comparatively new pair of French gloves. 'Don't they fit nicely?' she remarked. 'Oh, here?' she said, after a minute, 'No, I have not been here since I knew Sebastian; I often used to come here before that.' The situation struck Cecil as a trifle amusing, and he watched her with a faint smile, making patterns with his stick on the floor, as she hurried over the oysters and the brown bread and butter. Sebastian was alluded to, but merely in a general way. 'But there's something I want to tell you,' said Lucy; 'not here, you can drive me home; wait a minute, I have some money'; and she gave him two two-shilling pieces, which he slipt into his pocket; both laughed

---

[28] The Mitre Tavern, in Old Mitre Court, Fleet Street, was a favourite haunt of the poet and lexicographer, Samuel Johnson (1709–84), so is an appropriate watering-hole for a woman of Lucy's eighteenth-century allegiances. From here, she and Sebastian walk through Aldwych and along the Strand towards Trafalgar Square. They turn up Charing Cross Road towards Leicester Square before heading along Cranbourn Street to Coventry Street. This journey takes the couple through the heart of West London's theatre-land, an area Symons knew intimately.
[29] The Swiss entrepreneur Carol Gatti (1817–78) went from running a coffee stall to owning music halls, restaurants, and an ice importing business that made him a millionaire. After his death, his business empire was run by his family. Gatti's, a favourite resort of 1890s' bohemians, was at 463 Strand; the Gattis also owned a music hall in Villiers Street, near Charing Cross Station, that Symons often patronized.
[30] Stout is a strong, dark beer often served with live oysters, a popular 'street food' in 18th and 19th century London enjoyed by Samuel Johnson and his cat, Hodge. Eliot's 'The Love Song of J. Alfred Prufrock' (1917) notes the 'one night cheap hotels | And sawdust restaurants with oyster shells' that Eliot had frequented in London.

as he produced the coins, still in his hand, on the waiter's demand for the amount. They got into a cab, and Lucy, sitting straight upright, and looking right in front of her, her furs up to her ears, began to talk rapidly, not looking at him unless he turned to look after a woman who was passing on the pavement, when she gave him a little impatient nudge. Well, it appeared that she had found a new friend, a very nice man; it had been at the Empire, one night when she was sitting in the dress-circle; the acquaintance had begun almost by accident, and the man was immensely taken with her, so she said; and indeed he had proved it, for he had come up to tea, 'and he didn't … you know, merely a cup of tea,' she explained; after which he had sent her five pounds.[31] And they had philosophised together, and he had thought it was such a pity for her to go to the Empire; he had sent her ten pounds, afterwards, so she could stay away for a week. And he had wanted to come up and stay from Saturday to Monday; 'but, you see, Sebastian wasn't gone in time, so I had to put him off; however, he came up yesterday, and stayed.' And he had been quite dazzled by her books; there was a Homer, Pope's[32] you know, with her name in it; and he declared he would just like to see her discussing Homer with his father. In short, it was a serious affair; and he was very nice, and had heaps of money, only, there was one great trouble. He told her that he had been keeping a girl for the last five years, and, up to now, he had been faithful to her: she couldn't take him away from the girl. No, it was no use; she had never knowingly taken on with a man who was married or who kept a girl, and she never meant to. 'Cecil, you may say what you like, but it's my way of being good; and when I feel very wicked I think of that, and it helps me to feel I'm not altogether bad. I know it often doesn't do any good, and a man only goes after somebody else, but I'll never make another woman unhappy if I can help it, however much I lose by it.' So she had told him he was not to stay with her, but he could come and see her again, if he liked. Then James was coming home, too, in a few weeks' time; and altogether, wasn't she in luck? Cecil listened approvingly, laughing a little at her virtuous scruples, as he always did; and the cab drew up at the door. As they went upstairs together, the moonlight, for the first time since Cecil had known the place, lit up the staircase, over which he had so often stumbled; and, inside, the rooms had a curious empty look, now that Sebastian had gone. Lucy was in a very serious mood, talked of reducing her

---

[31] This was a significant sum of money in the 1890s (see Lucy's earlier earnings in the laundry) and the typical price of a sexual assignation with the expensive prostitutes who frequented the Empire Promenade.

[32] Pope published his translation of Homer's *Iliad* between 1715 and 1720. He also published a translation of the *Odyssey* in 1726, though he completed only half of the poem's twenty-four books and the others were translated by William Broome (1689–1745) and Elijah Fenton (1683–1730). An inescapable object of study in public schools, Pope's Homer became a standard work on the library shelves of any self-respecting gentleman; female enthusiasts were, understandably, rarer.

expenses while Sebastian was away; and she asked Cecil to go into the drawing room for five minutes while she got into bed, she was so tired. He came back five minutes after; and they smoked cigarettes until two o'clock in the morning, talking very seriously about books and general questions. Then she drew the bedclothes up to her chin and looked at him sleepily. 'You must go, now, Cecil, I'm so tired,' she said. 'Turn out the light.' He turned out the light, and bent over her as she lay with her face turned away, just visible in the fire-light. As he stooped down and put his lips against her cheek, a sharp scent of white heliotrope, that scent he remembered, came into his nostrils.[33] She turned up her mouth and kissed him softly, saying 'God bless you.' He had reached the door when she said, 'Why don't you say God bless you? Sebastian does, every night: You must say it.' He said 'God bless you,' and shut the bedroom-door behind him. Then he found his way out, in the dark, and once more met the moonlight on the stairs.

IX

One day Cecil turned up about three, and found her, as usual, in bed. Her eyes looked feverish; she was in a state of vague excitement, about nothing in particular, a mere matter of nerves. Presently, 'Would you like to see me in my tights?' she asked, and, not waiting for an answer, sprang up in bed and waved him out of the room. In a few minutes she called 'Cecil!' and he went back. She did not hear him come in. She had opened the door of the cupboard, in which there was a long narrow mirror, and she was gazing at herself in the glass, as she stood there in a ridiculous pose, in her violet tights, a gauze skirt, held out at arms length, and the gold wig which had cost thirty shillings. It offended his eye a little to see how awkwardly the tights fitted her, the chemise bundled down inside, padding her out at front and back; but her legs were charming, in their supple slimness, and he looked at them with a critical appreciation of their charm. The gaze with which she greeted herself in the glass was one of boundless adoration. He spoke to her, and she turned, affecting a pretty shyness as she met his glance, but soon she turned back to the mirror, and he came behind her, and put his arms round her, feeling her breasts pant under his hands; and he put his face down by hers, and the glass reflected both their faces, so curiously like each other, and now both equally flushed. The golden wig caught the softer curls of his hair, and tangled their heads together. Already she had forgotten him, though she was pressing his hands tighter against her breasts; she was absorbed in the delight of herself, the beauty of her own body, which at least had always been beautiful for her. He moved away from her, and she dropt the gauze which had been meant, he supposed, to break the shock; and then, in her violet tights, the golden wig

---

[33] See Symons's poem, 'White Heliotrope' (*London Nights*), in which the smell of this perfume triggers a reminiscence of a sexual encounter.

tossing, she began to caper before the glass, doing the few steps that she knew, with her favourite, formal reverence. She turned, and posed, and turned again, twisting her head off, almost, in her desire to see the curve of her legs in the back view. Her face, under the golden wig, smiled to face in the glass, voluptuously, enticingly. The eyes said, 'How beautiful you are! how beautiful!' and a curious wickedness, as of a temptress glorying in her power, mingled with the passionate admiration of herself. She reminded him for an instant of the half-crazy woman he had seen at the Moulin-Rouge, dancing in front of the mirror, under the musicians' gallery; the woman who always dances by herself, and who always looks at herself in the glass.[34] Never had Lucy seemed to him so sensual; never had he realized so clearly before that this charming girl, this cultivated woman, with her pruderies and her refinements, her books and her aspirations and her pictures, was after all (he said to himself now) merely a prostitute.

---

[34] This description recalls Symons's accounts of the dancer Jane Avril (1868–1943), whose performances led her to be nicknamed 'La Mélinite' after a brand of explosive. In 'La Mélinite: Moulin Rouge', the third part of *London Nights*'s 'Décor de Théâtre', Avril is described as dancing in a dream before a mirror, contemplating 'her morbid, vague, ambiguous grace' as she dances 'for her own delight'.

~

At the Alhambra:
Impressions and Sensations

This essay appeared in the fifth number of *The Savoy* in September 1896. Symons never reprinted it in its entirety, though a section from it was tacked on to 'The Russian Ballets' in *Dramatis Personae* (1923). The essay is therefore probably less well known than it deserves to be, for, as the ballet historian Ivor Guest, remarks, 'There exists no more illuminating account of the bustling world of sweat and tinsel to be found back-stage at the Alhambra'.[1]

Probably Symons's favourite theatre, the Alhambra stood on the east side of Leicester Square from 1856 until its demolition eighty years later. It was named after the Moorish palace in Grenada, and staged a wide variety of dramatic and musical entertainments, though Symons here foregrounds ballet above all else. In his guise as 'Silhouette', Symons regularly reviewed performances there, but he was a frequent patron when off-duty. Indeed, he was so familiar a presence that the theatre manager, John Hollingshead, nicknamed him 'l'enfant de la maison', and allowed him virtually free access to rehearsals and back-stage life. The soubriquet pleased him greatly: it was, he told Herbert Horne, a 'very pretty designation.'[2]

'At the Alhambra' differs from many of Symons's essays on travel, theatre, music or art because it often concentrates on observing events as they occur rather than dwelling upon their effect upon the viewer. Largely avoiding solipsism, it conveys life behind the scenes with a keen eye for piquant detail, evokes the beauty of ballet in performance, and succeeds in balancing recollections with commentary and analysis. Throughout the piece, Symons emerges as knowledge-able and well-informed, his accounts of the dancers' outfits generally avoiding the voyeurism one might have expected in a journal published by Leonard Smithers (who dealt in pornography), even as he admits to the lingering existence of the 'Puritan conscience' and the allure of 'painted women'. Being the editor of

---

[1] Guest, *Ballet in Leicester Square*, p. 7.
[2] Symons to Horne, *c.* March 1893, *Selected Letters*, p. 101.

The Savoy, Symons was able to grant himself more space and time than he ever received in the *Star*, but he retained something of his 'Silhouette' persona as a writer who is able to share his observations in ways which connect with his audience instead of becoming primarily self-interested.

The essay's title again foregrounds words of crucial importance to Symons, but it avoids getting drawn into abstraction, notably in its treatment of viewpoint. He is keen to distinguish vivid experience from its recollection and re-remembrance, with the lengthy paragraph a crucial means of dwelling within a moment instead of dissecting it. When he does reflect or reminisce, he does so through a change of focus, a method which is well suited to the essay's mixture of observation, evocation, and critical comment. As Karl Beckson points out, this 'simultaneous involvement and detachment of the writer' is 'characteristic of the self-reflexive art of Decadence' and had been shown in the poems of *London Nights* the previous year.[3]

Ballet's fusion of music, dance, and theatrical design make it, for Symons, the greatest of arts; its melding of aesthetic disciplines offering him a model for the interdisciplinary experiments of his own work. He also celebrates artificiality as something in itself rather than basing its success on mimetic assessment. The ideal spectator is aware of this and endorses it through colluding in the 'beautiful illusion' upon the stage, one enhanced by lighting and cosmetics. This was something to which he returned in 'The World as Ballet' (1898) where dance possesses 'the intellectual as well as sensuous appeal of a living symbol, which can but reach the brain through the eyes, in the visual, concrete, imaginative way'.[4] Such ideas had obvious significance for Yeats, though Symons's influence on him went largely unrecognized until Frank Kermode's *Romantic Image* appeared in 1957.

* * *

I

At the Alhambra I can never sit anywhere but in the front row of the stalls. As a point of view, the point of view considered in the abstract, I admit that the position has its disadvantages. Certainly, the most magical glimpse I ever caught of an Alhambra ballet was from the road in front, from the other side of the road, one night when two doors were suddenly flung open just as I was passing. In the moment's interval before the doors closed again, I saw, in that odd, unexpected way, over the heads of the audience, far off in a sort of blue mist, the whole stage, its brilliant crowd drawn up in the last pose, just as the curtain was beginning to

---

[3] Beckson, *Arthur Symons: A Life*, p. 150.
[4] Symons, 'The World as Ballet', in *Studies in Seven Arts*, p. 391.

descend. It stamped itself in my brain, an impression caught just at the perfect moment, by some rare felicity of chance. But that is not an impression that can be repeated. In the general way I prefer to see my illusions very clearly, recognizing them as illusions, and yet, to my own perverse and decadent way of thinking, losing none of their charm. I have been reproved, before now, for singing 'the charm of rouge on fragile cheeks,'[5] but it is a charm that I fully appreciate. Maquillage, to be attractive, must of course be unnecessary. As a disguise for age or misfortune, it has no interest for me.[6] But, of all places, on the stage, and of all people, on the cheeks of young people: there, it seems to me that make-up is intensely fascinating, and its recognition is of the essence of my delight in a stage performance. I do not for a moment want really to believe in what I see before me; to believe that those wigs are hair, that grease-paint a blush; any more than I want really to believe that the actor whom I have just been shaking hands with has turned into a real live emperor since I left him. I know that a delightful imposition is being practised upon me; that I am to see fairyland for a while; and to me all that glitters shall be gold. But I would have no pretence of reality: I do not, for my part, find that the discovery of a stage-trick lessens my appreciation of what that trick effects. There is this charming person, for instance, at the Alhambra: in the street she is handsome rather than pretty; on the stage she is pretty rather than handsome. I know exactly how she will look in her different wigs, exactly what her make-up will bring out in her and conceal; I can allow, when I see her on the stage, for every hair's-breadth of change: yet does my knowledge of all this interfere with my sensation of pleasure as I see her dancing on the other side of the footlights? Quite the contrary; and I will go further, and admit that there is a special charm to me in a yet nearer view of these beautiful illusions. That is why I like to alternate the point of view of the front row of the stalls with the point of view of behind the scenes.

There, one sees one's illusions in the making; but how exquisite in their frank artificiality, are these painted faces, all these tawdry ornaments, decorations, which are as yet only 'properties'! I have never been disappointed, as so many are disappointed, by what there is to be seen in that debatable land 'behind the scenes.' For one thing, I never expected to find an Arabian Nights' Entertainment of delightful splendour and delightful wickedness, and so I was never chagrined at not finding it. The coulisses of the Alhambra are, in themselves, quite prosaic. They form, of course, the three sides of a square, the outer rim; the fourth side being the footlights. On the prompt side is the stage-manager's chair, the row of

---

[5] The opening line of 'Maquillage' from *Silhouettes*. Symons dates the poem 18 September 1891.
[6] Symons is here indebted to Section X of Baudelaire's essay, 'The Painter of Modern Life' (1863), 'Woman'. 'Painting the face is not to be used with the vulgar, unavowable intention of imitating the fair face of nature, or competing with youth.' Charles Baudelaire, *Selected Writings on Art and Literature*, trans. by P. E. Charvet (London: Penguin, 1972), pp. 427–28.

brass handles which regulate the lights and ring down the curtain, and the little mirror, with a ledge running along below it, which (with the addition of a movable screen) constitute the dressing-room accommodation of the 'turns' who have to make a change of costume. Layer after layer of scenery is piled up against the wall at the side, and nearly the whole time there is a bustling of scene-shifters shoving along some great tottering framework, of which one sees only the canvas back and the narrow rim of wood. Turn to the right, pass under that archway, and the stone staircase going down leads to the canteen; that going up leads to the dressing- rooms of the *corps de ballet*. Another staircase on the other side of the stage leads to the dressing-rooms of the principals, the extra ladies, and the children. Downstairs are some more dressing-rooms for the supers and the male 'turns.' The back of the stage is merely a passage: it is occasionally a refuge from the stampede of scenery in a quick change.

It is ten minutes before the ballet is to commence. Some clowning comic people are doing their show in front of a drop-scene; behind, on the vacant space in the middle of the stage, the ladies of the ballet are beginning to assemble. They come down in twos and threes, tying a few final bows, buttoning a few overlooked buttons, drawing on their gloves, adjusting one another's coats and wigs. As I shake hands with one after another, my hands get quite white and rough with the chalk-powder they have been rubbing over their skin. Is not even this a charming sensation, a sensation in which one seems actually to partake of the beautiful artificiality of the place? All around me are the young faces that I know so well, both as they are and as the footlights show them. Now I see them in all the undisguise of make-up: the exact line of red paint along the lips, every shading of black under the eyes, the pink of the ears and cheeks, and just where it ends under the chin and along the rim of throat. In a plain girl make-up only seems to intensify her plainness; for make-up does but give colour and piquancy to what is already in a face, it adds nothing new. But in a pretty girl how exquisitely becoming all this is, what a new kind of exciting savour it gives to her real charm! It has, to the remnant of Puritan conscience or consciousness that is the heritage of us all, a certain sense of dangerous wickedness, the delight of forbidden fruit. The very phrase, painted women, has come to have an association of sin; and to have put paint on her checks, though for the innocent necessities of her profession, gives to a woman a sort of symbolic corruption. At once she seems to typify the sorceries and entanglements of what is most deliberately enticing in her sex —

'Femina dulce malum, pariter favus atque venenium' —[7]

---

[7] 'A woman is a sweet evil, at once honey-comb and venom'. The line is quoted twice in 'John Norton', one of the three novellas that comprises George Moore's *Celibates* (London: Walter Scott, 1895), pp. 342, 397, which is where Symons probably picked it up. He contributed an unsigned paragraph on the book to *The Athenæum*'s 'Literary Gossip' column on 6 October 1894 (p. 458) and was a close friend of the Irish novelist at this time. Moore attributes the

with all that is most subtle, and least like nature, in her power to charm. Then there is the indiscretion of the costumes, meant to appeal to the senses, and now thronging one with the unconcern of long use; these girls travestied as boys, so boyish sometimes, in their slim youth; the feminine contours now escaping, now accentuated. All are jumbled together, in a brilliant confusion; the hot faces, the shirt-sleeves of scene-shifters, striking rapidly through a group of princes, peasants, and fairies. In a corner some of the children are doing a dance; now and again an older girl, in a sudden access of gaiety, will try a few whimsical steps; there is a chatter of conversation, a coming and going; someone is hunting everywhere for a missing 'property'; someone else has lost a shoe, or a glove, or is calling for a pin to repair the loss of a button. And now three girls, from opposite directions, will make a simultaneous rush at the stage-manager. 'Mr Forde, I can't get on my wig!' 'Please, Mr Forde, may I have a sheet of notepaper?' 'Oh, Mr Forde, may Miss —- stay off? she has such a bad headache she can hardly stand.'[8] Meanwhile, the overture has commenced; and now a warning clap is heard, and all but those who appear in the first scene retreat hurriedly to the wings. The curtain is about to rise on the ballet.

To watch a ballet from the wings is to lose all sense of proportion, all knowledge of the piece as a whole; but, in return, it is fruitful in happy accidents, in momentary points of view, in chance felicities of light and shade and movement. It is almost to be in the performance oneself, and yet passive, a spectator, with the leisure to look about one. You see the reverse of the picture: the girls at the back lounging against the set scenes, turning to talk with someone at the side; you see how lazily the lazy girls are moving, and how mechanical and irregular are the motions that flow into rhythm when seen from the front. Now one is in the centre of a jostling crowd, hurrying past one on to the stage; now the same crowd returns, charging at full speed between the scenery, everyone trying to reach the dressing-room stairs first. And there is the constant shifting of scenery, from which one has a series of escapes, as it bears down unexpectedly, in some new direction. The ballet, half seen in the centre of the stage, seen in sections, has, in the glimpses that can be caught of it, a contradictory appearance of mere nature and of absolute unreality. And beyond the footlights, on the other side of the orchestra, one can see the boxes near the stalls, the men standing by the bar, an angle cut sharply off from the stalls, with the light full on the faces, the intent

---

poem, 'De meretrice' ['Of a whore'] to 'Marbodius', i.e. Bishop Marbod, Marbodus or Marbodius of Rennes (c. 1035–1123). Moore in turn probably took the poem from Jean-Paul Migne's magisterial *Patrologia Latina* published in 217 volumes between 1841 and 1855. A new edition of the collection began to be issued during the 1880s; the volume containing 'De meretrice' appeared in 1893.

[8] A. G. Forde, Stage-manager at the Alhambra, retired in 1898.

eyes, the gray smoke curling up from the cigarettes. It is all a bewilderment; but to me, certainly, a bewilderment that is always delightful.

II

To the amateur of what is more artificial in the art of illusion, there is nothing so interesting as a stage rehearsal, and there is no stage rehearsal so interesting as the rehearsal of a ballet. Coming suddenly out of the clear cold of a winter morning into the comparative warmth of the dimly-lighted Alhambra (it must have been three years ago, now, I think), I found that one of the rehearsals of a ballet named after *Aladdin*[9] was about to begin; and, standing at the far end of the hall, I saw the stage gradually filling with half-dressed figures, a few men in overcoats moving rapidly to and fro in their midst. Lit only by a T-light, these odd, disconcerting figures strolled about the stage, some arm in arm, some busily knitting; they formed into groups of twos and threes and half dozens, from which came the sound of a pleasant chatter, a brisk feminine laughter. I found my way between the lonely-looking stalls, disturbing the housekeeper at her work, and mounted to the stage. The stalls were covered in their white sheeting; white sheeting hung in long strips from boxes and balcony; here and there a black coat and hat stood out from the dingy monotony of white, or a figure flitted rapidly, a sudden silhouette, against the light of a window high up in the gallery. The T-light flickered unsteadily; a little chill light found its way through roof and windows, intensifying, by even so faint a suggestion of the outside world, all that curious unreality which is never so unreal as at the prosaic moments of a rehearsal.

I had the honour to know a good many ladies of the ballet, and there was no little news, of public and private interest, to be communicated and discussed. Thus I gathered that no one knew anything about the plot of the ballet which was being rehearsed, and that many were uncertain whether it was their fate to be a boy or a girl; that this one was to be a juggler, though she knew not how to juggle; and that one a fisher-boy, and that other a fisher-girl; and that Miss A had been put in a new place, and was disgusted; and Miss B, having also been put in a new place, was delighted; together with much information in no way bearing on the subject of the ballet. All at once the stage-manager clapped his hands; the ladies

---

[9] *Aladdin* was the Alhambra's 1892 Christmas production, opening on 19 December and running for 26 weeks. The scenario was by John Hollingshead, who reworked his 1871 adaptation of *Aladdin, oder Die Wunderlampe*, music by Gührich, first performed in 1834 and still in the repertory of Berlin's Royal Opera House fifty years later. The music for *Aladdin* was by the German composer, Georges Jacobi (1840–1906), choreography by Carlo Coppi (below). It starred Mademoiselle Marie as Aladdin, Pierini Legnani (below) as the Princess, and Fred Storey as the Magician.

rushed to their places; I retreated to a corner of the stage, behind the piano, at which sat a pianist and a violinist; and the ballet-master came forward, staff in hand, and took up his position on a large square piece of board, which had been provided for the protection of 'the boards' (technically speaking) against the incessant thump-thump of that formidable staff as it pounds away in time with the music. The rehearsal had begun.

Rehearsal costume, to the casual outside spectator, is rather curious. There is a bodice, which may be of any kind; there is a short petticoat, generally of white, with discreet linen drawers to match; the stockings are for the most part black. But a practising dress leaves room, in its many exceptions, for every variety of individual taste. A lively fancy sometimes expends itself on something wonderful in stockings, wonderful coloured things, clocked and patterned. Then there are petticoats plain and ornamented, limp and starched, setting tightly and flapping loosely; petticoats with frillings and edgings, petticoats of blue, of pink, of salmon colour, of bright red. But it is the bodice that gives most scope for the decorative instinct. Many have evidently been designed for the occasion; they are elaborately elegant, showy even. There are prints and stuffs and fancy arrangements in the way of blouses and jerseys and zouaves and Swiss bodices; with white shawls and outdoor jackets for the cold, and ribbons and bright ties for show.[10] The walking-ladies are in their walking-dresses; and it is with the oddest effect of contrast that they mingle, marching sedately, in their hats and cloaks, with these skipping figures in the undress of the dancing-school. Those who are not wanted cluster together at the sides, sitting on any available seats and benches, or squatting on the floor; or they make a dash to the dressing-rooms upstairs or to the canteen downstairs. One industrious lady has brought her knitting. It is stowed away for safety in some unused nook of the piano, which is rattling away by my side; presently it is hunted out, and I see her absorbed in the attempt to knit without looking at the stitches. Another has brought woolwork, which is getting almost too big to bring; several have brought books: the works of Miss Braddon, penny novelettes, and, yes, some one has actually brought the *Story of an African Farm*.[11] Occasionally a stage-carpenter or scene-shifter or limelight-man passes in the background; some of the new scenery is lying about, very Chinese in its brilliant red and blue lattice-work. And all the while the whole centre of the stage is in movement; the lines and circles cross and curve, hands lifted, feet lifted; and all

---

[10] Zouaves, French infantry regiments, wore open-fronted short jackets, loose-fitting trousers called 'serouel', and often affected oriental head gear and sashes.

[11] Mary Elizabeth Braddon (1835–1915), prolific writer of sensation novels and thrilling romances; author of *Lady Audley's Secret* (1862) among other works. *The Story of an African Farm* (1883), a novel by the South African writer, Olive Schreiner (1855–1920), with a markedly feminist outlook. It was much discussed during the 1890s. Symons's fellow poet, Ernest Dowson, adored it.

the while, in time with the music, the ballet-master pounds away with his stout staff, already the worse for wear, and shouts, in every language but English, orders which it is a little difficult to follow.[12]

As the bright, trickling music is beaten out on the perfunctory piano and violin, the composer himself appears, a keen profile rising sharply out of a mountainous furred overcoat. It was just then that the ballet-master had left his place, and was tripping lightly round the stage, taking the place of the absent premiere danseuse. It was only for a moment; then, after a rush at some misbehaving lady, a tempest of Italian, a growl of good-humoured fury, he was back on his board, and the staff pounded away once more. The *coryphées*, holding bent canes in their hands, turned and twirled in the middle of the stage; the *corps de ballet*, the children, the extra ladies, formed around them, a semicircle first, then a racing circle; they passed, re-passed, dissolved, re-formed, bewilderingly; with disconcerting rushes and dashes; turning upon themselves, turning round one another, advancing and retreating, in waves of movement, as the music scattered itself in waves of sound. Aimless, unintelligible it looked, this tripping, posturing crowd of oddly-dressed figures; these bright outdoor faces looked strange in a place where I was so used to see rouged cheeks and lips, powdered chins, painted eye-lashes, yellow wigs. In this fantastic return to nature I found the last charm of the artificial.[13]

III

The front row of the stalls, on a first night, has a character of its own. It is entirely filled by men, and the men who fill it have not come simply from an abstract aesthetic interest in the ballet. They have friends on the other side of the footlights, and their friends on the other side of the footlights will look down, the moment they come on the stage, to see who are in the front row, and who are standing by the bar on either side. The standing-room by the bar is the resource of the first-nighter with friends who cannot get a seat in the front row. On such a night the air is electrical. A running fire of glances crosses and re-crosses, above the indifferent, accustomed heads of the gentlemen of the orchestra; whom it amuses, none the less, to intercept an occasional smile, to trace it home. On the faces of the men in the front row, what difference in expression! Here is the eager, undisguised enthusiasm of the novice, all eyes, and all eyes on one; here is the

---

[12] Carlo Coppi was ballet-master at the Alhambra for more than a decade from 1891, and also arranged ballets for Drury Lane's pantomimes and Covent Garden operas. Ivor Guest notes that he had been principal mime at La Scala, Milan, and was 'a quiet, rather shy, benevolent-looking man with a beard, who wore a Holland suit and wielded a long stick at rehearsals'. *Ballet in Leicester Square*, p. 45.

[13] A persistent concern in Symons's writing of the period. See his poem, 'Violet: Proem' (*London Nights*), with its reference to 'a violet, planted here, | The artificial flower of my ideal.'

wary, practised attention of the man who has seen many first nights, and whose scarcely perceptible smile reveals nothing, compromises nobody, rests on all. And there is the shy, self-conscious air of embarrassed absorption, typical of that queer type, the friend who is not a friend of the ballet, and who shrinks somewhat painfully into his seat, as the dancers advance, retreat, turn, and turn again.

Let me recall a first night that I still, I suppose, remember: the first night of *Aladdin*. I have had to miss the dress rehearsal, so I am in all the freshness of curiosity as to the dresses, the effects, the general aspect of things. I have been to so many undress rehearsals that I know already most of the music by heart. I know all the dances, I know all the movements of masses. But the ballet, how that will look; but my friends, how they will look; it is these things that are the serious, the important things. And now the baton rises, and the drip, drip of the trickling music dances among the fiddles before the curtain has gone up on the fisherman's hut, and those dancing feet for which I am waiting. Already I see how some of my friends are going to look; and I remember now the musical phrase which I came to associate with that fisher dress, the passing of those slim figures. The Princess flashes upon us in a vision, twining mysteriously in what was then the fashion of the moment, the serpentine dance; and this dance transforms, by what she adds and by what she omits, a series of decorative poses into a real dance, for it is the incomparable Legnani.[14] Then the fisherman's hut, and all mortal things, vanish suddenly; and Aladdin comes down into a vast cave of livid green, set with stalactites, and peopled with brown demons, winged and crowned with fire; reminding one of the scene where Orfeo, in the opera of Gluck, goes down into hell.[15] Robed in white, the spirit of the Lamp leads on the *coryphées*, her genii; and they are here, they run forward, they dance in lines and circles, creatures with bat-like wings of pale green, shading into a green so dark as to be almost black. The Princess enters: it is 'a wave of the sea' that dances! And then, the scenery turning suddenly over and round, the cave suddenly changes into a palace. There is a dancing march, led by the children, with their toppling helmets, and soon, with banners, fans, gilt staves, a dancing crowd moves and circles, in beautiful white and gold, in purple and yellow, in terra-cotta, in robes that flower into chrysanthemums, and with bent garlands of leaves. I search through this bewildering crowd, finding and losing, losing and finding, the faces for which I search. The Princess is borne on in a palanquin; she descends, runs forward

---

[14] Pierina Legnani (1863–1930) was principal dancer at the Alhambra from 1888 until 1894, and once again in 1897. She was prima ballerina at La Scala and for the Tsar's Imperial Ballet in St Petersburg before her retirement in 1901. Widely considered one of the greatest ballerinas of all time, a number of her sequences remain in the repertoire, notably in the Black Swan's solo in Act III of Tchaikovsky's *Swan Lake* (1877) devised for the 1895 Petersburg production.
[15] *Orfeo ed Euridice* (1762), an opera by Christoph Wilibald Gluck (1714–87).

(Simeon Solomon's *Lady in a Chinese Dress*),[16] and in the quaintest little costume, a costume of a willow-pattern plate, does the quaintest little trotting and tripping dance, in what might be the Chinese manner. There is another transformation: a demon forest, with wickedly tangled trees, horrible creatures of the woods, like human artichokes, shimmering green human bats, delightful demons. The Princess, the Magician, Aladdin, meet: the Magician has the enchantment of his art, the Princess the enchantment of her beauty, Aladdin only the enchantment of his love. Spells are woven and broken, to bewitching motion: it is the triumph of love and beauty. There is another transformation: the diamond garden, with its flowers that are jewels, its living flowers. Colours race past, butterflies in pale blue, curious morbid blues, drowsy browns and pale greens, more white and gold, a strange note of abrupt black. The crystal curtain, a veil of diamonds, falls, dividing the stage, a dancing crowd before it and behind it, a rain of crystals around.[17] An electric angel has an apotheosis; and as the curtain falls upon the last grouping, I try, vainly, to see everyone at once, everyone whom I want to see. The whole front row applauds violently; and, if one observed closely, it would be seen that every man, as he applauds, is looking in a different direction.

IV

Why is it that one can see a ballet fifty times, always with the same sense of pleasure, while the most absorbing play becomes a little tedious after the third time of seeing? For one thing, because the difference between seeing a play and seeing a ballet is just the difference between reading a book and looking at a picture. One returns to a picture as one returns to nature, for a delight which, being purely of the senses, never tires, never distresses, never varies. To read a book, even for the first time, requires a certain effort. The book must indeed be exceptional that can be read three or four times; and no book ever was written that could be read three or four times in succession. A ballet is simply a picture in movement. It is a picture where the imitation of nature is given by nature itself; where the figures of the composition are real, and yet, by a very paradox of travesty, have a delightful, deliberate air of unreality. It is a picture where the colours change, recombine, before one's eyes; where the outlines melt into one another, emerge, and are again lost, in the kaleidoscopic movement of the dance. Here we need tease ourselves with no philosophies, need endeavour to read none of the riddles of existence; may indeed give thanks to be spared for one hour the imbecility of human speech. After the tedium of the theatre, where we are called

---

[16] An 1865 watercolour by Solomon (see 'The Life and Adventures of Lucy Newcome').

[17] This was a spectacular crystal curtain weighing 1½ tons with 75,000 faceted glass beads strung on 24 miles of wire. It was illuminated with coloured electric light and astonished and delighted audiences.

on to interest ourselves in the improbable fortunes of uninteresting people, how welcome is the relief of a spectacle which professes to be no more than merely beautiful; which gives us, in accomplished dancing, the most beautiful sight that we can see; which provides, in short, the one escape into fairy-land which is permitted by that tyranny of the real which is the worst tyranny of modern life.

And then there is another reason why one can see a ballet fifty times, a reason which is not in the least an aesthetic one, but on the contrary very human. I once took a well-known writer, who is one of the most remarkable women of our time, to see a ballet. She had never seen one, and I was delighted with her intense absorption in what was passing before her eyes. At last I said something about the beauty of a certain line of dancers, some effect of colour and order. She turned on me a half-laughing face: 'But it is the people I am looking at,' she said, 'not the artistic effect!' Since then I have had the courage to admit that with me too it is the people, and not only the artistic effect, that I like to look at.

~

Arles

By the late nineteenth century, the Provencal town of Arles had become a backwater. Long eclipsed by Marseilles, a dynamic replayed in the finale of 'An Autumn City', the coming of the railways severely reduced the river traffic that was its main income and its economic importance dwindled. Henry James found Arles strangely beguiling when he visited it in 1882, though he disliked the sharp, stony pavements — 'the rugosities of its dirty lanes affect the feet like knife-blades' — its 'torturous and featureless streets', 'puddles and shabby cafés'. 'Nothing could be more provincial than the situation of Arles at ten o'clock at night,' he wrote dolefully. 'As a city, indeed, Arles quite misses its effect in every way; and if it is a charming place, as I think it is, I can hardly tell the reason why.'[1] If a seasoned traveller such as James struggled to understand the peculiar charm of Arles, it is hardly surprising that Symons's Livia finds her experience of it bewildering and disappointing.

Its political and economic importance having dwindled, Arles became popular with artists, notably Vincent van Gogh, who lived there between February 1888 and May 1889 and produced over three hundred paintings and drawings while in residence, including the famous *Le Café de nuit* (1888). 'As long as autumn lasts I won't have enough hands, canvas or colours to paint the beautiful things that I see,' he told his brother in late September 1888, though he acknowledged that rain was inclined to make life difficult.[2] Unfortunately, his mental condition deteriorated during his residence in the town; it was in Arles that he severed his ear in December 1888, and he left after the townspeople had petitioned the authorities for his confinement.

Symons loved Arles, visiting the town en route to and from Italy and recording his impressions of it on a number of occasions. *Wanderings* reprints essays from 1891, 1898, and 1899, the second of which is reproduced here, and he also

---

[1] Henry James, 'Arles', in *A Little Tour in France* (1884; Boston and New York: Houghton, Mifflin and Co., 1900), pp. 258–67.
[2] Vincent to Theo van Gogh, 25 September 1888, vingoghletters.org, no. 687.

composed 'Beauty's Strangeness' there in October 1898, though this poem was not published until its inclusion in *Knave of Hearts*. Like many of Symons's travel essays, 'Arles' first appeared in the *Saturday Review* (22 October 1898), though it was somewhat slyly reprinted as 'An Autumn City' in *The Dome* in February 1899.

Symons's version of Arles is a highly selective one. There is no suggestion of the sordid, gas-lit night cafés depicted by van Gogh, or the touristic detail and attendant practicalities of James's account. Instead, Symons treats the town as the perfect setting for the melancholy weariness that afflicted him in the aftermath of the end of his affair with Lydia. The antithesis of the travel guide writer — he would never have received a commission from Baedeker — Symons avoided museums and historic buildings, preferring to simply walk the streets, soaking up atmosphere or, as his friends put it with gentle mockery, 'impreshuns and sensashuns', terms he was wont to overuse. His concern with the mood and the moment freed him from the necessities of background research, and allowed him to approach each city he visited in a state of heightened receptiveness, resulting in fascinating but profoundly idiosyncratic treatments of them. His evocation of a damp and seemingly deserted Arles is a case in point; it is very unlikely that many of his readers were inspired to visit the city, but that was hardly Symons's intention in advertising the sensitivity of his consciousness and the subtlety of his response to his surroundings.

'Arles' is patently a dry (or damp) run for 'An Autumn City', as much of it is transferred unblushingly from the essay to the similarly-titled story. At this point in his career, Symons was not stalked by bibliographers, and was far more able to reprint and reuse material than would be the case nowadays. It would seem that his visits to Arles made a profound impression on him, one which he brooded over in his travel essays and then pondered further in fiction, ruminating not only on the loss of Lydia but also on his own separation from other people and wider society.

* * *

When the soul of Autumn made for itself a body, it made Arles. I have never seen Arles when it was not grey and contentedly mournful, recollecting old things. All the beauty of that brooding over a great past has gone visibly to make up its one present greatness, the beauty of its women. They have the gravity, the unhasting passage through the world, of those who are conscious of a tradition. And they have something more than a casual, or merely personal, beauty; their beauty becomes collective, becomes one expression of Arles.

Avenues of trees from which the dust is never lifted, for they are dust-grey even in sunlight, close in almost the whole city, as with a leafy wall. The Avenue Victor-Hugo, which leads to the Aliscamps, has its long line of cafés, its attempts at animation; soldiers, *zouaves*,[3] are stationed in a great barrack; the carts come in from the country; in the evening the people walk there. At the side is the little melancholy public garden, with its paths curving upwards to the ruined walls and arches of the Roman theatre, its low balustrades of crumbling stone, its faint fountain, greenish grey; set there, in its loneliness, but a step out of the road, a road seeming to lead nowhere. Yes, to lead to the tombs, to that alley of tombs which Dante remembered when he saw the 'modo più amaro' by which the people in hell make alleys of living tombs:

Sì com' ad Arli ove'l Rodano stagna[4]

The tombs have been moved now, aside from the Aliscamps, into the little, secluded Allée des Tombeaux, where they line both sides of the way, empty stone trough after empty stone trough, with here and there a more pompous sarcophagus; there is a quiet path between them, leading to the canal and the bowling-green; and in the evening the old men come and sit among the tombs.

Everything in Arles seems to grow out of death, and to be returning thither. The place itself rises about the ruins; does not seem even yet detached from them. The amphitheatre fills a sort of public square, up to which one climbs through narrow streets; houses with closed shutters stand about it, as if not less empty of life. The ruins of the theatre look down on the public garden; one comes suddenly upon a Roman obelisk, fragments of the Roman walls; a Roman column has been built into the wall of one of the two hotels which stand in the Forum, now the Place du Forum; and the modern houses, the comparatively modern houses, have an air which is neither new nor old, but entirely sympathetic with what is old. They are faded, just a little dilapidated, not caring to distinguish themselves from the faint colours, the aged slumber, of the very ancient things about them.

And in the air itself there is something of decay. The smell of dead leaves is everywhere, the moisture of stone, the sodden dampness of earth, water forming in little pools on the ground, creeping out of the earth and into the earth again. Bright sun, sun which always scorches, alternates with pouring rain, and there is always uncertainty as to the fate of a day. I have never heard such thunder, or seen such lightning, as that which one night shook the old roof under which I lay, and blazed and flickered at the window until it seemed to be licking up the stones with liquid fire. The storm faded out in a morning of faint sunshine; only for the rain to cling furtively about the place all day.

To be in Arles for more than the day of a tourist's visit is to have dropped quietly out of the world to slumber for a while in a dead city. Wandering about those streets which bring one back always to one's starting-point, or along the boulevards which suggest the vague country, but set one no farther into it,

---

[3] French light infantry troops usually deployed in North Africa, known for their picturesque uniforms (see 'At the Alhambra').
[4] See note to 'An Autumn City'.

nothing seems to matter very much, for nothing very much seems to exist. With that sense of time's work on the world, which is part of the very air one breathes here, there comes a sort of merely sympathetic submission to things, a resignation to the uselessness of everything, which the first breath of sea-air at Marseilles would blow away, no doubt, but which is as genuine as any other effect on the nerves, while it is being endured.

To pass certain hours of the afternoon, when this gentle depression weighed most heavily, I used to attend Benediction[5] in the little church of Notre-Dame-la-Major, at the farthest corner of that oddly shaped square which goes up the hill from the amphitheatre. The first time I entered it, the church was quite dark, and I could only dimly see the high altar, draped in white, and with something white rising up from its midst, like a figure mysteriously poised among the unlighted candles. Hooded figures passed me, and knelt with bowed heads; presently a light passed along the church, and a lamp was let down by a chain, lighted, and drawn up again. Then a few candles were lighted, and I saw the priest kneeling motionless before the altar. The chanting was very homely, as in a village church, and with the village church's harmonium; but over the monotony of one repeated air, over and over and over again, deepened for me the sense of a religious harmony between this half-drowsy service and the slumbering city without. I waited until the service was over, the priests went out, the lamps and candles were extinguished, and the hooded figures, after a little silence, began to move again in the church.

But where, after all, Arles seems to withdraw into its most intimate self, is in the cloisters of Saint-Trophime. Every side dating from a different century, the north from the ninth, the east from the thirteenth, the west from the fourteenth, and the south from the sixteenth, they have gathered into this sadly battered court a little of the curious piety of age after age, working here to perpetuate, not only the legends of the Church, but the legends that have their home about Arles. Again and again, among these naive sculptures, one sees the local dragon, that man-eating Tarasque who has given its name to Tarascon.[6] The place is full of monsters, and of figures tortured into strange dislocations. Adam swings ape-like among the branches of the apple tree, biting at the leaves before he reaches the apple. Flames break out among companies of the damned, and the devil sits enthroned above his subjects. A gentle doctor of the Church, holding a book, and bending his head meditatively sideways, was shown to me as King Solomon; with, of course, in the slim saint on the other side of the pillar, the Queen of Sheba. Broken escutcheons, carved in stone, commemorate bishops on the walls. There is no order, or division of time; one seems shut off equally from the present and

---

[5] See note in 'An Autumn City'.
[6] See note in 'An Autumn City'.

from any appreciable moment of the past; shut in with the same vague, dateless Autumn that has moulded Arles into its own image.

An autumn city, hinting of every gentle, resigned, reflective way of fading out of life, of effacing oneself in a world to which one no longer attaches any value; always remembering itself, always looking into a dim mirror which reflects at least something of what it was, but mournfully veiled, Arles still sits in the midst of the rocky plains, by the side of the river, among its tombs.

~

Pachmann and the Piano

This essay was first printed in *The Academy* (24 May 1902) before being collected in *Plays, Acting and Music: A Book of Theory* the following year. It shows Symons at his best and worst, in that while he conveys quite passionately how Pachmann's playing of Chopin and Bach affects him, his evocation lacks precision and presupposes the reader's sympathy with his responses. The essay acknowledges some of the criticisms made of Pachmann's playing, but it gives them little sustained attention, preferring to evoke his musicianship through a series of parallels and images.

The problems faced by anyone writing about music, especially in the days before it could be easily recorded, are obvious. Addressing a non-specialist readership in *The Academy*, and lacking detailed knowledge of music theory, Symons found refuge in comparisons, analogies, and poetry, concentrating on the effect Pachmann's playing might produce upon a listener susceptible to its charm rather than trying to be overly analytical. There is something here of Shelley's reluctance to place the violet in the crucible in *A Defence of Poetry* (1821), as well as a defiant refusal to endorse more cerebral treatments of the keyboard. For Symons, touch rather than command of rhythm or textual fidelity, is all. When he is not being described as inhuman or elvish, Pachmann emerges as something of a savant, a romantic who conjures music into being through his sensitivity and vision, and though Symons does belatedly acknowledge the hours of practice required for such mastery, he does not dwell on the matter. With the essay citing the familiar Symons touchstones of Whistler and Verlaine, it is unsurprising that it should imply an analogous relationship between painting, poetry, and pianism. Whistler famously announced that 'the work of the master reeks not of the sweat of the brow — suggests no effort — and is finished from its beginning.'[1] Pachmann's performances are here made to appear similarly effortless, rather neglecting their lengthy preparatory work. As Whistler told the jury at the 1878 Ruskin libel trial, to produce a wonderful painting quickly

---

[1] James McNeill Whistler, *The Gentle Art of Making Enemies* (London: Heinemann, 1890), p. 115.

requires a lifetime of dedication and knowledge, even if the painting itself conceals the labour that went into it.

'Pachmann and the Piano' is well titled, as it is also a consideration of Symons's favourite music for the instrument. Like Shaw, he was unimpressed by displays of virtuosity for its own sake from the steel-fingered piano hammerers of the period, arguing instead for subtlety and restraint. He would surely have appreciated Alfred Cortot, and, had he been born later, the likes of Clifford Curzon. His reverence for Chopin is quite plain, and though his assessment that the four scherzi represent his finest achievement now seems rather wide of the mark, he was able to recognize that the small scale of a mazurka did not limit its interest or importance. He should therefore be acknowledged as anticipating some later trends in Chopin criticism, rejecting the image of him as a salon composer and disdaining the popular nicknames for his works. Nevertheless, in his identification of Chopin with morbidity, he is very much of his time.

The similarities between Pachmann and Christian Trevalga are readily apparent, though Pachmann possessed a humorous theatricality and *joie de vivre* wholly alien to Symons's creation and absent from his account. Born in Odessa of German parentage, Valdimir de Pachmann (1848–1933) was one of the finest pianists of his generation. He specialized in Chopin, challenging the idea that the composer's smaller works were too intimate for the concert hall. He made his London debut in 1883, and appeared there regularly thereafter, sometimes in joint recitals with his wife, Marguerite (a former pupil of his). Although his performances could be eccentric, as for instance when he demanded that the physically unprepossessing be removed from the front row of his audience, and led to James Huneker nicknaming him 'the chopinzee', his artistry won him worldwide renown, not least because of his extraordinary control of volume and nuance when playing 'Pachmannissimo'. He was the first pianist to play all of Chopin's Études and Preludes in the same concert (New York, 1900), and also one of the first to make regular recordings, almost always of Chopin, beginning in 1907. As this essay demonstrates, Symons was dazzled by him, but it was not simply amateurs who marvelled. The composer Kaikhosru Shapurji Sorabji (1892–1988) wrote an excellent summary of de Pachmann's art, remarking:

> The almost unlimited range of his gradations within a mezzo-forte and an unbelievable 'quasi-*niente*'; the amazing fluidity and limpidity of his '*jeu perlé*'; his delicious dainty staccato; the marvellous cantilena; the exquisite phrasing, and the wonderful delicate fantasy of the whole [...] made his playing of certain works of Chopin an enchantment and a delight.[2]

---

[2] Taken from Edward Blickstein's liner notes to Marston Record's edition of Pachmann's complete recordings, a treasure trove of Pachmann anecdotes as well as astute analyses of his art: http://www.marstonrecords.com/pachmann/pachmann_liner.htm.

Symons became friends with Pachmann and met up with him following his London concerts in 1915 and 1918. He wrote several other essays on him, all of which reiterate the ideas expressed in 'Pachmann and the Piano.' Karl Beckson's edition of Symons's letters quotes an unpublished memoir, dated 29 September 1918, in which he writes that Pachmann is:

> as wonderful as ever. I never saw him so mad as he is now after a year's seclusion. He began in a most uneasy manner — then seemed to say: 'I won't play the piano': put his hands in his pockets and goes back into the artists' room. He returns — plays Mozart divinely — Chopin as he always did. In one word: absolute perfection of this man of an abnormal and inhuman genius.[3]

Here Pachmann's eccentricities are acknowledged (they had undoubtedly become more pronounced than was the case in 1902), but are made to serve Symons's notion of genius and the artist's status as exempt from normal human concerns. In the last analysis, his on-stage antics, which may have served as an antidote to extreme nervousness, are very different from the existential crises which see Trevalga confined to the asylum.

* * *

I

It seems to me that Pachmann is the only pianist who plays the piano as it ought to be played. I admit his limitations, I admit that he can play only certain things, but I contend that he is the greatest living pianist because he can play those things better than any other pianist can play anything. Pachmann is the Verlaine of pianists, and when I hear him I think of Verlaine reading his own verse, in a faint, reluctant voice, which you overheard. Other players have mastered the piano, Pachmann absorbs its soul, and it is only when he touches it that it really speaks its own voice.

The art of the pianist, after all, lies mainly in one thing, touch. It is by the skill, precision, and beauty of his touch that he makes music at all; it is by the quality of his touch that he evokes a more or less miraculous vision of sound for us. Touch gives him his only means of expression; it is to him what relief is to the sculptor or what values are to the painter. To 'understand,' as it is called, a piece of music, is not so much as the beginning of good playing; if you do not understand it with your fingers, what shall your brain profit you? In the interpretation of music all action of the brain which does not translate itself perfectly in touch is useless. You may as well not think at all as not think in terms of your instrument, and the piano responds to one thing only, touch. Now Pachmann, beyond all other pianists, has this magic. When he plays it, the piano

---

[3] Symons, *Selected Letters*, pp. 234–35.

ceases to be a compromise. He makes it as living and penetrating as the violin, as responsive and elusive as the clavichord.

Chopin wrote for the piano with a more perfect sense of his instrument than any other composer, and Pachmann plays Chopin with an infallible sense of what Chopin meant to express in his mind. He seems to touch the notes with a kind of agony of delight; his face twitches with the actual muscular contraction of the fingers as they suspend themselves in the very act of touch. I am told that Pachmann plays Chopin in a morbid way. Well, Chopin was morbid; there are fevers and cold sweats in his music; it is not healthy music, and it is not to be interpreted in a robust way. It must be played, as Pachmann plays it, somnambulistically, with a tremulous delicacy of intensity, as if it were a living thing on whose nerves one were operating, and as if every touch might mean life or death.

I have heard pianists who played Chopin in what they called a healthy way. The notes swung, spun, and clattered, with a heroic repercussion of sound, a hurrying reiteration of fury, signifying nothing.[4] The piano stormed through the applause; the pianist sat imperturbably, hammering. Well, I do not think any music should be played like that, not Liszt even. Liszt connives at the suicide, but with Chopin it is a murder.[5] When Pachmann plays Chopin the music sings itself, as if without the intervention of an executant, of one who stands between the music and our hearing. The music has to intoxicate him before he can play with it; then he becomes its comrade, in a kind of very serious game; himself, in short, that is to say inhuman. His fingers have in them a cold magic, as of soulless elves who have sold their souls for beauty. And this beauty, which is not of the soul, is not of the flesh; it is a sea-change, the life of the foam on the edge of the depths. Or it transports him into some mid-region of the air, between hell and heaven, where he hangs listening. He listens at all his senses. The dew, as well as the raindrop, has a sound for him.

In Pachmann's playing there is a frozen tenderness, with, at moments, the elvish triumph of a gnome who has found a bright crystal or a diamond. Pachmann is inhuman, and music, too, is inhuman. To him, and rightly, it is a thing not domesticated, not familiar as a household cat with our hearth. When he plays it, music speaks no language known to us, has nothing of ourselves to tell us, but is shy, alien, and speaks a language which we do not know. It comes to us a divine hallucination, chills us a little with its 'airs from heaven' or elsewhere, and breaks down for an instant the too solid walls of the world, showing us the gulf.[6] When d'Albert plays Chopin's *Berceuse*, beautifully, it is a

---

[4] According to Shakespeare's Macbeth, life is 'a tale | Told by an idiot, full of sound and fury, | Signifying nothing' (V.v.ll.25–27).

[5] Ferenc Liszt (1811–86), Hungarian composer, virtuoso pianist, and influential teacher. He was a close friend of Chopin.

[6] This sentence splices two allusions to the first act of *Hamlet*. When the Prince is about to see the ghost for the first time, he says, 'Be thou a spirit of health or goblin damn'd, | Bring with thee airs from heaven or blasts from hell' (I.iv.l.41). Earlier, he has wished that 'this too too solid flesh would melt; | Thaw, and resolve itself into a dew' (I.ii.ll.129–30).

lullaby for healthy male children growing too big for the cradle.[7] Pachmann's is
a lullaby for fairy changelings who have never had a soul, but in whose veins
music vibrates; and in this intimate alien thing he finds a kind of humour.

In the attempt to humanise music, that attempt which almost every executant
makes, knowing that he will be judged by his success or failure in it, what is
most fatally lost is that sense of mystery which, to music, is atmosphere. In
this atmosphere alone music breathes tranquilly. So remote is it from us that
it can only be reached through some not quite healthy nervous tension, and
Pachmann's physical disquietude when he plays is but a sign of what it has cost
him to venture outside humanity, into music. Yet in music this mystery is a
simple thing, its native air; and the art of the musician has less difficulty in its
evocation than the art of the poet or the painter. With what an effort do we
persuade words or colours back from their vulgar articulateness into at least some
recollection of that mystery which is deeper than sight or speech. Music can never
wholly be detached from mystery, can never wholly become articulate, and it is
in our ignorance of its true nature that we would tame it to humanity and teach
it to express human emotions, not its own.

Pachmann gives you pure music, not states of soul or of temperament, not
interpretations, but echoes. He gives you the notes in their own atmosphere,
where they live for him an individual life, which has nothing to do with emotions
or ideas. Thus he does not need to translate out of two languages: first, from sound
to emotion, temperament, what you will; then from that back again to sound. The
notes exist; it is enough that they exist. They mean for him just the sound and
nothing else. You see his fingers feeling after it, his face calling to it, his whole
body imploring it. Sometimes it comes upon him in such a burst of light that he
has to cry aloud, in order that he may endure the ecstasy.[8] You see him speaking
to the music; he lifts his finger, that you may listen for it not less attentively. But
it is always the thing itself that he evokes for you, as it rises flower-like out of
silence, and comes to exist in the world. Every note lives, with the whole vitality
of its existence. To Swinburne every word lives, just in the same way; when he
says 'light,' he sees the sunrise; when he says 'fire,' he is warmed through all his
blood. And so Pachmann calls up, with this ghostly magic of his, the innermost
life of music. I do not think he has ever put an intention into Chopin. Chopin
had no intentions. He was a man, and he suffered; and he was a musician, and he
wrote music; and very likely George Sand,[9] and Majorca, and his disease, and

---

[7] Eugen d'Albert (1864–1932), Scottish-born pianist, composer and editor. Chopin, *Berceuse*
('lullaby' or 'cradle-song') in D Flat, Op. 57 (1843–44).
[8] Pachmann was notorious for crying out during ecstatic moments of performance. On occasion,
he would offer observations on the music itself, its other interpreters, or his own genius.
[9] George Sand, pseudonym of Amantine-Lucile-Aurore Dupin (1804–76), French novelist.
She had a ten-year-long liaison with Chopin (1837–47) which included a disastrous winter in
Majorca (1838–39), during which time he composed the 'Raindrop' Prelude in D Flat, Op. 28,
No. 15, and the *Scherzo in C Sharp Minor* (below).

Scotland, and the woman who sang to him when he died, are all in the music; but
that is not the question. The notes sob and shiver, stab you like a knife, caress you
like the fur of a cat; and are beautiful sound, the most beautiful sound that has
been called out of the piano. Pachmann calls it out for you, disinterestedly, easily,
with ecstasy, inevitably; you do not realise that he has had difficulties to conquer,
that music is a thing for acrobats and athletes. He smiles to you, that you may
realise how beautiful the notes are, when they trickle out of his fingers like singing
water; he adores them and his own playing, as you do, and as if he had nothing to
do with them but to pour them out of his hands. Pachmann is less showy with his
fingers than any other pianist; his hands are stealthy acrobats, going quietly about
their difficult business. They talk with the piano and the piano answers them. All
that violence cannot do with the notes of the instrument, he does. His art begins
where violence leaves off; that is why he can give you fortissimo without hurting
the nerves of a single string; that is why he can play a run as if every note had its
meaning. To the others a run is a flourish, a tassel hung on for display, a thing
extra; when Pachmann plays a run you realise that it may have its own legitimate
sparkle of gay life. With him every note lives, has its own body and its own soul,
and that is why it is worth hearing him play even trivial music like Mendelssohn's
'Spring Song' or meaningless music like Taubert's Waltz:[10] he creates a beauty
out of sound itself and a beauty which is at the root of music. There are moments
when a single chord seems to say in itself everything that music has to say. That
is the moment in which everything but sound is annihilated, the moment of
ecstasy; and it is of such moments that Pachmann is the poet.

   And so his playing of Bach, as in the *Italian Concerto in F*, reveals Bach as if
the dust had suddenly been brushed off his music.[11] All that in the playing of
others had seemed hard or dry becomes suddenly luminous, alive, and, above all,
a miracle of sound. Through a delicacy of shading, like the art of Bach himself
for purity, poignancy, and clarity, he envelops us with the thrilling atmosphere
of the most absolutely musical music in the world. The playing of this concerto
is the greatest thing I have ever heard Pachmann do, but when he went on to play
Mozart I heard another only less beautiful world of sound rise softly about me.
There was the 'glittering peace'[12] undimmed, and there was the nervous spring,
the diamond hardness, as well as the glowing light and ardent sweetness. Yet

---

[10] Felix Mendelssohn (1809–47), 'Frühlingslied' ('Spring Song'), one of the 'Songs Without
Words' for solo piano (Op. 62, No. 6, 1844). Wilhelm Taubert (1811–1891), German pianist
and composer. Symons may be referring to his 'Impromptu in the Form of a Waltz' in D minor
(Op. 117, 1876), a popular encore piece during the later nineteenth century.

[11] Johann Sebastian Bach (1685–1750), whose music, despite the best efforts of Mendelssohn,
had yet to achieve widespread popularity in Victorian and Edwardian Britain. The *Italian
Concerto in F* for solo harpsichord, BWV 971 (1735) boasts an especially beguiling central
andante in D minor perfectly suited to Pachmann's subtlety.

[12] A phrase from one of Goethe's letters ('Precisely in the darkness rises up for me clear,
glittering Peace') incorporated within Bettina von Arnim's *Die Günderode* (1840), which
Symons probably knew in the translation by Margaret Fuller (1842).

another manner of playing, not less appropriate to its subject, brought before me the bubbling flow, the romantic moonlight, of Weber;[13] this music that is a little showy, a little luscious, but with a gracious feminine beauty of its own. Chopin followed, and when Pachmann plays Chopin it is as if the soul of Chopin had returned to its divine body, the notes of this sinewy and feverish music, in which beauty becomes a torture and energy pierces to the centre and becomes grace, and languor swoons and is reborn a winged energy. The great third Scherzo was played with grandeur, and it is in the Scherzos, perhaps, that Chopin has built his most enduring work. The *Barcarolle*, which I have heard played as if it were Niagara and not Venice, was given with perfect quietude, and the second Mazurka of Op. 50 had that boldness of attack, with an almost stealthy intimacy in its secret rhythms, which in Pachmann's playing, and in his playing alone, gives you the dance and the reverie together. But I am not sure that the Etudes are not, in a very personal sense, what is most essential in Chopin, and I am not sure that Pachmann is not at his best in the playing of the Etudes.[14]

Other pianists think, perhaps, but Pachmann plays. As he plays he is like one hypnotised by the music; he sees it beckoning, smiles to it, lifts his finger on a pause that you may listen to the note which is coming. This apparent hypnotism is really a fixed and continuous act of creation; there is not a note which he does not create for himself, to which he does not give his own vitality, the sensitive and yet controlling vitality of the medium. In playing the Bach he had the music before him that he might be wholly free from even the slight strain which comes from the almost unconscious act of remembering. It was for a precisely similar reason that Coleridge, in whose verse inspiration and art are more perfectly balanced than in any other English verse, often wrote down his poems first in prose that he might be unhampered by the conscious act of thought while listening for the music.[15]

'There is no exquisite beauty,' said Bacon in a subtle definition, 'which has not some strangeness in its proportions.'[16] The playing of Pachmann escapes the insipidity of that beauty which is without strangeness; it has in it something fantastically inhuman, like fiery ice, and it is for this reason that it remains a thing

---

[13] Carl Maria von Weber (1786–1826), German composer, conductor, critic, and pianist. He composed two concertos for piano, and many brilliant short pieces. His *Konzertstück in F Minor*, Op. 79 J.282 (1821) for piano and orchestra proved especially influential, though his large hands made many of his compositions all but impossible for many pianists to perform.

[14] Symons is referring here to Chopin's *Barcarolle in F Sharp*, Op. 60, a stylized re-imagining of a Venetian gondolier's song which also mimics the movement of the gondola itself. The other works noted are Chopin's *Scherzo No. 3 in C Sharp Minor*, Op. 39 (1839) and the Mazurka in A Flat, Op. 50 No. 2 (1841–2).

[15] Samuel Taylor Coleridge (1772–1834), English Romantic poet.

[16] The English essayist and philosopher Francis Bacon (1561–1626) actually wrote that 'There is no excellent beauty which hath not some strangeness in the proportion' ('Of Beauty', *Essays* (1625)). The phrase was often quoted by Symons's mentor, Walter Pater.

uncapturable, a thing whose secret he himself could never reveal. It is like the secret of the rhythms of Verlaine, and no prosodist will ever tell us why a line like:

Dans un palais, soie et or, dans Ecbatane,[17]

can communicate a new shiver to the most languid or the most experienced nerves. Like the art of Verlaine, the art of Pachmann is one wholly of suggestion; his fingers state nothing, they evoke. I said like the art of Verlaine, because there is a singular likeness between the two methods. But is not all art a suggestion, an evocation, never a statement? Many of the great forces of the present day have set themselves to the task of building up a large, positive art in which everything shall be said with emphasis: the art of Zola, the art of Mr Kipling, in literature; the art of Mr Sargent in painting; the art of Richard Strauss in music.[18] In all these remarkable men there is some small, essential thing lacking; and it is in men like Verlaine, like Whistler, like Pachmann, that we find the small, essential thing, and nothing else.

II

The sounds torture me: I see them in my brain;
They spin a flickering web of living threads,
Like butterflies upon the garden beds,
Nets of bright sound. I follow them: in vain.
I must not brush the least dust from their wings:
They die of a touch; but I must capture them,
Or they will turn to a caressing flame,
And lick my soul up with their flutterings.

The sounds torture me: I count them with my eyes,
I feel them like a thirst between my lips;
Is it my body or my soul that cries
With little coloured mouths of sound, and drips
In these bright drops that turn to butterflies
Dying delicately at my finger tips?[19]

---

[17] 'In a silken, golden palace in Ecbatane', the opening line of 'Crimen amoris' from Paul Verlaine's *Jadis et Naguère* (1884).

[18] Symons largely ignored the poetry of Rudyard Kipling, though he was an early critic of his fiction ('*The Light That Failed* — and Why', *Anti-Jacobin* 11, 11 April 1891). He had little enthusiasm for the American artist, John Singer Sargent (1856–1925), and compared Richard Strauss (1864–1949) unfavourably with Wagner in *Studies in Seven Arts* (1906).

[19] Re-titled 'The Chopin Player', the poem is dedicated to Pachmann. Symons collected it in *The Fool of the World and Other Poems* (1906), though he dates it 26 October 1907 in his *Collected Works*.

III

Pachmann has the head of a monk who has had commerce with the Devil, and it is whispered that he has sold his soul to the diabolical instrument, which, since buying it, can speak in a human voice. The sounds torture him, as a wizard is tortured by the shapes he has evoked. He makes them dance for his pleasure, and you hear their breath come and go, in the swell and subsiding of those marvellous crescendoes and diminuendoes which set the strings pulsating like a sea. He listens for the sound, listens for the last echo of it after it is gone, and is caught away from us visibly into that unholy company.

Pachmann is the greatest player of the piano now living. He cannot interpret every kind of music, though his actual power is more varied than he has led the public to suppose. I have heard him play in private a show-piece of Liszt, a thunderous thing of immense difficulty, requiring a technique quite different from the technique which alone he cares to reveal to us; he had not played it for twenty years, and he played it with exactly the right crackling splendour that it demanded. On the rare occasions when he plays Bach, something that no one of our time has ever perceived or rendered in that composer seems to be evoked, and Bach lives again, with something of that forgotten life which only the harpsichord can help us to remember under the fingers of other players. Mozart and Weber are two of the composers whom he plays with the most natural instinct, for in both he finds and unweaves that dainty web of bright melody which Mozart made out of sunlight and Weber out of moonlight. There is nothing between him and them, as there is in Beethoven, for instance, who hides himself in the depths of a cloud, in the depths of wisdom, in the depths of the heart. And to Pachmann all this is as strange as mortal firesides to a fairy. He wanders round it, wondering at the great walls and bars that have been set about the faint, escaping spirit of flame. There is nothing human in him, and as music turns towards humanity it slips from between his hands. What he seeks and finds in music is the inarticulate, ultimate thing in sound: the music, in fact.

It has been complained that Pachmann's readings are not intellectual, that he does not interpret. It is true that he does not interpret between the brain and music, but he is able to disimprison sound, as no one has ever done with mortal hands, and the piano, when he touches it, becomes a joyous, disembodied thing, a voice and nothing more, but a voice which is music itself. To reduce music to terms of human intelligence or even of human emotion is to lower it from its own region, where it is Ariel.[20] There is something in music, which we can apprehend only as sound, that comes to us out of heaven or hell, mocking the human agency that gives it speech, and taking flight beyond it. When Pachmann plays a Prelude of Chopin, all that Chopin was conscious of saying in it will, no

---

[20] The airy spirit who serves Prospero in Shakespeare's *The Tempest* (1610–11).

doubt, be there; it is all there, if Godowsky[21] plays it; every note, every shade of expression, every heightening and quickening, everything that the notes actually say. But under Pachmann's miraculous hands a miracle takes place; mystery comes about it like an atmosphere, an icy thrill traverses it, the terror and ecstasy of a beauty that is not in the world envelop it; we hear sounds that are awful and exquisite, crying outside time and space. Is it through Pachmann's nerves, or through ours, that this communion takes place? Is it technique, temperament, touch, that reveals to us what we have never dreamed was hidden in sounds? Could Pachmann himself explain to us his own magic?

He would tell us that he had practised the piano with more patience than others, that he had taken more trouble to acquire a certain touch which is really the only way to the secret of his instrument. He could tell you little more; but, if you saw his hands settle on the keys, and fly and poise there, as if they had nothing to do with the perturbed, listening face that smiles away from them, you would know how little he had told you. Now let us ask Godowsky, whom Pachmann himself sets above all other pianists, what he has to tell us about the way in which he plays.

When Godowsky plays he sits bent and motionless, as if picking out a pattern with his fingers. He seems to keep surreptitious watch upon them, as they run swiftly on their appointed errands. There is no errand they are not nimble enough to carry without a stumble to the journey's end. They obey him as if in fear; they dare not turn aside from the straight path; for their whole aim is to get to the end of the journey, having done their task faultlessly. Sometimes, but without relaxing his learned gravity, he plays a difficult game, as in the Paganini variations of Brahms, which were done with a skill as sure and as soulless as Paganini's may have been.[22] Sometimes he forgets that the notes are living things, and tosses them about a little cruelly, as if they were a juggler's balls. They drop like stones; you are sorry for them, because they are alive. How Chopin suffers, when he plays the Preludes! He plays them without a throb; the scholar has driven out the magic; Chopin becomes a mathematician. In Brahms, in the G Minor Rhapsody, you hear much more of what Brahms meant to do; for Brahms has set strange shapes dancing, like the skeletons 'in the ghosts' moonshine' in a ballad of Beddoes;[23] and these bodiless things take shape in the music, as Godowsky plays it unflinchingly, giving it to you exactly as it is, without comment. Here his fidelity to every outline of form becomes an interpretation. But Chopin is so much more than form that to follow every outline of it may be to leave Chopin out of the outline.

---

[21] Leopold Godowsky (1870–1938), technically formidable Polish-American pianist and composer, who re-worked Chopin's studies in 53 *Studies on Chopin's Études* (1894–1914).
[22] Johannes Brahms, *Variations on a Theme of Paganini*, Op. 35 (1863). Niccolò Paganini (1782–1840), Italian violinist, guitarist, and composer. His astonishing virtuosity led to rumours that he had sold his soul to the Devil in return for his musical prowess.
[23] Brahms, *Rhapsody in G Minor*, Op. 79, No. 2 (1879). 'The Ghosts' Moonshine' is a poem by Thomas Lovell Beddoes (1803–49). Symons included an essay on him in *Figures of Several Centuries* (1916).

Pachmann, of all the interpreters of Chopin, is the most subtle, the one most likely to do for the most part what Chopin wanted. The test, I think, is in the Third Scherzo. That great composition, one of the greatest among Chopin's works, for it contains all his qualities in an intense measure, might have been thought less likely to be done perfectly by Pachmann than such Coleridge in music, such murmurings out of paradise, as the Etude in F Minor (Op. 25, No. 2) or one of those Mazurkas in which Chopin is more poignantly fantastic in substance, more wild and whimsical in rhythm, than elsewhere in his music; and indeed, as Pachmann played them, they were strange and lovely gambols of unchristened elves. But in the Scherzo he mastered this great, violent, heroic thing as he had mastered the little freakish things and the trickling and whispering things. He gave meaning to every part of its decoration, yet lost none of the splendour and wave-like motion of the whole tossing and eager sea of sound.

Pachmann's art, like Chopin's, which it perpetuates, is of that peculiarly modern kind which aims at giving the essence of things in their fine shades: 'la nuance encor!'[24] Is there, it may be asked, any essential thing left out in the process; do we have attenuation in what is certainly a way of sharpening one's steel to a very fine point? The sharpened steel gains in what is most vital in its purpose by this very paring away of its substance; and why should not a form of art strike deeper for the same reason? Our only answer to Whistler and Verlaine is the existence of Rodin and Wagner.[25] There we have weight as well as sharpness; these giants fly. It was curious to hear, in the vast luminous music of the *Rheingold*, flowing like water about the earth, bare to its roots, not only an amplitude but a delicacy of fine shades not less realised than in Chopin. Wagner, it is true, welds the lyric into drama, without losing its lyrical quality. Yet there is no perfect lyric which is made less by the greatness of even a perfect drama.[26]

Chopin was once thought to be a drawing-room composer; Pachmann was once thought to be no 'serious artist.' Both have triumphed, not because the taste of any public has improved, but because a few people who knew have whispered the truth to one another, and at last it has leaked out like a secret.

---

[24] A line from Verlaine's 'Art poétique' which Symons quoted regularly.

[25] Auguste Rodin (1840–1917), French sculptor about whom Symons wrote a number of critical essays. Richard Wagner (1813–83), German composer, conductor, essayist, and theorist of music and drama whose work was much discussed in late-Victorian Britain. In Wilde's *The Picture of Dorian Gray*, Lord Henry says, 'I like Wagner's music better than anybody's. It is so loud that one can talk the whole time without other people hearing what one says' (p. 41). Although he was never a wholly committed 'Wagnerite', Symons endorsed his theory of *gesamtkunstwerk*, the 'total work of art' and wrote about him at length in 'The Ideas of Richard Wagner' (*Studies in Seven Arts*) and 'Notes on Wagner at Bayreuth' (*Plays Acting and Music: A Book of Theory*, Second Edition (1909)). Of Wagner's thirteen operas, Symons was especially fond of *Tannhäuser* (1845), *Tristan und Isolde* (1865), and *Parsifal* (1882), attending performances at Bayreuth and Covent Garden, and enjoying radio broadcasts of his music in the years immediately prior to the Second World War.

[26] The opening work of Wagner's *Ring* Cycle, first performed in 1869, which retells Germanic myths in a quartet of music dramas.

Spiritual Adventures

~

A Prelude to Life

First published in *Spiritual Adventures*, 'A Prelude to Life' details the formative years of a rootless, largely self-educated aesthete and would-be writer before his literary career begins in earnest. Symons claimed it was 'simply a personal confession', though its relationship between lived and imaginative experience is complex from the outset.[1] Karl Beckson comments that it provides the only knowledge we have of Symons's early childhood, adding:

> Though ostensibly a fictionalized view of his early youth (influenced no doubt by Pater's 'imaginary portrait' titled 'A Child in the House' [*sic*] — in part meditative essay, in part retrospective autobiography, and in part evocative fiction) — 'A Prelude to Life' remains an invaluable source of information concerning his earliest years. Symons believed that it had sufficient factual truth to warrant inclusion in a projected volume of his memoirs that he prepared, without success, for publication in the 1930s.[2]

Autobiographical writing excavates and exhumes. It also builds (and falls off) bridges between the past it recollects and refashions and the present of its composition, making the two difficult to separate or distinguish. In a teleological and self-justificatory reading of his early life, Symons cultivated an air of detachment and not-belonging, portraying himself as a sensitive, imaginative child whose family barely understood him and whose intellectual, creative, and sexual ambitions soon separated him from conventional society. Stanford remarks that Symons possessed 'little self knowledge', meaning perhaps that although he found the scrutiny of his cultural engagement endlessly fascinating, he gave little thought to *why* he held the opinions he did, and did not seek to examine what might have prompted them.[3] For a post-Freudian audience, Symons's nightmares obviously indicate the irreconcilability of his Methodist

---

[1] Symons, 'The Genesis of Spiritual Adventures'.
[2] Beckson, *Arthur Symons: A Life*, p. 6. Beckson included the piece in his own edition of Symons's memoirs in 1977.
[3] Stanford, *Critics of the 'Nineties*, p. 115.

upbringing with his bohemian longings, but he seems not to have made any such connection, even before his breakdown.[4]

On one level, 'A Prelude to Life' operates in the familiar terrain of the *künstlerroman*; it might easily have borrowed a sub-title from Wordsworth and emphasized 'the growth of a poet's mind'. On another, however, Symons is more ambitious. His preference for impressionism over the minute detail of high-Victorian realist fiction left him uninterested in lengthy description of people or places. What he sought instead was to evoke how his encounters with a thunderstorm, or Chopin's piano music, or the London crowds, made him feel. He would discourse at length on the effect of such stimuli, but made no attempt to convert an audience to his opinion. What mattered was the depiction of perceptual nuance, not the sharing of that perception by others. 'Sensation' was therefore a key word for Symons, and one which occurs repeatedly throughout his writing. He used it not in the sense of the 'sensation fiction' popular during his youth but, following on from Walter Pater's *Marius the Epicurean* (1885), subtitled 'His Sensations and Ideas', with reference instead to his own emotions and perceptions. He remained preoccupied by these throughout his life, leaving many vivid accounts of his reactions to art, cities, women, the sea, drama, dance, literature, and confinement. However, these sensations were largely divorced from any psychological basis, being attributed instead to the influences of art and culture. Aesthetic connoisseurship became prioritized over self-insight, a process which in time led Symons to see things not as they might appear to be in themselves but in terms of artistic productions of proven value. He could, for instance, liken a sunset to a Wagnerian orchestra, a comparison whose success requires an element of synaesthesia, a visit to Bayreuth, and the reader's complicity in assuming the superiority of art to nature and of the German composer's music to (say) Elgar or Saint-Saëns.[5]

'A Prelude to Life' is as self-conscious a construction as anything Symons ever wrote, despite (or even because of) the seemingly casual progress of its events. Its reminiscences (or fictionalized quasi-reminiscences) flow in loosely chronological order, though there are no firm temporal markers and no explanations for the abrupt changes of scene, as for instance, the sudden references to Coventry and Chester, actually a consequence of Symons's father taking up new parishes. There is also little in the way of dialogue, for here as elsewhere in the collection, the world of thought and feeling is prized above social interaction. 'A Prelude' is a series of impressions which pass before the reader not in dumb show, as the sins of the world pass before Dorian Gray, but in the way in which, in the story's

---

[4] Coincidentally, Freud's *Three Essays on the Theory of Sexuality* first appeared in 1905, though they were not immediately translated into English.
[5] Symons, 'Valencia', *Saturday Review*, 14 January 1899, pp. 41–42. Reprinted in *Cities and Sea-Coasts and Islands* (London: W. Collins, 1918), pp. 106–13.

beautifully-worked concluding image, the bubbles in an Irish stream run past a snapping dog. 'Of the varied life of society, and of man's other activities and studies — politics, history, philosophy and science — he appears to possess no interest and no knowledge,' writes Stanford. 'He has nothing but his sensibility; lonely, discriminating, exquisite. All his writing is one man's record — that of one man hardly aware of the social ties which bind him to the body of mankind within a common culture.'[6] Would Symons have seen this judgement as negative? Having worked so hard to fashion such an image in 'A Prelude to Life', probably not. It is unlikely however that he would have endorsed Barbara Charlesworth's view that in this 'quasi-autobiography', Symons portrays himself as 'thoroughly spoiled, completely self-involved, resentful of his parents' poverty and of the fact that they were "surrounded by commonplace, middle-class people"'. Such egoism, exaggerated or otherwise, is 'nearly monstrous', she concludes.[7]

***

I

I am afraid I must begin a good way back if I am to explain myself to myself at all satisfactorily. I can see how the queer child I was laid the foundation of the man I became, and yet I remember singularly little of my childhood. My parents were never very long in one place, and I have never known what it was to have a home, as most children know it; a home that has been lived in so long that it has got into the ways, the bodily creases, of its inhabitants, like an old, comfortable garment, warmed through and through by the same flesh. I left the town where I was born when I was one year old, and I have never seen it since. I do not even remember in what part of England my eyes first became conscious of the things about them. I remember the hammering of iron on wood, when a great ship was launched in a harbour; the terrifying sound of cannons, as they burst into smoke on a great plain near an ancient castle, while the soldiers rode in long lines across the grass; the clop-clop of a cripple with a wooden leg; with my intense terror at the toppling wagons of hay, as I passed them in the road. I remember absolutely nothing else out of my very early childhood; I have not even been told many things about it, except that I once wakened my mother, as I lay in a little cot at her side, to listen to the nightingales, and that Victor Hugo once stopped the nurse to smile at me, as she walked with me in her arms at Fermain Bay, in Guernsey.[8] If I have been a vagabond, and have never been able to root myself in

---

[6] Stanford, *Critics of the 'Nineties*, p. 115.

[7] Barbara Charlesworth, *Dark Passages: The Decadent Consciousness in Victorian Literature* (Madison and Milwaukee: University of Wisconsin Press, 1965), pp. 102–03.

[8] Victor Hugo (1802–85), French novelist and poet, author of *Les Misérables* (1862). Hugo lived in Guernsey from 1855 until 1870, exiling himself from France during the rule of

any one place in the world, it is because I have no early memories of any one sky or soil. It has freed me from many prejudices in giving me its own unresting kind of freedom; but it has cut me off from whatever is stable, of long growth in the world.

I could not read until I was nine years old, and I could not read because I resolutely refused to learn. I declared that it was impossible; that I, at all events, never could do it; and I made the most of a slight weakness in my eyes, saying that it hurt them, and drawing tears out of my eyes at the sight of a book. I liked being read to, and I used to sit on the bed while my sister, who often had to lie down to rest, read out stories to me. I had a theory that a boy must never show any emotion, and the pathetic parts of *Uncle Tom's Cabin* tried me greatly.[9] On one occasion I felt my sobs choking me, and the passion of sorrow, mingled with the certainty that my emotion would betray itself, sent me into a paroxysm of rage, in which I tore the book from my sister's hands, and attacked her with my fists.[10]

I never learned to read properly until I went to school at the age of nine. I had been for a little while to a dame's school, and learned nothing. I could only read easy words, out of large print books, and I was totally ignorant of everything in the world, when I suddenly found I had to go to school. I was taken to see the schoolmaster, whom I hated, because I had been told he had only one lung, and I heard them explaining to him how backward I was, and how carefully I had to be treated. When the day came I left the house as if I were going to the scaffold, walked very slowly until I had nearly reached the door of the school, and then, when I saw the other boys hurrying in with their satchels, and realised that I was to be in their company, to sit on a form side by side with strangers, who knew all the things I did not know, I turned round and walked away much more quickly than I had come. I took some time in getting home, and I had to admit that I had not been to school. In the afternoon I was sent back, not alone. I have no recollection of more than the obscure horror of that first day at school. I went home in the evening with lessons that I knew had to be learned. Life seemed suddenly to have become serious. Up to then I had always fancied that the grave things people said to me had no particular meaning for me; for other people, no doubt, but not for me. I had played with other boys on the terrace facing the sea; I had seen them going off to school, and I had not had to go with them. Now

---

Napoleon III and only returning after he had been overthrown in the Franco-Prussian War (1870).

[9] *Uncle Tom's Cabin; or, Life Among the Lowly* (1852), an anti-slavery novel by Harriet Beecher Stowe (1811–96).

[10] Symons's sister, Anna (1864–1933), lived with her father until his death, and then joined the Sisters of the Poor of the West London Mission. In a letter of April 1900 to his future wife, Rhoda, Symons recalled that as a child, he 'argued [himself] frantic' with her (*Selected Letters*, p. 6).

everything had changed. There was no longer any sea; I had to live in a street; I had lessons to learn, and other people were to be conscious how well I learned them.

It was that which taught me to read. What had seemed to me not worth doing when I had only myself to please, for I could never realise that my parents, so to speak, counted, became all at once a necessity, because now there were others to reckon with. It was discovered that in the midst of my unfathomable ignorance I had one natural talent; I could spell, without ever being taught. I saw other boys poring over the columns of their spelling-books, trying in vain to get the order of the letters into their heads. I never even read them through; they came to me by ear, instinctively. Finding myself able to do without trying something that the others could not succeed in doing at all, I felt that I could be hardly less intelligent than they, and I felt the little triumph of outdoing others. I began to learn greedily.

The second day I was at school I found the schoolroom door shut when I came into the playground, and I was told that I could not come in. I climbed the gymnasium ladder and looked through the window. Two boys were having a furious fight, and the bigger boys of the school were gravely watching it. I was completely fascinated; it was a new sensation. That day a boy bigger than myself jeered at me. I struck him. There was a rapid fight before all the school, and I knocked him down. I never needed to fight again, nor did I.

When I had once begun to learn, I learned certain things very quickly, and others not at all. I never understood a single proposition of Euclid;[11] I never could learn geography, or draw a map. Arithmetic and algebra I could do moderately, so long as I merely had to follow the rules; the moment common sense was required I was helpless. History I found entertaining, and I could even remember the dates, because they had to do with facts which were like stories. French and Latin I picked up easily, Greek with more difficulty. German I was never able to master; I had an instinctive aversion to the mere sound of it, and I could not remember the words; there were no pegs in my memory for them to hang upon, as there were for the words of all the Romance languages. When a thing did not interest me, nothing could make me learn it. I was not obstinate, I was helpless. I have never been able to make out why geography was so completely beyond my power. I have travelled since then over most of Europe, and I have learned geography with the sight of my eyes. But with all my passion for places I have never been able to find my way in them until I have come to find it instinctively, and I suppose that is why the names in the book or on the map said nothing to me. At an examination when I was easily taking half the prizes, I have read through my papers in geography and in Euclid, and taken them up to the

---

[11] Euclid or Euclid of Alexandria (fl. 300 BC), a Greek mathematician known as the Father of Geometry. His teachings were a key component of a middle-class Victorian boy's education. Symons's difficulties with geography are reprised in 'The Childhood of Lucy Newcome'.

head-master's desk, and handed them back to him, calmly telling him that I could not answer a single question. I was never able to go in for matriculation, or any sort of general public examination, to the great dissatisfaction of my masters, because, while I could have come out easily at the top in most of the subjects, there were always one or two in which I could do nothing.

I was not popular, at any of my schools, either with the boys or with the masters, but I was not disliked. I neither hated out-of-door games nor particularly cared for them. I rather liked cricket, but never played football. I was terribly afraid of making a mistake before other people, and would never attempt anything unless I was sure that I could do it. I did not make friends readily, and I was somewhat indifferent to my friends. I cannot now recollect a single school-friend at all definitely, except one strange little creature, with the look and the intelligence of a grown man; and I remember him chiefly because he seemed to care very much for me, not because I ever cared much for him. He had a mathematical talent which I was told was a kind of genius, but, even then, he was only just kept alive, and he died in boyhood. He seemed to me different from any one else I knew, more like a girl than a boy; someone to be pitied. I remember his saying goodbye to me when they took him away to die.

What the masters really thought of me I never quite knew. I looked upon them as a kind of machine, not essentially different from the blackboard on which they wrote figures in chalk. They sometimes made mistakes about things which I knew, and this gave me a general distrust of them. I took their praise coolly, as a thing which was my due, and I was quite indifferent to their anger. I took no pains to conceal my critical attitude towards them, and one classical master in particular was in terror of me. He was not a sound scholar, and he knew that I knew it. Every day he watched me out of the corner of his eye to see if I was going to expose him, and he bribed me by lending me books which I wanted to read. I loathed him, and left him alone. One day he carried his deceit too far; there was an inquiry, and he disappeared. I have no doubt my criticism was often unjust; I had the insolence of the parvenu in learning. It had come to me too late for me to be able to take it lightly. I corrected the dictation, put Maréchal for 'Marshal' because the word was used in reference to Ney,[12] who I knew was a Frenchman; and was furious when my pedantry lost me a mark

During all this time I was living in the country, in small country towns in the South of England, places to which Blackmore and Kingsley had given a sort of minor fame.[13] I remember long drives by night over Dartmoor, and the sea at

---

[12] Michel Ney (1769–1815), French military commander during the Revolutionary and Napoleonic Wars and one of Napoleon's eighteen Marshals of France.
[13] R[ichard] D[oddridge] Blackmore (1825–1900), novelist, poet and author of the perennially popular *Lorna Doone, A Romance of Exmoor* (1869). Charles Kingsley (1819–75), novelist and Christian Socialist, author of *The Water Babies* (1863).

Westward Ho.[14] Dartmoor had always a singular fascination for me, partly because of its rocky loneliness, the abrupt tors on which one could so easily be surprised in the mist, and partly because there was a convict prison there, in a little town which we often had occasion to visit. The most exquisite sensation of pleasure which the drinking of water has ever given me was one hot day on Dartmoor, when I drank the coldest water there ever was in the world out of the hollow of my hand under a little Roman bridge that we had to cross in driving to Princetown. The convict settlement was at Princetown, and as we came near we could see gangs of convicts at work on the road.[15] Warders with loaded muskets walked up and down, and the men, in their drab clothes marked in red with the broad-arrow, shovelled and dug sullenly, like slaves. I thought every one of them had been a murderer, and when one of them lifted his head from his work to look at us as we passed I seemed to see some diabolical intention in his eyes. I still remember one horrible grimace, done, I suppose, to frighten me. I feared them, but I pitied them; I felt certain that someone was plotting how to escape, and that he would suddenly drop his shovel and begin to run, and that I should see the musket pointed at him and hear the shot, and see the man fall. Once there was an alarm that two convicts had escaped, and I expected at every moment to see them jump out from behind a rock as we drove back at night. The warders had been hurrying through the streets, I had seen the bloodhounds in leash; I sickened at the thought of the poor devils who would be captured and brought back between two muskets. Once I saw an escaped convict being led back to prison; his arms were tied with cords, he had a bloody scar on his forehead, his face was swollen with heat and helpless rage.

But I have another association with Princetown besides the convicts. It was in the house of one of the warders that I first saw *Don Quixote*.[16] We had gone in to get some tea, and, as we waited in the parlour, and my father talked with the man, a grave, powerful person dressed in dark-blue clothes, I came upon a book and opened it, and began to read. I thought it the most wonderful book I had ever seen; I could not put it down, I refused to be separated from it, and the warder said he would lend it to me, and I might take it back with me that night. There was a thunderstorm as we drove back over the moor in the black darkness; I

---

[14] Westward Ho! A village in north Devon which took its name from Charles Kingsley's 1855 novel of the same name, set in nearby Bideford. It is the only place in Britain to have a name ending in an exclamation mark, though Symons does not give it.

[15] Dartmoor Prison, which opened in 1809, was originally built to house French prisoners during the Napoleonic Wars, though it also held American sailors following the 1812 Anglo-American War. It was refashioned as a convict prison in 1850 and remains in use today. Princetown was established in 1785 and named after the then Prince of Wales (afterwards George IV).

[16] *The Ingenious Gentleman Don Quixote of la Mancha*, a 1615 novel by Miguel de Cervantes Saavedra (1547–1616) that is a cornerstone of the European novelistic tradition.

remember the terror of the horse, my father's cautious driving, for the road was narrow and there was a ditch on each side; the rain poured, and the flashes of lightning lit up the solid darkness of the moor for an instant, and then left us in the hollow of a deeper darkness. I clutched the book tight under my overcoat; the majesty of the storm mingled in my head with the heroic figure of which I had just caught a glimpse in the book; I sat motionless, inexpressibly happy, and when we reached home I had to waken myself out of a dream.

The dream lasted until I had finished the book, and after. I cannot remember how I felt, I only know that no book had ever meant so much to me. It was *Don Quixote* which wakened in me the passion for reading. From that time I read incessantly, and I read everything. The first verse I read was Scott, and from Scott I turned to Byron[17], at twelve or thirteen, as to a kind of forbidden fruit, which must be delicious because it is forbidden. I had been told that Byron was a very, very great poet, and a very, very wicked man, an atheist, a writer whom it was dangerous to read. At school I managed to get hold of a Byron, which I read surreptitiously at the same moment that I was reading 'The Headless Horseman.'[18] I thought 'The Headless Horseman' very fine and gory, but I was disappointed in the Byron, because I could not find *Don Juan* in it. I knew, through reading a religious paper which condemned wickedness in great detail, that *Don Juan* was in some way appallingly wicked. I wanted to see for myself, but I never, at that time, succeeded in finding an edition immodest enough to contain it.

II

While all this, and much more that I have forgotten, was building up about me the house of life that I was to live in, I was but imperfectly conscious of more than a very few things in the external world, and but half awake to more than a very few things in the world within me. I lived in the country, or at all events with lanes and fields always about me; I took long walks, and liked walking; but I never was able to distinguish oats from barley, or an oak from a maple; I never cared

---

[17] Sir Walter Scott (1771–1832), Scottish narrative poet and novelist, author of *Kenilworth* (1821) and other works, a central figure in the development of historical fiction, keenly read and imitated throughout the Victorian period. George Gordon, sixth baron Byron (1788–1824), Scottish Romantic poet, widely popular for his exotic tales in verse. His scandalous private life and liberal political convictions made him a problematic figure for many Victorian readers though inspirational for bohemians such as Symons. His epic, unfinished satire, *Don Juan* (1819–24), and many of his political poems were often expunged from collections of his more 'acceptable' love poetry.

[18] The headless horseman menaces Ichabod Crane in 'The Legend of Sleepy Hollow', a story in *The Sketch Book* (1820) by the American writer Washington Irving (1783–1859). It was much imitated by later writers of ghostly tales and 'penny dreadfuls'.

for flowers, except slightly for their colour, when I saw many of them growing together; I could not distinguish a blackbird from a thrush; I was never conscious in my blood of the difference between spring and autumn.[19] I always loved the winter wind and the sunlight, and to plunge through crisp snow, and to watch the rain through leaves. But I would walk for hours without looking about me, or caring much for what I saw; I was never tired, and the mere physical delight of walking shut my eyes and my ears. I was always thinking, but never to much purpose; I hated to think, because thinking troubled me, and whenever I thought long my thoughts were sure to come round to one of two things: the uncertainty of life, and the uncertainty of what might be life after death. I was terribly afraid of death; I did not know exactly what held me to life, but I wanted it to last forever. I had always been delicate, but never with any definite sickness; I was uneasy about myself because I saw that others were uneasy about me, and my voracious appetite for life was partly a kind of haste to eat and drink my fill at a feast from which I might at any time be called away. And then I was still more uneasy about hell.

My parents were deeply religious; we all went to church, a Nonconformist church,[20] twice on Sunday; I was not allowed to read any but pious books or play anything but hymns or oratorios on Sunday; I was taught that this life, which seemed so real and so permanent to me, was but an episode in existence, a little finite part of eternity. We had grace before and after meals; we had family prayers night and morning; we seemed to live in continual communication with the other world. And yet, for the most part, the other world meant nothing to me. I believed, but could not interest myself in the matter. I read the Bible with keen admiration, especially Ecclesiastes; the Old Testament seemed to me wholly delightful, but I cared less for the New Testament; there was so much doctrine in it, it was so explicit about duties, about the conduct of life. I was taught to pray to God the Father, in the name of God the Son, for the inspiration of God the Holy Ghost. I said my prayers regularly; I was absolutely sincere in saying them; I begged hard for whatever I wanted, and thought that if I begged hard enough my prayer would be answered. But I found it very difficult to pray. It seemed to

---

[19] Such indifference to nature underpinned many of Symons's writings during his heyday. In the 1896 revised preface to his second collection, *Silhouettes*, for example, he insisted that artificiality was the basis of art, and that 'There is no necessary difference in artistic value between a good poem about a flower in the hedge and a good poem about the scent in a sachet.'

[20] Nonconformists are Protestants who do not belong to the official British Protestant Church, the Church of England or Anglican Church, and who tend to privilege scriptural over ecclesiastical authority. The term was originally applied to those Anglicans who, arguing over the legitimacy of certain church ceremonies, refused to accede to the 1662 Act of Conformity, but by the nineteenth century it had become synonymous with 'dissenter'. The terms were typically applied to Unitarians, Presbyterians, Baptists, Quakers, and, with especial significance for Symons, Methodists.

me that prayer was useless unless it were uttered with an intimate apprehension of God, unless an effort of will brought one mentally into His presence. I tried hard to hypnotise myself into that condition, but I rarely succeeded. Other thoughts drifted through my mind while my lips were articulating words of supplication. I said, over and over again, 'O Lord, for Jesus' sake!' and even while I was saying the words with fervour I seemed to lose hold of their meaning. I was taught that being clever mattered little, but that being good mattered infinitely. I wanted to want to be good, but all I really wanted was to be clever. I felt that this in itself was a wickedness. I could not help it, but I believed that I should be punished for not being able to help it. I was told that if I was very good I should go to heaven, but that if I was wicked I should go to hell. I saw but one alternative.

And so the thought of hell was often in my mind, for the most part very much in the background, but always ready to come forward at any external suggestion. Once or twice it came to me with such vividness that I rolled over on the ground in a paroxysm of agony, trying to pray God that I might not be sent to hell, but unable to fix my mind on the words of the prayer. I felt the eternal flames taking hold on me, and some foretaste of their endlessness seemed to enter into my being. I never once had the least sensation of heaven, or any desire for it. Never at any time did it seem to me probable that I should get there.

I remember once in church, as I was looking earnestly at the face of a child for whom I had a boyish admiration, that the thought suddenly shot across my mind: 'Emma will die, Emma will go to heaven, and I shall never see her again.' I shivered all through my body, I seemed to see her vanishing away from me, and I turned my eyes aside, so that I could not see her. But the thought gnawed at me so fiercely that a prayer broke out of me, silently, like sweat: 'O God, let me be with her! O God, let me be with her!' When I came out into the open air, and felt the cold breeze on my forehead, the thought had begun to relax its hold on me, and I never felt it again, with that certainty; but it was as if a veil had been withdrawn for an instant, the veil which renders life possible, and, for that instant, I had seen.

When my mother talked to me about pious things, I felt that they were extraordinarily real to her, and this impressed me the more because her thirst for this life was even greater than mine, and her hold on external things far stronger.[21] My father was a dryly intellectual, despondent person, whose whole view of life was coloured by the dyspepsia which he was never without, and the sick headaches which laid him up for a whole day, every week or every fortnight. He

---

[21] Symons's engagement with what he called 'the visible world', a term he took from Théophile Gautier (1811–72), intensified during the years of his friendship with Yeats and the writing of *The Symbolist Movement in Literature*. Gautier's remark, 'Je suis un homme pour qui le monde visible existe,' was recorded in the Goncourt Brothers' Journal (1 May 1857), first published in 1888.

was quite unimaginative, cautious in his affairs, a great reader of the newspaper; but he never seemed to me to have had the same sense of life as my mother and myself. I respected him, for his ability, his scholarship, and his character; but we had nothing akin, he never interested me. He was severely indulgent to me; I never knew him to be unkind, or even unreasonable. But I took all such things for granted, I felt no gratitude for them, and I was only conscious that my father bored me. I had no dislike for him; an indifference, rather; perhaps a little more than indifference, for if he came into the room, and I did not happen to be absorbed in reading, I usually went out of it. We might sit together for an hour, and it never occurred to either of us to speak. So when he spoke to me of my soul, which he did seriously, sadly, with an undertone of reproach, my whole nature rose up against him. If to be good was to be like him, I did not wish to be good.[22]

With my mother, it was quite different. She had the joy of life, she was sensitive to every aspect of the world; she felt the sunshine before it came, and knew from what quarter the wind was blowing when she awoke in the morning. I think she was never indifferent to any moment that ever passed her by; I think no moment ever passed her by without being seized in all the eagerness of acceptance. I never knew her when she was not delicate, so delicate that she could rarely go out of doors in the winter; but I never heard her complain, she was always happy, with a natural gaiety which had only been strengthened into a kind of vivid peace by the continual presence of a religion at once calm and passionate. She was as sure of God as of my father; heaven was always as real to her as the room in which she laughed and prayed. Sometimes, as she read her Bible, her face quickened to an ecstasy. She was ready at any moment to lay down the book and attend to the meanest household duties; she never saw any gulf between meditation and action; her meditations were all action. When a child, she had lain awake, longing to see a ghost; she had never seen one, but if a ghost had entered the room she would have talked with it as tranquilly as with a living friend. To her the past, the present, and the future were but moments of one existence; life was everything to her, and life was indestructible. Her own personal life was so vivid that it never ceased, even in sleep. She dreamed every night, precise, elaborate dreams, which she would tell us in the morning with the same clearness as if she were telling us of something that had really happened. She was never drowsy, she went to sleep the moment her head was laid on the pillow, she awoke instantly wide awake. There were things that she knew and things that she did not know, but she was never vague. A duty was as clear to her as a fact; infinitely tolerant to others, she expected from herself perfection, the utmost perfection of which her nature was capable. It was because my mother talked to me of the other world that I felt, in

---

[22] Beckson points out that 'Symons's relationship with his father seems quite different from this one-sided portrait, for Revd Symons took an interest in his son's literary career and, indeed, helped him read the proofs of his first volume of verse' (*Arthur Symons: A Life*, p. 10).

spite of myself, that there was another world. Her certainty helped to make me the more afraid.

She did not often talk to me of the other world. She preferred that I should see it reflected in her celestial temper and in a capability as of the angels. She sorrowed at my indifference, but she was content to wait; she was sure of me, she never doubted that, sooner or later, I should be saved. This, too, troubled me. I did not want to be saved. It is true that I did not want to go to hell, but the thought of what my parents meant by salvation had no attraction for me. It seemed to be the giving up of all that I cared for. There was a sort of humiliation in it. Jesus Christ seemed to me a hard master.

Sometimes there were revival services at the church, and I was never quite at my ease until they were over. I was afraid of some appeal to my emotions, which for the moment I should not be able to resist. I knew that it would mean nothing, but I did not want to give in, even for a moment. I felt that I might have to resist with more than my customary indifference, and I did not like to admit to myself that any active resistance could be necessary. I knelt, as a stormy prayer shook the people about me into tears, rigid, forcing myself to think of something else. I saw the preacher move about the church, speaking to one after another, and I saw one after another get up and walk to the communion rail, in sign of conversion. I wondered that they could do it, whatever they felt; I wondered what they felt; I dreaded lest the preacher should come up to me with some irresistible power, and beckon me up to that rail. If he did come, I knelt motionless, with my face in my hands, not answering his questions, not seeming to take the slightest notice of him; but my heart was trembling, I did not know what was going to happen; I felt nothing but that horrible uneasiness, but I feared it might leave me helpless, at the man's mercy, or at God's perhaps.

As we walked home afterwards, I could see the others looking at me, wondering at my spiritual stubbornness, wondering if at last I had felt something. To them, I knew, I was like a man who shut his eyes and declared that he could not see. 'You have only to open your eyes,' they said to the man. But the man said, 'I prefer being blind.' It was inexplicable to them. But they were not less inexplicable to me.

III

From the time when *Don Quixote* first opened my eyes to an imaginative world outside myself, I had read hungrily; but another world was also opened to me when I was about sixteen. I had been taught scales and exercises on the piano; I had tried to learn music, with very little success, when one day the head-master of the school asked me to go into his drawing-room and copy out something for him. As I sat there copying, the music-master, a German, came in and sat down at the piano. He played something which I had never heard before, something which seemed to me the most wonderful thing I had ever heard. I tried to go on copying, but I did not know what I was writing down; I was caught into an ecstasy, the sound seemed to envelop me like a storm, and then to trickle through me like raindrops shaken from wet leaves, and then to wrap me again in a tempest which was like a tempest of grief. When he had finished I said, 'Will you play that over again?' As he played it again I began to distinguish it more clearly; I heard a slow, heavy trampling of feet, marching in order, then what might have been the firing of cannon over a grave, and the trampling again. When he told me that it was Chopin's 'Funeral March',[23] I understood why it was that the feet had moved so slowly, and why the cannon had been fired; and I saw that the melody which had soothed me was the timid, insinuating consolation which love or hope sometimes brings to the mourner. I asked him if he would teach me music and if he would teach me that piece. He promised to teach me that piece, and I learned it. I learned no more scales and exercises; I learned a few more pieces; but in a little while I could read at sight; and when I was not reading a book I was reading a piece of music at the piano. I never acquired the technique to play a single piece correctly, but I learned to touch the piano as if one were caressing a living being, and it answered me in an intimate and affectionate voice.

Books and music, then, together with my solitary walks, were the only means of escape which I was able to find from the tedium of things as they were. I was passionately in love with life, but the life I lived was not the life I wanted. I did not know quite what I wanted, but I knew that what I wanted was something very different from what I endured. We were very poor, and I hated the constraints of poverty. We were surrounded by commonplace, middle-class people, and I hated commonplace and the middle classes. Sometimes we were too poor even to have a servant, and I was expected to clean my own boots. I could not endure getting my hands or my shirt-cuffs dirty; the thought of having to do it disgusted me every day. Sometimes my mother, without saying anything to me, had cleaned my boots for me. I was scarcely conscious of the sacrifices which she and the others were continually making. I made none, of my own accord, and I felt aggrieved if I had to share the smallest of their privations.

From as early a time as I can remember, I had no very clear consciousness of anything external to myself; I never realised that others had the right to expect from me any return for the kindness which they might show me or refuse to me, at their choice. I existed, others also existed; but between us there was an impassable gulf, and I had rarely any desire to cross it. I was very fond of my

---

[23] The 'Marche funèbre: Lento', composed in 1837, became the third movement of Frédéric Chopin's *Piano Sonata No. 2 in B flat minor*, Op. 35 (1839), often known as the 'Funeral March'. For Chopin's wider importance for Symons, see 'Pachmann and the Piano' and 'Christian Trevalga'. Lhombreaud suggests the German teacher was 'Mr Thur' and that the event occurred in December 1880. *Arthur Symons*, p. 13.

mother, but I felt no affection towards anyone else, nor any desire for the affection of others. To be let alone, and to live my own life forever, that was what I wanted; and I raged because I could never entirely escape from the contact of people who bored me and things which depressed me. If people called, I went out of the room before they were shown in; if I had not time to get away, I shook hands hurriedly, and slipped out as soon as I could. I remember a cousin who used to come to tea every Sunday for two or three years. My aversion to her was so great that I could hardly answer her if she spoke to me, and I used to think of Shelley, and how he too, like me, would 'lie back and languish into hate.'[24] The woman was quite inoffensive, but I am still unable to see her or hear her speak without that sickness of aversion which used to make the painfulness of Sunday more painful.

People in general left me no more than indifferent; they could be quietly avoided. They meant no more to me than the chairs on which they sat; I was untouched by their fortunes; I was unconscious of my human relationship to them. To my mother every person in the world became, for the moment of contact, the only person in the world; if she merely talked with any one for five minutes she was absorbed to the exclusion of every other thought; she saw no one else, she heard nothing else. I watched her, with astonishment, with admiration; I felt that she was in the right and I in the wrong; that she gained a pleasure and conferred a benefit, while I only wearied myself and offended others; but I could not help it. I felt nothing, I saw nothing, outside myself.

I always had a room upstairs, which I called my study, where I could sit alone, reading or thinking. No one was allowed to enter the room; only, in winter, as I always let the fire go out, my mother would now and then steal in gently without speaking, and put more coals on the fire. I used to look up from my books furiously, and ask why I could not be left alone; my mother would smile, say nothing, and go out as quietly as she had come in. I was only happy when I was in my study, but, when I had shut the door behind me, I forgot all about the tedious people who were calling downstairs, the covers of the book I was reading seemed to broaden out into an enclosing rampart, and I was alone with myself.

At my last school there was one master, a young man, who wrote for a provincial newspaper, of which he afterwards became the editor, with whom I made friends. He had read a great deal, and he knew a few literary people; he was equally fond of literature and of music. Some school composition of mine had interested him in me, and he began to lend me books, and to encourage me in trying to express myself in writing. I had already run through Scott and Byron, with a very little Shelley, and had come to Browning,[25] whom he detested. When

---

[24] The poet Percy Bysshe Shelley (1792–1822) much disliked his wife Mary's stepmother, the bookseller and translator Mary Jane Godwin, and used this phrase of her on several occasions.
[25] Robert Browning (1812–89) had survived early unpopularity and romantic controversy to become widely feted in late-Victorian England. The Browning Society was formed in 1881.

I was laid up with scarlatina[26] he sent me over a packet of books to read; one of them was Swinburne's *Poems and Ballads*,[27] which seemed to give voice to all the fever that I felt just then in my blood. I read *Wuthering Heights* at the same time and Rabelais a little time afterwards. I read all the bound volumes of the *Cornhill Magazine* from the beginning right through, stories, essays, and poems, and I remember my delight in *Harry Richmond*, at a time when I had never heard the name of George Meredith.[28] I read essays signed 'R.L.S.', from which I got my first taste of a sort of gipsy element in literature which was to become a passion when, later on, *Lavengro* fell into my hands.[29] The reading of *Lavengro* did many things for me. It absorbed me from the first page, with a curiously personal appeal, as of someone akin to me, and when I came to the place where Lavengro learns Welsh in a fortnight, I laid down the book with a feeling of fierce emulation. I had often thought of learning Italian: I immediately bought an Italian Bible, and

---

The young Symons was extremely enthusiastic about his work and wrote a number of dramatic monologues that bear his influence.

[26] Scarlatina, now called Scarlet Fever, was a dangerous illness before the advent of antibiotics. It causes a severe sore throat, a high temperature, and a widespread rash. It can also lead to hallucinations and paranoia.

[27] *Poems and Ballads, First Series* (1866), the first collection by Algernon Swinburne (1837–1909), caused outrage and alarm with its frank depictions of sensuality and erotic cruelty, and was hardly approved reading for the sons of clergymen.

The opening stanza of its first poem, 'A Ballad of Life' depicts a woman whose beauty 'fervent as a fiery moon, | Made my blood burn and swoon | Like a flame rained upon.' Although Symons's mature work has little in common with Swinburne's in stylistic terms, he strongly agreed with Swinburne's separation of art from morality and his conception of the artist as operating outside the constraints of bourgeois convention. He once remarked that 'there was a period in everyone's life when one thought Swinburne's poetry not only the best, but the only poetry worth reading. It seemed to annihilate all other verse.' Maurice Baring, *The Puppet Show of Memory* (London: Heinemann, 1922), p. 155.

[28] *Wuthering Heights* (1847), the only novel by Emily Brontë (1818–48). Symons included a poem, 'Emily Brontë', in *The Fool of the World* (1906).

François Rabelais (*c.* 1494–*c.* 1553), French satirist, creator of *Gargantua* (1534) and *Pantagruel* (1532 or 1533).

The *Cornhill Magazine* (1860–1975) was a high quality literary journal initially edited by the novelist W. M. Thackeray (1811–63).

George Meredith (1828–1909), Victorian novelist and poet, regarded as 'modern' and controversial for his depiction of marriage and sexuality in works such as the sonnet sequence *Modern Love* (1862), a favourite of Symons's. His novel, *The Adventures of Harry Richmond* was serialized in the *Cornhill* from September 1870 to November 1871.

[29] The essays of Robert Louis Stevenson (1850–94) appeared as *Virginibus Puerisque* ('Of Boys and Girls') in 1881 and *Familiar Studies of Men and Books* in 1882. Symons is perhaps referring to 'Walking Tours' in the first of these collections.

Lavengro: The Scholar, The Gypsy, The Priest (1851) and its sequel, *The Romany Rye* (1857), novels of Romany life by George Borrow (1803–81). The title 'Lavengro' is Romany for 'he who is expert with words'. Symons remained fascinated by gypsies and their lore for the rest of his life, notably through his friendship with the artist Augustus John (1878–1961).

a grammar; I worked all day long, not taking up *Lavengro* again, until, at the end
of the fortnight which I had given myself, I could read Italian. Then I finished
Lavengro.

Lavengro took my thoughts into the open air, and gave me my first conscious
desire to wander. I learned a little Romany, and was always on the lookout for
gipsies. I realised that there were other people in the world besides the
conventional people I knew, who wore prim and shabby clothes, and went to
church twice on Sundays, and worked at business and professions, and sat down
to the meal of tea at five o'clock in the afternoon. And I realised that there was
another escape from these people besides a solitary flight in books; that if a book
could be so like a man, there were men and women, after all, who had the interest
of a book as well as the warm advantage of being alive. Humanity began to exist
for me.

But with this discovery of a possible interest in real people, there came a deeper
loathing of the people by whom I was surrounded. I had for the most part been
able to ignore them; now I wanted to get away, so that I could live my own life,
and choose my own companions. My vague notions of sex became precise,
became a torture.

When I first read Rabelais and the *Poems and Ballads*, I was ignorant of my
own body; I looked upon the relationship of man and woman as something
essentially wicked; my imagination took fire, but I was hardly conscious of any
physical reality connected with it. I was irrepressibly timid in the presence of a
woman; I hardly ever met young people of my own age; and I had a feeling of the
deepest reverence for women, from which I endeavoured to banish the slightest
consciousness of sex. I thought it an inexcusable disrespect; and in my feeling
towards the one or two much older women who at one time or another had a
certain attraction for me, there was nothing, conscious at least, but a purely
romantic admiration. At the same time I had a guilty delight in reading books
which told me about the sensations of physical love, and I trembled with ecstasy
as I read them. Thoughts of them haunted me; I put them out of my head by an
effort, I called them back, they ended by never leaving me.

I think it was a little earlier than this that I began to walk in my sleep, and to
have nightmares; but it was just then that I suffered most from those obscure
terrors of the night. Once, when I was a child, I remember waking up in my
nightshirt on the drawing-room sofa, and being wrapped up in a shawl and
carried upstairs by my father, and put back into bed. I had come down in my
sleep, opened the door, and walked into the room without seeing any one, and
laid myself down on the sofa. I did not often dream, but, whenever I dreamed, it
was of infinite spirals, up which I had to climb, or of ladders, whose rungs
dropped away from me as my feet left them, or of slimy stone stairways into cold
pits of darkness, or of the tightening of a snake's coils around me, or of walking
with bare feet across a floor curdling with snakes. I awoke, stifling a scream, my

hair damp with sweat, out of impossible tasks in which time shrank and swelled in some deadly game with life; something had to be done in a second, and all eternity passed, lingering, while the second poised over me like a drop of water always about to drip: it fell, and I was annihilated into depth under depth of blackness.[30]

Into these dreams of abstract horror there began to come a disturbing element of sex. My books and my thoughts haunted me; I was restless and ignorant, physically innocent, but with a sort of naïve corruption of mind. All the interest which I had never been able to find in the soul, I found in what I only vaguely apprehended of the body. To me it was something remote, evil, mainly inexplicable; but nothing I had ever felt had meant so much to me. I never realised that there was any honesty in sex, that nature was after all natural. I reached stealthily after some stealthy delight of the senses, which I valued the more because it was a forbidden thing. Love I never associated with the senses, it was not even passion that I wanted; it was a conscious, subtle, elaborate sensuality, which I knew not how to procure. And there was an infinite curiosity, which I hardly even dared dream of satisfying; a curiosity which was like a fever. I was scarcely conscious of any external temptations. The ideas in which I had been trained, little as they had seemed consciously to affect me, had given me the equivalent of what I may call virtue, in a form of good taste. I was ashamed of my desires, of my sensations, though I made no serious effort to escape them; but I knew that, even if the opportunity were offered, something, some scruple of physical refinement, some timidity, some unattached sense of fitness, would step in to prevent me from carrying them into practice.

IV

Every now and then my father used to talk to me seriously, saying that I should have to choose some profession, and make my own living. I always replied that there was nothing I could possibly do, that I hated every profession, that I would rather starve than soil my hands with business, and that so long as I could just go on living as I was then living, I wanted nothing more. I did not want to be a rich man, I was never able to realise money as a tangible thing, I wanted to have just enough to live on, only not at home; in London. My father did not press the

---

[30] Throughout his life Symons was plagued by nightmares in which the serpent was a recurring image. He composed his poem 'The Andante of Snakes' on 7 July 1904, including it in *The Fool of the World*. Following his breakdown, the serpent is increasingly associated with women, sex, and Satan. For further evidence of his strange fascination with snakes, see his letter to Rhoda Bowser (17 April 1900) describing an encounter with a Grass Snake and proposing a visit to see the serpents at London Zoo (*Selected Letters*, pp. 158–59).

matter; I could see that he dreaded my leaving home, and he knew that, for the time, going to London was out of the question.

One summer I went down to a remote part of England to stay with some of my relations. I had seen none of them since I was a child, I knew nothing about them, except that some were farmers, some business people; there was an astronomer, an old sea-captain, and a mad uncle who lived in a cottage by himself on a moor near the sea, and grew marvellous flowers in a vast garden. I stayed with a maiden aunt, who was like a very old and very gaunt little bird; she was deaf, wrinkled, and bent, but her hair was still yellow, her voice a high piping treble, and she ran about with the tireless vivacity of a young girl. She had been pretty, and had all the little vanities of a coquette; she wore bright, semi-fashionable clothes, and conspicuous hats. She had much of the natural gaiety of my mother, who was her elder sister; and she was infinitely considerate to me, turning out one of her little rooms that I might have it for a study. She liked me to play to her, and would sit by the side of the old piano listening eagerly. The mad uncle was her brother, and he would come in sometimes from his cottage, bringing great bundles of flowers. He was very kind and gentle, and he would sometimes tell me of the letters he had been writing to the Prince of Wales[31] on the subject of sewage, and of how the Prince of Wales had acknowledged his communications. He had many theories about sewage; I have heard that some of them were plausible and ingenious; and he was convinced that his theories would someday be accepted, and that he would become famous. I believe his brain had been turned by an unlucky passion for a beautiful girl; he was only in an asylum for a short time; and for the most part lived happily in his cottage among his flowers, developing theories of sewage, and taking sun-baths naked in the garden.

The people of whom I saw most were some cousins: the father kept a shop, and they all helped in the business. They were very kind, and did all they could for me by feeding me plentifully and taking me for long drives in the country, which was very hilly and wooded, and sometimes to the sea, which was not too far off to reach by driving. We had not an idea in common, and I always wondered how it was possible that my aunt, who was my mother's eldest sister, could ever have married my uncle. He was a kind man, and, in his way, intelligent; but he talked incessantly, insistently, and with something unctuous in his voice and manner; he came close to me while he spoke, and tapped my shoulder with his fingers or my leg with his stick. I could not bear him to touch me; sometimes he dropped his h's, and, as I heard them drop, I saw the old man looking fixedly into my face with his large, keen, shifting eyes.

One of the daughters had something inquiring in her mind, a touch of rebellious refinement; she had enough instinct for another kind of life to be at

---

[31] Queen Victoria's eldest child, Edward (1841–1910), was a dissolute figure of whom his mother despaired. Following her death, he reigned as Edward VII from 1902 until his death.

least discontented with her own; with her I could talk. But the others fitted into their environment without a crease or a ruffle. They went to the shop early in the morning, slaved there all day, taught in the Sunday-School on Sundays, said the obvious things to one another all day long, were perfectly content to be where they were, do what they did, think what they thought, and say what they said. Their house reflected them like a mirror. Everything was clean and new, there was plenty of everything; and I used to sit in their drawing-room looking round it in a vain attempt to find a single thing which I could have lived with, in a house of my own.

I went home from the visit gladly, glad to be at home again. We were living then in the Midlands, and I used to spend whole days at Kenilworth, at Warwick, at Coventry; I knew them from Scott's novels, but I had never seen a ruined castle, a city with ancient buildings, and I began to feel that there was something else to be seen in the world besides the things I had dreamed of seeing. I took a boat at Leamington, and rowed up the river as far as the chain underneath Warwick Castle. I do not know why I have always remembered that moment, as if it marked a date to me. It was with a full enjoyment of the contrast that I found them busy preparing for a *fête* when I got back to Leamington; stringing up the Chinese lanterns to the branches of the trees, and putting out little tables on the grass. At Coventry I loved going through the narrow streets, looking up at the windows which leaned together under their gabled roofs. I saw Lady Godiva borne through the streets, more clothed than she appears in the pictures, in the midst of a gay and solemn procession, tricked out in old-fashioned frippery.[32] And I spent a long day there, one of the days of the five-day fair, which feasted me with sensations on which I lived for weeks. It was the first time I had ever plunged boldly into what Baudelaire[33] calls 'the bath of multitude'; it intoxicated me, and seemed, for the first time in my life, to carry me outside myself. I pushed my way through the crowds in those old and narrow streets, in an ecstasy of delight at all that movement, noise, colour, and confusion. I seemed suddenly to have become free, in contact with life. I had no desire to touch it too closely, no fear of being soiled at its contact; a vivid spirit of life seemed to come to me, in my solitude, releasing me from thought, from daily realities.

---

[32] An eleventh century Anglo-Saxon noblewoman, who allegedly rode naked through the streets of the town to win her tenants remission from her husband's punitive taxes. 'Peeping Tom', who dared to watch her as she did so, was struck blind. One can imagine Symons's interest in a legend involving female performance, nudity, and the punishment of sin.

[33] Baudelaire was a lifelong influence on Symons, who often quoted his prose-poem 'Les Foules' ('Crowds') from *Le Spleen de Paris* (1862) in his city writings. It was one of twelve pieces included in his translation, *Poems in Prose from Charles Baudelaire*, published in November 1905. 'It is not given to every man to take a bath of multitude: to play upon crowds is an art,' the piece begins. *Poems in Prose from Baudelaire* (London: Elkin Mathews, 1905), p. 28.

Once I went as far as Chester. It was the Cup day, and there was an excursion. I watched the race, feeling a momentary excitement as the horses passed close to me, and the pellets of turf shot from their heels into the air above my head; the crowd was more varied than any crowd I had ever seen, and I discovered a blonde gipsy girl, in charge of a cocoanut-shy, who let me talk a little Romany with her.[34] I thought Chester, with its arcades and its city-walls, the most wonderful old place I had ever seen. As I walked round the wall, a woman leaned out of a window and called to me: I thought of Rahab in the Bible, and went home dreaming romantically about the harlot on the wall.[35]

One day, as I was walking along a country road, I was stopped by a sailor, who asked me how far it was to some distant place. He was carrying a small bundle, and was walking, he told me, until he came to a certain sea-port. He did not beg, but accepted gladly enough what I gave him. He had been on many voyages, and had picked up a good many words of different languages, which he mispronounced in a scarcely intelligible jargon of his own. He had been left behind by his ship in Russia, where he had stayed on account of a woman: she could speak no English, and he but little Russian; but it did not seem to have mattered. It was the first time I had seemed to come so close to the remote parts of the world; and as he went on his way, he turned back to urge me to go on some voyage which he seemed to remember with more pleasure than any other: to the West Indies, I think. I began to pore over maps, and plan to what parts of the world I would go.

Meanwhile, little by little, I was beginning to live my own life at home; I played the piano on Sundays, to whatever tune I liked; I read whatever I liked on Sundays; and, finally, I ceased to go to church. Latterly I had come to put my boredom there to some purpose: I followed the lessons word by word in Bibles and Testaments in many languages, and, while the sermon was going on I kept my Bible quietly open on my knees, and read on, chapter after chapter, while the preacher preached I knew not what: I never heard a word of it, not even the text. I read, not for the Bible's sake, but to learn the language in which I was reading it. My parents knew this, but after all it was the Bible, and they could hardly object to my reading the Bible. Sometimes I scribbled down ideas that came into my head; sometimes I merely sat there, with a stony inattention, showing, I fancy, in my face, all the fierce disgust that I felt. During the sermon I always found it quite easy to abstract my attention; during the hymns I amused myself by criticising

---

[34] This is a rare reference by Symons to a sporting event. The Chester Cup was established in 1824, became the Chester Trades' Cup in 1874 and the Chester Cup ten years later. A race for thoroughbreds over four years of age, it is held in May.

[35] Rahab is the prostitute who, as recorded in the Book of Joshua, assists the Israelites in their attack on Jericho. Symons caused considerable offence with his poetic accounts of encounters with prostitutes in 'Stella Maris' (*Yellow Book* I, April 1894) and *London Nights*.

the bad rhymes and false metaphors; but during prayer-time, though I kept my eyes wide open, and sat as upright as I dared, I could hardly help hearing what was said. What was said, very often, made me ashamed, as if I were unconsciously helping to repeat absurdities to God.

When I told my parents that I could go to church no longer, I had no definite reason to allege, except that the matter did not interest me. I did not doubt the truth of the Christian religion; I neither affirmed nor denied; it was something, to me, beside the question. I could argue about dogma; I defended a liberal interpretation of doctrines; I insisted that there were certain questions which we were bound to leave open. But I was not alienated from Christianity by intellectual difficulties; it had never taken hold of me, and I gave up nothing but a pretence in giving up the sign of outward respect for it. My parents were deeply grieved, but, then as always, they respected my liberty.

The first time I remember going to London, for I had been there when a child, was by an excursion, which brought me back the same night. Of the day, or of what I did then, I can recall nothing; daylight never meant so much to me as the first lighting of the lamps. I found my way back to King's Cross,[36] in some bewilderment, to find that one train had gone, and that the next would leave me an hour or two more in London. I walked among the lights, through hurrying crowds of people, in long, dingy streets, not knowing where I was going, till I found myself outside a great building which seemed to be a kind of music-hall. I went in; it was the Agricultural Hall,[37] and some show was being given there. There were acrobats, gymnasts, equilibrists, performing beasts; there was a vast din, concentrating all the noises of a fair within four walls; people swarmed to and fro over the long floor, paying more heed to one another than to the performance. I scrutinised the show and the people, a little uneasily; it was very new to me, and I was not yet able to feel at home in London. I found my way to the station like one who comes home, half dizzy and half ashamed, after a debauch.

The next time I went to London, I went for a week. I stayed in a lodging-house near the British Museum,[38] a mean, uncomfortable place, where I had to be

---

[36] King's Cross Station, in London's Euston Road, was built in 1851–52 and was the London terminus for the Great Northern Railway. It is named after a monument to George IV which stood nearby between 1830 and 1845.

[37] The Royal Agricultural Hall opened in Islington in 1862, initially as a venue for agricultural shows, though it was soon hosting a wide variety of other entertainments.

[38] The British Museum in Holborn opened in 1759. Between 1852 and 1857, the courtyard was converted into a Reading Room graced with an enormous copper dome designed by Sidney Smirke (1798–1877). This became the centre of scholarly activity in the capital, though some found it oppressive: there are memorable depictions of it in Gissing's novel, *New Grub Street* (1891). Symons used it a great deal in his research for *William Blake* (1907) and his critical anthology, *The Romantic Movement in English Poetry* (1909).

indoors by midnight. During the day I read in the Museum; the atmosphere weighed upon me, and gave me a headache every day; the same atmosphere weighed upon me in the streets around the Museum; I was dull, depressed, anxious to get through with the task for which I had come to London, anxious to get back again to the country. I went back with a little book-learning, of the kind that I wanted to acquire; I began to have books sent down to me from a Library in London; I worked, more and more diligently, at reading and studying books; and I began to think of devoting myself entirely to some sort of literary work. It was not that I had anything to say, or that I felt the need of expressing myself. I wanted to write books for the sake of writing books; it was food for my ambition, and it gave me something to do when I was alone, apart from other people. It helped to raise another barrier between me and other people.

I went up to London again for a longer visit, and I stayed in a lodging-house in one of the streets leading from the Strand to the Embankment, near the stage-door of one of the theatres.[39] A little actress and her mother were staying in the house, and I felt that I was getting an intimate acquaintance with the stage, as I sat up with the little actress, after her mother had gone to bed, and listened timidly to her stories of parts and dresses and the other girls. She was quite young, and still ingenuous enough to look forward to the day when she would have her name on the placards in letters I forget how many inches high. I had been to my first theatre, it was Irving in *King Lear*,[40] and now I was hearing about the stage from one who lived on it. A little actress, afterwards famous for her beauty, and then a child with masses of gold hair about her ears, lived next door, at another lodging-house, which her mother kept. I watched for her to pass the window, or for a chance of meeting her in the street. When I went back again to the country, it

---

[39] The Strand is a thoroughfare linking Westminster with the City. In the 1890s, it was the centre of London's theatre-land, and boasted more theatres than any other street in the capital. 'No sensation is so familiar to me as that emptiness of the Strand just before the people come out of the theatres,' Symons wrote in *London: A Book of Aspects* (*Cities and Sea-Coasts and Islands*, pp. 179–80). His poem, 'In the Strand', dated 9 May 1889 and collected in *Knave of Hearts* (1913), depicts a ruined woman who 'craves the bestial wages' of sin from the street's passers-by.

The Embankment, properly the Albert, Victoria, and Chelsea Embankments, runs alongside the Thames in West London for over three miles. Built between 1868 and 1874, it was considered a marvel of civil engineering, though by the 1890s, it had acquired a reputation for attracting the homeless and suicidal.

[40] Henry Irving, born John Henry Brodribb (1838–1905), widely considered the finest Victorian actor. He was particularly associated with Shakespearean tragedies such as *King Lear* (1604–05) and in 1895, became the first actor to receive a knighthood. Symons enjoyed his performances and was flattered when, in 1888, he was asked to annotate *Twelfth Night* for the 'Henry Irving Shakespeare' series. He also provided notes for *Antony and Cleopatra*, *Hamlet*, *Henry VIII*, *King Lear*, *Macbeth*, and *Measure for Measure*, (1889–90). He reviewed several of Irving's performances, and included an essay on him in *Plays, Acting, and Music*.

was with a fixed resolve to come and live in London, where, it seemed, I could, if I liked, be something more than a spectator of the great, amusing crowd. The intoxication of London had got hold of me; I felt at home in it, and I felt that I had never yet found anywhere to be at home in.

I lived in London for five years, and I do not think there was a day during those five years in which I did not find a conscious delight in the mere fact of being in London. When I found myself alone, and in the midst of a crowd, I began to be astonishingly happy. I needed so little at the beginning of that time. I have never been able to stay long under a roof without restlessness, and I used to go out into the streets, many times a day, for the pleasure of finding myself in the open air and in the streets. I had never cared greatly for the open air in the country, the real open air, because everything in the country, except the sea, bored me; but here, in the 'motley'[41] Strand, among these hurrying people, under the smoky sky, I could walk and yet watch. If there ever was a religion of the eyes, I have devoutly practised that religion. I noted every face that passed me on the pavement; I looked into the omnibuses, the cabs, always with the same eager hope of seeing some beautiful or interesting person, some gracious movement, a delicate expression, which would be gone if I did not catch it as it went. This search without an aim grew to be almost a torture to me; my eyes ached with the effort, but I could not control them. At every moment, I knew, some spectacle awaited them; I grasped at all these sights with the same futile energy as a dog that I once saw standing in an Irish stream, and snapping at the bubbles that ran continually past him on the water. Life ran past me continually, and I tried to make all its bubbles my own.

---

[41] Motley —exhibiting a great diversity of elements.

~

Esther Kahn

'Esther Kahn' is a surprising attempt to pair Symons's fascination with the stage with the representation of a woman's consciousness. It was first published in the New York magazine, *Smart Set* 8 (October 1902). According to the section of Symons's memoirs Karl Beckson entitles 'An Actress in Whitechapel', it was inspired by a performance of *Romeo and Juliet* in the East End of London in June 1890. Symons had recently read *The Picture of Dorian Gray* (in its magazine version) and claims 'what happened to Dorian happened to me.' The 'lovely' young female lead 'excited in me an abstract passion,' he recalls. 'She expressed the supreme ecstasy of her passion, both in voice and face.' After the performance, the 'villainous Jew' who ran the theatre invited Symons backstage to meet her. Her name was Rachel Kahn. Symons was star-struck, but the conversation was interrupted almost immediately by Rachel's drunken mother. Symons invited Rachel to his rooms at Fountain Court, but whether she attended, or even existed in the first place, is unknown. The entire account so determinedly parallels Wilde's description of Sibyl Vane that it is impossible to tell where fact ends and fiction begins.[1] Perhaps Symons conflated the event with another of his 'Unspiritual Adventures', an encounter with a teenage music-hall performer called Gladys Fane (or Vane), whom he met when staying in a London rooming-house in the summer of 1889 and with whom he had his first affair.[2]

The version of events in 'The Genesis of Spiritual Adventures' is a little different. The story was inspired, Symons admits, by one of his 'nocturnal expeditions from Fountain Court to the Docks', but there is no mention of a trip to the theatre. Instead, 'giv[ing] the notes as I made them', Symons describes how

---

[1] Symons, 'An Actress in Whitechapel', *The Memoirs of Arthur Symons*, pp. 75–7. I can find no record of a London production of the play which matches this one, or of an actress called Rachel Kahn.

[2] Beckson, *Arthur Symons*, p. 49. Princeton University holds an unpublished manuscript headed 'This is one of my Unspiritual Adventures, Gladys Vane, Savoy Buildings, July 24, 1889'. The girl's name was surely a stage-name. T. Wemyss Reid's *Gladys Fane: A Story of Two Lives* was a bestseller of the 1880s and early 1890s.

he found himself on 'a broad and dimly-lighted street' where he was drawn to a brightly-lit window. Untroubled by any ethical considerations, he peered in and watched a Jewish family 'eagerly discussing something' at the supper table. One of them was 'a young girl of delicately Jewish beauty' who sat 'motionless, absorbed, lost in some vague reverie, her head lifted, her eyes gazing into space, her lips slightly parted.' Her attitude leads Symons to compare her with Thérèse in the 1873 stage version of Zola's *Thérèse Raquin* — another example of his tendency to use artistic analogues as the touchstones of individual perception — and at last he wanders off, wondering 'what is she thinking?' and 'haunted by the clear pallor of that strange and mystic face, those visionary eyes, that immovable attitude.'[3] The East End setting is a familiar one in the 'slum fiction' of the 1890s. Symons used similar descriptions in his 'East and West End Silhouettes' (collected in his *Memoirs*) and seems especially influenced by Arthur Morrison's *Tales of Mean Streets* (1894 — Esther lives on a 'mean street') and the work of Israel Zangwill (1864–1926), who chronicled East End Jewish life in such novels as *Children of the Ghetto* (1892), a work Symons admired. In the wake of Tsarist pogroms during the 1880s, London's East End had seen high levels of Eastern European Jewish immigration. Many of these immigrants worked in the textile industry, either from home or in sweatshops.

The relationship between Dorian and Sibyl Vane in *The Picture of Dorian Gray* collapses when Sibyl's experience of love makes her unable to counterfeit such emotion when performing Shakespeare. Young and beautiful, with an exquisite voice, 'consummate art-instinct', and 'personality', Sibyl seems to be 'a born artist', but her relationship with Dorian renders her performance embarrassingly stagy and 'unbearably artificial'.[4] In 'Esther Kahn' however, the relationship between art and life is less destructive. Esther is positively encouraged to fall in love. As another character tells her, 'you think you can act, and you have never felt anything worse than a cut finger.' Rather than experience being the enemy of art, and its opposite pole, as is the case in Wilde, Symons makes art capable of absorbing and then distilling genuine emotion into altogether more intoxicating spirit. When her lover betrays her, preferring Italian beauty and passion to Jewish 'cleverness', Esther is able to sublimate her anger and disappointment into dramatic art, producing a stunning performance but also finding a way of bottling the experience inside herself so that she might drink from it as required. Esther's triumph seems based upon prototypical method acting rather than on what Haygarth the playwright, an obvious Symons surrogate, has taught her: female

---

[3] Symons, 'The Genesis of Spiritual Adventures'.
[4] Wilde, *The Picture of Dorian Gray*, pp. 49, 67, 72. One assumes that this remark implies the existence of 'bearable' artificiality, presumably that which is profoundly artificial while seeming wholly 'natural'.

sensibility and 'startling intuitions' triumph over the male dramatist's formal schooling as emotion becomes transmuted into art.

Haygarth 'not only knew what should be done, but exactly why it should be done', and though he is 'one of those creative critics who can do every man's work but their own', he has a great deal of wisdom to impart.[5] He and Esther embark on an ambitious programme of theatrical education, studying the speaking of verse, training the voice, watching the leading European actresses of the day, Eleonora Duse, Gabrielle Réjane, and Sarah Bernhardt, and the particularly stylized manner of English stage performance, which 'maintained itself at so stiff a distance from nature.' The theatre of the 1890s saw marked departures from older conventions, with the rise of more naturalistic styles of writing and acting, fresh ideas about lighting and set design, and continued debate about drama's permissible subject matter, all beneath the watchful and censorious eye of the Lord Chamberlain. Symons followed these developments keenly. Like Haygarth, his own career as a dramatist had as yet borne little fruit. By 1902, he had managed to stage only *The Minister's Call*, an adaptation of a Frank Harris story that failed to impress its critics in 1892, but this did not prevent him from writing voluble dramatic criticism and thinking long and hard about the art of the stage. As elsewhere in his work, it was the European avant-garde which represented the alternative to native experimentation. He celebrated Ibsen, Jarry, Maeterlinck, and D'Annunzio, and spent hours in London and Paris theatres.[6] 'Esther Kahn' demonstrates Symons's extensive knowledge of these in providing the dual perspectives of actress and writer. There is, as one might expect, no concern with the unenlightened view from the stalls, for the theatre's patrons exist solely to applaud Esther's genius, not to scrutinize or debate it.

The plot of 'Esther Kahn', with its nods to Du Maurier's *Trilby* (1894) and many other works which focus on pairing of artistic and sentimental education, might easily have taken a melodramatic turn. A more popularly-minded writer would have presented the 'scene of unmeasured violence' between Haygarth and Esther at length, but Symons summarizes rather than dramatizes the fateful encounter, resisting any confusion of stage with page. The story's carefully preserved distance from such extravagant emotionalism is wholly appropriate, for Esther's final triumph derives very much from her ability to subordinate her feelings to the needs of theatrical performance.

---

[5] Symons reused the description of Haygarth in 'A Study in Morbidity', a typescript now held at Princeton but published as 'A Study in Morbidity: Herbert Horne', in *The Memoirs of Arthur Symons* (pp. 125–28).

[6] John Stokes provides valuable context for Symons's enthusiasm for radical theatre and performance in his essay, 'The Legend of Duse', in *Decadence and the 1890s*, ed. by Ian Fletcher (London: Arnold, 1979), pp. 151–72.

Avoiding intrusive narration and moral judgement, Symons leaves his readers to draw their own conclusions about his characters, making it difficult for those a century later to determine whether their attitudes are being endorsed or undermined. Haygarth's views on women are shared by Daniel Roserra in 'An Autumn City' and Henry Luxulyan, both of whom espouse views akin to Symons's own. Haygarth is a 'devoted, discreet amateur of woman' who 'appreciated women really for their own sakes'; his pride in Esther 'was like his pride in a play that he had written finely, and put aside'. It is difficult to see such views finding favour with feminist readers of either sex, but at the same time it is by no means easy to judge the extent to which Haygarth's proprietorial view of Esther is supported by Symons himself. Laurel Brake has observed how *The Savoy* was 'full of male discourse, and misogyny', short stories, poems, and drawings which 'treat performing women' as the 'object of the gaze of males', and there are many instances in Symons's poems and essays of his fascination with watching dancers, singers, and actresses.[7] 'Esther Kahn' is however, different from a poem such as *London Nights*'s 'La Mélinite: Moulin Rouge' in its concern with the psychology of the performer rather than her appearance or her effect on others. Only at the end of the story does Symons fall back into his familiar ways. 'She had never been more restrained, more effortless', he writes. '[S]he seemed scarcely to be acting; only, a magnetic current seemed to have been set in motion between her and those who were watching her.' As 'Silhouette', Symons was accustomed to making such comments, but he was unable to make the imaginative leap required to convey Esther's experience through access to her own consciousness and, perhaps recognizing his limitations, shifted his focus instead to Haygarth's eyes 'fixed on the stage'. He hails the fact that she 'had made his play' and 'had made herself a great actress', an order of phrasing which suggests his fundamentally egotistical outlook and might lead readers to think she was well rid of him.

The final image is of Esther 'weeping uncontrollable tears', her private self being very different from her assured theatrical one. As she speculates whether or not to 'take back her lover', Symons's skilled use of free indirect style makes it all-but impossible to distinguish between the narrator's summary of her feelings and the feelings themselves. Her 'deliberate, automatic nature' has undergone 'a kind of release', but the agent of that release is uncertain. Is it the fulfilment of her theatrical ambitions, the intense upset of her broken relationship, or the galvanising effects of jealousy when besting her Italian rival? Here, as in the 'Lucy Newcome' stories, Symons makes a determined attempt to delineate female subjectivity, striking a quite different note from the treatment of women elsewhere in his output. As Margaret Stetz notes, the story was progressive in its

---

[7] Laurel Brake, *Subjugated Knowledges*, pp. 151, 153.

serious attention to a woman's 'professional ambitions', especially as the woman
in question was a Jew. However, 'it was also backward-looking in its reaffirmation
of the old cliché that the true source of education for a woman artist could only
be heterosexual experience and disappointment in love.'[8]

Esther Kahn is the only one of Symons's works to have been adapted for the
cinema. Directed by Arnaud Desplechin, who also co-wrote the screenplay, it was
shown at the Cannes Film Festival in 2000, though not released in Britain or the
United States until 2002. Summer Phoenix played Esther, Ian Holm was Nathan
Quellen, and Fabrice Desplechin Philip Haygarth.

* * *

Esther Kahn was born in one of those dark, evil-smelling streets with strange
corners which lie about the Docks. It was a quiet street, which seemed to lead
nowhere, but to stand aside, for some not quite honest purpose of its own. The
blinds of some of these houses were always drawn; shutters were nailed over some
of the windows. Few people passed; there were never many children playing in
the road; the women did not stand talking at their open doors. The doors opened
and shut quietly; dark faces looked out from behind the windows; the Jews who
lived there seemed always to be at work, bending over their tables, sewing and
cutting, or else hurrying in and out with bundles of clothes under their arms,
going and coming from the tailors for whom they worked. The Kahns all worked
at tailoring: Esther's father and mother and grandmother, her elder brother and
her two elder sisters. One did seaming, another button-holing, another sewed on
buttons; and, on the poor pay they got for that, seven had to live.

As a child Esther had a strange terror of the street in which she lived. She was
never sure whether something dreadful had just happened there, or whether it
was just going to happen. But she was always in suspense. She was tormented
with the fear of knowing what went on behind those nailed shutters. She made
up stories about the houses, but the stories never satisfied her. She imagined some
great, vague gesture; not an incident, but a gesture; and it hung in the air
suspended like a shadow. The gestures of people always meant more to her than
their words; they seemed to have a secret meaning of their own, which the words
never quite interpreted. She was always unconsciously on the watch for their
meaning.

At night, after supper, the others used to sit around the table, talking eagerly.
Esther would get up and draw her chair into the corner by the door, and for a
time she would watch them, as if she were looking on at something, something
with which she had no concern, but which interested her for its outline and

---

[8] Margaret D. Stetz, *Gender and the London Theatre, 1880–1920* (Buckingham: Rivendale Press,
2004), p. 59.

movement. She saw her father's keen profile, the great, hooked nose, the black, prominent, shifty eye, the tangled black hair straggling over the shirt-collar; her mother, large, placid, with masses of black, straight hair coiled low over her sallow cheeks; the two sisters, sharp and voluble, never at rest for a moment; the brother, with his air of insolent assurance, an immense self-satisfaction hooded under his beautifully curved eyelids; the grandmother, with her bent and mountainous shoulders, the vivid malice of her eyes, her hundreds of wrinkles. All these people, who had so many interests in common, who thought of the same things, cared for the same things, seemed so fond of one another in an instinctive way, with so much hostility for other people who were not belonging to them, sat there night after night, in the same attitudes, always as eager for the events of today as they had been for the events of yesterday. Everything mattered to them immensely, and especially their part in things; and no one thing seemed to matter more than any other thing. Esther cared only to look on; nothing mattered to her; she had no interest in their interests; she was not sure that she cared for them more than she would care for other people; they were what she supposed real life was, and that was a thing in which she had only a disinterested curiosity.

Sometimes, when she had been watching them until they had all seemed to fade away and form again in a kind of vision more precise than the reality, she would lose sight of them altogether and sit gazing straight before her, her eyes wide open, her lips parted. Her hand would make an unconscious movement, as if she were accompanying some grave words with an appropriate gesture; and Becky would generally see it, and burst into a mocking laugh, and ask her whom she was mimicking.

'Don't notice her,' the mother said once; 'she's not a human child, she's a monkey; she's clutching out after a soul, as they do. They look like little men, but they know they're not men, and they try to be; that's why they mimic us.'

Esther was very angry; she said to herself that she would be more careful in future not to show anything that she was feeling.

At thirteen Esther looked a woman. She was large-boned, with very small hands and feet, and her body seemed to be generally asleep, in a kind of brooding lethargy. She had her mother's hair, masses of it, but softer, with a faint, natural wave in it. Her face was oval, smooth in outline, with a nose just Jewish enough for the beauty of suave curves and unemphatic outlines. The lips were thick, red, strung like a bow. The whole face seemed to await, with an infinite patience, some moulding and awakening force, which might have its way with it. It wanted nothing, anticipated nothing; it waited. Only the eyes put life into the mask, and the eyes were the eyes of the tribe; they had no personal meaning in what seemed to be their mystery; they were ready to fascinate innocently, to be intolerably ambiguous without intention; they were fathomless with mere sleep, the unconscious dream which is in the eyes of animals.

Esther was neither clever nor stupid; she was inert. She did as little in the house as she could, but when she had to take her share in the stitching she stitched more neatly than any of the others, though very slowly. She hated it, in her languid, smouldering way, partly because it was work and partly because it made her prick her fingers, and the skin grew hard and ragged where the point of the needle had scratched it. She liked her skin to be quite smooth, but all the glycerine she rubbed into it at night would not take out the mark of the needle. It seemed to her like the badge of her slavery.

She would rather not have been a Jewess; that, too, was a kind of badge, marking her out from other people; she wanted to be let alone, to have her own way without other people's help or hindrance. She had no definite consciousness of what her own way was to be; she was only conscious, as yet, of the ways that would certainly not be hers.

She would not think only of making money, like her mother, nor of being thought clever, like Becky, nor of being admired because she had good looks and dressed smartly, like Mina. All these things required an effort, and Esther was lazy. She wanted to be admired, and to have money, of course, and she did not want people to think her stupid; but all this was to come to her, she knew, because of some fortunate quality in herself, as yet undiscovered. Then she would shake off everything that now clung to her, like a worn-out garment that one keeps only until one can replace it. She saw herself rolling away in a carriage towards the west; she would never come back. And it would be like a revenge on whatever it was that kept her stifling in this mean street; she wanted to be cruelly revenged.

As it was, her only very keen pleasure was in going to the theatre with her brother or her sisters; she cared nothing for the music-halls, and preferred staying at home to going with the others when they went to the Pavilion or the Foresters. But when there was a melodrama at the Standard, or at the Elephant and Castle, she would wait and struggle outside the door and up the narrow, winding stairs, for a place as near the front of the gallery as she could get.[9] Once inside, she would never speak, but she would sit staring at the people on the stage as if they hypnotised her. She never criticised the play, as the others did; the play did not

---

[9] Symons knew all these venues intimately and reviewed performances at them during his time as 'Silhouette', the *Star*'s music hall correspondent. For The Pavilion, see 'The Life and Adventures of Lucy Newcome'. The Foresters, in Cambridge Heath Road, Whitechapel, opened in 1870 and closed in 1917. It was the scene of Dan Leno's first significant London engagement — before becoming the greatest of pantomime dames, Dan Leno (orig. George Wild Galvin, 1860–1904) was paid £5 a week for clog dancing and comic songs in 1885. The Royal Standard Music Hall, close to where Victoria station now stands, opened in 1863, was lavishly remodelled in 1886, and closed in 1910, at which point it was replaced by the Victoria Palace Theatre. The Elephant and Castle in New Kent Road, built on the site of a theatre of the same name destroyed by fire in 1878, opened in 1879 and was converted to a cinema in 1928.

seem to matter; she lived it without will or choice, merely because it was there and her eyes were on it.

But after it was over and they were at home again, she would become suddenly voluble as she discussed the merits of the acting. She had no hesitations, was certain that she was always in the right, and became furious if any one contradicted her. She saw each part as a whole, and she blamed the actors for not being consistent with themselves. She could not understand how they could make a mistake. It was so simple, there were no two ways of doing anything. To go wrong was as if you said no when you meant yes; it must be wilful.

'You ought to do it yourself, Esther,' said her sisters, when they were tired of her criticisms. They meant to be satirical, but Esther said, seriously enough: 'Yes, I could do it; but so could that woman if she would let herself alone. Why did she try to be something else all the time?'

Time went slowly with Esther; but when she was seventeen she was still sewing at home and still waiting. Nothing had come to her of all that she had expected. Two of her cousins, and a neighbour or two, had wanted to marry her; but she had refused them contemptuously. To her sluggish instinct men seemed only good for making money, or, perhaps, children; they had not come to have any definite personal meaning for her. A little man called Joel, who had talked to her passionately about love, and had cried when she refused him, seemed to her an unintelligible and ridiculous kind of animal. When she dreamed of the future, there was never any one of that sort making fine speeches to her.

But, gradually, her own real purpose in life had become clear. She was to be an actress. She said nothing about it at home, but she began to go round to the managers of the small theatres in the neighbourhood, asking for an engagement. After a long time the manager gave her a small part. The piece was called *The Wages of Sin*, and she was to be the servant who opens the door in the first act to the man who is going to be the murderer in the second act, and then identifies him in the fourth act.[10]

Esther went home quietly and said nothing until supper-time. Then she said to her mother: 'I am going on the stage.'

'That's very likely,' said her mother, with a sarcastic smile; 'and when do you go on, pray?'

'On Monday night,' said Esther.

'You don't mean it!' said her mother.

'Indeed I mean it,' said Esther, 'and I've got my part. I'm to be the servant in *The Wages of Sin*.'

---

[10] This fictitious play sounds very like many late-Victorian melodramas, though its title, adapted from 'The wages of sin *is* death' (Romans 6. 23), hints at the perception of the theatre as an immoral place for women and at Esther's transgression in leaving her home for the stage.

Her brother laughed. 'I know,' he said, 'she speaks two words twice.'

'You are right,' said Esther; 'will you come on Monday, and hear how I say them?'

When Esther had made up her mind to do anything, they all knew that she always did it. Her father talked to her seriously. Her mother said: 'You are much too lazy, Esther; you will never get on.' They told her that she was taking the bread out of their mouths, and it was certain she would never put it back again. 'If I get on,' said Esther, 'I will pay you back exactly what I would have earned, as long as you keep me. Is that a bargain? I know I shall get on, and you won't repent of it. You had better let me do as I want. It will pay.'

They shook their heads, looked at Esther, who sat there with her lips tight shut, and a queer, hard look in her eyes, which were trying not to seem exultant; they looked at one another, shook their heads again, and consented. The old grandmother mumbled something fiercely, but as it sounded like bad words, and they never knew what Old Testament language she would use, they did not ask her what she was meaning.

On Monday Esther made her first appearance on the stage. Her mother said to her afterwards: 'I thought nothing of you, Esther; you were just like any ordinary servant.' Becky asked her if she had felt nervous. She shook her head; it had seemed quite natural to her, she said. She did not tell them that a great wave of triumph had swept over her as she felt the heat of the gas footlights come up into her eyes, and saw the floating cluster of white faces rising out of a solid mass of indistinguishable darkness. In that moment she drew into her nostrils the breath of life.

Esther had a small part to understudy, and before long she had the chance of playing it. The manager said nothing to her, but soon afterwards he told her to understudy a more important part. She never had the chance to play it, but, when the next piece was put on at the theatre, she was given a part of her own. She began to make a little money, and, as she had promised, she paid so much a week to her parents for keeping her. They gained by the bargain, so they did not ask her to come back to the stitching. Mrs Kahn sometimes spoke of her daughter to the neighbours with a certain languid pride; Esther was making her way.

Esther made her way rapidly. One day the manager of a West End theatre came down to see her; he engaged her at once to play a small but difficult part in an ambitious kind of melodrama that he was bringing out. She did it well, satisfied the manager, was given a better part, did that well, too, was engaged by another manager, and, in short, began to be looked upon as a promising actress. The papers praised her with moderation; some of the younger critics, who admired her type, praised her more than she deserved. She was making money; she had come to live in rooms of her own, off the Strand; at twenty-one she had done, in a measure, what she wanted to do; but she was not satisfied with herself. She had always known that she could act, but how well could she act? Would she never be able to act any better than this? She had drifted into the life of the stage as naturally as if she had never known anything else; she was at home, comfortable, able to do what many others could not do. But she wanted to be a great actress.

An old actor, a Jew, Nathan Quellen, who had taken a kind of paternal interest in her, and who helped her with all the good advice that he had never taken to himself, was fond of saying that the remedy was in her own hands.

'My dear Esther,' he would tell her, smoothing his long grey hair down over his forehead, 'you must take a lover; you must fall in love; there's no other way. You think you can act, and you have never felt anything worse than a cut finger. Why, it's an absurdity! Wait till you know the only thing worth knowing; till then you're in short frocks and a pinafore.'[11]

He cited examples, he condensed the biographies of the great actresses for her benefit. He found one lesson in them all, and he was sincere in his reading of history as he saw it. He talked, argued, protested; the matter seriously troubled him. He felt he was giving Esther good advice; he wanted her to be the thing she wanted to be. Esther knew it and thanked him, without smiling; she sat brooding over his words; she never argued against them. She believed much of what he said; but was the remedy, as he said, in her own hands? It did not seem so.

As yet no man had spoken to her blood. She had the sluggish blood of a really profound animal nature. She saw men calmly, as calmly as when little Joel had cried because she would not marry him. Joel still came to see her sometimes, with the same entreaty in his eyes, not daring to speak it. Other men, very different men, had made love to her in very different ways. They had seemed to be trying to drive a hard bargain, to get the better of her in a matter of business; and her native cunning had kept her easily on the better side of the bargain. She was resolved to be a business woman in the old trade of the affections; no one should buy or sell of her except at her own price, and she set the price vastly high.

Yet Quellen's words set her thinking. Was there, after all, but one way to study for the stage? All the examples pointed to it, and, what was worse, she felt it might be true. She saw exactly where her acting stopped short.

She looked around her with practical eyes, not seeming to herself to be doing anything unusual or unlikely to succeed in its purpose. She thought deliberately

---

[11] For Symons, life and art were not mutually exclusive, personal experience being transformed into art by the skill of the poet. It was a rather different story where women were concerned, since Symons typically praises his favourite performers, Eleonora Duse, for example, for their ability to perform rather than to create. The emotional basis of the performance is less important than the version apprehended by the audience. Duse, he said, did not rely upon nature. Rather, she 'controlled' it 'into the forms of her desire, as the sculptor controls the clay under his (*sic*) fingers. She is the artist of her own soul, and it is her force of will, her mastery of herself, not her abandonment to it, which make her what she is' ('Eleonora Duse' in *Studies in Seven Arts*, p. 214).

over all the men she knew; but who was there whom it would be possible to take seriously? She could think of only one man: Philip Haygarth.

Philip Haygarth was a man of five-and-thirty, who had been writing plays and having them acted, with only a moderate success, for nearly ten years. He was one of the accepted men, a man whose plays were treated respectfully, and he had the reputation of being much cleverer than his plays. He was short, dark, neat, very worldly-looking, with thin lips and reflective, not quite honest eyes. His manner was cold, restrained, with a mingling of insolence and diffidence. He was a hard worker and a somewhat deliberately hard liver. He avoided society and preferred to find his relaxation among people with whom one did not need to keep up appearances, or talk sentiment, or pay afternoon calls. He admired Esther Kahn as an actress, though with many reservations; and he admired her as a woman, more than he had ever admired anybody else. She appealed to all his tastes; she ended by absorbing almost the whole of those interests and those hours which he set apart, in his carefully arranged life, for such matters.

He made love to Esther much more skilfully than any of her other lovers, and, though she saw through his plans as clearly as he wished her to see through them, she was grateful to him for a certain finesse in his manner of approach. He never mentioned the word 'love,' except to jest at it; he concealed even the extent to which he was really disturbed by her presence; his words spoke only of friendship and of general topics. And yet there could never be any doubt as to his meaning; his whole attitude was a patient waiting. He interested her; frankly, he interested her: here, then, was the man for her purpose. With his admirable tact, he spared her the least difficulty in making her meaning clear. He congratulated himself on a prize; she congratulated herself on the accomplishment of a duty.

Days and weeks passed, and Esther scrutinised herself with a distinct sense of disappointment. She had no moral feeling in the matter; she was her own property, it had always seemed to her, free to dispose of as she pleased. The business element in her nature persisted. This bargain, this infinitely important bargain, had been concluded, with open eyes, with a full sense of responsibility, for a purpose, the purpose for which she lived. What was the result?

She could see no result. The world had in no sense changed for her, as she had been supposing it would change; a new excitement had come into her life, and that was all. She wondered what it was that a woman was expected to feel under the circumstances, and why she had not felt it. How different had been her feeling when she walked across the stage for the first time! That had really been a new life, or the very beginning of life. But this was no more than a delightful episode, hardly to be disentangled from the visit to Paris which had accompanied it. She had, so to speak, fallen into a new habit, which was so agreeable, and seemed so natural, that she could not understand why she had not fallen into it before; it was a habit she would certainly persist in, for its own sake. The world remained just the same.

And her art: she had learned nothing. No new thrill came into the words she spoke; her eyes, as they looked across the footlights, remembered nothing, had nothing new to tell.

And so she turned, with all the more interest, an interest almost impersonal, to Philip Haygarth when he talked to her about acting and the drama, when he elaborated his theories which, she was aware, occupied him more than she occupied him. He was one of those creative critics who can do every man's work but their own. When he sat down to write his own plays, something dry and hard came into the words, the life ebbed out of those imaginary people who had been so real to him, whom he had made so real to others as he talked. He constructed admirably and was an unerring judge of the construction of plays. And he had a sense of acting which was like the sense that a fine actor might have, if he could be himself and also someone looking on at himself. He not only knew what should be done, but exactly why it should be done. Little suspecting that he had been chosen for the purpose, though in so different a manner, he set himself to teach her art to Esther.[12]

He made her go through the great parts with him; she was Juliet, Lady Macbeth, Cleopatra; he taught her how to speak verse and how to feel the accent of speech in verse, another kind of speech than prose speech; he trained her voice to take hold of the harmonies that lie in words themselves; and she caught them, by ear, as one born to speak many languages catches a foreign language.[13] She went through Ibsen as she had gone through Shakespeare; and Haygarth showed her how to take hold of this very different subject-matter, so definite and so elusive.[14] And they studied good acting-plays together, worthless plays that gave

---

[12] Symons reworks the melodrama of George Du Maurier's *Trilby* by making Haygarth a practical teacher rather than a mesmerist (though he invokes the hypnotist image later in the story), and also explores the Pygmalion myth a decade before Shaw's play of the same name. Haygarth's views clearly echo the dramatic theory Symons was evolving in the early twentieth century. Rhoda Symons had theatrical ambitions, and Symons acknowledged her influence on his views in the preface to *Studies in Seven Arts*.

[13] There may be an echo here of the relationship between George Bernard Shaw (1856–1950) and Florence Farr (1860–1917), the actress and occultist whom Symons knew through her friendship with Yeats. As both Irishmen were pursuing Farr, Symons may have heard rather jaundiced accounts of Shaw's training methods from his rival. Farr, Yeats, and Arnold Dolmetsch explored the relationship of music to speech, Yeats producing the essay 'Speaking to the Psaltery' which Symons reviewed in *The Academy* (31 May 1902), together with an account of Farr's demonstration of her methods. The review was reprinted in slightly edited form as 'The Speaking of Verse' (*Plays, Acting and Music*).

[14] The work of the Norwegian dramatist Henrik Ibsen (1828–1906) had been hugely controversial in England during the 1890s, and, championed by Shaw and others, it remained the benchmark of theatrical modernity in the early years of the new century. The unflinching realism and provocative sexual politics of *A Doll's House* (1879) and *Hedda Gabler* (1890) provoked disgust or adulation, according to taste. Symons saw the former, in William Archer's translation, in London in June 1889, and *Ghosts* (1881) in Paris the following year, reviewing

the actress opportunities to create something out of nothing. Together they saw Duse and Sarah Bernhardt; and they had seen Réjane[15] in Paris, in crudely tragic parts; and they studied the English stage, to find out why it maintained itself at so stiff a distance from nature. She went on acting all the time, always acting with more certainty; and at last she attempted more serious parts, which she learned with Haygarth at her elbow.

She had to be taught her part as a child is taught its lesson; word by word, intonation by intonation. She read it over, not really knowing what it was about; she learned it by heart mechanically, getting the words into her memory first. Then the meaning had to be explained to her, scene by scene, and she had to say the words over until she had found the right accent. Once found, she never forgot it; she could repeat it identically at any moment; there were no variations to allow for. Until that moment she was reaching out blindly in the dark, feeling about her with uncertain fingers.

And, with her, the understanding came with the power of expression, sometimes seeming really to proceed from the sound to the sense, from the gesture inward. Show her how it should be done, and she knew why it should be done; sound the right note in her ears, arrest her at the moment when the note came right, and she understood, by a backward process, why the note should sound thus. Her mind worked, but it worked under suggestion, as the hypnotists say; the idea had to come to her through the instinct, or it would never come.

As Esther found herself, almost unconsciously, becoming what she had dreamed of becoming, what she had longed to become, and, after all, through Philip Haygarth, a more personal feeling began to grow up in her heart toward this lover who had found his way to her, not through the senses, but through the mind. A kind of domesticity had crept into their relations, and this drew Esther nearer to him. She began to feel that he belonged to her. He had never, she knew, been wholly absorbed in her, and she had delighted him by showing no jealousy,

---

it for the *Pall Mall Gazette* (5 June 1890). He published many pieces on Ibsen, beginning with 'Henrik Ibsen' (*Universal Review*, 15 April 1889). His review of Olga Nethersole in *The Lady from the Sea* appeared in *The Academy* (10 May 1902), suggesting Ibsen was much on his mind when writing 'Esther Kahn'. His most lengthy consideration of the playwright was 'Henrik Ibsen' (*Quarterly Review*, October 1906), reprinted in *Figures of Several Centuries* (1916).

[15] Eleonora Duse (1859–1924), internationally-renowned Italian actress revered by Symons who specialized in Ibsen and modern European drama. Sarah Bernhardt (1844–1923), French actress often considered the greatest *tragedienne* of her time. Gabrielle Réjane (1856–1920), another French actress, one who, at her best, rivalled Bernhardt. Symons wrote essays on each performer in *Plays, Acting and Music*, summing them up in 'Sarah Bernhardt': 'After all, though Réjane skins emotions alive, and Duse serves them up to you on golden dishes, it is Sarah Bernhardt who prepares the supreme feast.' In Dowson and Moore's *A Comedy of Masks* (1893), two theatregoers wonder 'How is that French actresses have such beautiful voices?' and decide that their favourite has 'the voice of a true Parisian *femme de siècle, fin de siècle*' (p. 67).

no anxiety to keep him. As long as she remained so, he felt that she had a sure hold on him. But now she began to change, to concern herself more with his doings, to assert her right to him, as she had never hitherto cared to do. He chafed a little at what seemed an unnecessary devotion.

Love, with Esther, had come slowly, taking his time on the journey; but he came to take possession. To work at her art was to please Philip Haygarth; she worked now with a double purpose. And she made surprising advances as an actress. People began to speculate: had she genius, or was this only an astonishingly developed talent, which could go so far and no farther?

For, in this finished method, which seemed so spontaneous and yet at the same time so deliberate, there seemed still to be something, some slight, essential thing, almost unaccountably lacking. What was it? Was it a fundamental lack, that could never be supplied? Or would that slight, essential thing, as her admirers prophesied, one day be supplied? They waited.

Esther was now really happy, for the first time in her life; and as she looked back over those years, in the street by the Docks, when she had lived alone in the midst of her family, and since then, when she had lived alone, working, not finding the time long, nor wishing it to go more slowly, she felt a kind of surprise at herself. How could she have gone through it all? She had not even been bored. She had had a purpose, and now that she was achieving that purpose, the thing itself seemed hardly to matter. Her art kept pace with her life; she was giving up nothing in return for happiness; but she had come to prize the happiness, her love, beyond all things.

She knew that Haygarth was proud of her, that he looked upon her talent, genius, whatever it was, as partly the work of his hands. It pleased her that this should be so; it seemed to bind him to her more tightly.

In this she was mistaken, as most women are mistaken when they ask themselves what it is in them that holds their lovers. The actress interested Haygarth greatly, but the actress interested him as a problem, as something quite apart from his feelings as a man, as a lover. He had been attracted by the woman, by what was sombre and unexplained in her eyes, by the sleepy grace of her movements, by the magnetism that seemed to drowse in her. He had made love to her precisely as he would have made love to an ignorant, beautiful creature who walked on in some corner of a Drury Lane melodrama. On principle, he did not like clever women. Esther, it is true, was not clever, in the ordinary, tiresome sense; and her startling intuitions, in matters of acting, had not repelled him, as an exhibition of the capabilities of a woman, while they preoccupied him for a long time in that part of his brain which worked critically upon any interesting material. But nothing that she could do as an artist made the least difference to his feeling about her as a woman; his pride in her was like his pride in a play that he had written finely, and put aside; to be glanced at from time to time, with cool satisfaction. He had his own very deliberate theory of values, and one value was never allowed to interfere with another. A devoted, discreet amateur of woman, he appreciated women really for their own sakes, with an unflattering simplicity. And for a time Esther absorbed him almost wholly.

He had been quite content with their relations as they were before she fell seriously in love with him, and this new, profound feeling, which he had never even dreaded, somewhat disturbed him. She was adopting almost the attitude of a wife, and he had no ambition to play the part of a husband. The affections were always rather a strain upon him; he liked something a little less serious and a little more exciting.

Esther understood nothing that was going on in Philip Haygarth's mind, and when he began to seem colder to her, when she saw less of him, and then less, it seemed to her that she could still appeal to him by her art and still touch him by her devotion. As her warmth seemed more and more to threaten his liberty, the impulse to tug at his chain became harder to resist. His continued, unvarying interest in her acting, his patience in helping her, in working with her, kept her for some time from realising how little was left now of the more personal feeling. It was with sharp surprise, as well as with a blinding rage, that she discovered one day, beyond possibility of mistake, that she had a rival, and that Haygarth was only doling out to her the time left over from her rival.

It was an Italian, a young girl who had come over to London with an organ-grinder, and who posed for sculptors, when she could get a sitting. It was a girl who could barely read and write, an insignificant creature, a peasant from the Campagna, who had nothing but her good looks and the distinction of her attitudes. Esther was beside herself with rage, jealousy, mortification; she loved, and she could not pardon. There was a scene of unmeasured violence. Haygarth was cruel, almost with intention; and they parted, Esther feeling as if her life had been broken sharply in two.

She was at the last rehearsals of a new play by Haygarth, a play in which he had tried for once to be tragic in the bare, straightforward way of the things that really happen. She went through the rehearsals absent-mindedly, repeating her words, which he had taught her how to say, but scarcely attending to their meaning. Another thought was at work behind this mechanical speech, a continual throb of remembrance, going on monotonously. Her mind was full of other words, which she heard as if an inner voice were repeating them; her mind made up pictures, which seemed to pass slowly before her eyes: Haygarth and the other woman. At the last rehearsal Quellen came round to her, and, ironically as she thought, complimented her on her performance. She meant, when the night came, not to fail: that was all.

When the night came, she said to herself that she was calm, that she would be able to concentrate herself on her acting and act just as usual. But, as she stood in the wings, waiting for her moment to appear, her eyes went straight to the eyes of the other woman, the Italian model, the organ-grinder's girl, who sat, smiling contentedly, in the front of a box, turning her head sometimes to speak to someone behind her, hidden by the curtain. She was dressed in black, with a rose in her hair: you could have taken her for a lady; she was triumphantly beautiful. Esther shuddered as if she had been struck; the blood rushed into her forehead and swelled and beat against her eyes. Then, with an immense effort, she cleared her mind of everything but the task before her. Every nerve in her body lived with a separate life as she opened the door at the back of the stage, and stood, waiting for the applause to subside, motionless under the eyes of the audience. There was something in the manner of her entrance that seemed to strike the fatal note of the play. She had never been more restrained, more effortless; she seemed scarcely to be acting; only, a magnetic current seemed to have been set in motion between her and those who were watching her. They held their breaths, as if they were assisting at a real tragedy; as if, at any moment, this acting might give place to some horrible, naked passion of mere nature. The curtain rose and rose again at the end of the first act; and she stood there, bowing gravely, in what seemed a deliberate continuation, into that interval, of the sentiment of the piece. Her dresses were taken off her and put on her, for each act, as if she had been a lay-figure. Once, in the second act, she looked up at the box; the Italian woman was smiling emptily, but Haygarth, taking no notice of her, was leaning forward with his eyes fixed on the stage. After the third act he sent to Esther's dressing-room a fervent note, begging to be allowed to see her. She had made his play, he said, and she had made herself a great actress. She crumpled the note fiercely, put it carefully into her jewel-box, and refused to see him. In the last act she had to die, after the manner of the Lady of the Camellias, waiting for the lover who, in this case, never came.[16] The pathos of her acting was almost unbearable, and, still, it seemed not like acting at all. The curtain went down on a great actress.

Esther went home stunned, only partly realising what she had done, or how she had done it. She read over the note from Haygarth, unforgivingly; and the long letter that came from him in the morning. As reflection returned, through all the confused suffering and excitement, to her deliberate, automatic nature, in which a great shock had brought about a kind of release, she realised that all she had wanted, during most of her life, had at last come about. The note had been struck, she had responded to it, as she responded to every suggestion, faultlessly;

---

[16] *The Lady of the Camellias*, English translation of *La dame aux camélias*, a novel by Alexandre Dumas, *fils* (1824–95), published in 1848 and swiftly adapted for the stage. The story of the doomed love between the courtesan, Marguerite Gautier, and her young admirer, Armand Duval culminates in the heroine's death from tuberculosis. The role was popular with Duse, Bernhardt (Symons saw her perform it in 1889), and Réjane. Despite the heroine's incurable respiratory disease, the story was hugely successful in its operatic adaptation, Verdi's *La Traviata* (1853). Symons translated the novel for Heinemann in 1900; he had visited Dumas with Havelock Ellis in April 1890.

she knew that she could repeat the note, whenever she wished, now that she had once found it. There would be no variation to allow for, the actress was made at last. She might take back her lover, or never see him again, it would make no difference. It would make no difference, she repeated, over and over again, weeping uncontrollable tears.

~

Christian Trevalga

A portrait of a Cornish pianist sliding towards insanity, 'Christian Trevalga' is filled with detail of personal significance to its author, augmenting 'A Prelude to Life' in interesting and revealing ways. Unpublished before its appearance in *Spiritual Adventures*, it was probably written in April 1902, since in a letter of 2 May of that year, Symons told the American novelist and music critic James Gibbons Huneker:

> I try feebly now and then to say something about music, but I haven't enough knowledge to be able to do much. All the same, you might glance at a sort of imaginary portrait called 'Christian Trevalga,' a study of a musical temperament, which is to come out one of these days in the *Fortnightly Review*.[1]

The story derived in part from Symons attending a performance by Vladimir de Pachmann in February 1902. Pachmann was 'the greatest living pianist', he declared, because he specialized in Chopin (Symons's favourite composer) and prized tonal nuance and subtlety of expression above solipsistic dexterity.[2] Trevalga's technique and intentions seem modelled on Pachmann's, though he has none of the comic eccentricities which led the latter to be nicknamed 'the Chopinzee'. His vision of smoke rising from the keyboard during a performance of Chopin's *Études* is, however, apparently taken from the pianist's own experience, being 'word for word what he told me one night when I was dining with him.'[3] Symons's essay, 'Pachmann and the Piano' (1902), provides detailed evidence of his fascination with the musician.

If Trevalga's style owes much to Pachmann's example, his background and general outlook are closer to Symons himself. Symons admitted that 'I bring myself into this narrative, and Vladimir de Pachmann.' Trevalga's Spanish mother is inspired by the fact that Symons's mother 'had a Spanish name, Lydia

---

[1] Symons, *Selected Letters*, p. 165.
[2] Symons, 'Pachmann, "Parsifal" and the Pathetic Symphony', *The Academy*, 22 February 1902, p. 200. This was later reworked for *Plays, Acting, and Music*.
[3] Symons, 'The Genesis of Spiritual Adventures'.

Pascoe'. Mrs Symons also 'had a way of moulding bread into little figures, little nude figures, exquisitely proportioned'. Trevalga shares with Pachmann and Symons the gift of perfect pitch, but his implied promiscuity echoes the author's: 'Is it necessary to say,' Symons wrote, that the story's sexual content 'represents myself and my adventures during the years when I lived in Fountain Court?' The belief that 'to love a woman is, for an artist, to change one's religion' is 'Trevalga's comment and mine', Symons adds, and suggests that he may already have felt his marriage to Rhoda was a mistake, a view reinforced by the similarity of Rhoda's name to that of the luckless Rana Vaughan.[4]

'A Prelude to Life' recounted something of Symons's early enthusiasm for the piano and his discovery of Chopin. Although he received no formal musical training, he became a useful pianist, one capable of playing through the piano scores of Wagner's *Parsifal* and *Tristan and Isolde*, as well as Richard Strauss's *Feuersnot*.[5] He also possessed a talent for improvisation. His memoirs recall 'a famous and infamous Night House in Paris' where 'As people took turns at the piano, I often took mine; and, with the atrocious heat that went from my head to my heels and to the end of my finger-tips, I made mad music rise out of the notes I touched'. This, he adds, 'maddened the dancers' and made him 'perhaps too often turn my head to observe their furious extravagances.' In a rare moment of modesty, he admitted that 'I never acquired the technique to play a single piece correctly, but I learned to touch the piano as if one were caressing a living being […] it answered me in an intimate and affectionate voice.'[6]

'Christian Trevalga' moves in more rarefied climes, the fiercely-competitive world of London's music schools and concert halls. Some of its details may have been supplied by Rhoda, who had been a violin student at the Royal College of Music, others from Symons's frequent presence at recitals; its treatment of the pressures weighing on solo artists are more convincingly realized than the struggles of an apprentice actress in 'Esther Kahn'. Nevertheless, for all that Symons was a lifelong enthusiast where music was concerned, listening to radio concerts even during the Second World War, he struggled to find a critical language that could comment effectively on its performance. As the essay on Pachmann proves, he often falls back on artistic analogies or accounts of his own reactions to what he hears, and his musical reviews, while often vivid, lack the informed precision of George Bernard Shaw or Robert Hichens. In 'On Writing about Music' (1903), he suggests that 'music is the one absolutely disembodied art, when it is heard, and no more than a proposition of Euclid, when it is written.' 'Music has indeed a language,' he went on, 'but it is a language in which birds and other angels may talk, but out of which we cannot translate their meaning.'[7]

4 Symons, 'The Genesis of Spiritual Adventures'.
5 Symons, 'The Problem of Richard Strauss', *Studies in Seven Arts*, pp. 212–13.
6 Symons, 'Marcelle and Other Parisian Diversions', in *The Memoirs of Arthur Symons*, p. 146.
7 Symons, 'On Writing about Music', *Plays, Acting, and Music*, pp. 139–40.

The story's sexual politics, notably Trevalga's fear of women and the effect they have upon the male creative consciousness are examined at greater length in 'Henry Luxulyan', being much to the fore around the time of Symons's marriage. One wonders whether Rana has something of Rhoda Bowser in being sensitive to art but unable to produce it. In October 1901, Symons published an essay on Keats in the *Monthly Review* that pondered women at length. 'Have you ever thought of the frightful thing it is to shift one's centre?' he asked. 'That is what it is to love a woman. One's nature no longer radiates freely, from its own centre; the centre itself is shifted, is put outside one's self. Up to then, one may have been unhappy, one may have failed, many things may seem to have gone wrong. But at least there is this security: that one's enemies were all outside the gate. With the woman whom one loves one admits all one's enemies.'[8]

Like 'Esther Kahn', 'Christian Trevalga' showed Symons's skill in handling free indirect style, but the musician's story is more fragmentary as befits its narrative of disequilibrium and collapse, particularly in its concluding pages. The notion of the artist who creates something he considers to be extraordinary only for it to be misunderstood, ridiculed, abused, or thought mad by its observers is probably drawn from Balzac's 'Le chef-d'oeuvre Inconnu' ('The Unknown Masterpiece', 1831), though it was a popular topic during the *fin de siècle* as the avant-garde became increasingly antagonistic towards those perceived as philistines. It was a recurrent theme for Henry James, but receives its finest expression in Arthur Machen's *The Hill of Dreams* (wr. 1895–1897, publ. 1907). The jottings salvaged from the asylum are offered as evidence of Trevalga's madness, but their content echoes both the uncomprehending reaction to Balzac's Frenhofer and Symons's own musical essays. As so often in *Spiritual Adventures*, fiction seems to prophesy what Symons would soon endure.

* * *

He had never known what it was to feel the earth solid under his feet.[9] And now, while he waited for the doctor who was to decide whether he might still keep his place in the world, and make what he could of all that remained to him of his life, the past began to come back to him, blurred a little in his memory, and with whole spaces blotted out of it, but in a steady return upon himself, as the past, it is said, comes back to a drowning man at the instant before death. There was that next step to take, the step that frightened him; was it into another, more painful, kind

---

[8] 'John Keats', *Monthly Review* 5 (October 1901), pp. 139–55.
[9] Symons quoted this passage with explicit reference to his breakdown in *Confessions* (1930): 'Was I not really in the situation of my Christian Trevalga?' (*Memoirs*, p. 234). In 'The Genesis of *Spiritual Adventures*', he writes: 'That has been one of my most curious impressions: and that is one reason why I never ventured near the edge of a cliff, as I had the nervous fear that I might fall into the sea'.

of oblivion? He was still an artist, his fingers were still his own; but had the man all gone out of him, the power to live for himself, when his fingers were no longer on the keyboard? That was to be decided; and the past was trying to make its own comment on the situation.

Christian Trevalga was born in a little sea-coast village in Cornwall, and the earliest thing he remembered was the sharp, creaking voice of the sea-gulls, as they swept past him at the edge of the cliff, high up over the sea.[10] He was conscious of it, because it hurt him, sooner than he was conscious of the many voices of the sea, which, all through his childhood, sang out of the midst of all his dreams. Pain always meant more to him than pleasure, though, indeed, he was not always sure if the things that hurt him were not the things he cared for most.

He was thirty-six now, and he had never gone back to the village since he left it, at the age of sixteen, to come to London and try to win a scholarship at the College.[11] His father was a gentleman, who had come down in the world; drink, gambling, and a low kind of debauchery brought him down; and when he came back from Spain in a certain year, sobered, something of a wreck, and married to a slow-witted Spanish woman whom he had found no one knew where, he had only an old-fashioned, untidy, but large and rambling, house on a cliff to live in, on the outskirts of a village, most of which had once belonged to him. Debts and mortgages left just enough to live on uncomfortably; he was not exacting now, and the place was good for an idle, helpless man, who was tired of what he called living, and had taken a late fancy to the open air, and, as soon as the child was old enough, to the companionship of his child. His wife sat indoors all day, crouching over the fire, except when the summer heat was extreme, and then she lay on the grass, under an umbrella. When they sat at table her fingers were always crumbling the bread into tiny crumbs, and often, at tea-time especially, she would take a large slice of bread and mould it into little figures, little nude figures exquisitely proportioned, with all the modelling of the limbs and shoulder-blades.

---

[10] Trevalga is a village on the north Cornish coast between Boscastle and Tintagel, an area Symons knew well and which he described in a number of travel essays, notably 'Cornish Sketches' (October 1904), collected in *Cities and Sea-Coasts and Islands*.

[11] Symons was 36 when he wrote this story.

'The College' is the Royal College of Music (RCM), founded in 1882 by the Prince of Wales (later Edward VII). Its first director was Sir George Grove (1820–1900), who led it until his retirement in 1894 and is best known as the founding editor of *Grove's Dictionary of Music and Musicians*, the first volume of which appeared in 1878. The RCM grew out of the short-lived National Training School for Music (NTSM), established in 1876, which was inspired by the Prince Consort's proposal that scholarships be available for the training of professional musicians. The Royal Academy of Music did not provide training for those seeking to become professional performers. It is therefore significant that Trevalga studied at the RCM — he seeks to interpret and transmit music by others rather than composing it himself.

Sometimes she would do more than a single figure, a little well, for instance, and a woman kneeling at the brink, and leaning over it, with her arms outstretched. She loved the little figures, and talked about them very seriously, criticising their defects, not content with the lines that she had got, seeing them with subtler curves than any she had been able to get. She would like to have kept some of them, but, though she soaked them in milk, they would always crumble away as soon as the bread dried. Christian stared at her when her fingers were busy; he was puzzled, not exactly happy; he generally ran away and left her for his father, who was not so queer, half-absorbed, and busy about nothing.

His father had a great fondness for music, but he could not play any instrument, only whistle. He whistled elaborate tunes, with really a kind of skill.[12] There was a good old Broadwood piano[13] in the house, and, from as long ago as he could remember, Christian had been put on the music-stool, and told to play what his father whistled. The first time he was put there he picked out every note correctly, with one finger. The father caught him up in his exuberant way: 'You will be a great musician, my boy!' he said. The mother nodded over the fire, and looked down at her tiny fingers, which could pick out form as the child, it seemed, could pick out sound.

Christian lived at the piano, playing all the music that he could find in the house, and making up a strange, formless music of his own when there was nothing else to play. His ear, from the first, was faultless; if a poker fell in the fireplace he could tell you the pitch of the note which it sounded. He was always listening, and sounds, with him, often became visible, or at least reflected themselves upon his brain in contours and patterns. The wind at night, when it flapped at the windows with the sound of a sail flapping, seemed to surround the house with realisable forms of sound. The music which he played on the piano made lines, whenever he thought of it; never pictures. His mother, who did not seem to herself to know or care anything about music, sometimes described a little scene which the music he had been playing called up to her, but he could never see things in that way. When he played the first ballade of Chopin, for instance, she saw two lovers, sheltering under trees in a wood, out of the rain

---

[12] Christian's father is in some ways a *déclassé* bohemian unconcerned with social niceties, since whistling was often associated with ungentlemanly behaviour. By the 1890s, 'Madge', the etiquette-advisor of *Truth* magazine, counselled that 'whistling and singing are incompatible with the conduct of a gentleman in the street, though this by no means applies to a quiet country road, where ceremonious bearing is not required.' *Manners for Men* (London: James Bowden, 1897), p. 19.

[13] John Broadwood (1732–1812), a Scottish harpsichord and later piano manufacturer, established his business in London in the mid-1770s. His firm's instruments were renowned throughout the world and played by Mozart, Haydn, Beethoven, Chopin, and Liszt. Broadwood made pianos for every British monarch from George II to George VI. Symons and his wife owned a Broadwood decorated by Edward Burne-Jones.

which was falling around them, and she followed their emotions, as the music interpreted them to her.[14] But he did not understand music like that; what was mathematical in it he saw as pattern, but the emotion came to him in an almost equally abstract way, as musical emotion, beginning and ending in the music itself, and not needing to have any of one's own feelings put into it. It was the music itself that cried and wept, and tore one; the passions of abstract sound.

For, he knew from the beginning, the soul of music is something more than the soul of humanity expressing itself in melody, and the life of music something more than an audible dramatisation of human life. Beethoven, let us say, is angry with the world, Schumann dreams about the roots of a flower; and they sit down to make music under that impulse.[15] Well, the anger will be there, and the flower coming up out of the earth, but the music itself will have forgotten both the dream and the feeling, the moment it begins to speak articulately in sound. It will have its own message, as well as its own language, and you will not be able to write down that message in words, any more than your words can be translated into that language.

And so Christian, with his divination of what music really means, was never able to attach any expressible meaning to the pieces he played, and became tongue-tied if any one asked him questions about them. The emotion of the music, the idea, the feeling there, that was what moved him; and his own personal feelings, apart from some form of music which might translate them into a region where he could recognise them with interest, came to mean less and less to him, until he seemed hardly to have any personal feelings at all. It was natural to him to be kind, people liked him and often imagined that he responded to their liking; but, at many periods of his life, accused him of gross unkindness, or even treachery, and he had not been conscious of the affection or of its betrayal.

And outward things, too, as well as people, meant very little to him, and meant less and less as time went on. What he saw, when he went for long walks with his father, had vanished from his memory before he had returned to the house; it was as if he had been walking through underground passages, with only a little

---

[14] Frederic Chopin, *Ballade No. 1 in G Minor*, Op. 23 (1831). Its dramatic finale has occasionally been compared to a sudden downpour, though the composer never attached a programme to the piece. Chopin was Symons's most beloved composer, and during the 1890s and 1900s he often attended performances of his music. Trevalga is here caught between a 'romantic' conception of natural genius, in which, as Keats said, poetry comes 'as leaves to a tree,' a diligent work ethic, and a distinction between the emotional connotations of music appreciated by audiences and the abstractions understood by musicians themselves. The latter is an early indication of his inability to form meaningful relationships with other people, particularly women.

[15] Ludwig van Beethoven (1770–1827) and Robert Schumann (1810–56), German composers, virtuoso pianists, and key figures in the evolution of Romanticism. Symons had a great fondness for the latter's *Piano Concerto in A minor*, Op. 54 (1845).

faint light on the roadway in front of his feet. He knew all the sea-cries, but never seemed to notice the movement, the colour, of the sea; the sunsets over the sea left him indifferent; he looked, with the others, but said nothing, and seemed to see nothing.[16]

When he had decided that he was going to be a great pianist, and this was when he was about ten, he had settled down to the hard work which that meant, with an enthusiasm so profound and tenacious that it looked like stolidity. They gave him a room at the top of the house, where he could practise without disturbing anybody, and he shut himself in there, until he was dragged out unwillingly to his meals, grudging the time when he had to sit quiet at the table. 'What are you always thinking about?' they would ask him, as he frowned silently over his food; but he was thinking about nothing, he wanted to get back to the bar in the middle of which he had been interrupted. The cadence seemed to hang in space, swinging like a spider, and unable to catch the cornice on the other wall.

He was sixteen when he went up to London for the first time, and it had been arranged that he should take lodgings in Bloomsbury, and try to hear some of the great pianists, and, if possible, get some help privately, before he tried for the scholarship.[17] He got a bedroom at the top of a house in Coptic Street, and hired a piano, which took up most of the space left over by the bed; and he began to go to the shilling seats at concerts, especially when there was any piano music to be heard.[18] Just then several of the most famous pianists were in London; he went to hear them, at first with a horrible apprehension, and then more boldly, as he saw what could be learned from them, and yet seemed to fancy that they, too, might have found something to learn from him. He heard their thunders, and laughed: that was not his idea of the instrument, a thing, in their hands, that could overtop an orchestra playing *fortissimo*. He saw these athletes fight with the poor

---

[16] Symons never valued mimetic art, which imitated the natural or external world, as much as he did that which came from within. He had little interest in Victorian realist fiction, arguing that Symbolism offered a superior mode in which 'the visible world is no longer a reality, and the unseen world no longer a dream.' 'Introduction', *The Symbolist Movement in Literature*, p. 6.

[17] During the early 1880s, London concert-goers could hear such luminaries as Anton Rubinstein (see below), de Pachmann, Clara (Wieck) Schumann (1819–96), the widow of Robert, Liszt's favourite female pupil, Sophie Menter (1846–1918), Charles Hallé (1819–95), founder of the Hallé Orchestra, the exciting Polish pianist Natalia Janotha (1856–1932), and Hans von Bülow (1830–94), also a conductor and critic who had been married to Liszt's daughter, Cosima.

[18] Originally built following the Great Fire of 1666, Coptic Street was known as Duke Street until 1894, when the confusion caused by London's plethora of similarly named thoroughfares became insurmountable. Its new name was inspired by the arrival of a valuable collection of Coptic manuscripts at the nearby British Museum in 1893. Symons's willingness to place fictional characters in topographically exact locales, and even have them meet figures from real life reflects the evolution of realist art during the 1880s and 1890s.

instrument as if they fought with a dangerous wild beast. Some used it as an anvil to hammer sparks out of it; the chords rang and rebounded as if iron had struck iron; it was the new art of attack, and piano-makers were strengthening their defences daily. Some displayed an incredible agility, and invented all sorts of ugly difficulties, in order to overcome them; they reminded him of the dancing girls he had read of, who used, at Roman feasts, to leap head-foremost into the midst of a circle of sword-blades, and dance there on their hands, and leap out again.[19] He knew that he could not do any of these things, as he heard them done; but was that really the way to treat music, or the way to treat the piano?

Christian Trevalga remembered all this as he sat waiting for the doctor in his rooms in Piccadilly; and it came to him like the first act of a play which he was still watching, without knowing how the curtain was to come down. That year in London, the loneliness, poverty, labour of it; the great day of the competition, when he played behind the curtain, and Rubinstein,[20] sitting among the professors, silenced every hesitation with his strong approval; the three years of hard daily work, the painful perfecting of everything that he had sketched out for himself; life, as he had lived it, a queer, silent, sullen, not unattractive boy, among the students in whom he took so little interest; all this passed before him in a single flash of memory. He had gone abroad, at the expense of the college; had travelled in Germany and Austria; had extorted the admiration of Brahms, who had said, 'I hate what you play, and I hate how you play it, but you play the piano!'[21]

---

[19] Few of these stunts are musically valuable, but they are often astonishing in their technical demands and sheer audacity. Liszt transcribed orchestral works both to display his virtuosity and, increasingly, to communicate their meaning and effects in a non-orchestral performance, but his rivals and successors subordinated musical concerns to narcissistic showboating. There are many startling examples in Harold C. Schonberg, *The Great Pianists* (1964). Trevalga (and Symons) are horrified by such vulgarity.

The piano-hammering described here was much associated with the Polish players Theodore Leschetitzsky (1830–1915) and his pupil Jan Paderewski (1860–1941). Symons admired the latter, feeling that 'he gives you thunder as if heard through clouds' (*Plays, Acting, and Music*, p. 160). George Bernard Shaw was less impressed with Leschetitzsky and his followers — Paderewski was a 'harmonious blacksmith who puts a concerto on the piano as upon an anvil', while his mentor's fingers were like 'steel hammers'. *GBS On Music* (London: Penguin, 1962), p. 16.

[20] Anton Grigorevitch Rubinstein (1829–94), Russian virtuoso pianist, teacher, and composer. He was pianist to the Russian court, founded the St Petersburg conservatory in 1862, taught Tchaikovsky composition and performed throughout Europe and the United States, touring England several times between 1841 and 1886. Despite their initial popularity, few of his many compositions have endured.

[21] Johannes Brahms (1833–97), German composer and pianist. Despite writing in classical forms rather than composing programme music, Brahms's work was essentially romantic: he was a fervent admirer of Beethoven, and his First Symphony (1857) is often nicknamed

Tschaikowsky[22] was in Vienna; he had taken a warm personal liking to the unresponsive young Englishman, who seemed to be always frowning, and looking at you distrustfully from under his dark, overhanging eyebrows. It was not to the musician that he was unresponsive, as he was to the musician in Brahms, the German doctor of music in spectacles, that peered out of those learned, intellectual scores. He felt Tschaikowsky with his nerves, all that suffering music without silences, never still and happy, like most other music, at all events sometimes. But the man, when he walked arm in arm with him, seemed excessive, a kind of uneasy responsibility.

Then he had come back to London, lived and worked there, given concerts, made his fame in the world, seen himself triumph, watching his own career with an absolute certainty of being able to do what he wanted. And all the time he had been, as he was that day at the college when he won the scholarship, playing behind a curtain. He knew that on the other side of the curtain was the world, with many things to do besides listening to him, though he could arrest it when he liked, and make it listen; then it went on its way again, and the other things continued to occupy it. Well, for him, where were those other things? They hardly existed. The great men who had given him their friendship, all the people who came to him because they admired him, those who came to him because his playing seemed to speak to them from somewhere inside their own hearts, in the little voices of their blood, the women who, as it seemed, loved him: why was it that he could not be as they were, respond to them in their own language, which was that of humanity itself, admire, like, love them back?

He had tried to find himself, to become real, by falling in love. Women had not found it difficult to fall in love with him; his reticence, his enigmatical reluctance to speak out, the sympathetic sullenness of his face, a certain painful sensibility which shot like distressed nerves across his cheeks and forehead and tugged at the restless corners of his eyelids, seemed to attract them as to something which they could perhaps find out, and then soothe, and put to rest. He had no morals, and was too indifferent to refuse much that was offered to him. When it was a simple adventure of the flesh, he accepted it simply, and, without knowing it, won the reputation of being both sensual and hard-hearted, a sort of coldly passionate creature, that promised everything in the sincerity of

---

'Beethoven's Tenth'. He was strongly antipathetic to the 'new music' associated with Liszt and Wagner, so his response to Trevalga's performance is wholly in character.

[22] Pyotr Ilyich Tchaikovsky (1840–93), Russian pianist, composer, and conductor, known for such tuneful, colourfully scored, and fervidly emotional works as the ballet, *Swan Lake*, Op. 20 (1877) and the *Sixth Symphony in B Minor*, Op. 74 (1893). A homosexual, Tchaikovsky may have deliberately contracted cholera to avoid a scandal — it has also been suggested that he was poisoned in order to hush up sexual indiscretions related to the aristocracy. Writing in the aftermath of the Wilde affair, Symons veils the issue of whether the composer's sexuality has any bearing on his reaction to Trevalga.

one moment, and broke every promise in the sincerity of the next. He did not go out of his way to find a woman who did not seem to suggest herself to him; and when he mistook what was, perhaps, real love for something else, all he wanted, he was genuinely sorry, and, at least once, almost fancied that he was going to answer in key at last.

He had met Rana Vaughan at the college, where she was trying, impossibly, to learn the piano. She had the artist's soul, and long, white fingers, which seemed eager to touch the ivory and ebony of the instrument; only, the soul and the fingers never could agree among themselves, there was some stoppage of the electric current between them. The piano never responded to her, but she knew, better than all the professors, how it should respond; and Trevalga's playing was the only playing she had ever liked. She adored him because he could do what she wanted, above all things, to do; and it was with almost a vicarious ecstasy that she listened to him. She admired, pitied, wanted to help him; exulted in him, became his comrade, perhaps (he wondered?) loved him, or would have loved him if he would have let her. He, who could talk to no one else, could talk to her; and she brought him a warmth and reality of life which he had never known. In her, for a time, he seemed to touch real things; and, for a time, the experience quickened him.

She cared intensely for the one thing he cared for, and not less intensely (and here was the wonder to him) for all the other things that existed outside his interests. For her, life was everything, and everything was a part of life. She would have given everything she had to become a great player; but, if you found your way down to the root of things, her feeling for music was neither more nor less than her feeling for every form of art, and her feeling for art, which was unerring, was the same thing as her feeling for skating or dancing. She got as much pleasure from bending a supple binding in her hand as from reading the poems inside it. She made no selections in life, beyond picking out all the beautiful and pleasant things, whatever they might be. Trevalga studied her with amazement; he felt withered, shrivelled up, in body and soul, beside her magnificent acceptance of the world; she vitalised him, drew him away from himself; and he feared her. He feared women.

To live with a woman, thought Christian, in the same house, the same room with her, is as if the keeper were condemned to live by day and sleep by night in the wild beast's cage. It is to be on one's guard at every minute, to apprehend always the claws behind the caressing softness of their padded coverings, to be continually ready to amuse one's dangerous slave, with one's life for the forfeit. The strain of it, the trial to the nerves, the temper! it was not to be thought of calmly. He looked around him, and saw all the other keepers of these ferocious, uncertain creatures, wearing out their lives in the exciting companionship; and a dread of women took the place of his luxurious indifference, as he imagined himself actually playing the part, too.

It would be, he saw, a conflict of egoisms,[23] and he could not afford to risk his own. Woman, as he saw her, is the beast of prey: rapacious of affection, time, money, all the flesh and all the soul, one's nerves, one's attention, pleasure, duty, art itself! She is the rival of the idea, and she never pardons. She requires the sacrifice of the whole man; nothing less will satisfy her; and, to love a woman is, for an artist, to change one's religion.

Christian had tried honestly to explain himself to Rana, but the girl would not understand him. She cared for his art as much as he did; she would never come between him and his art; she would hate him if he preferred her to his art. She said all that, sincerely; but he shook his head obstinately, a little sadly, knowing that for him possible things were impossible. The mere presence of any one he cared for, all the more if he cared for her a great deal, disturbed him, upset his life. And he must keep his life intact while he might.

After all, he considered, what was he? Caged already, for another kind of slavery, the prisoner of his own fingers, as they worked, independently of himself, mechanically, doing their so many miles of promenade a day over the piano. He was such another as the equilibrist whirling around his fixed bar, or swinging from trapeze to trapeze in the air; a specialist in a particular kind of muscular movement, which in him communicated itself to the mechanism of an instrument of sound. For ever on the trapeze of sound, his life, the life of his reputation, risked whenever he went through his performance before the public; yes, he was only a kind of acrobat, doing tricks with his fingers.

As he looked fairly at all his imprisonments, dreading the worst, the no longer solitary imprisonment, he realised that he had no outlook, that he would never be able to look through the bars. 'I have only felt,' he said to himself, 'I have never thought, and I have felt only one thing very acutely, music.' He was almost frightened as he saw, in a flash, within that narrow limits this one interest, this exercise of one instinct, caged him. Other men were curious about many things; the world existed for them, not only as substance, but as a matter for thought; there were all the destinies of nations and of mankind to think about, and he had never thought about them.[24] He wondered what people meant when they spoke about general interests. Were they a kind of safety valve, for the lack of which he was bound, sooner or later, to come to grief?

Occupied more and more nervously with himself, shutting himself up for days and nights, almost without food, in an agony of attack on some difficulty hardly tangible enough to be put into words, he let Rana Vaughan drift away from him,

---

[23] A familiar concern in 1890s' fiction. See, for example, Crackanthorpe's tale of dysfunctional marriage, 'A Conflict of Egoisms', in *Wreckage* (1893).
[24] Aside from his hysterical opposition to women's suffrage, Symons was generally uninterested in international or domestic politics. He was sympathetic to elements of Yeats's nationalism but tended to see the artist as independent of the state, and free of responsibilities toward it.

with an unavowed sense of failure, of having lost something which he could not bring himself to take, and which might yet have saved him. She parted from him, at the last, angrily, her pity worn out, her admiration stained with contempt. He remembered the look of her face, flushed, indignant, as, withdrawn now wholly into herself, she said good-bye for the last time. With her went his last hold on the world.

Gradually sound began to take hold of him, like a slave who has overcome his master. The sensation of sound presented itself to him continually, not in the form of memory, nor as the suggestion of a composition, but in a disquieting way, like some invisible companion, always at one's side, whispering into one's ears.[25] He was not always able to distinguish between what he actually heard, a noise in the street, for instance, which came to him for the most part with the suggestion of a cadence, which his ear completed as if it had been the first note of a well-known tune, and what he seemed to hear, through noise or silence, in some region outside reality. 'So long as I can distinguish,' he said to himself, 'between the one and the other, I am safe; the danger will be when they become indistinguishable.'

He had realised a certain danger, always. He felt that he was a piece of mechanism which was not absolutely to be trusted. There had been something wrong from the beginning; the works did not wear evenly; one part or another was bound to use itself up before its time; and then, well, not even a shock would be needed to set everything out of order: it was only a question of time.

He began to watch himself more closely, to watch for the enemy; and now a kind of expectant uneasiness came of itself to suggest otherwise imperceptible pains and troubles of sound. He was always listening, with a frequent precipitation of pulses, to nothing, to something about to come, to the fancy of music. The days dragged, and yet some feverish idea seemed always to be hurrying him along; he was restless whenever his fingers were not on the keys of the piano.

One day, at a concert, while he was playing one of Chopin's studies, something in the curve of the music, which he had always seen as a wavy line, going on indefinitely in space, spreading itself out elastically, but without ever forming a pattern, seemed to become almost externally visible, just above the level of the strings on the open top of the piano.[26] It was like grey smoke, forming and unforming as if it boiled up softly out of the pit where the wires were coiled up. It was so distinct that he shut his eyes for a moment, to see if it would be there

---

[25] This conceit may have been recalled by Eliot in *The Waste Land* (1922): 'Who is the third who walks always beside you? [...] who is that on the other side of you?' (ll. 359, 365).

[26] Chopin composed two sets of studies, Op. 10 (1829–32) and Op. 25 (1832–36). Each comprises 12 virtuoso pieces which embed the confrontation of a technical challenge within music of more 'poetic' character. They therefore contain both elements of Trevalga's character, though unlike him, they manage to fuse the two to perfection.

when he opened them again. It was still there, getting darker in colour, and more distinct. He looked out of the corner of his eyes, to see if the people sitting near him had noticed anything; but the people sitting near him had their eyes fixed on his fingers, from which he seemed, as usual, to be quite detached; they evidently saw nothing. He smiled to himself, half apologetically; the piece had come to an end, and he was bowing to the applause; he walked boldly off the platform.

When he came back to play again, he looked nervously at the top of the piano, but there was nothing to be seen. He sat down, and bent over the keyboard, and his hands began to run to and fro softly. When he looked up he saw what he was playing as clearly as he could have seen the notes if they had been there: but the wavy line was upright now, and drifted upwards swiftly, vanishing at a certain point; it swayed to and fro like a snake beating time to the music of the snake-charmer; and he looked at it as if it understood him, and nodded his head to it, to show that he understood.[27] By this time it seemed to him quite natural, and he forgot that there had ever been a time when he had not seen the music like that.

On his way home after the concert, it occurred to him that something unusual had happened, but he could not remember what it was. He dined by himself, and after dinner went out into the streets, and walked in the midst of people, as he liked to do, that he might take hold of something real.[28] But he could not concentrate his mind, he seemed somehow to be slipping away from himself, dissolving into an uneasy vacancy. The people did not seem, very real that night: he stopped for a long time at the corner of the pavement, near Piccadilly Circus, and tried to see what was going on around him. It was quite useless. The confusing lights, the crush and hurry of figures wrapped in dark clothes, the noise of the horses' hoofs striking the stones, the shouts of omnibus-conductors and newsboys, all the surge and struggle of horrible exterior forces, seeming to be tightened up into an inextricable disorder, but pushing out with a hundred arms this way and that, making some sort of headway against the opposition of things, brought over him a complete bewilderment. 'I can see no reason,' he said to himself, 'why I am here rather than there, why these atoms which know one another so little, or have lost some recognition of themselves, should coalesce in this particular body, standing still where all is in movement.' He looked at the horses pulled back roughly at a cross-current, and tossing back their heads as the hind-legs grew convulsively

---

[27] The materialization of music is one of the hallucinations that torments Septimus Smith in Virginia Woolf's *Mrs Dalloway* (1925). Symons was plagued by serpent-related nightmares (see 'A Prelude to Life'), and had watched snake-charming acts in London and Parisian theatres. He once told Yeats that he was in love with a 'serpent-charmer,' a new sensation he briefly found exhilarating.

[28] For Symons and the Baudelairean idea of the 'crowd bath', see 'A Prelude to Life'.

rigid, and he felt sorry for them, and wondered why the driver was driving them and why they were not driving the driver. Someone ran violently against him, and apologised. The shock did nothing to wake him up; he noticed it, waited for the effect, and was surprised that no effect came. 'Decidedly,' he said to himself, 'I am losing my sense of material things, for, slight as it always has been, I have always resented being pushed into the mud.'

He went home, and opened the piano; but he was afraid of it, and shut it up, and went to bed. He slept well, but he dreamed that he was on the island of Portland, among the convicts; there was a woman with him, who seemed to be Rana, and they had tea at a farm, high up among trees; and then he went away and forgot her, and found himself in a lonely place where there were a number of cucumber-frames on the ground, and several convicts were laid out asleep in each, half-naked, and packed together head to heel.[29] Then he remembered the woman, and went back to the farm where he had left her; but she was no longer there, she had gone to look for him, and he thought she must have lost her way among the convicts. He was greatly distressed, but he found he was walking with her along Piccadilly, and she told him that she had been waiting for him a long time in an omnibus which had stopped at the corner of the Circus.

When he awoke in the morning he was relieved to find that his brain seemed to have become quite clear, surprisingly clear, as if the fog that had been gathering about him had lifted; and he sat at the piano playing for many hours, and when he had finished playing he heard still more ravishing sounds in the air, a music which was like what Chopin might have written in Paradise. Tears of delight came into his eyes; he sat listening in an ecstasy. Now everything had come right; all the trouble and confusion had gone out of the sounds; they no longer teased him with their muttering, coming and going elusively; they were all about him, they flooded the air, they were like pure joy, speaking at last its own language.

And for days after that he went about with a strange, secret smile on his face, more than reconciled to his new companion, enamoured of him; and at last he could keep the secret no longer, but had to tell everyone he met of this miracle that now went with him wherever he went. When he stopped listening, and played the music that he had known before this new music spoke to him, he seemed to play better than he had ever played before. Only, when he had stopped playing, he sank back sleepily into his ecstatic oblivion, not distinguishing between those he talked with in his dream (the Chopin out of Paradise) and the few remaining friends, who now came about him pityingly, and tried to do what they could for him. Their coming awakened him a little; he awoke enough to realise that they thought him mad; and it was with a very

---

[29] Portland Prison, on the Isle of Portland, Dorset, opened in 1848. It is now a Young Offenders' Institution.

lucid fear that he waited now for the doctor who was to decide finally whether he might still keep his place in the world.

Five years later, when Christian Trevalga died in the asylum at ——, some loose scraps of paper were found, on which he had jotted down a few disconnected thoughts about music. They are, perhaps, worth giving, for they are more explicit than he ever cared, or was able, to be when he was quite sane; and, fragmentary as they are, may help to complete one's picture of the man.

'It has been revealed to me that there is but one art, but many languages through which men speak it. When the angels talk among themselves, their speech is art; for they do not talk as men do, to discuss matters or to relate facts, but to express either love or wisdom.[30] It is partly the beauty of their voices which causes whatever they say to assume a form of beauty. Music comes nearer than any other of the human languages to the sound of these angelic voices. But painting is also a language, and sculpture, and poetry; only these have more of the atmosphere of the earth about them, and are not so clear. I have heard pictures which spoke to me melodiously, and I have listened to the faultless rhythm of statues; but it was as an Englishman who knows French and Italian quite well follows a conversation in those languages. He has to substitute one sound for another in his mind.[31]

'When I am playing the piano I am always afraid of hurting a sound. I believe that sounds are living beings, flying about us like motes in the air, and that they suffer if we clutch them roughly. Have you ever tried to catch a butterfly without brushing the dust off its wings? Every time I press a note I feel as if I were doing that, and it is an agony to me. I am certain that I have hurt fewer sounds than any other pianist.[32]

---

[30] A remark probably inspired by Symons's reading of William Blake, the poet, artist, and mystic he and Yeats had been studying since the mid-1890s. Some of Blake's drawings appeared in *The Savoy* and helped to ensure that it was not stocked by W. H. Smith, an act which hastened the journal's collapse. For further details of Symons's interest in Blake, see 'The Death of Peter Waydelin'.

[31] Symons spoke French and Italian well, and like Trevalga, searched for a way of melding differing forms of art. In *London: A Book of Aspects*, he described this as 'gradually trying to paint, or to set to music, to paint in music, perhaps, those sensations which London awakened in me.' *Cities and Sea-Coasts and Islands*, p. 199.

[32] The continued strengthening of the concert grand piano encouraged its abuse by performers and would also see its redefinition as a percussion instrument by the likes of Béla Bartók (1881–1945). Symons preferred a less vigorous style in which the instrument was caressed rather than hit, an approach exemplified by Pachmann.

'Chopin's music screams under its breath, like a patient they are operating upon in the hospital. There are flowers on the pillow, great sickly pungent flowers, and he draws in their perfume with the same breath that is jarred down below by the scraping sound of the little saw.[33]

'Chopin always treats the piano like a gentleman. He never gives it a note that it cannot sing, he is always scrupulous towards its whims, he indulges it like a spoilt child. Schumann comes back cloudily out of a dream, and sets down the notes as he heard them, upon paper; then he leaves the piano to make the best of it.

'Most modern music is a beggar for pity. The musician tries to show us how he has suffered, and how hopeless he is. He sets his toothache and his heartache to music, putting those sufferings into the music, without remembering that sounds have their own agonies, which alone they can express in a perfect manner. He forgets also that joy is the natural speech of music, and that when he comes to sound for the expression of his joy he is asking it to sing out of its own heart.[34]

'I remember I once heard a Siamese band playing on board the yacht of the King of Siam. It played its own music, of which I could make nothing; and also passages from our operas. How can the same ears hear in two different ways? And how far behind these Eastern musicians are we, who cannot even understand their music when it is played to us! Some day someone will dig down to the roots, and turn up music as it is before it is tamed to the scale.[35]

---

[33] This blends Baudelaire, the hothouse scenes of Huysmans' *A Rebours* (*Against Nature*, 1884) and perhaps the then unpublished novel by Swinburne, issued posthumously as *Lesbia Brandon* (1952). It thus links the story with the 'decadence' with which Symons had been associated during the 1890s, a connection he worked hard to repudiate.

[34] A possible recollection of Robert Burns's claim, 'For my own part I never had the least thought or inclination of turning Poet till I got heartily in Love, and then Rhyme and Song were, in a manner, the spontaneous language of my heart.' (First Commonplace Book, 1783).

[35] A Javanese gamelan orchestra had caused a sensation at the Paris Exposition in 1889, profoundly influencing the young Claude Debussy (1862–1918) who was more than capable of hearing 'in two different ways'. Symons and Trevalga, by contrast, find non-Western music bewildering. Symons admired Javanese dancers on his first trip to Paris in September 1889, but evoked their accompanying music as 'the clang of metal, beaten drums, | Dull, shrill, continuous, disquieting' ('Javanese Dancers', *The Book of the Rhymers' Club*, 1892).

'It is strange, I never used to think about music: I accepted it by an act of faith; I was too near it to look all round it. But lately, I do not know why, I have been forced to think out many of the things which I used to know without thinking. It all comes to the same thing in the end; one form or another of knowledge; and does it matter if I can explain it to you or not?'

~

The Childhood of Lucy Newcome

'The Childhood of Lucy Newcome' is the first of three stories about a young woman's drift into prostitution which Symons considered publishing as a longer work. He seems to have envisaged a deliberately fragmented and elliptical novel which offered perspectives on the main character's sensations and experiences rather than a more formally plotted realist schema. Symons proposed:

> A novel in chapters, à la Goncourt, some of them merely the noting of a significant sensation — as her horror of being in the house by herself, or her favourite reading. Note them from time to time, separately, as they come to my knowledge. Her childhood. Try first a chapter or two on her desertion after the birth of her child, the laundry, the old man, the baby's death. Give up the idea of writing entirely from the facts, and make it a living thing, a study of character, studied of course after the real person. Get what details I can, and then work on them. Show a woman affectionate, slightly but not greatly sensual, capable of loving but not with passion, and easily changing, carrying her home instincts with her wherever she goes. Quite a new study of a courtesan as a very average human being, singularly without bad instincts. Pictures of average life going on in that particular circle, with all its incidents.[1]

While his contemporaries negotiated with the naturalism of Zola and Maupassant, Symons was generally more attracted to the more detached style of Flaubert and the Goncourt brothers, whom he praised in 'The Decadent Movement in Literature' and in a number of other essays between 1894 and 1896.[2] The project was obviously of great importance to Symons as he considered publishing it on several occasions over a forty year period, and also incorporated elements of it into his unpublished memoirs.

'The Childhood of Lucy Newcome' was first published in the final issue of *The Savoy* in December 1896. The journal had been ailing since the autumn, and

---

[1] Symons, 'Original Preface' to 'Pages From the Life of Muriel Broadbent', p. 1.
[2] See 'The Goncourts' (*Saturday Review*, 29 December 1894, pp. 701–02), his obituary of Edmond de Goncourt (*The Athenæum*, 25 July 1896, p. 129), and 'A Literary Causerie: On Edmond de Goncourt', *The Savoy* No. 5 (September 1896), pp. 85–87.

Symons provided the entire text for the concluding number, probably because Leonard Smithers, the magazine's publisher, was no longer able to pay contributors their agreed rates. Pieces by Crackanthorpe and Edgar Jepson were returned despite having been accepted earlier in the year, and it may be that Symons included 'The Childhood of Lucy Newcome' to fill the pages freed up by the excision of these contributions. The final issue of *The Savoy* also included a tribute to Pater which recycled material from Symons's 1887 review of *Imaginary Portraits*. 'The Childhood' is far closer to Pater's methods than 'Pages from the Life of Lucy Newcome', suggesting it was written later and that it may not even have been composed when the first 'Lucy' story appeared that spring.

The three 'Lucy Newcome' stories were probably composed between late 1894 and the end of 1898, with the first two being published in *The Savoy*. Symons was therefore spared editorial compromises, and was also allowed greater latitude than he would have been granted in some of the journal's rivals. Alan Johnson notes how portions of the unpublished 'Life and Adventures' made their way into early drafts of 'Henry Luxulyan', with Lucy becoming 'Dorothie Lister' and playing the role played by 'Clare' in the final version. After the publication of *Spiritual Adventures* however, Symons abandoned the novel for a decade, returning to it only in 1915, when he was about to republish 'The Goncourts' in *Figures of Several Centuries*. He and his patron, John Quinn, made an unsuccessful attempt to get it into print despite Thomas Hardy advising against the idea. It was then, as Johnson says, 'defictionalized' and incorporated within Symons's planned volume of memoirs, though its frank treatment of prostitution drew objections from Jonathan Cape's reader as late as 1933. Symons was still not finished with the project, seeking a publisher for 'The Life and Adventures' under the new title, 'A Strange Woman's Story', but without success.[3]

The life of the 'fallen woman' was a staple of Victorian fiction and art, though by the 1890s the stock narrative of earlier periods had moved away from cautionary tale into the morally ambivalent realm of novels such as *Tess of the D'Urbervilles* (1891) and Moore's *Esther Waters* (1894), and shorter fiction such as Crackanthorpe's 'Battledore and Shuttlecock' (*Sentimental Studies*, 1895). To a certain extent, Symons profited from this attitudinal shift, and the increasing frankness that accompanied it, for it licensed an ambitious attempt to represent the consciousness of a sexually active single woman. This is, however, a daunting challenge for even the most experienced male novelist, and there are times when, for all his professed determination not to 'write entirely from the facts', Symons has nothing else to fall back upon.

The first 'Lucy Newcome' story is another version of 'A Prelude to Life', with the focus on Lucy's early 'sensations and impressions' instead of the young

---

[3] Alan Johnson, 'Symons' "Novel à la Goncourt"', *Journal of Modern Literature* 9 (1981), pp. 50–64 (p. 52).

writer's. It shows Lucy's tastes, outlook, and attitudes, and the effect on her of significant events. Much of it came directly from Muriel herself. 'I invented almost nothing,' Symons recalled, 'except here and there some poignant situation.'[4] After such a start to Lucy's life, it is something of a shock to see her in the squalid circumstances documented in subsequent episodes, but by publishing 'Pages from the Life' before 'The Childhood', and by never succeeding in publishing the final instalment at all, Symons was unable to present the novel in the form he would have wished. It is hoped that the present edition will rectify this to some extent, and allow the three stories to be read in conjunction.

* * *

The house which Lucy Newcome remembered as her home, the only home she ever had, was a small house, hardly more than a cottage, with a little, neat garden in front of it, and a large, untidy garden at the back. There was a low wooden palisade cutting it off from the road, which, in that remote suburb of the great town, had almost the appearance of a road in the country. The house had two windows, one on each side of the door, and above that three more windows, and attics above that. The windows on each side of the door were the windows of the two sitting-rooms; the kitchen, with its stone floor, its shining rows of brass things around the walls, its great dresser, was at the back. It was through the kitchen that you found your way into the big garden, where the grass was always long and weedy and ill-kept, and so all the pleasanter for lying on; and where there were a few alder-trees, a pear-tree on which the pears never seemed to thrive, for it was quite close to Lucy's bedroom window, a flower-bed along the wall, and a great, old sundial, which Lucy used to ponder over when the shadows came and stretched out their long fingers across it. The garden, when she thinks of it now, comes to her often as she saw it one warm Sunday evening, walking to and fro there beside her mother, who was saying how good it was to be well again, or better: this was not long before she died; and Lucy had said to herself, What a dear little mother I have, and how young, and small, and pretty she looks in that lilac bodice with the bright belt round the waist! Lucy had been as tall as her mother when she was ten, and at twelve she could look down on her quite protectingly.

Her father she but rarely saw; but it was her father whom she worshipped, whom she was taught to worship. The whole house, she, her mother, and Linda, the servant, who was more friend than servant (for she took no wages, and when she wanted anything, asked for it), all existed for the sake of that wonderful, impracticable father of hers; it was for him they starved, it was to him they looked

---

4 Symons, 'The Genesis of Spiritual Adventures'.

for the great future which they believed in so implicitly, but scarcely knew in what shape to look for. She knew that he had come of gentlefolk, in another county, that he had been meant for the Church, and, after some vague misfortune at Cambridge, had married her mother, who was but seventeen, and of a class beneath him, against the will of his relations, who had cast him off just as, at twenty-one, he had come into a meagre allowance from the will of his grandfather. He had been the last of eleven children, born when his mother was fifty years of age, and he had inherited the listless temperament of a dwindling stock.[5] He had never been able to do anything seriously, or even to make up his mind quite what great thing he was going to do. First he had found a small clerkship, then he had dropped casually upon the post which he was to hold almost to the time of his death, as secretary to some Assurance Society, whose money it was his business to collect. He did the work mechanically; at first, competently enough; but his heart was in other things. Lucy was never sure whether it was the great picture he was engaged upon, or the great book, that was to make all the difference in their fortunes. She never doubted his power to do anything he liked; and it was one of her privileges sometimes to be allowed to sit in his room (the sitting-room on the left of the door, where it was always warmer and more comfortable than anywhere else in the house), watching him at his paints or his manuscripts, with great serious eyes that sometimes seemed to disquiet him a little; and then she would be told to run away and not worry mother.

The little mother, too, she saw less of than children mostly see of their mothers; for her mother was never quite well, and she would so often be told: 'You must be quiet now, and not go into your mother's room, for she has one of her headaches,' that she gradually accustomed herself to do without anybody's company, and then she would sit all alone, or with her doll, who was called Arabella, to whom she would chatter for hours together, in a low and familiar voice, making all manner of confidences to her, and telling her all manner of stories. Sometimes she would talk to Linda instead, sitting on the corner of the kitchen fender; but Linda was not so good a listener, and she had a way of going into the scullery, and turning on a noisy stream of water, just at what ought to have been the most absorbing moment of the narrative.

Lucy was a curious child, one of those children of whom nurses are accustomed to say that they will not make old bones. She was always a little pale, and she would walk in her sleep; and would spend whole hours almost without moving, looking vaguely and fixedly into the air: children ought not to dream like that!

---

[5] *Fin-de-siècle* fiction abounds in questions of heredity and depictions of decayed or corrupted stock. For an aesthete such as Symons, the opening section of *A Rebours* was of particular importance, though in this story, there may also be echoes of *Tess of the D'Urbervilles*.

She did not know, herself, very often, what she was dreaming about; it seemed to her natural to sit for hours doing nothing.

Often, however, she knew quite well what she was dreaming about; and first of all she was dreaming about herself. Really, she would explain if you asked her, she did not belong to her parents at all; she belonged to the fairies; she was a princess; there was another, a great mother, who would come some day and claim her. And this consciousness of being really a princess was one of the joys of her imagination.[6] She had composed all the circumstances of her state, many times over, indeed, and always in a different way. It was the heightening she gave to what her mother had taught her: that she was of a better stock than the other children who lived in the other small houses all round, and must not play with them, or accept them as equals. That was to be her consolation if she had to do without many of the things she wanted, and to be shabbily dressed (out of old things of her mother's, turned and cut and pieced together), while perhaps some of those other children, who were not her equals, had new dresses.

And then she would make up stories about the people she knew, the ladies to whom she paid a very shifting devotion, very sincere while it lasted. One of her odd fancies was to go into the graveyard which surrounded the church, and to play about in the grass there, or, more often, gather flowers and leaves, and carry them to a low tomb, and sit there, weaving them into garlands. These garlands she used to offer to the ladies whose faces she liked, as they passed in and out of the church. The strange little girl who sat among the graves, weaving garlands, and who would run up to them so shyly, and with so serious a smile, offering them her flowers, seemed to these ladies rather a disquieting little person, as if she, like her flowers, had a churchyard air about her.

Blonde, tall, slim, delicately-complexioned, with blue eyes and a wavering, somewhat sensuous mouth, the child took after her father; and he used to say of her sometimes, half whimsically, that she was bound to be like him altogether, bound to go to the bad.[7] The big, brilliant man, who had made so winning a

---

[6] Such beliefs would be examined at length by Sigmund Freud in 'Family Romances' (1909), where he suggests that 'a quite peculiarly marked imaginative activity is one of the essential characteristics of neurotics and also of all comparatively highly gifted people.' 'Family Romances', in *The Standard Edition of the Complete Psychological Works of Sigmund Freud*, Volume IX (1906–1908), p. 237.

[7] This description is reminiscent of Symons himself. In *Everyman Remembers* (London: J. M. Dent, 1931), Ernest Rhys remembered the young Symons as 'almost pretty to look upon — rosy cheeks, light brown hair, blue eyes, and peculiarly white skin' (p. 110). Yvette Guilbert's *The Song of My Life* (London: Harrap, 1929) recalled how Symons in his late twenties had 'fair hair plastered on his temples, a narrow thin face, rather pink on the cheekbones, thick, rather sensual, very red lips, wet and shiny; restless, darting eyes, now looking blue, now black'. She added that 'when he spoke and tried to overcome his terrible shyness he would blush like a young girl' (p. 313).

failure of life, so popular always, and the centre of a little ring of intellectual people, used sometimes to let her stay in the room of an evening, while he and his friends drank their ale and smoked pipes and talked their atheistical philosophy. These friends of her father used to pet her, because she was pretty; and it was one of them who paid her the first compliment she ever had, comparing her face to a face in a picture. She had never heard of the picture, but she was immensely flattered; for she did not think a painter would ever paint anyone who was not very pretty. She listened to their conversation, much of which she could not understand, as if she understood every word of it; and she wondered very much at some of the things they said. Her mother was a Catholic, and, though religion was rarely referred to, had taught her some little prayers; and it puzzled her that all this could be true, and yet that clever people should have doubts of it. She had always learned that cleverness (book-learning, or any disinterested journeying of the intellect) was the one important thing in the world. Her father was clever: that was why everything must bow to him. There must be something in it, then, if these clever people, if her father himself, doubted of God, of heaven and hell, of the good ordering of this world. And she announced one day to the pious servant, who had told her that God sees everything, that when she was older she meant to get the better of God, by building a room all walls and no windows, within which she would be good or bad as she pleased, without his seeing her.

Lucy was never sent to school, like most children; that was partly because they were very poor, but more because her father had always intended to teach her himself, on a new and liberal scheme of education, which seemed to him better than the education you get in schools.[8] And sometimes, for as much as a few weeks together, he would set her lessons day by day, and be excessively severe with her, not permitting her to make a single slip in anything he had given her to learn. He would even punish her sometimes, if she still failed to learn some lesson perfectly; and that seemed to her a mortal indignity; so that one day she rushed out into the garden, and climbed up into a tree, and then called out, tremulously but triumphantly: 'If you promise not to punish me, I'll come down; but if you don't, I'll throw myself down!'

She always disliked learning lessons, and those fits of scrupulousness on his part were her great dread. They did not occur often; and between whiles he was very lenient, ready to get out of the trouble of teaching her on the slightest excuse; only too glad if she did not bother him by coming to say her lessons. Both were

---

[8] There was considerable opposition to the series of Education Acts which overhauled the English school system from 1870 onwards. Teaching was often considered (by conservatives and artistic radicals alike) to be overly reliant on the rote-learning of facts, and was also felt to privilege the acquisition of basic practical skills of reading, writing, and numeracy over creativity, interpretation, and analysis.

quite happy then; she to be allowed to sit in his room with her lesson-book on her knees, dreaming; he not to be hindered in the new sketch he was making or the notes he was preparing for that great book of the future, perhaps out of one of those old, calf-covered books which he used to bring back from second-hand shops in the town, and which Lucy used to admire for their ancient raggedness, as they stood in shelves round the room, brown and broken-backed.

And then if she had not her geography to learn by heart (those lists of capes and rivers and the population of countries, which she could indeed learn by heart, but which represented nothing to her of the actual world itself) she had of course all the more time for her own reading.[9] When she had outgrown that old fancy about the fairies, and about being a princess, she cared nothing for stories of adventure; but little for the material wonders of the 'Arabian Nights'; somewhat more for the *Pilgrim's Progress*,[10] in which she always lingered over that passage of the good people through the bright follies of Vanity Fair; but most of all for certain quiet stories of lovers, in which there was no improbable incident, and no too fantastical extravagance of passion; but a quiet probable fidelity, plenty of troubles, and of course a wedding at the end.[11] One book, 'The Story of Mrs Jardine,' she was never tired of reading; and she liked almost all the stories in the bound volumes of the *Argosy*.[12] Then there was a little book of poetical selections; she never could remember the name of it afterwards; and there were the songs of

---

[9] 'I could never learn geography or draw a map,' Symons recalls in 'A Prelude to Life'.

[10] *The Pilgrim's Progress from This World to That Which Is to Come; Delivered under the Similitude of a Dream* (1678) is a Christian allegory by John Bunyan (1628–88). Vanity Fair is a frivolous, idly amusing place established by Christian's enemies, the fiendish Beelzebub, Apollyon, and Legion, in the town of Vanity. It lasts all year round and sells houses, lands, trades, places, honours, preferments, titles, countries, kingdoms, lusts, pleasures, and delights of all kinds. Christian's fellow pilgrim, Faithful, is there burned to death by Judge Hategood. *Vanity Fair* is also the title of Thackeray's satirical novel of nineteenth-century high society (1847–48), whose anti-heroine, Becky Sharp, leads a frequently disreputable life. Ironically, Lucy may take her surname from Thackeray's sentimental account of the Victorian bourgeoisie, *The Newcomes* (1855).

[11] *Arabian Nights Entertainments* or *The Thousand and One Nights* is a collection of Egyptian, Syrian, Persian, and perhaps Indian tales which began to take shape during the fourteenth century. It was translated into French during the early eighteenth century; selections from this appeared in English throughout the eighteenth and nineteenth centuries, although a substantial English version did not appear until the late 1830s. The first complete, unexpurgated English versions did not appear until John Payne produced a limited edition for the Villon Society (1882–84) and Sir Richard Burton produced another subscription-only version between 1885–88.

[12] 'The Story of Mrs Jardine' is probably *Young Mrs Jardine* (1879) by Dinah Craik (1826–87).
  The Argosy: A Magazine of Tales, Travels, Essays and Poems was a monthly magazine that ran from 1865 (the year of Symons's birth) to 1901. It was owned and edited by the sensation novelist Mrs Henry Wood from 1867 to 1887, and was a vehicle for her fiction throughout this period. An argosy is a large and abundantly-laden merchant ship.

Thomas Moore, and, above all, there was Mrs Hemans.[13] Those gentle and lady-like poems 'of the affections,' with their nice sentiments, the faded ribbons of their second-hand romance, seemed to the child like a beautiful glimpse into the real, tender, not too passionate world, where men and women loved magnanimously, and had heroic sufferings, and died, perhaps, but for a great love, or a great cause, and always nobly. She thought that the ways of the world blossomed naturally into Casabiancas and Gertrudes and Imeldas, who were faithful to death, and came into their inheritance of love or glory beyond the grave.[14] She used to wonder if she, too, like Costanza, had a 'pale Madonna brow'; and she wished nothing more fervently than to be like those saintly and affectionate creatures, always so beautiful, and so often (what did it matter?) unfortunate, who took poison from the lips of their lovers, and served God in prison, and came back afterwards, spirits, out of the angelical rapture of heaven, to be as some rare music, or subtle perfume, in the souls of those who had loved them. Many of these poems were about death, and it seemed natural to her, at that time, to think much about death, which she conceived as a quite peaceful thing, coming to you invisibly out of the sky, and which she never associated with the pale faces and more difficult breathing of those about her. She had never known her mother to be quite well; and when, on her twelfth birthday, her mother called her into her room, where she lay in bed now so often, and talked to her more solemnly than she had ever talked before, saying that if she became very ill, too ill to get up at all, Lucy was to look after her father as carefully as she herself had looked after him, always to look after him, and never let him want for anything; even then it did not seem to the child that this meant more than a little more illness; and it was so natural for people to be ill.

And so, after all, the end came almost suddenly; and the first great event of her childhood took her by surprise. The gentle, suffering woman had been failing for many months, and when, one afternoon in early March, the doctor told her to take to her bed at once, life seemed to ebb out of her daily, with an almost visible haste to be gone.[15] Whenever she was allowed to come in, Lucy would curl herself up on the foot of the bed, never taking her eyes off the face of the dying woman, who was for the most part unconscious, muttering unintelligible words sometimes, in a hoarse voice, broken by coughs, and breathing, all the time, in great, heavy breaths, which made a rattle in her throat. When she was in the next

---

[13] Thomas Moore (1779–1852), Irish poet and songwriter, famous for his *Irish Melodies* (1808–34) including lyrics such as 'The Harp that once through Tara's Halls' and 'The Last Rose of Summer'. Felicia Hemans (1793–1835), English poet and translator.

[14] 'Casabianca', better known by its opening line, 'The boy stood on the burning deck,' appears in Hemans's *The Forest Sanctuary* (1829). 'Gertrude, or Fidelity till Death', 'Imelda', and 'Constanza' are from her *Records of Women* (1828).

[15] Lydia Symons, Arthur's mother, died in Willesden on 16 March, 1896.

room, Lucy could hear this monotonous sound going on, almost as plainly as in the room itself. It was that sound that frightened her, more than anything; for, when she was sitting on the bed, watching the face lying among the pillows (drawn, and glazed with a curious flush, as it was), it seemed, after all, only as if her mother was very, very ill, and as if she might get better, for the lips were still red, and sucked in readily all the spoonsful of calves-foot jelly, and brandy and water, which were really just keeping her alive from hour to hour. On Friday night, in the middle of the night, as Lucy was sleeping quietly, she felt, in her dream, as it seemed to her, two lips touch her cheek, and, starting awake, saw her father standing by the bedside. He told her to get up, put on some of her things, and come quietly into the next room. She crept in, huddled up in a shawl, very pale and trembling, and it seemed to her that her mother must be a little better, for she drew her breath more slowly and not quite so loudly. One arm was lying outside the clothes, and every now and then this arm would raise itself up, and the hand would reach out, blindly, until the nurse, or her father, took it and laid it back gently in its place. They told her to kiss her mother, and she kissed her, crying very much, but her mother did not kiss her, or open her eyes; and as she touched her hair, which was coming out from under her cap, she felt that it was all damp, but the lips were quite dry and warm. Then they told her to go back to bed, but she clung to the foot of the bed, and refused to go, and the nurse said, 'I think she may stay.' The tears were running down both her cheeks, but she did not move, or take her eyes off the face on the pillow. It was very white now, and once or twice the mouth opened with a slight gasp; once the face twitched, and half turned on the pillow; she had to wait before the next breath came; then it paused again; then, with an effort, there was another breath; then a long pause, a very slow breath, and no more. She was led round to kiss her mother again on the forehead, which was quite warm; but she knew that her mother was dead, and she sobbed wildly, inconsolably, as they led her back to her own room, where, after they had left her, and she could hear them moving quietly about the house, she lay in bed trying to think, trying not to think, wondering what it was that had really happened, and if things would all be different now.

And with her mother's death it seemed as if her own dream-life had come suddenly to an end, and a new, more desolate, more practical life had begun, out of which she could not look any great distance. After the black darkness of those first few days; the coming of the undertakers, the hammering down of the coffin, the slow drive to the graveside, the wreath of white flowers which she shed, white flower by white flower, upon the shining case of wood lying at the bottom of a great pit, in which her mother was to be covered up to stay there for ever; after those first days of merely dull misery, broken by a few wild outbursts of tears, she accepted this new life into which she had come, as she accepted the black clothes which Linda the servant, now more a friend than ever, had had made for her. Her father could no longer bear to sleep in the room in which his wife had died, so

Lucy gave up her own room to him, and moved into the room that had been her mother's; and it seemed to bring her closer to her mother to sleep there. She thought of her mother very often, and very sadly, but the remembrance of those almost last words to her, those solemn words on her twelfth birthday, that she was to look after her father as her mother had looked after him, and never let him want for anything, helped her to meet every day bravely, because every day brought some definite thing for her to do. She felt years and years older, and quietly ready for whatever was now likely to happen.

For a little while she saw more of her father, for they had their mid-day meal together now, and she used to come and sit at the table when he was having his nine o'clock meat supper, with which he had always indulged himself, even when there was very little in the house for the others. He still took it, and his claret with it, which the doctor had ordered him to take; but he took it with scantier and scantier appetite; talking less over his wine, and falling into a strange and brooding listlessness. During his wife's illness he had let his affairs drift; and the society of which he was the secretary had overlooked it, as far as they could, on account of his trouble. But now he attended to his duties less than ever; and he was reminded, a little sharply, that things could not go on like this much longer. He took no heed of the warning, though the duns were beginning to gather about him.[16] When there was a ring at the door, Lucy used to squeeze up against the window to see who it was; and if it was one of those troublesome people whom she soon got to know by sight, she would go to the door herself, and tell them that they could not see her father, and explain to them, in her grave, childish way, that it was no use coming to her father for money, because he had no money just then but he would have some at quarter-day, and they might call again then. Sometimes the men tried to push past her into the hall, but she would never let them; her father was not in, or he was very unwell, and no one could see him; and she spoke so calmly and so decidedly that they always finished by going away. If they swore at her, or said horrid things about her father, she did not mind much. It did not surprise her that such dreadful people used dreadful language.[17]

In telling the duns that her father was very unwell, she was not always inventing. For a long time there had been something vaguely the matter with him, and ever since her mother's death he had sickened visibly, and nothing would rouse him from his pale and cheerless decrepitude. He would lie in bed till four, and then come downstairs and sit by the fireplace, smoking his pipe in silence,

---

[16] Duns are those who importune for the payment of bills (Anglo-Saxon, <*dunan*, to din or clamour).

[17] Much of Lucy's early life, including the garden in which she languishes, recalls that of reminiscent of Isabel Sleaford in Mary Braddon's *The Doctor's Wife* (1864). This would be very appropriate in an English reworking of radical French fiction, as Braddon's novel was itself a conscious retelling of Flaubert's *Madame Bovary* (1857).

doing nothing, neither reading, nor writing, nor sketching. All his interest in life seemed to have gone out together; his very hopes had been taken from him, and without those fantastic hopes he was but the shadow of himself. It scarcely roused him when the directors of his society wrote to him that they would require his services no longer. When they sent a man to unscrew the brass plate on the door, on which there were the name of the society and the amount of its capital, he went outside and stood in the garden while it was being done. Then he gave the man a shilling for his trouble.

Soon after that, he refused to eat or get up, and a great terror came over Lucy lest he, too, should die; and now there was no money in the house, and the duns still knocked at the door. She begged him to let her write to his relations, but he refused flatly, saying that they would not receive her mother, and he would never see them, or take a penny of their money as long as he lived. One day a cab drove up to the door, and a hard-featured woman got out of it. Lucy, looking out of the bedroom window, recognised her aunt, Miss Marsden, her mother's eldest sister, whom she had only seen at the funeral, and to whose grim face and rigid figure she had already taken a dislike. It appeared that Linda, unknown to them, had written to tell her into what desperate straits they had fallen; and her severe sense of duty had brought her to their help.

And the aunt was certainly good to them in her stern, unkindly way. The first thing she did was to send for a doctor, who shook his head very gravely when he had examined the patient; and spoke of foreign travel, and other impossible, expensive remedies. That was the first time that Lucy ever began to long for money, or to realise exactly what money meant. It might mean life or death, she saw now.

Her father now lay mostly in bed, very weak and quiet, and mostly in silence; and whether his eyes were closed or open, he seemed to be thinking, always thinking. He liked Lucy to come and sit by him; but if she chattered much he would stop her, after a while, and say that he was tired, and she must be quiet. And then sometimes he would talk to her, in his vague, disconnected way, about her mother, and of how they had met, and had found hard times together a great happiness; and he would look at her with an almost impersonal scrutiny, and say: 'I think you will live happily, not with the happiness that we had, for you will never love as we loved, but you will find it easy to like people, and many people will find it easy to like you; and if you have troubles they will weigh on you lightly, for you will live always in the day, that is, without too much memory of the day that was, or too much thought of the day that will be to-morrow.' And once he said: 'I hardly know why it is I feel so little anxiety about your future. I seem somehow to know that you will always find people to look after you. I don't know why they should, I don't know why they should.' And then he added, after a pause, looking at her a little sadly, 'You will never love nor be loved passionately, but you have a face that will seem to many, the first time they see you, like the face of an old and dear friend.'

Sometimes, when he felt a little better, the sick man would come downstairs, and at times he would walk about in the garden, stooping under his great-coat and leaning upon his stick. One very bright day in early February he seemed better than he had been since his illness had come upon him, and as he stood at the window looking at the white road shining under the pale sun, he said suddenly: 'I feel quite well today, I shall go for a little walk.' His eyes were bright, there was a slight flush on his cheek, and he seemed to move a little more easily than usual. 'Lucy,' he said, 'I think I should like some claret with my supper to-night, like old times. You must go into the town and get me some: I suppose there is none in the house.' Lucy took the money gladly, for she thought: 'He is beginning to be better.' 'Get it from Allen's,' he called after her, as she went to put on her hat and jacket; 'it won't take so very much longer to go there and back, and it will be better there.' When she came downstairs her aunt was helping him to put on his coat. 'Don't wait for me,' he said, smiling, and tapping her cheek with his thin, chilly fingers; 'I shall have to walk slowly.' She went out, and turning, as she came to the bend in the road, saw him come out of the gate, leaning on his stick, and begin to walk slowly along in the middle of the road. He did not look up, and she hurried on.

It was the last time she ever saw him. The house, when she returned to it, after her journey into town, had an air of ominous quiet, and she saw with surprise that her father's hat and coat were lying in a heap across the chair in the hall, instead of hanging neatly upon the hat-pegs. As she closed the door behind her, she heard the bedroom door opened, and her aunt came quickly downstairs with a strange look on her face. She began to tremble, she knew not why, and mechanically she put the bottle of wine on the floor by the side of the chair; and her aunt, though she would always have everything put in its proper place, did not seem to notice it; but took her into the sitting-room, and said: 'There has been an accident; no, you must not go upstairs'; and she said to herself, seeming to hear her own words at the back of her brain, where there was a dull ache that was like the coming-to of one who has been stunned: 'He is dead, he is dead.' She felt that her aunt was shaking her, and wondered why she shook her, and why everything looked so dim, and her aunt's face seemed to be fading away from her, and she caught at her; and then she heard her aunt say (she could hear her now), 'I thought you were going to faint: I'll have no fainting, if you please; I must go up to him again.' So he was not dead, after all; and she listened, with a relief which was almost joy, while her aunt told her rapidly what had happened: how the mail-cart had turned a corner at full speed just as he was walking along the road, more tired than he had thought, and he had not the strength to pull himself out of the way in time, and had been knocked down, and the wheel had just missed him, but he had been terribly shaken, and one of the horse's hoofs had struck him on the face. They hoped it was nothing serious; he seemed to feel little pain; but he had said: 'Don't let Lucy come in; she musn't see me like this.'

Lucy had been so used to obey her father, his commands had always been so capricious, that she obeyed now without a murmur. She understood him; the fastidiousness which was part of his affection, and which made him refuse to be seen, by those he loved, under a disfigurement which time would probably heal, was one of the things for which she loved him, for it was part of her pride in him.

The doctor had come and gone; he had been very serious, she had seen his grave face, and had overheard one or two of his words to her aunt; she had heard him say: 'Of course, it is a question of time.' Night came on, and she sat in the unlighted room alone, and looking into the fire, in which the last dreams of her childhood seemed to flicker in little wavering tongues of flame, which throbbed, and went out, one after another, in smoke or ashes. She cried a little, quietly, and did not wipe away the tears; but sat on, looking into the fire, and thinking. She was crying when her aunt came downstairs, and told her that she must go to bed; he was resting quietly, and they hoped he would be better in the morning.

She slept heavily, without dreams; and the hour seemed to her late when she awoke in the morning. It was Linda, not her aunt, who came into the room, and took her in her arms, and cried over her, and did not need to tell her that she had no father. He had died suddenly in his sleep, and just before he turned over on his side for the last rest, he had said to her (she thought drowsily): 'I am very tired; if anything happens, cover my face.' When Lucy crept into the room, on tip-toe, his face was covered. It was a white, shrouded thing that lay there, not her father. The terror of the dead seized hold upon her, and she shrieked, and Linda caught her up in her arms, and carried her back to her room, and soothed her, as if she had been a little, wailing child.

At the funeral she saw, for the first time, her father's relations, the rich relations who had cast him off; and she hated them for being there, for speaking to her kindly, for offering to look after her. She was rude to them, and she wished to be rude. 'My father would never touch your money,' she said, 'and I am sure he wouldn't like me to, and I don't want it. I don't want to have anything to do with you.' She clung to the severe aunt who had been good to her father; and she tried to smile on her other uncle and aunt, and on her cousin, who was not many years older than she was: he had seemed to her so kind, and so ready to be her friend. 'I will go with my aunt,' she said. The rich relatives acquiesced, not unwillingly. They did not linger in the desolate house, where this unreasonable child, as they thought her, stood away from them on the other side of the room. She seemed to herself to be doing the right thing, and what her father would have wished; and she saw them go out with relief, not giving a thought to the future, only knowing that she had buried her childhood, on that day of the funeral, in the grave with her father.

~

The Death of Peter Waydelin

A depiction of the dissonant relationship between art and life, this story first appeared as 'Peter Waydelin's Experiment' in the American *Lippincott's Monthly Magazine* for February 1904. Once again, it is easy to discern the presence of an author-surrogate in the narrator, a man who, like Symons, visits Sussex and Moscow, has a wide knowledge of London's music halls and an appreciation of modern art, though Waydelin himself seems to combine aspects of Beardsley and Whistler. Indeed, the critic of the *Chicago Daily Tribune* saw the story less as 'piece of fiction' than 'a mephitic biographical study [...] a page from the peculiar memoirs of Aubrey Beardsley, that young depicter of ancient and evil things, who died in the youth of his monstrous genius.'[1]

Symons characterized the story as 'a morbid analysis of diseased nerves and of a depraved imagination' which 'had no other basis than my recollections of Toulouse-Lautrec and Aubrey Beardsley.' Acknowledging the vicious edge of its descriptions, Symons admitted that it was 'conceived cruelly', and also that it was 'the only one of the stories [in *Spiritual Adventures*] which is realistic.' By this, he seems to have meant that it was drawn from what he had seen happen to others rather than what had been impressed upon himself. 'I made it out of the many curious and sinister incidents I had seen in the East End and in Soho,' he said, a comment which might have placed the story in Wilde's 'great and daily increasing school of novelists for whom the sun always rises in the East-End' had it been written in the hey-day of 'slum fiction'.[2]

Turning to the protagonist, Symons writes, 'Waydelin accepted his fate, because his existence had turned back upon him, in the invariable way of those who have failed in achieving what they set their hearts on doing.'[3] His illness is at once an allusion to Beardsley's tuberculosis and a more symbolic ailment that

---

[1] Elia W. Peattie, 'Brilliant New Fiction for the Holidays', *Chicago Daily Tribune* (16 December 1905), p. 9.

[2] Wilde, 'The Decay of Lying, An Observation', *Collected Works* (London: HarperCollins, 1994), pp. 1074–75.

[3] Symons, 'The Genesis of Spiritual Adventures'.

signals the gulf between the body and the imagination or soul: like Aschenbach in Thomas Mann's *Death in Venice* (1912), Waydelin discovers 'art is an intensified life. By art one is more deeply satisfied and more rapidly used up.'[4] The painter has consciously decided to live in squalid surroundings because they are the essential stimulus his art requires: 'I never wanted to be happy,' he says. The investigative journalists of the period, for example, Jack London in *The People of the Abyss* (1903), also attempt to live 'as like a native as I could, and with no return ticket in my pocket,' but their intention in descending into the nether world was to reveal the horrors of metropolitan poverty in order to bring about its amelioration. Waydelin has no such political mission. His aim is for his aesthetic vision to supplant the vulgarity and coarseness of lived experience, but he pays a heavy price for his 'experiment', as does his wife, Clara. He never lets her know what he truly thinks about her, keeps from her the full extent of his illness and paints a brutal portrait of her which she calls 'a horrid thing'. Although Waydelin says she is 'a very nice woman and an excellent model', he has 'no gift for domesticity', and the narrator is conspicuous snobbish and judgemental towards her, wholly complicit in his friend's strategy. When Clara enters her husband's room during his final moments of consciousness, he attempts to sketch the 'grotesque horror' of her terror and incomprehension, before dropping his pencil and lapsing into unconsciousness. Until his final moment, he refuses to place human concerns before artistic ones.

Like 'Esther Kahn', 'The Death of Peter Waydelin' transforms the familiar narratives of popular fiction — here, the artist who dies before he can complete his masterpiece — into something more sophisticated. Symons does this by placing aesthetic debate rather than human relationships at the centre of the story. As a young man he had been unimpressed by Kipling's *The Light that Failed* (1891) and he had seen numerous plays which depicted the artist torn between, as Yeats might put it, 'perfection of the life, or of the work'.[5] Both he and Waydelin opt for the latter, and the story might be read in allegorical terms. A recent study has called it 'the perfect example of a condensed *Künstlerroman*', offering as it does 'the topoi of the self-destructive genius, Symbolist vision, avant-gardism and bohemianism'. It offers too 'a most vivid encapsulation of the culture of the 1890s', in a story which allows Symons to exploit the opportunities afforded by imaginary portraiture in moving fluidly between character study, auto-biographical reminiscence, and aesthetic debate.[6] As John M. Munro concludes,

---

[4] Thomas Mann, *Death in Venice and Other Stories*, trans. by David Luke (London: Vintage, 2003), pp. 208–09.

[5] Symons, '*The Light that Failed* — and Why', *Anti-Jacobin* 11, 11 April 1891, pp. 264–65; Yeats, 'The Choice', *The Winding Stair and Other Poems* (1933). Symons's views of other 'artist novels' such as James's *The Tragic Muse* (1890), or Dowson and Moore's *A Comedy of Masks* (1893), are not recorded.

[6] Boyiopoulos, Choi, and Tildesley, eds, *The Decadent Short Story*, p. 379.

'The point Symons makes is that the price of dedication and sincerity is self-annihilation.'[7]

* * *

Peter Waydelin, the painter of those mysterious, brutal pictures, who died last year at the age of twenty-four, spent a week with me at Bognor, trying to get better, a little while before it was quite certainly too late; and we had long talks of a very intimate kind as we lay and lounged about the sand from Selsey to Blake's Felpham, along that exquisite coast.[8] To him, if he were to be believed, all that meant very little; he hated nature, he was always assuring you; but at Bognor nature deals with its material so much in the manner of art that he can hardly have been sincere in not feeling the colour-sense of those arrangements of sand, water, and sky which were perpetually changing before him.[9] One of our conversations that I remembered best, because he seemed to put more of himself into it than usual, took place one afternoon in June as we lay on the sand about half-way towards Selsey, beyond the last of those troublesome groins, and I remember that as I listened to him, and heard him defining so sincerely his own ideas of art, I was conscious all the time of a magnificent silent refutation of some of those ideas, as nature, quietly expressing herself before us, transformed the whole earth gradually into a new and luminous world of air. He did not seem to see the sunset; now and then he would pick up a pebble and throw it vehemently, almost angrily, into the water. We were talking of art. He began to explain to me what art meant to him, and what it was he wanted to do with his own art. I remember almost the very words he used, sometimes so serious, sometimes so petulant and boyish. I was interested in his ideas, and the man too interested me; so young and so experienced, so mature already and so enthusiastic under his cynicism. He puzzled me: it was as if there were a clue wanting; I could not get further with him than a certain point, frank, self-explanatory even, as he seemed to be. Of himself he never spoke, only of his ideas. I knew vaguely that he had been in Paris, and I supposed that he had been living there for some time. I had

---

[7] John M. Munro, *Arthur Symons* (New York: Twayne, 1969), p. 108.

[8] Selsey and Bognor (Bognor Regis since 1929) are coastal towns in West Sussex, popular with day-trippers from London. Symons was an occasional visitor to the Sussex coast, usually when he was finding London unduly oppressive but was unable to get back to Cornwall. William Blake, the subject of a critical study by Symons (1907), lived in the nearby village of Felpham from 1800 until 1803. Symons's poem, 'Felpham' written in Bognor in July 1903 and included in *The Fool of the World*, has as its epigraph Blake's line, 'Away to sweet Felpham, for Heaven is there', a line from 'To my Dear Friend, Mrs Anna Flaxman' (1800).

[9] Symons wrote several poems he termed 'colour studies'. The best of these, 'At Dieppe', dedicated to the artist Walter Sickert and written in September 1893, appeared in *London Nights* (1895). It opens: 'The grey-green stretch of sandy grass, | Indefinitely desolate; | A sea of lead, a sky of slate'.

met him in London, in the street, quite casually, and he had looked so ill that I had asked him there and then to come with me to Bognor, where I was going. He agreed willingly, and was at the station with his bag the next day. I never ask people about their private affairs, and his talk was entirely about pictures, his own chiefly, and about ideas. As he talked I tried to piece together the man and his words. What was it in this man, who was so much a gentleman, that drew him instinctively, whenever he took up a brush or a pencil, towards gross things, things that he painted as if he hated them, but painted always? Was it a theory or an enslavement? and had he, in order to interpret with so cruel a fidelity so much that was factitious and dishonourable in life, sunk to the level of what he painted? I could not tell. He was not obviously the man of his pictures, nor was he obviously the reverse. I felt in those pictures, and I felt equally, but differently, in the man, a fundamental sincerity; after that came I know not how much of pose, perhaps merely the defiant pose of youth. He was a problem to me, which I wanted to think out; and I listened very attentively to everything that he said on that afternoon when he was so much more communicative than usual.

'All art, of course,' he said, 'is a way of seeing, and I have my way. I did not get to it at once. Like everybody else, I began by seeing too much. Gradually I gave up seeing things in shades, in subdivisions; I saw them in masses, each single. It takes more choice than you think, and more technical skill, to set one plain colour against another, unshaded, like a great, raw morsel, or a solid lump of the earth. The art of the painter, you observe, consists in seeing in a new, summarising way, getting rid of everything but the essentials; in seeing by patterns. You know how a child draws a house? Well, that is how the average man thinks he sees it, even at a distance. You have to train your eye not to see. Whistler sees nothing but the fine shades, which unite into a picture in an almost bodiless way, as Verlaine writes songs almost literally "without words." You can see, if you like, in just the opposite way: leaving in only the hard outlines, leaving out everything that lies between. To me that is the best way of summarising, the most abbreviated way. You get rid of all that molle,[10] sticky way of work which squashes pictures into

---

[10] 'Molle', French for 'soft', but also the Peruvian mastic-tree, hence artists' slang (pronounced 'molly') for mastic or varnish. Although Symons was not an admirer of the Pre-Raphaelites' closely-observed realism, he (and Beardsley) sympathized with their revolt against the conventions of the Royal Academy, particularly the tradition of working from a brown ground, the use of dark varnish on finished works, and the official disdain for medieval art. Many early Pre-Raphaelite paintings gain their bright and vivid colours from being painted on white grounds, i.e. a canvas which has been painted white before work begins on the painting proper. There are clear analogies between this practice and Beardsley's fondness for white paper, though the touchstones here are the American painter James McNeill Whistler (1834–1903, who painted 'The Beach at Selsey Bill', c. 1865) and the French poet, Paul Verlaine (1844–96), both of whom Symons idolized. In his study of Beardsley, Symons observed that 'there was a very serious and adequate theory of art at the back of all his destructive criticisms.' *Aubrey Beardsley*, p. 14.

cakes and puddings, and of that stringy way of work which draws them out into tapes and ribbons. It is a way of seeing square, and painting like hits from the shoulder.

'I wonder,' he went on, after a moment, 'how many people think that I paint ugly pictures, as they call them, because I am unable to paint pretty ones? Perhaps even you have never seen any of my quite early work: Madonnas for Christmas cards and hallelujah angels for stained-glass windows.[11] They were the prettiest things imaginable, immensely popular, and they brought me in several pounds. I take them out and show them to people who complain that I have no sense of beauty, and they always ask me pityingly why I have not gone on turning out these confectionaries.'

'I contend that I have never done anything which is without beauty, because I have never done anything which is without life, and life is the source and sap of beauty. I tell you that there is not one of those grimacing masks, those horribly pale or horribly red faces, plastered white or red, leering professionally across a gulf of footlights, or a café-table, that does not live, live to the roots of the eyes, somewhere in the soul, I think! And if beauty is not the visible spirit of all that infamous flesh, when I have sabred it like that along my canvas, with all my hatred and all my admiration of its foolish energy, I at least am unable to conjecture where beauty has gone to live in the world.'

He looked at me almost indignantly, as if he took me for one of his critics. I said nothing, and he went on:

'I have done nothing, believe me, without being sure that I was doing a beautiful thing.[12] People don't see it, it seems. How should they, when we do our best to train them up within the prison walls of a Raphael æsthetics, when we send them to the Apollo Belvedere, instead of to the marbles of Ægina?[13] Our

---

[11] Beardsley joked that 'If I am not grotesque, I am nothing.' Edward Burne-Jones, whose work influenced his early drawings, made many stained-glass designs, perhaps the most notable of which are in the cathedral in his home town of Birmingham. Unsurprisingly, an artist of Beardsley's reputation did not receive ecclesiastical commissions, though he did design a Christmas card for the first number of The Savoy. This should have been issued in December 1895, but because of controversy surrounding Beardsley's cover design for the magazine, it was not available until January 1896, too late for the remunerative festive market. This may have been a sore point for Symons, as it prevented the journal getting off to a sound start and may have indirectly undermined its long term prospects.

[12] In the 'Preface' to The Picture of Dorian Gray, Wilde asserts that 'The artist is the creator of beautiful things.' That he and Beardsley had very different ideas about what constituted beauty is shown by their contretemps concerning Beardsley's illustrations for Salomé (1894).

[13] Waydelin's Pre-Raphaelite sympathies are evident in his scepticism towards the official enshrining of Raphael (1483–1520) and his methods. The Apollo Belvedere, or Pythian Apollo, is a classical marble statue now in the Vatican which was rediscovered in Italy during the late 15th century. Depicting Apollo as an archer, it was (and is) often regarded as the finest statue of antiquity, and has been widely studied and imitated since the 18th century. Aegina was the island which rivalled Athens during the fifth century BC. There are many examples of its marble

academies shut out nine parts of beauty and imprison us with the poor tenth, which we have never even the space to frequent casually and grow familiar with. How much of the world itself do you think exists as a thing of beauty for the average man? Why, he has to know if the most exquisite leaf in the world, the thing I came upon just now in the lane, belongs to a flower or a weed before he can tell whether he ought to commend it for existing. I hate nature, because fools prostrate themselves before sunsets; as if there is not much better drawing in that leaf than in all the Turners of the sky. You see, one has to quote Turner to apologise for a sunset!'[14]

He laughed, really without malice, waving his hand towards the sky with a youthful impertinence. For a little while he was silent, and then, in a different tone, he said:

'I wonder if it is possible to paint what one doesn't like, to take one's models as models, and only know them for the hours during which they sit to you in this attitude or that. I don't believe that it is. Much of our bad painting comes from respectable people thinking that they can soil their hands with paint and not let the dye sink into their innermost selves. Do you know that you are the only man of my own world that I ever see, or have seen for years now? People call me eccentric; I am only logical. You can't paint the things I paint, and live in a Hampstead villa. You must come and see me some day: will you take the address? 3 Somervell Street, Islington. It's not much like a studio. However, there's 'Collins's' at hand, and I live there a good deal, you know. I lived in the Hampstead Road for some time on account of the 'Bedford.' But 'Collins's' suits me and my models better.'[15]

---

sculpture in the British Museum. Waydelin's preferences again show his opposition to received aesthetic standards and beliefs. See also Pater's essay, 'The Marbles of Aegina', first published in the *Fortnightly Review* (April 1880) and reprinted in his posthumously-published *Greek Studies* (1895).

[14] Joseph Mallord William Turner (1775–1851), British land and seascape painter famous for his spectacular images of sunset. In the 1904 version of the story, Symons has 'in order to apologise for a sunset'. In Wilde's 'The Decay of Lying', Mrs Arundel praises a sunset which is simply 'a Turner of a bad period, with all the painter's worst faults exaggerated and over-emphasised.'

[15] Collins' Music Hall in Islington Green opened in 1863 and was substantially reworked in 1897. At this time it boasted a 4 ft by 3 ft iron-framed sign made of coloured glass illuminated by gas jets. The building burned down in 1958.

The Bedford Music Hall was in Camden High Street. Opened in 1861, it was demolished in July 1898 and replaced by the lavish Bedford Palace of Varieties in February 1899. It was briefly a cinema during the 1930s, and though it reverted to theatre and variety, closed in 1959 and was demolished ten years later. Symons would have known both these venues well, though the 1890s' artist most closely associated with paintings of music hall performance is not Beardsley but Walter Sickert (1860–1942).

He broke off with an ambiguous laugh, flung his last stone into the water, and jumped up, as if to end the conversation. Something in the way he spoke made me feel vaguely uneasy, but I was used to his exaggerations, his way of inventing as he went along. Was I, after all, any nearer to his secret, to himself as he really was?

Waydelin went back to London and I to Russia, which I shall always remember, after that terrible summer under the gold and green domes of Moscow, as the hottest country in which I have ever been.[16] When I came back to London I thought of Waydelin, made plan after plan to visit him, when one evening in November I received a brief note in his handwriting, asking me if I would come and see him at once, as he was very ill, and wanted to see me on a matter of business. I started immediately after dinner and got to Islington a little after nine. The street was one of those drab, hopeless streets to which a Russian observer has lately attributed the 'spleen' from which all Englishmen are thought to suffer.[17] There was a row of houses on each side of the way, every house exactly like every other house, each with its three steps leading to the door, its bow window on one side, its strip of dingy earth in which there were a few dusty stalks between the lowest step and the railing, the paint for the most part peeling off the door, the bell-handle generally hanging out from its hole in the wall. I rang at No. 3. I had to wait for some time, and then the door was opened by an impudent-looking servant girl in a very untidy dress. I asked for Waydelin. 'Mrs Waydelin, did you say?' said the girl, leering at me; then, calling over my head to the driver of a four-wheeler which just then drew up at the door, 'Wait five minutes, will you?' she turned to me again: 'Mr Waydelin? I don't know if you can see him.' I told her impatiently that I had come by appointment, and she held the door open for me to come in. She knocked at a room on the first floor. 'Come in,' said a shrill voice that I did not know, and I went in.

It was a bedroom; a woman, with her bodice off, was making-up in front of the glass, and in a corner, with the clothes drawn up to his chin, a man lay in bed. The cheeks were covered by a three days' beard; they were ridged into deep hollows; large eyes, very wide open, looked out under a mass of uncombed hair, and as the face turned round on the pillow and looked at me without any change of expression I recognised Peter Waydelin. The woman, seeing me in the glass,

---

[16] Symons went to Moscow during a heat wave in August 1897 — it was the hottest summer for 37 years — and was unimpressed. His account of his visit first appeared in the tri-lingual magazine *Cosmopolis* three months later, and was later included in *Cities* (1903). 'Moscow has all the barbarism of a civilisation which is but two centuries old,' he wrote (*Cities*, p. 173).

[17] The Russian is Alexander Herzen (1812–70), who lived in London from 1852–64, and whose memoirs provide compelling accounts of the plight of the imaginative intellectual in the metropolis. Symons probably knew these through French translations as they were widely read on the continent. They were, however, unavailable in English until Constance Garnett's translation of them as *My Life and Thoughts: The Memoirs of Alexander Herzen* in 1922.

nodded at my reflection, and said, as she drew a black pencil through her eyelashes: 'You'll excuse me, won't you? I have to be at the hall in ten minutes. Don't stand on ceremony; there's Peter. He'll be glad to see you, poor dear!' She spoke in a common and affected voice, and I thought her a deplorable person, with her carefully curled yellow hair, her rouged and powdered cheeks, her mouth glistening with lip salve, her big, empty blue eyes with their blackened under-lids, her fat arms and shoulders, the tawdry finery of her costume, half on and half off the body. I moved towards the bed, and Waydelin looked up at me with a queer, mournful smile.

'It was good of you to come,' he said, stretching out a long, thin hand to me; 'Clara has to go out, and we can have a talk. How do you like the last thing I've done?'

I lifted the drawing which was lying on the bed. It was a portrait of the woman before the glass, just as she looked now, one of the most powerful of his drawings, crueller even than usual in its insistence on the brutality of facts: the crude contrasts of bone and fat, the vulgar jaw, the brassy eyes, the reckless, conscious attitude. Every line seemed to have been drawn with hatred.[18] I looked at Mrs Waydelin. She had finished dressing, and she came up to the bedside to say good-bye to Peter. 'Horrid thing,' she said, nodding her head at the drawing; 'not a bit like me, is it? I assure you none of them like it at the hall. They say it doesn't do me justice. I'm sure I hope not.' I bowed and murmured something. 'Goodbye, Peter,' she said, smiling down at him in a kindly, hurried way, 'I'll come back as soon as I can,' and with a nod to me she was out of the room.

Peter drew himself slowly up in the bed, pointed to a shawl, which I wrapped round his shoulders, and then, looking at me a little defiantly, said: 'My theory, do you remember? of living the life of my models! She is a very nice woman and an excellent model, and they appreciate her very much at 'Collins's'; but it appears that I have no gift for domesticity.'

I scarcely knew what to say. While I hesitated he went on: 'Don't suppose I have any illusions, or, indeed, ever had. I married that woman because I couldn't help doing it, but I knew what I was doing all the time. Have you ever been in Belgium? There is stuff they give you there to drink called Advokat, which you begin by hating, but after a time you can't get on without it. She is like Advokat.'[19]

'You are ill, Waydelin,' I said, 'and you speak bitterly. I don't like to hear you speak like that about your wife.'

---

[18] This portrait of Mrs Waydelin recalls Beardsley's controversial drawing, 'The Fat Woman', a caricature of Whistler's wife, Trixie. Pulled from the *Yellow Book* when John Lane discovered its inspiration, it later appeared in *Today* (21 May 1894), illustrating a feature entitled 'A New Master of Art: Mr Aubrey Beardsley'.

[19] An alcoholic drink made from eggs, sugar, and brandy. An acquired taste.

Waydelin stared at me curiously. 'So you are going to defend her against my brutality,' he said. 'I will give you every opportunity. Did you know I was married?'

I shook my head.

'I have been married three years,' he said, 'and I never told even you. I know you did not take me at my word when I talked about how one had to live in order to paint as I painted, but I did not tell you half. I have been living, if you like to call it so, systematically, not as a stranger in a foreign country which he stares at over his Baedeker, but as like a native as I could, and with no return ticket in my pocket.[20] Why shouldn't one be as thorough in one's life as in one's drawing? Is it possible for one to be otherwise, if one is really in earnest in either? And the odd thing is, as you will say, I didn't live in that way because I wanted to do it for my art, but something deeper than my art, a profound, low instinct, drew me to these people, to this life, without my own will having anything to do with it. My work has been much more sincere than anyone suspected. It used to amuse me when the papers classed me with the Decadents of a moment, and said that I was probably living in a suburban villa, with a creeper on the front wall. I have never cared for anything but London, or in London for anything but here, or the Hampstead Road, or about the Docks. I never really chose the music-halls or the public-houses; they chose me. I made the music-halls my clubs; I lived in them, for the mere delight of the thing; I liked the glitter, false, barbarous, intoxicating, the violent animality of the whole spectacle, with its imbecile words, faces, gestures, the very heat and odour, like some concentrated odour of the human crowd, the irritant music, the audience! I went there, as I went to public-houses, as I walked about the streets at night, as I kept company with vagabonds, because there was a craving in me that I could not quiet. I fitted in theories with my facts; and that is how I came to paint my pictures.'[21]

As he spoke, with bitter ardour, I looked at him as if I were seeing him for the first time. The room, the woman, that angry drawing on the bed, and the dishevelled man dying there, just at the moment when he had learnt everything that such experiences could teach him, fell of a sudden into a revealing relation with each other. I did not know whether to feel that the man had been heroic or a fool; there had been, it was clear to me, some obscure martyrdom going on, not the less for art's sake because it came out of the mere necessity of things. A great

---

[20] The German publishing house, founded by Karl Baedeker in 1827, remains a leading publisher of travel guides. During the 1890s, 'Baedeker' was almost a proprietary eponym. The books are known for their reliability and accuracy, but although Symons doubtless used them in his European journeys, he rarely acknowledged the fact, tending to see the use of such guides as the hallmark of the inexperienced traveller or worse, tourist.

[21] Symons included the claim that he 'never really chose the music-halls' in his unpublished reminiscences. See *The Memoirs of Arthur Symons*, p. 109.

pity came over me, and all I could say was, 'But, my dear friend, you have been very unhappy!'

'I never wanted to be happy,' said Waydelin; 'I wanted to live my own life and do my own work; and if I die to-morrow (as likely enough I may), I shall have done both things. My work satisfies me, and, because of that, so does my life.'

'Are you very ill?' I asked.

'Dead, relatively speaking,' he said in his jaunty way, which death itself could not check in him; 'I'm only waiting on some celestial order of precedence in these matters, which, I confess, I don't understand. So it was good of you to come; I would like to arrange with you about what is to be done with my work, presently, when they will have to accept me. I always said that I had only to die in order to be appreciated.'

I had a long talk with him, and I promised to carry out his wishes. All the money that his pictures brought in was to go to his wife, but, as he said, she would not know what to do with them if they were left in her own hands, not even how to turn them into money. He was quite certain that they would sell; he knew exactly the value of what he had done, and he knew how and when work finds its own level.

I sat beside the bed, talking, for more than two hours. He could no longer do much work, he said, and he hated being alone when he was not working. But it amused him to talk, for a change. 'Clara talks when she is here,' he said, with one of his queer smiles. I promised to come back and see him again. 'Come soon,' he said, 'if you want to be sure of finding me.'

I went back two days afterwards, a little later in the evening so that I need not meet Mrs Waydelin, and he seemed better. He had shaved, his hair was brushed and combed, and he was sitting up in bed, with the shawl thrown lightly about his shoulders.

'Would you like to know,' he began, almost at once, 'how I came to paint in what we will call, if you please, my final manner? One day, at the theatre, I saw Sada Yacco.[22] She taught me art.'

'What do you mean?' I said.

'Look here,' he went on, 'they say everything has been done in art. But no, there is at least one thing that remains for us. Have you ever seen Sada Yacco? When I saw her for the first time I said to myself, "I have found out the secret of Japanese art." I had never been able to understand how it was that the Japanese, who can

---

[22] Sada Yacco (1871–1946), Japanese geisha, dancer, and actress. She performed in London at the Coronet Theatre, Notting Hill Gate, in May and June of 1900. Symons probably saw her there, though he did not publish his views of her performance in essay form. 'I give here my impressions of Sada Yacco,' he said in 'The Genesis of Spiritual Adventures'. Beardsley was a great admirer of Japanese art and design, especially in its erotic manifestations, and had Yacco visited London earlier, he would surely have been interested in her performances.

imitate natural things, a bird, a flower, the rain, so perfectly, have chosen to give us, instead of a woman's face, that blind oval, in which the eyes, nose, and mouth seem to have been made to fit a pattern. When I saw Sada Yacco I realised that the Japanese painters had followed nature as closely in their woman's faces as in their birds and flowers, but that they had studied them from the women of the Green Houses[23], the women who make up, and that Japanese women, made up for the stage or for the factitious life of the Green Houses, look exactly like these elegant, unnatural images of the painters.[24] What a new kind of reality that opened up to me, as if a window had suddenly opened in a wall! Here, I said to myself, is something that the painters of Europe have never done; it remains for me to do it. I will study nature under the paint by which woman, after all, makes herself more woman; the ensign of her trade, her flag as the enemy.[25] I will get at the nature of this artificial thing, at the skin underneath it, and the soul under the skin. Watteau and the Court painters have given us the dainty, exterior charm of the masquerade, woman when she plays at being woman, among "lyres and flutes."[26] Degas, of course, has done something of what I want to do, but only a part, and with other elements in his pure design, the drawing of Ingres, setting itself new tasks, exercising its technique upon shapeless bodies in tubs, and the strained muscles of the dancer's leg as she does "side-practice."[27] What I am going to do is to take all the ugliness, gross artifice, crafty mechanism, of sex disguising itself for its own ends: that new nature which vice and custom make out of the honest curves and colours of natural things.

'Well, I have tried to do that; in all my best work, my work of the last two or three years, I have done it. I am sure that what I have done is a new thing, and I think it is the one new thing left to us Western painters.'

'I am beginning to understand you,' I said, 'and I have not always found it easy. When I admire you, it has so often seemed to me irrational. I am gradually finding

---

[23] 'Green Houses', a loose translation of the Japanese *seirō*, a courtesan's residence. Waydelin is incorrectly eliding courtesans and geisha.

[24] Japanese art, ceramics, design, and ornament were increasingly in vogue in Europe from the 1860s onwards. Whistler was strongly influenced by Japanese painting, while Beardsley was drawn to Japanese graphic design and decorated his rooms with sexually explicit *shunga* ('picture of spring') prints, with which he enjoyed startling his visitors.

[25] A comment clearly informed by the sections on women and cosmetics in Charles Baudelaire's essay, 'La Peintre du vie moderne' ('The Painter of Modern Life', 1863), a totemic text for Symons and alluded to in 'At the Alhambra: Impressions and Sensations'.

[26] Jean-Antoine Watteau (1684–1721) was a favourite painter of Beardsley and Conder, but Symons is here combining Pater's evocation of him in 'A Prince of Court Painters' from *Imaginary Portraits* with the famous description of 'La Gioconda' from his essay 'Leonardo da Vinci' (1869), reprinted in *The Renaissance* (1873). See too 'For a Picture of Watteau', the final poem in *Silhouettes*.

[27] For Degas, see 'The Extra Lady'. Jean Auguste Dominique Ingres (1780–1867), French academic painter known for his portraits, nudes, and superb draughtsmanship.

out your logic. Do you remember those talks we used to have at Bognor, one in particular, when you told me about your way of seeing?'

'Yes, yes,' he said, 'I remember, but there was one thing I am almost sure I did not tell you, and it is curious. I don't understand it myself. Do you know what it is to be haunted by colours? There is something like a temptation of the devil, to me, in the colour green. I know it is the commonest colour in nature, it is a good, honest colour, it is the grass, the trees, the leaves, very often the sea. But no, it isn't like that that it comes to me. To me it is an aniline dye, poisoning nature.[28] I adore and hate it. I can never get away from it. If I paint a group outside a café at Montmartre by gas-light or electric light, I paint a green shadow on the faces, and I suppose the green shadow isn't there; yet I paint it. Some tinge of green finds its way invariably into my flesh-colour; I see something green in rouged cheeks, in peroxide-of-hydrogen hair; green lays hold of this poor, unhappy flesh that I paint, as if anticipating the colour-scheme of the grave. I know it, and yet I can't help doing it; I can't explain to you how it is that I at once see and don't see a thing; but so it is.[29]

'And it grew upon me too like an obsession. I always wanted to keep my eyes perfectly clear, so that I could make my own arrangements of things for myself, deliberately; but this, in some unpleasant way, seemed horribly like "nature taking the pen out of one's hand and writing," as somebody once said about a poet. I would rather do all the writing myself; the more so, as I have to translate as I go.'

He broke off suddenly, as if a wave of exhaustion had come over him. His eyes, which had been very bright, had gone dull again, and he let his head droop till the chin rested on his breast.

'I have tired you,' I said, 'you must not talk any more. Try to go to sleep now, and I will come back another day.'

'Tomorrow?' he said, looking at me sleepily.

I promised. When I went back the next day he was weaker, but he insisted on sitting up and talking. He spoke of his wife, without affection and without bitterness; he spoke of death, with so little apprehension, or even curiosity, that I was startled. His art was still a much more realisable thing to him.

---

[28] Aniline was first isolated by destructive distillation of indigo during the 1820s. Further experimentation, notably by the eighteen year-old William Henry Perkin (who was trying to produce synthetic quinine) led in 1856 to the creation of Mauveine (or mauvine), the first synthetic dye. Its impact on clothing, soft furnishings, and interior decor was widespread and immediate.

[29] The colour green gained a sinister allure during the *fin de siècle* because of absinthe, the wormwood-based spirit popular in bohemian circles. The greenish tinge which pervades Van Gogh's 'Le Café de nuit' (1888) is often attributed to the artist's absinthe consumption. Symons is also recalling Toulouse Lautrec's oil paintings, which often employed a greenish tinge, as for instance in the portrait of Jane Avril (1892). In 'The Genesis of Spiritual Adventures' he remarks that the discussion 'refers to Lautrec without mentioning his name'.

'Do you believe in God, religion, and all that?' he said. 'To tell you the honest truth, I have never been able to take a vital interest in those or any other abstract matters: I am so well content with this world, if it would only go on existing, and I don't in the least care how it came into being, or what is going to happen to it after I have moved on. I suppose one ought to feel some sort of reverence for something, for an unknown power, at least, which has certainly worked to good purpose. Well, I can't. I don't know what reverence is. If I were quite healthy, I should be a pagan, and choose, well! Dionysus Zagreus, a Bacchus who has been in hell, to worship after my fashion, in some religious kind of "orgie on the mountains." That is how somebody explains the origin of religion, or was it of religious hymns? I forget; but, you see, having had this rickety sort of body to drag about with me, I have never been able to follow any of my practical impulses of that sort, and I have had to be no more than an unemployed atheist, ready to gibe at the gods he doesn't understand.[30]

'I am afraid even in art,' he went on, as if leaving unimportant things for the one thing important, 'I don't find it easy to look up to anybody, at least in a way that anybody can be imagined as liking. I have never gone very much to the National Gallery, not because I don't think Venetian and Florentine pictures quite splendid, painted when they were, but because I can get nothing out of them that is any good for me, now in this all but twentieth century.[31] You won't expect me, of all people, to prate about progress, but, all the same, it's no use going to Botticelli for hints about modern painting.[32] We have different things to look at, and see them differently. A man must be of his time, else why try to put his time on the canvas? There are people, of course, who don't, if you call them painters:

---

[30] Beardsley converted to Roman Catholicism in March 1897 but before then (and indeed afterwards) his art was often regarded as pagan, blasphemous, or even Satanic; the critic Roger Fry called him 'the Fra Angelico of Satanism' and Symons suggested that the artist was 'Anima naturalitur pagana' ('a naturally pagan soul') (Aubrey Beardsley, p. 11). The discussion of the origins of religion here draws on the classicist, Gilbert Murray, Pater's 'Denys l'Auxerrois', whom Symons had characterized as Dionysus Zagreus in his 1887 review of Imaginary Portraits, Pater's 1876 essay, 'A Study of Dionysus', repr. in Greek Studies, and J. G. Frazer's The Golden Bough (two volume edition 1890, three volume 1900), which was becoming widely influential by the early twentieth century. Dionysos, the god of wine, is here linked with scenes of unrestrained licentious excess.

Zagreus was the 'first-born Dionysos', who presided over the Orphic Mysteries. The son of Zeus and Persephone (whom Zeus seduced in the form of a snake), he was killed and dismembered by the Titans. Zeus retrieved his heart and fed it in a potion to Semele, his mortal love. It was from this that she conceived the younger Dionysos, a reincarnation of the first though with a mixture of human and divine qualities that his predecessor had not possessed.

[31] For the National Gallery, see 'The Life and Adventures of Lucy Newcome'. Late-Victorian radicals found it somewhat staid. Despite having grown up in Brighton and being resident in London, Beardsley told Robert Ross in 1892 that he had never been to it. Ross, Aubrey Beardsley, p. 17.

[32] For Botticelli, see 'The Life and Adventures of Lucy Newcome'.

Watts, Burne-Jones, Moreau, that sort of hermit-crab.[33] But I am talking about painting life and making it live. If it comes to making pictures for churches and curiosity shops!'

He spoke eagerly, but in a voice which grew more and more tired, and with long pauses. I was going to try to get him to rest when the front door opened noisily and I heard Mrs Waydelin's voice in the hall. I heard other voices, men's and women's, feet coming up the stairs. I looked apprehensively at Waydelin. He showed no surprise. I heard a door open on the landing; then, a moment after, it was shut, and Mrs Waydelin came into the bedroom, flushed and perspiring through the paint, and ran up to the bed. 'I have brought a few friends in to supper,' she said. 'They won't disturb you, you know, and I couldn't very well get out of it.'

She would have entered into explanations, but Waydelin cut her short. 'I have not the least objection,' he said. 'I must only ask you to apologise to them for my absence. I am hardly entertaining at present.'

She stared at him, as if wondering what he meant; then she asked me if I would join her at supper, and I declined; then went to the dressing-table, took up a pot of vaseline[34] and looked at her eyelashes in the glass; then put it down again, came back to the bed, told Peter Waydelin to cheer up, and bounced out of the room.

I could see that Waydelin was now very tired and in need of sleep. I got up to go. The partition between the two rooms must have been very thin, for I could hear a champagne-cork drawn, the shrill laughter of women, men talking loudly, and chairs being moved about the floor. 'I don't mind,' he said, seeing what I was thinking, 'so long as they don't sing. But they won't begin to sing for two hours yet, and I can get some sleep. Good-night. Perhaps I shall not see you again.'

'May I come again?' I said.

'I always like seeing you,' he said, smiling, and thereupon turned over on the pillow, just as he was, and fell asleep.

---

[33] George Frederic Watts (1817–1904), English painter and sculptor, whose work Symons disliked. Edward Burne-Jones (1833–98), English painter and illustrator whose medievalism inspired Beardsley's drawings for Thomas Malory's *Morte d'Arthur* (1893). He at first encouraged Beardsley, but relations between them cooled as the older artist began to see Beardsley's work as parodying everything he held dear.

Gustave Moreau (1826–98), reclusive French symbolist painter, known for his visionary mythological scenes and a favourite artist of Jean Des Esseintes in Huysmans' *A Rebours*. Symons believed Burne-Jones and Moreau felt 'life is a thing to be escaped from, not turned to one's purpose' and that they consequently painted 'pictures of pictures' rather than 'the modern world'. *Studies in Seven Arts*, p. 106.

A hermit crab is a marine crustacean that inhabits the discarded shells of molluscs rather than having one of its own.

[34] The first known reference to the name Vaseline was by Robert Chesebrough in his US patent for the process of making petroleum jelly in 1872. It is widely used as a cleanser and make-up remover.

I looked at his face as he lay there, with the shawl about his shoulders and his hands outside the bedclothes. The jaw hung loose, the cheeks were pinched with exhaustion, sweat stood out about the eyes.[35] The sudden collapse into sleep alarmed me. I could not leave him in such a state, and with no one at hand but those people supping in the next room. I sat down in a corner near the bed and waited.

As I sat there listening to the exuberant voices, I wondered by what casual or quixotic impulse Waydelin had been led to marry the woman, and whether the woman was really heartless because she sat drinking champagne with her friends of the music-hall while her husband, a man of genius in his way, lay dying in the next room. I forced myself to acknowledge that she had probably no suspicion of how near she was to being a widow, that Waydelin would deceive her to the end in this matter, and the last thing in the world he would desire would be to see Mrs Waydelin in tears at the foot of the bed.

As time went on the supper-party got merrier, but Waydelin did not stir, and I sat still in my corner. It was probably in about two hours, as he had foreseen, that a chord was struck on the piano, and a man began to sing a music-hall song in a rough, facile voice. At the sound Waydelin shivered through his whole body and woke up.[36] In a very weak voice he asked me for water. I brought him a glass of water and held it to his lips. He drank a little and then pushed it away and began shivering again. 'Let me send for a doctor,' I said, but he seized my hand, and said violently that he would see no doctor. In the next room the piano rattled and all the voices joined in the chorus. I distinguished the voice of Mrs Waydelin. He seemed to be listening to it, and I said, 'Let me call her in.' 'Poor Clara may as well amuse herself,' he said, with his odd smile. 'What is the use? I feel very much as if I am going to die. Will it bother you: being here, I mean?' His voice seemed to grow weaker as he spoke, and his eyes stared.[37] I left him and went hastily into the other room. The singer stopped abruptly, and the girl at the piano turned round. I saw the remains of supper on the table, the empty glasses and bottles, the chairs tilted back, the cigars, tobacco-smoke, the flushed faces, rings, artificial curls; and then Mrs Waydelin came to me out of the midst of them, looking almost frightened, and said, 'What's the matter?' 'Get rid of these people at once,' I said in a low voice, 'and send for a doctor.' Her face sobered instantly, she took

---

[35] Beardsley anticipated his death in several drawings, notably 'The Death of Pierrot' and its accompanying caption from the sixth *Savoy* (August 1896), which depicts members of the *commedia dell'arte* gathering at the bedside of the 'white frocked clown of Bergamot'. Unlike Mrs Waydelin's friends, they are hushed and reverent.

[36] The juxtaposition of the raucous music-hall song and the dying consumptive may have been suggested by Crackanthorpe's 'Modern Melodrama' (*Yellow Book*, April 1894), in which a dying woman hears 'Daisy, Daisy' being bawled in the street below her sick-room.

[37] Waydelin's death represents a significant artistic advance on one of Symons's superficially similar juvenile poems, 'A Café Singer' (*Days and Nights*, 1889).

one step to the bell, was about to ring it, then turned and said to one of the men, 'Go for a doctor, Jim,' and to the others, 'You'll go, all of you, quietly?' and then she came with me into the bedroom.

Waydelin lay shivering and quaking on the bed; he seemed very conscious and wholly preoccupied with himself. He never looked at the woman as she flung herself on the floor by the bedside and began to cry out to him and kiss his hand. The tears ran down over her cheeks, leaving ghastly furrows in the wet powder, which clotted and caked under them. The curl was beginning to come out of her too yellow hair, which straggled in wisps about her ears. She sobbed in gulps, and entreated him to look at her and forgive her. At that he looked, and as he looked life seemed to revive in his eyes. He motioned to me to lift him up. I lifted him against the pillows, and in a weak voice he asked me for drawing-paper and a pencil. 'Don't move,' he said to his wife, who knelt there struck into rigid astonishment, with terror and incomprehension in her eyes. The pose, its grotesque horror, were finer than the finest of his inventions. He made a few scrawls on the paper, trying to fix that last and best pose of his model. But he could no longer guide the pencil, and he let it drop out of his hand with a look of helplessness, almost of despair, and sank down in the bed and shut his eyes. He did not open them again. The doctor came, and tried all means to revive him, but without success. Something in him seemed consciously to refuse to come back to life. He lay for some time, dying slowly, with his eyes fast shut, and it was only when the doctor had felt his heart and found no movement that he knew he was dead.

~

An Autumn City

'An Autumn City' brings together two of Symons's most intense passions: his love of the 'dead city', Arles, about which he wrote several essays, and 'Lydia', the dancer with whom he had a turbulent affair and with whom he was obsessed for the rest of his life. He described it as 'an ironical story of two temperaments that have a curious way of clashing', a description which hardly conveys the narrative's melancholy power. Daniel Roserra, the protagonist, 'who tended his soul like one might tend an orchid', is imbued with 'something of myself', he wrote, while Livia contains 'traces of what was once enigmatical and passionate in a wonderful girl, of mixed blood' — Lydia was half-Spanish — 'who was my mistress for many years'. She was a composite figure, also derived from 'a married woman, whose temperament was totally different'.[1] The story is another that treads a thin and wavering line between autobiography, fiction and a particular kind of fantasy, being filled with material that invites biographical interpretation. That Symons incorporated descriptions of Arles from his non-fictional accounts of the town only strengthens the similarity between himself and Roserra, the wealthy and leisured Cornishman who shares so many of Symons's views and is, in many ways, the cosmopolitan connoisseur he would like to have been. The preface to *Cities* (1903) further reinforces their similarities. 'For me,' Symons wrote, 'cities are like people, with souls and temperaments of their own, and it has always been one of my chief pleasures to associate with the souls and temperaments congenial to me among cities.'[2] Roserra's opinion is almost identical.

Written in the aftermath of the end of Symons's affair with 'Lydia', the story broods on what might have happened had the idealized Symons been able to marry her.[3] To judge from Symons's recollections, she seems to have been far less

---

[1] Symons, 'The Genesis of Spiritual Adventures'.
[2] Symons, *Cities*, p. v.
[3] Beckson notes a single sheet of paper in Box 1 of the Symons Archive at Princeton with the date 31 January 1896 and typed words, 'The last night Lydia ever slep[t] with me was that night'. *Arthur Symons: A Life*, p. 133. He wrote about their final night together in more detail in *Amoris Victimia* [*sic*] (privately printed, 1940), pp. 20–22, accompanying his recollections with a photograph of her. The Arthur Symons Papers at Princeton contain a number of other images of 'Lydia', pictures Symons had kept for half a century.

capable of appreciating his creative and intellectual life than Muriel Broadbent, and perhaps the story allows the reader to credit Symons with a little more self-knowledge than Derek Stanford does. Although it is reductive to read it as simply an alternative history of Symons's failed relationship with his former mistress, it surely feeds off his pondering of what may have transpired had their lives together taken a different course. Would she, like Rhoda, have been able to travel with him to the cultural centres of Europe, or enjoy the quiet and neglected backwaters? It seems unlikely, and the story's chilling final line implies that the passionate relationship between 'the dancer' and 'the dreamer', as Symons put it in one of his poems, would not have lasted long when exposed to the fierce heat of Marseilles or the 'penitential chilliness' of Arles.

Symons again uses free indirect style with considerable subtlety throughout the story, making it difficult to distinguish between the narrator's views and those of Roserra. He does not attempt to delve deeply into Livia's consciousness however, for the story relies upon Roserra's attempts to 'study' her and somehow understand her personality through prolonged observation rather than asking anything so vulgar as a direct question. The implication is that Roserra and his creator have boundless depths but Livia (and women in general?) only has surfaces, however glittering and alluring those surfaces may be. They certainly cannot be understood by men on anything other than the most trivial level, an intimation which makes the ambitious 'Lucy Newcome' project, or even 'Esther Kahn', all the more surprising. Like a number of modernist writers, Symons uses free indirect style to create a problematic relationship between the narrator and the characters, and he also expects the reader to assume an active rather than passive role, reading between the lines, as it were, to become a shaper rather than receiver of meaning. As with 'Esther Kahn', it is now difficult to know quite how far we are being encouraged to endorse Roserra's perceptions. Can a man of such worldly experience really be ignorant of the true nature of that 'magnetic current' which draws him towards a sexually desirable and charismatic young woman?

'An Autumn City' first appeared in *The Weekly Critical Review*, where it appeared in three instalments on 25 June, 2 July, and 9 July 1903. It is not to be confused with Symons's earlier travel essay, 'An Autumn City' (*The Dome*, February 1899), which is reprinted in the present volume as 'Arles'.

* * *

To Daniel Roserra life was a matter of careful cultivation. He respected nature, for what might be cunningly extracted from nature; provided only that one's aim was a quite personal thing, willingly subject to surroundings on its way to the working out of itself. He tended his soul as one might tend some rare plant; careful above most things of the earth it was to take root in. And so he thought much of the influence of places, of the image a place makes for itself in the consciousness, of all that it might do in the formation of a beautiful or uncomely disposition. Places had virtues of their own for him; he supposed that he had the quality of divining their secrets; at all events, if they were places to which he could possibly be sensitive. Much of his time was spent in travelling, in a leisurely way, about Europe; not for the sake of seeing anything in particular, for he had no interest in historical associations or in the remains of ugly things that happened to be old, or in visiting the bric-a-brac museums of the fine arts which make some of the more tolerable countries tedious. He chose a city, a village, or a seashore for its charm, its appeal to him personally; nothing else mattered.

When Roserra was forty he fell in love, quite suddenly, though he had armed himself, as he imagined, against such disturbances of the aesthetic life, and was invulnerable. He had always said that a woman was like a liqueur: a delightful luxury, to be taken with discretion. He feared the influence of a companion in his delicate satisfactions: he realised that a woman might not even be a sympathetic companion. He had, it is true, often wished to try the experiment, a risky one, of introducing a woman to one of his friends among cities; it was a temptation, but he remembered how rarely such introductions work well among people. Would the cities be any more fortunate?

When, however, he fell in love, all hesitation was taken out of his hands by the mere force of things. Livia Dawlish[4] was remarkably handsome, some people thought her beautiful; she was tall and dark, and had a sulky, enigmatical look that teased and attracted him. Some who knew her very well said that it meant nothing, and was merely an accident of colour and form, like the green eye of the cat or the golden eye of the buffalo. Roserra tried to study her, but he could get no point of view. He felt something that he had never felt before, and this something was like a magnetic current flowing subtly from her to him; perhaps, like the magnetic rocks in the 'Arabian Nights,' ready to draw out all the nails and bolts of his ship, and drown him among the wrecked splinters of his life.[5]

He was rich, not too old, of a good Cornish family; he could be the most charming companion in the world; he knew so many things and so many places and was never tedious about them: Livia thought him on the whole the most suitable husband whom she was likely to meet. She was happy when he asked her to marry him, and she married him without a misgiving. She was not reflective.

---

4 Dawlish is a seaside town in South Devon. The pairing of Cornwall and Devon symbolizes the misalliance of the lovers, the more so since the distinction between the two counties is often too subtle to be appreciated by their non-residents.

5 Though the collection was a rich repository of stories and motifs for Western writers, Victorian translations only appeared in private editions because of the dangers of prosecution for obscenity. This may have heightened their appeal for Symons. The magnetic island appears in 'The Third Kalandar's Tale' and is a mountain gifted by Allah with the power of lodestone. Here it is used as a metaphor for Livia's erotic allure.

After the marriage they went straight to Paris, and Roserra was surprised and delighted to find how childishly happy Livia could be among new surroundings. She had always wanted to see Paris, because of its gaiety, its bright wickedness, its names of pleasure and fashion. Everything delighted her; she seemed even to admire a little indiscriminatingly. She thought the Sainte-Chapelle the most beautiful thing in Paris.[6]

They went back to London with more luggage than they had brought with them, and for six months Livia was quite happy. She wore her Paris hats and gowns, she was admired, she went to the theatre; she seemed to get on with Roserra even better than she had expected.

During all this time Roserra seemed to have found out very little about his wife. It gave him more pleasure to do what she wanted than it had ever given him to carry out his own wishes. So far, they had never had a dispute; he seemed to have put his own individuality aside as if it no longer meant anything to him. But he had not yet discovered her individuality from among her crowds of little likes and dislikes, which meant nothing. Nothing had come out yet from behind those enigmatical eyes; but he was waiting; they would open, and there would be treasure there.

Gradually, while he was waiting, his old self began to come back to him. He must do as he had always wanted to do: introduce the most intimate of his cities to a woman. Autumn was beginning; he thought of Arles, which was an autumn city, and the city which meant more to him than almost any other. He must share Arles with Livia.

Livia had heard of the Arlesiennes,[7] she remembered Paris, and, though she was a little reluctant to leave the new London into which she had come since her marriage, she consented without apparent unwillingness.

They went by sea to Marseilles, and Livia wished they were not going any further. Roserra smiled a little satisfied smile; she was so pleased with even slight, superficial things, she could get pleasure out of the empty sunlight and obvious sea of Marseilles. When the deeper appeal of Arles came to her, that new world in which one went clean through the exteriorities of modern life, how she would respond to it!

---

[6] The Sainte-Chapelle is a medieval royal chapel, begun in 1239 by Louis IX and consecrated in 1248. It was built to hold the king's collection of holy relics, which included a purported Crown of Thorns, and located near the Palais de la Cité, on the Ile de la Cité in the heart of Paris. Damaged during the French Revolution, it was restored during the nineteenth century and completed in 1855. It is famed for its Gothic architecture and its collection of thirteenth-century stained glass. Undoubtedly a beautiful place, it is too much of a tourist trap to appeal to Roserra.

[7] Perhaps Roserra introduced Livia to Georges Bizet's tuneful incidental music for Alphonse Daudet's *L'Arlésienne* ('The Girl from Arles', 1872), which is often performed as a pair of suites (1872, 1879). Some of its material is drawn from folk melodies.

They reached Arles in the afternoon, and drove to the little old-fashioned house which Roserra had taken in the square which goes uphill from the Amphitheatre, with the church of Notre Dame la Major in the corner. Livia looked about her vividly as the cab rattled round twenty sharp angles, in the midst of narrow streets, on that perilous journey. Here were the Arlesiennes, standing at doorways, walking along the pavements, looking out of windows. She scarcely liked to admit to herself that she had seen prettier faces elsewhere. The costume, certainly, was as fine as its reputation; she would get one, she thought, to wear, for amusement, in London. And the women were a noble race; they walked nobly, they had beautiful black hair, sometimes stately and impressive features. But she had expected so much more than that; she had expected a race of goddesses, and she found no more than a townful of fine-looking peasants.[8]

'Do not judge too quickly,' said Roserra to her; 'you must judge neither the place nor the people until you have lived yourself into their midst. The first time I came here I was disappointed. Gradually I began to see why it was that even the guide-books tell you to come to this quiet, out-of-the-way place, made up of hovels that were once palaces.'[9]

'I will wait,' said Livia contentedly. The queer little house, with its homely furniture, the gentle, picturesque woman who met her at the door, amused her.[10] It was certainly an adventure.

Next day, and the days following, they walked about the town, and Roserra felt that his own luxuriating sensations could hardly fail to be shared by Livia, though she said little and seemed at times absent-minded. They strolled among the ruins of the theatre begun under Augustus, and among the coulisses of the great amphitheatre;[11] they sat on the granite steps; they went up the hundred steps of the western tower. From the cloisters of St. Trophime they went across to the museum opposite, where a kindly little dwarf showed them the altar to Leda, the

---

[8] 'I had expected a cluster of goddesses,' Symons writes in his 1891 essay on Arles, 'and I found a company of fine-looking peasants', *Wanderings*, p. 17. 'Arles is the one place in the world to which one goes, and admits that one goes, for the sake of the women,' Symons writes in his 1899 Arles essay. 'The fame of the women of Arles has gone over the whole world [...] They walk with a magnificent composure [...] Here is a townful of peasant women who are like a townful of artists' models' (*Wanderings*, pp. 27–28). 'Arles has the extraordinary distinction of existing on the fame of its beautiful women,' he added in 'Aspects of Cornwall' (1913) (*Wanderings*, p. 254). Even Henry James was struck by the beauty of Arlesian women, describing one at length in the 'Arles' section of *A Little Tour in France* (1884).

[9] 'The first time I was in Arles,' wrote Symons in 1899, 'I was a little disappointed [...]. But now, on my third visit to Arles, I am beginning to understand the Arlésiennes' (*Wanderings*, p. 27).

[10] Symons uses 'amuse' here and elsewhere in the story in its older sense: to occupy in a pleasing or engaging fashion.

[11] Augustus: the first Roman emperor, who ruled from 27 BC until 14 AD. A coulisse is the space between pieces of theatrical scenery, through which actors can enter and exit.

statue of Mithras, and the sarcophagi with the Good Shepherd.[12] He sold them some photographs of Arlesian women: one was very beautiful. 'That is my sister,' he said shyly.[13]

When the soul of Autumn made for itself a body, it made Arles. An autumn city, hinting of every gentle, resigned, reflective way of fading out of life, of effacing oneself in a world to which one no longer attaches any value; always remembering itself, always looking into a mournfully veiled mirror which reflects something at least of what it was, Arles sits in the midst of its rocky plains, by the side of its river, among the tombs. Everything there seems to grow out of death, and to be returning thither. The town rises above its ruins, does not seem to be even yet detached from them. The remains of the theatre look down on the public garden; one comes suddenly on a Roman obelisk and the fragments of Roman walls; a Roman column has been built into the wall of one of the two hotels which stand in the Forum, now the Place du Forum; and the modern, the comparatively modern houses, have an air which is neither new nor old, but entirely sympathetic with what is old. They are faded, just a little dilapidated, not caring to distinguish themselves from the faint colours, the aged slumber, of the very ancient things about them.

Livia tried to realise what it was that charmed Roserra in all this. To her there was no comfort in it; it depressed her; in the air itself there was something of decay. There was a smell of dead leaves everywhere, the moisture of stone, the sodden dampness of earth, water forming into little pools on the ground, creeping out of the earth and into the earth again. There was dust on everything; the trees that close in almost the whole city as with a leafy wall were dust-grey even in sunlight. The Aliscamps seemed to her drearier than even a modern cemetery, and she wondered what it was that drew Roserra to them, with a kind of fascination. On the way there, along the Avenue Victor Hugo, there were some few signs of life; the cafés, the Zouaves[14] going in and out of their big barrack, the carts coming in from the country; and in the evening the people walked there. But she hated the little melancholy public garden at the side, with its paths curving

---

[12] St Tromphine (or Tromphinus) is the legendary first bishop of Arles (c. 250 AD). His church in Arles, a former cathedral, was built between the twelfth and fifteenth centuries.

In Greek mythology, Leda was the daughter of Thestius, King of Aetolia, raped by Zeus in the form of a swan and mother of Clytemnestra, Helen of Troy, and the twins Castor and Polydeuces. She has often been depicted in paintings and sculpture, and is the subject of Yeats's 'broken sonnet', 'Leda and the Swan' (1924). Mithras was originally an Indo-Iranian god of light and truth, whose male cult came to Rome during the second half of the first century BC. He was often depicted slaying a bull, and his worship was especially associated with soldiers.

[13] In his 1891 essay on Arles, Symons writes, 'a kindly dwarf showed me the statue of Mithras … Then he sold me photographs of the Arlésian women. "C'est ma soeur," he said, pointing to one. She did not resemble her brother.' 'Arles I: A Night at Arles', *Wonderings*, p. 16.

[14] Zouaves are French light infantry troops usually deployed in North Africa.

upwards to the ruined walls and arches of the Roman theatre, its low balustrades of crumbling stone, its faint fountains, greenish grey. It was a place, she thought, in which no one could ever be young or happy; and the road which went past it did but lead to the tombs. Roserra told her that Dante, when he was in hell, and saw the 'modo più amaro' in which the people there are made into alleys of living tombs, remembered Arles:

'Sì com' ad Arli ove'l Rodano stagna.'[15]

She laughed uneasily, with a half shudder. The tombs are moved aside now from the Aliscamps, into the little secluded Allée des Tombeaux, where they line both sides of the way, empty stone trough after empty stone trough, with here and there a more pompous sarcophagus. There is a quiet path between them, which she did not even like to walk in, leading to the canal and the bowling-green; and in the evening the old men creep out and sit among the tombs.

At first there was bright sunshine every day, but the sun scorched; and then it set in to rain. One night a storm wakened her, and it seemed to her that she had never heard such thunder, or seen such lightning, as that which shook the old roof under which she lay, and blazed and flickered at the window until it seemed to be licking up the earth with liquid fire. The storm faded out in a morning of faint sunshine; only the rain clung furtively about the streets all day.

Day after day it rained, and Livia sat in the house, listlessly reading the novels which she had brought with her, or staring with fierce impatience out of the window.[16] The rain came down steadily, ceaselessly, drawing a wet grey curtain over the city. Roserra liked that softened aspect which came over things in this uncomfortable weather; he walked every day through the streets in which the water gathered in puddles between the paving-stones, and ran in little streams down the gutters; he found a kind of autumnal charm in the dripping trees and soaked paths of the Aliscamps; a peaceful, and to him pathetic and pleasant, odour of decay. Livia went out with him once, muffled in a long cloak, and keeping her whole face carefully under the umbrella. She wanted to know where he was taking her, and why; she shivered, sneezed, and gave one or two little coughs. When she saw the ground of the Aliscamps, and the first trees began to drip upon her umbrella with a faint tap-tapping on the strained silk, she turned resolutely, and hurried Roserra straight back to the house.

---

[15] A reference to the sarcophagi of the groaning heretics in Canto IX of Dante's *Inferno* (*c.* 1307–20). 'Even as at Arles, where stagnant flows the Rhone' (H. W. Longfellow translation, 1867).

[16] In the summer of 1904, while working on *Spiritual Adventures*, Symons wrote an untitled, somewhat Hardyean poem which he did not publish until the essay in which it appears, 'A Valley in Cornwall', was collected in *Cities and Sea-Coasts and Islands*. It depicts a similar scene to the one evoked here, with a woman staring out at a storm: 'Only you at the window, with rueful lips | Half pouting, | Stand dumb and doubting, | And drum with your finger-tips.' It was reprinted as the third of the 'Songs of Poltescoe Valley' in *Poems*, Volume II (1924).

After that she stayed indoors day after day, getting more irritable every day. She took up one book after another, read a little, and then laid it down. She walked to and fro in the narrow room, with nothing, as she said, to think about, and nothing to see if she looked out of the window. There was the square, every stone polished by the rain; the other houses in the square, most of them shuttered; the little church in the corner, with its monotonous bell, its few worshippers. She knew them all; they were mostly women, plain, elderly women; not one of them had any interest, or indeed existence, for her. She wondered vaguely why they went backwards and forwards, between their houses and the church, in such a regular way. Could it really amuse them? Could they really believe certain things so firmly that it was worth while taking all that trouble in order to be on the right side at last? She supposed so, and ended her speculations.

When Roserra was with her, he annoyed her by not seeming to mind the weather. He would come in from a walk, and, if she seemed to be busy reading, would sit down cheerfully by the stove, and really read the book which he had in his hand. She looked at him over the pages of hers, hating to see him occupied when she could not fix her mind on anything. She felt imprisoned; not that she really wanted to go out: it was the not being able to that fretted her.

About the time when, if she had been in London, she would have had tea, the uneasiness came over her most actively. She would go upstairs to her room, and sit watching herself pityingly in the glass; or she would try on hat after hat, hats which had come from Paris, and were meant for Paris or London, hats which she could not possibly wear here, where her smallest and simplest ones seemed out of place. Sometimes she brought herself back into a good temper by the mere pleasurable feel of the things; and she would run downstairs forgetting that she was in Arles.

One afternoon, when she was in one of her easiest moods, Roserra persuaded her to attend Benediction[17] with him at the church of Notre Dame la Major, in the corner of the square. The church was quite dark, and she could only dimly see the high-altar, draped in white, and with something white rising up from its midst, like a figure mysteriously poised among the unlighted candles. Hooded figures passed, and knelt with bowed heads; presently a light passed across the church, and a lamp was let down by a chain, lighted, and drawn up again to its place. Then a few candles were lighted, and only then did she see the priest

---

[17] Benediction of the Blessed Sacrament, commonly referred to as Benediction and known in France as Salut, is a Roman Catholic service usually held in the afternoon or evening. Hymns, litanies, or canticles are sung before the Blessed Sacrament (the Host and Eucharistic wine). This is displayed upon the altar in a monstrance and surrounded by candles. At the end of the service, the priest, his shoulders enveloped in a veil made from silk or cloth-of-gold, lifts the monstrance and silently makes the sign of the cross over the kneeling congregation. Benediction may conclude other services, but here appears as a rite complete in itself. Roserra seems attracted to it for aesthetic rather than religious reasons.

kneeling motionless before the altar. The chanting was very homely, like that in a village church; there was even the village church's harmonium; but the monotony of one air repeated over and over again brought even to Livia some sense of a harmony between this half-drowsy service and the slumbering city outside. They waited until the service was over, the priests went out, the lamps and the candles were extinguished, and the hooded figures, after a little silence, began to move again in the dimness of the church.

Sometimes she would go with Roserra to the cloisters of St. Trophime, where Arles, as he said, seemed to withdraw into its most intimate self. The oddness of the whole place amused her. Every side was built in a different century: the north in the ninth, the east in the thirteenth, the west in the fourteenth, and the south in the sixteenth; and the builders, century by century, have gathered into this sadly battered court a little of the curious piety of age after age, working here to perpetuate, not only the legends of the Church, but the legends that have their home about Arles. Again and again, among these naïve sculptures, one sees the local dragon, the man-eating Tarasque who has given its name to Tarascon.[18] The place is full of monsters, and of figures tortured into strange dislocations. Adam swings ape-like among the branches of the apple-tree, biting at the leaves before he reaches the apple. Flames break out among companies of the damned, and the devil sits enthroned above his subjects. A gentle Doctor of the Church holding a book, and bending his head meditatively sideways, was shown to Livia as King Solomon; with, of course, in the slim saint on the other side of the pillar, the Queen of Sheba.[19] Broken escutcheons, carved in stone, commemorate bishops on the walls. There is no order, or division of time; one seems shut off equally from the present and from any appreciable moment of the past; shut in with the same vague and timeless Autumn that has moulded Arles into its own image.

But it was just this, for which Roserra loved Arles above all other places, that made Livia more and more acutely miserable. Wandering about the streets which bring one back always to one's starting-point, or along the boulevards which

---

[18] The Tarasque was a Provencal monster said to live on a rock in the midst of the Rhône. It was a fearsome creature, something like a dragon with a lion's head, six short bear-like legs, the body of ox, a turtle's shell, and a scaly tail that ended in a scorpion's sting. It was tamed by the hymns and prayers of St Martha, who led it back to the city of Nerluc where, unresisting, it was killed by the townspeople. Martha's preaching converted them to Christianity, whereupon repenting of their treatment of the unfortunate beast, they changed the town's name to Tarascon.

[19] According to the Book of Kings, Solomon was the son of David, builder of the First Temple in Jerusalem, a man noted for his wisdom, wealth, and authorship of the Song of Solomon. Later works attributed great occult powers to him. The Queen of Sheba heard of Solomon's great wisdom and journeyed to Jerusalem with gifts of spices, gold, precious stones and beautiful wood and to test him with questions (1 Kings 10. 1–13). Later commentators often see a sexual union between the two monarchs, though the Old Testament gives no suggestion of any such relationship.

suggest the beginning of the country, but set one no further into it, nothing seems to matter very much, for nothing seems very much to exist. In Livia, as Roserra was gradually finding out, there was none of that sympathetic submissiveness to things which meant for him so much of the charm of life. She wanted something definite to do, somewhere definite to go; her mind took no subtle colour from things, nor was there any active world within her which could transmute everything into its own image. She was dependent on an exterior world, cut to a narrow pattern, and, outside that, nothing had any meaning for her. He began to wonder if he had made the irremediable mistake, and, in his preoccupation with that uneasy idea, everything seemed changed; he, too, began to grow restless.

Meanwhile Livia was deciding that she certainly had made a mistake, unless she could, after all, succeed in getting her own way; and to do that she would have to take things into her own hands, much more positively than she had yet done. She would walk with him when it was fine, because there was nothing else to do. Once they walked out to the surprising remains of the abbey of Mont-Major, and it began to rain, and they lingered uncomfortably about the ruins and in the subterranean chapel. She walked back with him, nursing a fine hatred in silence. She turned it over in her heart, and it grew and gathered, like a snowball rolled over and over in the snow. It was comprehensive and unreasoning, and it forgot the small grievance out of which it rose, in a sense of the vast grievance into which it had swollen. To Roserra such moods, which were now becoming frequent, were unintelligible, and he suffered from them like one who has to find his way through a camp of his enemies in the dark.

When they got back to the house, Livia would silently take up a book and sit motionless for hours, turning over the pages without raising her eyes, or showing a consciousness of his presence. He pretended to do the same, but his eyes wandered continually, and he had to read every page twice over. He wanted to speak, but never knew what to say, when she was in this prickly state of irritation. To her, his critical way of waiting, and doing nothing, became an oppression. And his silence, and what she supposed to be his indifference, grew upon her like a heavy weight, until the silent woman, who sat there reading sullenly, felt the impulse to rise and fling away the book, and shriek aloud.

Livia did not say that she wished to go away from Arles, anywhere from Arles, but the desire spoke in all her silences. She made no complaint, but Roserra saw an unfriendliness growing up in her eyes which terrified him. She held him, as she had held him since their first meeting, by a kind of magnetism which he had come to realise was neither love nor sympathy. He felt that he could hate her, and yet not free himself from that influence. What was to be done? He would have to choose; his life of the future could no longer be his life of the past. His introduction of a woman to his best friend had been unfortunate, as such introductions always are, in one way or another. He had tended his soul for more than half a lifetime, waited upon it delicately, served it with its favourite food;

and now something stronger had come forward and said: No more. What was it? He had no wish to speculate; it mattered little whether it was what people called his higher nature, or what they called his lower nature, which had brought him to this result. At least he had some recompense.

When he told Livia that he had decided to go back to Marseilles ('Arles does not suit you,' he said; 'you have not been well since we came here') Livia flung herself into his arms with an uncontrollable delight. On the night before they left, he sat for a long time, alone, under the Allée des Tombeaux. When he came back, Livia was watching for him from the window. She ran to the door and opened it.

It was midday when they reached Marseilles. The sun burned on the blue water, which lay hot, motionless, and glittering. There was not a breath of wind, and the dust shone on the roads like a thick white layer of powder. The light beat downwards from the blue sky, and upwards from the white dust of the roads. The heat was enveloping; it wrapped one from head to foot like the caress of a hot furnace. Roserra pressed his hands to his forehead, as he leaned with Livia over the terrace above the sea; his head throbbed, it was an effort even to breathe. He remembered the grey coolness of the Allée des Tombeaux, where the old men sat among the tombs. A nausea, a suffocating nausea, rose up within him as he felt the heat and glare of this vulgar, exuberant paradise of snobs and tourists. He sickened with revolt before this over-fed nature, sweating the fat of life. He looked at Livia; she stood there, perfectly cool under her sunshade, turning to watch a carriage that came towards them in a cloud of dust. She was once more in her element, she was quite happy; she had plunged back into the warmth of life out of that penitential chillness of Arles; and it was with real friendliness that she turned to Roserra, as she saw his eyes fixed upon her.

~

Seaward Lackland

Unpublished before its appearance in *Spiritual Adventures*, 'Seaward Lackland' may have been Hardy's favourite of Symons's stories, but at first sight it is very much the 'odd one out' where the collection is concerned: the life and spiritual crises of a pilchard fisherman seem far removed from those of the artists and intellectuals elsewhere in the book. However, although the story does not invite the biographical speculations of 'Christian Trevalga' or 'An Autumn City', it nevertheless explores aspects of its creator through its Cornish setting and its engagement with Methodist teachings whose impact Symons always struggled to acknowledge and either properly assimilate or reject.

In his essay on the stories, Symons writes that '"Seaward Lackland" is almost wholly imaginary. I only rarely put anything of myself into it. Yet there was my reading my Bible, my wanderings on the cliffs and my adventures with the fishermen in their boats.'[1] He then discusses the sea in Carbis Bay and along the coast at Trevalga in a way which is very reminiscent of the essays on the Cornish coast he collected in *Cities and Sea-Coasts and Islands* (1918) and *Wanderings* (1931), mentioning in passing that he had attended the chapel in Carbis Bay when a boy, just as Seaward does. This tantalizing glimpse of Symons's childhood throws into relief the account given in 'A Prelude to Life', where the narrator notes his Nonconformist background and its focus on the world to come rather than 'this life, which seemed so real and so permanent to me'. 'It seemed to me that prayer was useless unless it were uttered with an intimate apprehension of God, unless an effort of will brought one mentally into his presence,' Symons writes, an egotistical underestimation of the powers of the Almighty. 'I did not want to be saved,' he adds. 'It is true that I did not want to go to hell, but the thought of what my parents meant by salvation had no attraction for me. It seemed to be the giving up of all that I cared for.' This 'spiritual stubbornness' made the emotional atmosphere of 'revival services' very challenging for him, as

---

[1] Symons, 'The Genesis of Spiritual Adventures'. As a minister's son, the young Symons may well have occupied a privileged position in St Ives. One wonders whether he was considered a lucky charm by fishermen, though it is unlikely that he took part in many fishing expeditions.

he feared that it would sway his reason and push him into the arms of a faith for which he had no sympathy. 'I was not alienated from Christianity by intellectual difficulties; it had never taken hold of me,' he concludes, though to judge from the content of the nightmares that troubled him throughout his life, he had obviously absorbed its serpent symbolism.

There is no question of Seaward Lackland approaching Christianity from the standpoint of 'A Prelude to Life'. John Wesley preached in Cornwall over thirty times during the second half of the eighteenth century, and by the Victorian era, the county was a Methodist stronghold, the 1851 Census showing that of the 50% of people attending religious services there, 32% were Methodist. Superstitious coastal communities cross-fertilized Christian teachings with plentiful maritime myths and legends. Methodism was very much the preserve of the poor, though its teachings appealed to a wide range of people ill at ease with the doctrines and management of the Anglican church. 'A Prelude to Life' depicts a 'dryly intellectual, despondent person, whose whole view of life was coloured by the dyspepsia he was never without,' but Symons's father was a popular and respected minister during his period in St Ives, and may have encountered such zealots as Seaward Lackland, just as Mr Curnock does in his son's story. Symons tried to shut his ears to the message preached in the chapels, but he nonetheless imbibed something of their atmosphere, and the intense preoccupations of those who worshipped in them.

'Seaward Lackland' is singularly unlike Pater in style, but along with the 'The Childhood of Lucy Newcome' and perhaps 'Esther Kahn', it is the story in which Symons best disguises his own concerns. For all that he insisted it contained little of himself, it shows what he might have become had he been stirred by revivalist preaching. It also dramatizes at one remove some of the theological and eschatological anxieties which tormented him during his adolescence, and which continued to rumble away long after the publication of the story. Structurally, it follows 'Esther Kahn' in working its way to a moment of crisis arising from public performance, and as in that story, offers the reader no excerpts of its script or sermon. However, where the actress overcomes her personal torment in order to shine upon the stage, Seaward first bewilders and then enrages his listeners, finishing the story as an outcast. As Karl Beckson observes, Seaward's wondering whether 'a mere man could imitate that supreme surrender' is 'an indication of the sin of pride rather than the certainty of faith'.[2]

Like many of Symons's favourite writers, Seaward is misunderstood by the public and by conventional authority. The minister who is with him as he dies 'shook his head sorrowfully' when Seaward explains that his disastrous sermon came about 'Because I loved God more than I loved myself.' His reaction is hardly

---

[2] Beckson, *Arthur Symons: A Life*, p. 221.

surprising when, Max Saunders notes, for Seaward, 'the fulfilment of his damnation is supposed to be the proof of the strength of his faith.'[3] Lackland and Waydelin may be strange bedfellows, but they invite allegorical interpretation as artists and visionaries whose engagement with the world moves from the quotidian to the transcendent. Seaward's particular brand of fervent, ecstatic but self-destructive mysticism also makes him oddly allied with the writers discussed in *The Symbolist Movement*. Symons hailed Mallarmé's shrinking from 'that handing over of his naked soul to the laughter of the multitude', and thereby keeping the 'secret' of his art. Seaward's exposure of his innermost beliefs is very much a 'handing over of his naked soul', and shows the folly of so doing.[4] Nevertheless, there is a central distinction between the two, in that Mallarmé's 'secret' is kept by means of the deliberate mystification of language and typography, whereas Seaward's is incommunicable because it lies beyond his powers of expression. The most poignant image in the story is therefore not the death scene with which it concludes, but Seaward silent in the deserted chapel, 'standing before the open Bible in the pulpit.'

* * *

Seaward Lackland was born on a day of storm, when his father was out at sea in his fishing-boat; and the mother vowed that if her husband came home alive the boy should be dedicated to the Lord. Isaac Lackland was the only one of his mates who came home alive out of the storm; and the boy got the queer name of Seaward because his mother had looked out to sea, as soon as she had strength enough to be propped up in bed, praying for her husband every minute of the time until he came back. She could see the sea through the little leaded windows of the cottage which stood right on the edge of the cliff above Carbis Bay.[5] The child's earliest recollection was of the shape and colour of the waves, between the diamond leadings, as he was held up to the window in his mother's arms. It was like looking at pictures in frames, he thought afterwards.

The child was dedicated to the Lord. Isaac knelt down by the bedside and prayed over him as Mary held him in her arms, and when he got up from his knees he said: 'Mary, if the boy lives, please God, he shall have his schooling; and I wouldn't say but he might make a fine preacher of the Gospel.'

[3] Saunders, *Self Impression*, p. 253.

[4] Symons, 'Stéphane Mallarmé', *The Symbolist Movement in Literature*, p. 62.

[5] Carbis Bay lies a mile south-east of St Ives, then a fishing port and now a holiday and artistic centre. It is part of the larger St Ives Bay. Beckson describes it as Symons's 'spiritual home' (*Arthur Symons: A Life*, p. 221). It was here that he composed the notorious 'Stella Maris' (*Yellow Book*, April 1894). See too 'At Carbis Bay', dated 26 November 1893 and included in *London Nights*.

'It was little schooling Peter ever had,' said his wife.

'Peter was wanted in the boat; this youngster can wait.'

'Oh, Isaac, do you think he'll go to America, when he's grown up, like Peter?'

'No, Mary, he'll not go farther than Land's End by land, or Mount's Bay by sea, if what I feel is the truth.'[6] We've given him to the Lord, and I say the Lord will lend him to us.

Mary said under her breath, 'Oh, please, Lord Jesus,' several times over, with her eyes tight shut, as she did when she seemed to pray best. Her first son had been drowned at sea, her second had run away from home and gone to America; and she hardly dared think of what would happen to this one. But they had done what they could. Would not God watch over him, and would he not be kind to her because she had given up some of her rights in the child?

The child grew strong and gentle; he learned quickly what he was taught, and when he had learned it he would set himself to think out what it really meant, and why it meant that and not something else. He was always good to his mother, and as soon as he had learned to read he would read to her out of a few books which she cared for, the Bible chiefly, and Bogatzky's *Golden Treasury*, and the *Pilgrim's Progress*.[7] Through reading it over and over to his mother, he got to know a good part of the Bible by heart, and he was always asking what this and that puzzling passage meant exactly, and, when he got no satisfying answer, trying to puzzle out a meaning for himself.

Every day he went in to the Wesleyan day-school at St Ives, and as he walked there and back along the cliff-path, generally alone, all sorts of whimsical ideas turned over in his head, ideas that came to him out of books, and out of what people said, and out of the queer world in which he found himself, half land and half water. It was always changing about him and yet always there, in the same place, with its regular and yet unaccountable tides and harvests.[8] Sometimes there

---

[6] Land's End is the most westerly point in England. Mount's Bay is the largest bay in Cornwall and dotted with settlements, the most populous of which is Penzance. Its unpredictable tides and currents made it a dangerous place for sailors throughout the nineteenth century.

[7] *Güldenes Schatz-Kästlein der Kinder Gottes* ('Little Golden Treasure Chest of God's Children'), a collection of devotional texts for children including Biblical quotations, prose reflections, and verse assembled by Carl Heinrich von Bogatzky (1690–1774) and first published in 1718. Translated into many European languages, it remained popular for well over a century, though its inclusion here demonstrates Cornwall's provincialism as well as the piety of the Lackland family. For *The Pilgrim's Progress*, see 'The Childhood of Lucy Newcome'.

[8] Wesleyans follow the teachings of John Wesley (1703–91) and his brother, Charles (1707–88), reformers of the Protestant church whose ideas were termed 'Methodist' because of the way in which 'rule' and 'method' governed their approach. Methodism deliberately engaged with the poor and socially marginal who were bypassed by the established church during the eighteenth century, and was popular throughout south west England. It maintains that entry to Heaven is not the prerogative of a chosen elect but is available to all those who are justified (that is, pardoned or forgiven their sins) by their faith. Believers are sanctified by the Holy

was a storm at sea and all the boats did not come back, and the people he had talked with yesterday had gone, like the stone he kicked over the cliff in walking, or he saw them carried up the beach with covered faces. Death is always about the life of fishermen, and he saw it more visibly and a thing more natural and expected than it must seem to most children.

He had always loved the sea, and it was his greatest delight to be taken out when the pilchards were in the bay, and to sit in the boat watching the silver shoals as they crowded into the straining net. He waited for the cry of 'Heva!' from the watchman on the hill, and often sat beside him, or stared out to sea through his long telescope, longing to be the first to catch the moving glitter of silver.[9] He talked with the men 'like a grown-up chap' they said, and they talked with him as if he were a man, telling him stories, not the stories they would have told children, but things out of their own lives, and ideas that came into their heads as they lay out at sea all night in the drift-boats.

There was one old man with whom the boy liked best to talk, because he had been a sailor in his youth and had gone through all the seas and landed at many ports, and had been shipwrecked on a wild island and lived for a year among savages, and he was not like the other men, who had always been fishers, and thought Plymouth probably as good as London.[10] Old Minshull seemed to the boy a very clever as well as a far-travelled person, and he discussed some of his difficulties with him and got help, he thought, from the old man.

His difficulties were chiefly religious ones. He knew much more about the Bible than about the world, and his imagination was constantly at work on those absorbing stories in Kings and Judges, and all sorts of cloudy pictures which he made up for himself out of obscure hints in the Prophets and the Apocalypse.[11] The old Cornishman knew his Bible pretty well, but not so well as the boy; and the boy would bring the book out on the cliff and read over some of the confusing things; murders, with God's approval, it seemed, and treacheries which set nations free, and are called 'blessed,' and the sins of the saints; and then mysterious curses and unintelligible idolatries, and the Scarlet Woman and Jonah's whale.[12] He

Spirit, whom God grants to those who repent and believe that through their faith, they can overcome sin. Everyone is entitled to God's grace. Seaward Lackland has an adversarial, even confused relationship to these tenets.

[9] 'Heva' or 'hevva' is Cornish for a shoaling of fish. The Cornish language was in decline by the time Symons was born, but he certainly knew some words of it.

[10] Plymouth is a major port and naval centre in south Devon, approximately 80 miles (c. 130 km) from St Ives.

[11] Books of the Old Testament, which, to judge from 'A Prelude to Life', Symons preferred to the New.

[12] The Scarlet Woman, a figure who haunted Symons's imagination throughout his life, is also known as the Whore of Babylon. She appears in the Book of Revelation (ch. 17–18); her full title is Mystery, Babylon the Great, the Mother of Harlots and Abominations of the Earth. Dressed in purple and scarlet robes and draped with jewels, she rides a seven-headed beast.

liked best the Old Testament, and had formed a clear idea of God the Father as a perfectly just but constantly avenging deity; it pained him if he could not bring everything into agreement with this idea; and in the New Testament he was often perplexed by what Jesus seemed to do and undo in the divine affairs. The old sailor turned over all these matters in his head; they were new to him, but he faced them, and he was sometimes able to suggest just the common-sense way out of the difficulty.

When Mary Lackland thought the boy old enough to understand the full meaning of it, she told him how, on the day of his birth, he had been dedicated to God, and she told him that he was never to forget this, but to think much of God's claims upon him, and to be certain of a special divine guardianship. He listened gravely, and promised. From that time he began to look on God, not with less awe, but with a more intimate sense of his continual presence, and a kind of filial feeling grew up in him quite simply, a love of God, which came as a great reality into his life. He felt that he must never dishonour this divine father, either by anything he did or by the way in which he thought of him even. Did not God, in a sense, depend on him as a father depends on his son, to keep his honour spotless, to be more jealous of that honour than of his own? That, or something like it, only half-defined to himself, was what he felt about God, to whom his whole life had been dedicated.

When he had finished his schooling, the boy joined his father in the boats, first, only by day, in the pilchard fishery, and then in the drift-boats that went far out, at night, in the herring season. His father was a silent man and rarely spoke to him; the other men half feared and half despised him, because he would not drink or play cards with them, and seemed to be generally either reading or thinking. He thought a great deal in those long nights, and when he was eighteen he began to be seriously alarmed because, so far as he knew, he was not converted.

He knew that he tried to do what was right, that he kept all the commandments, prayed night and morning, and that he had this instinctive love of God; but, according to the Methodists, all that was not enough. There must be a moment, they held, in every man's life when he becomes actively conscious of salvation; for every man there is a road to Damascus.[13] Seaward Lackland had not yet come to that great crisis, and he waited for it, wondering what it was and when he would come to it.

Jonah appears in The Second Book of Kings (14. 25) and the Book of Jonah. He is a Hebrew prophet who initially defies God's will, and is swallowed by a whale (or large fish) in whose belly he prays for forgiveness. After three days, the whale vomits him forth to continue God's work. The figure of Jonah became proverbial, especially in seafaring communities, for carrying bad luck.

[13] The scene of Saul's conversion from zealous Pharisee to the Christian Paul, told in Paul's letters and in the Acts of the Apostles. The phrase, along with the allied notion of 'seeing the light', is widely used to refer to sudden realizations and changes of mind.

He began to be troubled about his sins. The Bible said that every evil thought was a sin, and he did not know how many evil thoughts had come into his mind since he had become conscious of good and evil. A heavy burden of guilt weighed upon him; he could not put it aside; the more he thought of God, the more conscious did he become of that awful gulf which lay between him and God. Conversion, he had heard, bridged that gulf, or your sins fell off into it and were no more seen, even if, somewhere out of sight, they still existed, and would exist through all eternity. He would have despaired but for the hope of that miracle. And if I die, he said to himself, before I am converted?

He had always gone regularly to chapel on Sundays and as often as he could on week-days, but now he began to stay to the prayer-meetings after the service, and the minister at St. Ives noticed him, and often prayed with him and talked with him, but to no avail. A year went by, and he grew more despondent; even his love for God seemed to be slackening. One winter evening he heard that a famous revivalist was coming to Lelant.[14] He thought he would go and hear him, then something seemed to urge him not to go; and he walked half-way there, and then back again, unable to make up his mind. Then, thinking that it was the devil who was trying to keep him away, he turned and walked resolutely to Lelant.

When he reached the chapel the service had begun. They were singing 'Jesu, lover of my soul,'[15] and the preacher was standing inside the communion-rail (he liked to be nearer the people than he could be in the pulpit), and, as Seaward had the first glimpse of his face, he was singing as if every word of the hymn meant something wonderful to him. His eyes were wide open and shining; he held the closed hymn-book in both hands, rigid in front of him, and the people seemed already to have begun to feel that magnetic influence which he rarely failed to establish between himself and his hearers. After the hymn he stretched out his hand with a sudden gesture, and the people stood motionless for a moment and then gradually sank down on their knees as he began to pray rapidly. He seemed to be talking with God as if God were there in the midst of them, and as he passed from supplication into a kind of vivid statement, meant for the people rather than for the ear of God, there seemed to be a dialogue going on, as if the answers which he gave were hardly his own answers. He ended abruptly, and, without the harmonium, started an almost incoherent marching-song which was well known at all revivals. 'Hallelujah, send the glory!' he sang, and the voices of the people rose louder and louder and feet began to beat time to the heavy swing of the tune. Then he read the lesson and, without a pause, gave out the text, and began to speak.

---

[14] A small village on Carbis Bay, within walking distance of St Ives.
[15] A hymn by Charles Wesley in his *Hymns and Spiritual Songs* (1753) which employs maritime imagery.

Seaward Lackland had stepped into a pew near the door, and in the furthest corner of the chapel. Something in the preacher's voice had thrilled him, and he could not take his eyes off the long lean face, with its eyes like two burning coals, as it seemed to him, under a high receding forehead, from which the longish hair was brushed straight back. A huge moustache seemed to eat up the whole lower part of the face; and, as the man spoke, you saw nothing but the eyes and the quivering moustache. He began quietly, but, from the first, in the manner of one who has some all-important, and perhaps fatal, secret to tell. An uneasiness spread gradually through the chapel, which increased as he went on, with more urgency. People shifted in their seats, looked sideways at their neighbours, as if they feared to have betrayed themselves. Seaward felt himself turning hot and cold, for no reason that he could think of, and he took out his handkerchief and wiped his forehead. Near him he saw a young woman begin to cry, quite quietly, and a man not far off drew long breaths, that he could hear, almost like groans. The preacher's voice sounded like pathetic music, and he heard the tones rather than the words, tones which seemed to plead with him like music, asking something of him, as music did; and he wanted to respond; and he realised that it was his sin that was keeping him back from somehow completing the harmony, and he heard the preacher's voice talking with his soul, as if no one were there but they two. And God? God, perhaps.

By this time many people in the chapel were weeping, men groaned heavily, some jumped up crying 'Hallelujah!' and when the preacher ended and said, 'Now let us have silent prayer,' and came down into the aisle, and moved from pew to pew, one after another, as he spoke to them, got up, and went to the communion-rail, and knelt there, some of them with looks of great happiness. As Seaward saw the preacher coming near him, he felt a horrible fear, he did not know of what; and he rose quietly and stepped out into the night. But there, as he stood listening to some exultant voices which he still heard crying 'Hallelujah!' and as he felt the comfort of the cool air about him, and looked up at the stars and the thin white clouds which were rushing across the moon, a sense of quiet and well-being came over him, and he felt as if some bitter thing had been taken out of his soul, and he were free to love God and life at the same time, and not, as he had done till then, with alternate pangs of regret. 'If God so loved the world,'[16] he found himself repeating; and the whole mercy of the text enveloped him. He walked home along the cliff like one in a dream: he only hoped not to waken out of that happiness.

From this time, year by year, Seaward Lackland grew more eager to do some work for God. He had made few friends among the young men and women of his own age; to the women he seemed at once too cold and too earnest, and the men were not quite certain of the comradeship of one who had so much book-

---

[16] 'For God so loved the world, that he gave his only begotten Son, that whosoever believeth in him should not perish, but have everlasting life.' John 3. 16.

learning, and who was so full of strange ideas. He did not mean to be unfriendly, but he had not the qualities that go to the easy making of friendships; and he found no one, neither man nor woman, with whom he had anything in common. The men respected him, for he was a good fisherman; but the women had for the most part a certain contempt for this large-boned, dull-eyed, heavy-jawed young man, who was never at his ease when he was with them, and who waited on no occasions for meeting them when they might have liked his company. The minister at St. Ives had noticed him and asked him sometimes to come and have a talk with him in his study. One day Lackland, warmed out of his reserve, had been talking so well that the minister said to him: 'I think we must have you as a local preacher, Lackland. What do you say to it?' He said quietly: 'I would like to try, sir.'

A few weeks afterwards, when the quarterly 'plan' was handed in at the Lacklands' cottage, and Mrs Lackland had unfolded it eagerly, to see who were appointed to take the services at Carbis, she came suddenly upon a name which startled her so much, that the broad sheet of paper fluttered off her knees to the floor. 'My boy,' she said, as Seaward picked it up, and handed it back to her with a smile, 'I have been praying for this ever since I dedicated you to the Lord. Now I hardly know what there is left for me to pray for.'

'Pray that I may be steadfast in the faith, mother,' said Seaward.

'I will, my son; but I wouldn't mind trusting him for that.'

Everybody in the village was in Carbis Chapel to hear Seaward Lackland's first sermon. He was not afraid of them; he had something to say, and he was to speak for God; he said quietly all that was in his mind to say.

After the sermon, while he was walking across to the cottage with his father and mother, both very happy, and saying nothing at all, one or two of the older people stayed behind to discuss the sermon. 'Do you think he is quite orthodox?' said one of them, dubiously. 'I don't know,' said another; 'there were some ideas, sure enough, I never heard before; but I wouldn't say for that they weren't orthodox.' 'We must be careful,' said a third; 'these young people think too much.' 'A great deal too much,' said the first, 'once you begin to think for yourself, what's to stop you?'

———————————

From the time of his first sermon Seaward Lackland looked upon his dedication to God as not only complete, but, in a sense, accepted. He had offered himself as an interpreter of the will of God to men, and power was put into his hand. Now, he said to himself, if I should prove a backslider, that would be a calamity for God also. The thought of his sins, which he believed God to have pardoned, came back to him again and again; he saw them still existing, like atoms which refused to go out into nothingness; even if pardoned, not literally extinct. What if his soul were one day to reinherit them, to slip back into their midst, having let go of the hand of God, which needed at all times to hold him up out of that deadly gulf? And now that he, who needed help so much, had taken it upon him to try to help others, could he be sure that he was rightly helping them? Could he, in all obedience, be sure that he was interpreting the divine will aright?

He had never found help in any book but the Bible. Once or twice he had borrowed a commentary from the minister at St Ives, but he could not read these dry and barren discourses, which seemed to tell you so many unnecessary things, but never the things that you wanted to know. He put them aside, and the conviction came to him that with prayer and thought everything would explain itself to him. Did not the Holy Ghost still descend into men's minds, illuminating that patient darkness? He waited more and more expectantly on that divine light, and it seemed to come to him with a more punctual answer. At night, on the water, while the other men lay across the seats, smoking their pipes in silence, he would withdraw into his own mind until visible things no longer existed, and he was alone in a darkness which began to glow with soft light. Only then did he seem to see quite clearly, and what he saw was not always what he had reasoned out for himself; but it was a solution, and it came irresistibly.

Once, when he had fallen asleep, he dreamed a dream from which he awoke with a cry of terror. In his dream he had seen an evil spirit (it had the appearance of a man, but he knew it to be an evil spirit because of the infinitely evil joy which shone through the melancholy of its eyes), and he was sitting talking with the evil spirit on the edge of a tall cliff above the sea; and it said to him: Do you know that Seaward Lackland is damned? and he said No, and it said: He is damned because he has sinned the sin against the Holy Ghost; and the evil joy began to grow and grow in its eyes, and it was watching him as if to discover whether he knew that he himself was Seaward Lackland, and he tried to say No again, more loudly, and as he drew back, the cliff began to crumble away, but very slowly, so that a hundred years might have passed while he felt himself slipping down into the gulf of the sea; and his own cry awakened him.

He knew that he had been dreaming, but the dream might have been a message. He knew the text in the Bible, and he had often wondered what it meant. Had not Jesus said: 'All manner of sin and blasphemy shall be forgiven unto men: but the blasphemy against the Holy Ghost shall not be forgiven unto men'?[17] It was the most terrible saying in the Bible. What was the sin which even God could not forgive? He remembered that reiteration in Matthew: 'And whosoever speaketh a word against the Son of Man, it shall be forgiven him: but whosoever speaketh against the Holy Ghost, it shall not be forgiven him, neither in this world, nor in the world to come.' Might it not be possible for a man to sin that

---

[17] Matthew 12. 31–32.

sin in ignorance? Would his ignorance avail him, if he had actually sinned it? These thoughts troubled him strangely, and he tried to put them away from him.

They came back to him again, and more searchingly. Since his conversion he had been as much troubled by the thought of his past sins as he had been before that change occurred. They were put away; yes, but was it not a kind of putting off the payment of a debt which might be still accumulating? And now, if there was one sin which could never be atoned for, and if he had committed that one sin? It was possible, and the thought filled him with horror.

One July night, when the boats were away in the North Sea, he set himself to think the whole matter out; he would get at the truth, and not endure this doubt and trouble any longer. He was sitting in the stern of the boat, the other men were talking in low voices, but he was used not to hear them. He put his elbows on his knees, and bowed his head over till his hands met above it. He shut his eyes and stared hard into the darkness under his eyelids. The boat rocked gently: he wanted to keep quite still, so that he might think, and he put his feet against the sides of the boat, steadying himself.

As he sat there, annihilating thought that he might think the more deeply, it seemed to him after a time as if all his past life came back to him under a new aspect, as something which had been wrong from the beginning. Had he not, as a child, been angry, greedy, loving only his own pleasure, ungrateful to those who had refused him any of his desires for his own good? Had he not been heedless and self-willed as a young man, had he not even made a boast of his own righteousness after he had found Christ? Was there a day since he had come to a knowledge of good and evil when he had not sinned at least in thought? He imagined God adding up all those sins, from the animal sins of childhood to the sins of the mature mind. 'The Lamb's book of life':[18] he remembered the words, and they became terrible to him, for he saw all the pages in which his account was written. For him it would be the book of eternal death.

He lifted his head and looked up. God was up there, beyond that roof which was his pavement. He was afraid of the great loneliness which lay between him and God.

He looked around. The drift-net lay out for a mile along the water, its brown corks heaving gently, at regular intervals. Other boats lay alongside, with their nets adrift; some of the boats were silent, the men all asleep; from others he heard voices, a sudden laugh, and then silence. The water was all about him, and the water was friendly, a great breathing thing, that had him in its arms. He only felt at home when he was on the water, because the water was so living, and the land lay like a dead thing, always the same, but for the change of its coverings. There

---

[18] 'And all that dwell upon the earth shall worship him, whose names are not written in the book of life of the Lamb slain from the foundation of the world.' Revelation 13. 8.

was in the Bible one of those hard sayings: that in heaven 'there shall be no more sea.'[19] It was too difficult for him to understand.

The sea comforted him a little, but he said to himself: 'I do not want to be dandled to sleep like a child; I want to see the truth.' Had he, or had he not, among the numberless sins, which he had seen God adding up in his book, committed the one sin which should never be pardoned? He did not know what that sin was, but, he argued, my ignorance makes no difference. If I pick toad-stools for mushrooms, and eat them, I shall pay the penalty, just the same as if I had eaten them on purpose. The Bible, it was true, did not tell you, as far as he could discover; but there must be people who knew. There was the minister, who had a reference Bible,[20] and knew Hebrew. He would certainly know.

'When we get back to St Ives,' said Lackland to himself, 'I will go and see Mr Curnock; meanwhile the less I think about this the better.' But there was one thought that he could not put out of his mind. Suppose he had not sinned the unpardonable sin, had he not sinned so often, and so deeply, that God ought not to pardon him, if he were really a just judge, and not swayed, as men are, by a pity which is only one form of partiality? He had always conceived sternly of God; the Jehovah of the Old Testament was always before him, a mighty avenger, a God of battles and judgments, inexorably just. If God was also love, God might forgive him; he would want to forgive him; but would it be right to accept mercy, if that mercy lowered his creator in his own eyes? The thought stung him, raced through him like poison; he could not escape from it. His old sense of honour towards God came back on him with redoubled force. If God were just, God would not forgive him. Did he not love God so much that he would suffer eternal misery, gladly, in order that God might be just?

When the boats went home with their fish, Lackland had only one thought: to go and see Mr Curnock at St Ives. He walked in from Carbis that evening, and found the minister alone in his study. Mr Curnock respected him; he had gone steadily on, year after year, preaching whenever he was wanted, and though one or two people had complained that his sermons were not strictly orthodox, most of the people spoke well of him; many said that he had helped them. On that night he was very serious, and he seemed to be hesitating to say all that he had to say. At last he admitted that it was the text in the Bible which was troubling him.

Mr Curnock went up to his shelves and looked along them. 'I know,' he said, 'that many people have been needlessly disturbed about that saying. And, as the Bible does not tell us, we cannot be quite certain what that sin is. But if I can find one or two passages that recur to me, in some of the people who have written

---

[19] 'And I saw a new heaven and a new earth: for the first heaven and the first earth were passed away; and there was no more sea.' Revelation 21. 1.
[20] A reference Bible contains annotation and commentary alongside the text, rather than being an additional volume.

about the Gospels, I think they will throw some light on the matter.' He took down a big black book, and turned over the pages. 'Here, for instance: "Not a particular *act* of sin but a *state* of wilful, determined opposition to the Holy Spirit, is meant." That is very much what I should imagine to be the truth. But it is a little vague, perhaps?'

'I don't thoroughly see it,' said Lackland. 'The Bible says "blasphemy against the Holy Ghost."'

'Well now,' said the minister, taking down another book, 'here is a translation from a Spaniard of the sixteenth century, who has been called "a Quaker before his time." He puts things quaintly, but I like him better than the formal people. Let me see: "Whence, considering that …" No, that doesn't concern us; here it is: "do I come to understand that a man then sins against the Holy Spirit, when, with mental malignity he persuades men that the works of the Holy Spirit are the works of the devil, he being soul-convinced of the contrary." Is that clear?'[21]

'That's clearer,' said Lackland.

'He goes on, on the next page,' said Mr Curnock, '"And I understand that sin against the Holy Ghost that worked in Christ was inexcusable, for it could not spring save from the most depraved minds, obstinate in depravity."' Mr Curnock shut the book, and put it back in its place. 'Now, do you see,' he said, sitting down by the table, 'this awful sin, such as it is, could not be sinned unconsciously; its very essence is that it is a deliberate rejection of what we know to be truth. I might almost say that to sin it, a man must make up his mind that he will do so.'

'I think I see,' said Lackland, staring before him; 'and I was wrong there, for certain: I never committed that sin. But, all the same, I don't feel quite clear yet.'

'Why is that?' said the minister.

'Have you never thought, sir,' said Lackland, 'that the only return we can make to God for his love to us, is to love him more than we love ourselves?'

'But certainly,' said Mr Curnock.

'Well,' said Lackland, 'do you see it might be that a good Christian would think most of saving his own soul.'

'That is his duty,' said Mr Curnock.

'But are they both true?' said Lackland.

'Both things you have said are perfectly true,' said Mr Curnock; 'only, I see no contradiction between them.'

'Thank you, sir,' said Lackland, getting to his feet; 'I'll go and think it all over; I'm not very ready at thinking, I have to set my mind to things slowly; and you've given me a good lot to think over. Goodnight, Mr Curnock.'

---

[21] 'The phrase 'a Quaker before his time' suggests Symons took the quotation from James Fitzmaurice-Kelly, *A History of Spanish Literature* (1898) where it is applied to the Spanish religious writer, Juan de Valdés (c. 1509–41).

'And now, my dear Lackland,' said the minister, as he opened the door of the house, 'above all, don't worry over a text which none of us are very sure about. Be certain of one thing, that God's mercy is infinite, and that he'll bring you through.'

Lackland walked slowly away from the door, along the terrace above the sea, and then more rapidly, as he came out on the rough path along the cliff. The wind blew sharply against him; the moon glittered in the sky, among a multitude of glittering stars; and he heard the sea screaming and tearing at the pebbles, as he sat down on the edge of the cliff, just before getting to Carbis Bay, and looked along the uneasy water, which quivered all over with little waves, hunching themselves up, one after another, and leaping forward, all in a white froth, as they struck upon the beach. 'They are like the lives of men,' thought Lackland; 'all that effort, a struggling onward, a getting to the journey's end: see, that wave is making for just that old tin can, and it has hit it, and the can rolls over and remains, and the wave is gone.' He drew his breath in sharply, drawing up the salt smell of the sea into his nostrils, and sat there for a long time thinking.

No, he had not committed the sin against the Holy Ghost: God could still pardon him. But was it right, was it just, that God should pardon him? One after another of the hard sayings of the Old Testament came into his mind: it was clearly impossible to fulfil every one of those obligations; he could but strive towards them, and fail, and fall back on the mercy of God. At that thought something rose up in him like a pride on behalf of God, and he said to himself: 'I will never ask God to stoop in order that I may rise.' As he said the words he looked round him; the aspect of the place, which he had known all his life, seemed to change, to become dim, to become mysteriously distinct, and he saw that he was sitting where he had sat with the evil spirit in his dream. He got up hastily and went indoors.

Night after night Seaward Lackland went out with the fishing-boats; he did his share of the work just as usual, took his share of the profits, slept by day, and sat awake by night; and, to all about him, he was the same man as before. But an ecstasy was growing up within him which kept his own ears shut to everything but one interior voice; he was meditating a great sacrifice; and a great happiness began to inhabit his soul. 'If God so loved the world,' he repeated, as he had repeated it on the night of his conversion, 'that he gave his only begotten Son ...' He brooded over the words, wondering if a mere man could imitate that supreme surrender. He was only a poor fisherman; the disciples had been that, and Jesus had called them to leave their fathers and their nets and follow him. Both his father and mother were dead; no one in the world depended on him; he was free to give up the world, if he chose, for God. The thought intoxicated him; he saw nothing but the thought, like a light beckoning to him in the darkness: perhaps calling him to destruction. The pride of a vast magnanimity thrilled through him: he would sin the one sin that God could not pardon, in order that God should deal with him according to his justice, and not according to his mercy. He would, as he had dreamed when a child, prefer God's honour to his own; he would give up heaven in order that God might be worthy of his own idea of him. I will sin, he said to himself, the sin against the Holy Ghost, and I will do it for the love of God.

When he had made up his mind, and was full of an exultant inner peace because of it, he still waited and pondered, not knowing quite how he would do the thing he had decided to do. It must be done publicly, and he must suffer for it here, as he was to suffer for it hereafter. It must be done in Carbis Chapel, when his turn came to preach there.

It was some time before his turn came, and he waited with a feverish impatience. He tried to think out what he should say, but he could not imagine anything that seemed to him sufficiently 'obstinate in depravity.' He remembered the phrase, 'when, with mental malignity, he persuades men that the works of the Holy Spirit are the works of the devil';[22] and he tried to work out an argument, at which he shuddered, which would seem to show Jesus as one working miracles with the help of Satan. At first he could not put two words together, but gradually the task became easier; strange arguments came into his head, which seemed almost plausible to himself; he wondered if it was actually the devil, for his own ends, helping him. He did not write down a word, though he was accustomed to write every word of his sermons; every word, as he thought it, stamped itself in his mind, like a seal pressed into burning wax.

The night before the Sunday on which he was to preach his last sermon, he lay in bed trying to sleep, but unable to close his eyes on the darkness that seemed to palpitate about him. He got out of bed, threw open the window, and leaned out. The night was quite black, he could see nothing, but he could hear the waves splashing upon the sand down below in the bay. A chill wind bit at his face, and made his body shiver. He shut the window, and lay down in bed again, staring for the dawn. He felt cold right through to the heart, and he felt horribly alone. By to-morrow night he would have cut himself adrift; he would be like that seaweed which the sea was tossing upon the sand, and dragging away from the sand. For God's sake he would have cast off God, and he had no other friend. To-morrow he would have none. His resolution never wavered, but he no longer wished the dawn to come quickly; he would have liked, when he saw the first light on the window-panes, to have held back the dawn.

He was to preach in the evening, and in the morning he sat in the chapel and heard the minister from St. Ives telling of the mercy of God. His text was: 'I say unto you that likewise joy shall be in heaven over one sinner that repenteth, more

---

[22] Symons took these quotations from Edward Boehemer's 1882 translation of Juan de Valdés's Commentary upon the Gospel of St Matthew.

than over ninety and nine just persons which need no repentance.'[23] He spoke of salvation for all; not a word was said about that one exception. Lackland felt a bitter smile twitching at the corners of his lips.

At night he made his own tea as usual, and walked up and down the room, often looking at the clock, until it was time to go across to the chapel. He saw the people passing his window on their way; some of them looked in, saw him, and nodded in a friendly manner. He looked again at the clock; now it was time for him to go, and he went into a corner of the room, knelt down, and prayed to God for strength to deny him. Then he walked rapidly across to the chapel.

The chapel was very full, it seemed to him oppressively hot, and he felt the blood flushing his forehead. Many of the people remembered afterwards that they had noticed something strange in his manner from the moment in which he set foot on the steps of the pulpit. They were quick to recognise the outward signs of a flame lighted within; and they anticipated a fine sermon. His first prayer was very short, but it was like a last confession. Each word seemed to live with a sharp, painful life of its own; the words cried out, and called down heaven for an answer. The text was a verse out of the twenty-fourth chapter of St. Matthew: 'Then if any man shall say unto you, Lo, here is Christ, or there; believe it not.'[24] It was not the first time he had chosen a strange text. He began slowly, and with an unusual solemnity. It seemed to him that they were not understanding him aright. As he went on, his voice, which had at first been low, grew louder; he spoke as if he were hurrying through some message which had been laid upon him to deliver; yet with the calmness of one who has mastered his own fever. He was speaking the most terrible words they had ever heard, and they were at first too bewildered even to think. As he went on, they began to look at one another, wondering if he were mad or they; one or two women near the door got up quietly and went out; men stirred in their seats; a great shudder went through the whole congregation. Blasphemies such as they had never dreamed of filled their ears, dazed their senses; and Seaward Lackland stood there calmly, like a martyr, one of them said afterwards; the sweat stood out on his forehead, but he spoke in an even voice: was it Seaward Lackland or was it the devil who stood there denying God, denying the Holy Spirit? There were those who looked up at the ceiling above them, thinking that the roof would fall in and bury them with the blasphemer. But as heaven did not stir in its own defence, it was for them to assume the defence of heaven. An old class leader stood up in his pew, near the communion-rail, and turning his back on the preacher, said in a loud voice: 'I entreat you all to listen to this man no longer, but to go instantly home, and pray God Almighty to forgive you for what you have heard this day.' Lackland stood silent, and everyone in the chapel got up and went quickly out, the old class-leader the last; and Lackland

---

[23] Luke 15. 7.
[24] Matthew 24. 23. See too Mark 13. 21.

was left alone in the chapel, standing before the open Bible in the pulpit. He fell on his knees and covered his face with his hands: 'O God, forgive me,' he prayed, 'for what I have done for thee today.'

From that day Seaward Lackland was an outcast in the village. The mates with whom he shared the boat and the nets refused to go to sea in his company, lest they should share a judgment reserved for him, and all be drowned together. He accepted his fate without protest, and, as one thing after another slipped out of his hands, made no complaint. When there was nothing else for him to do, he drove a cart which used to carry the fish from the boats to the salting-cellars, and afterwards from the cellars to the railway station, where they were sent in barrels to the nearest port for Genoa and Leghorn. He was too poor now to live in his cottage, and housed with some others as poor as himself, in a half-fallen shanty on the way to Lelant. Even his housemates mocked him, and held themselves more decent folks than he. It was thought that his brain had weakened, for he became more and more eccentric in his ways, and got to talk with himself, for hours together, in a low voice, but with the gestures of one explaining something to an unseen disputant. One day as he was racing up the hill by the side of his cart, urging on the horses, his foot slipped, and he fell under the near wheel, which had crushed into his breast-bone before the horses could be stopped. He was carried back, and laid on his ragged bed; and was just able to ask those about him to fetch the minister from St Ives. He was not quite dead when the minister came, and he said 'Amen,' simply, to the prayer which the minister offered up for him. Then, as he seemed anxious to say something, the minister stooped down, and, to help him, said: 'Perhaps you want to tell us why you sinned against God ...' he was going to add, 'and that you repent of it, and hope for salvation,' but the dying man, in a very faint but ecstatic voice, said: 'Because I loved God more than I loved myself'; and so died, with a great joy on his face. But the minister shook his head sorrowfully, not understanding what he meant.

~

Extracts from the Journal of Henry Luxulyan

The final story in *Spiritual Adventures*, the previously-unpublished 'Henry Luxulyan' was, said Symons, 'mostly founded on actual facts' and 'not entirely imaginary.' 'I put much of my own temperament into it,' he admitted, 'many of my impressions and adventures.'[1]

The 'facts' of the story were supplied by Symons's friend, La Comtesse Victor Sallier de la Tour, a socialite, patron of the arts and hunter of literary lions, during his sojourn with her in 1898.[2] As Symons concedes, Luxulyan is another of this collection's problematic authorial doubles, with the summary of his early life and character bearing obvious comparison with 'A Prelude to Life', and many of his attitudes being those Symons expressed elsewhere. His name links him, like Trevalga and Roserra, to Cornwall, the only place in England, barring London, to which Symons felt any sense of attachment. Luxulyan is a village known for its china clay and granite quarries, as well as being a familiar Cornish surname; Lord Luxellian marries Elfride Swancourt, the heroine of Hardy's *A Pair of Blue Eyes* (1873), a novel set largely in Boscastle ('Castle Boterel'), only a few miles north of the village of Trevalga. In 'Henry Luxulyan', Cornwall serves as an

---

[1] Symons, 'The Genesis of Spiritual Adventures'.

[2] An accomplished musician, artist and linguist, the Comtesse (née Mathilde Ruinard de Brimond, 1852–1912), was a friend of Symons until her death in March 1912 - her domestic circumstances were very different from those of Baroness von Eckenstein. Symons spent six weeks with her at her château in the Auvergne in August/September 1898, writing essays on Verlaine and other French writers, telling Yeats she was 'the best of companions' and her home 'a continual delight' (*Arthur Symons: A Life*, p. 177). She painted a flattering portrait of him, signed 'Mahaut', which hung in his cottage for many years. Long believed to be lost, it surfaced in 1982 and was sold at Bonhams in October 2005. The Comtesse also enabled Symons to stay at the Benedictine monastery in Monserrat in October 1898, a sojourn which produced several poems and his essay 'Monserrat' (*Saturday Review*, 5 November 1898). After visiting Venice in the summer of 1903, Symons and Rhoda stayed with the Comtesse in Rome that December. Symons sent the Comtesse a confused plea for help during his illness, but never saw her again once he had been returned to England.

antidote to London, just as it was for Symons, who would frequently visit the Cornish coast when the London smog (or his business and romantic commitments) became unduly oppressive.

With so much of his history and opinions on display, it is little wonder that Symons chose to employ a nameless narrator, a countryman of Luxulyan, who burns letters unread, changes names, and leaves no allusion 'to circumstances which it is likely that anyone could easily identify.' Adopting the format of a journal also serves as a disguise of sorts, in that it allows him to concentrate on psychology rather than exterior concerns, as well as licensing gaps, silences, and omissions which leave so much unsaid, particularly where Luxulyan's earlier life is concerned. In doing so, Symons followed the example of Pater's 'A Prince of Court Painters' to some extent, though he also seems inspired by the use of the diary in Gothic and sensation fiction from *The Woman in White* to *Dracula*. It is well suited to the horrible story of the Baroness's disfigurement, as well as making it impossible for Luxulyan (or the reader) to know her innermost thoughts and desires.

The story shows Symons's ability to rework both elements of his life and the familiar components of Victorian fiction and reportage, such as financial ruin or vitriol attack. The collapse of the Argonaut is derived from that of Jabez Balfour's Liberator Building Society, the great financial scandal of the 1890s, while the disfiguring of the Baroness has its roots in the acid attacks of Gissing's *The Nether World* (1889) and Stevenson's *The Ebb-Tide* (1894) as well as being a feature of papers such as the *Illustrated Police News*.[3] Symons may also be drawing upon the French tradition of the *conte cruel* associated with writers such as Villiers de l'Isle-Adam and Jean Lorrain who combined an admiration for Poe with a markedly misogynistic streak. In their work, lovers often revenge themselves upon unfaithful partners in horrible and/or ingenious ways. In this respect, it is telling that the incident is revisited in the final story Symons published, 'The Sinister Guest', fourteen years later. The genre was not popular in less-permissive late-Victorian England, though isolated examples of it did appear. Perhaps the nastiest is Conan Doyle's 'The Case of Lady Sannox' from *Round the Red Lamp* (1894), though here the disfigurement is caused by surgical knives rather than sulphuric acid

There are many curiously prophetic moments in *Spiritual Adventures*, none more so than this story's pairing of Venice with madness. Symons first visited Venice in March 1894, and wrote a number of essays and poems about his

---

[3] The vitriol attack remained a staple of sensation and crime fiction for years afterwards. See for example, Conan Doyle's 'The Adventure of Illustrious Client' from *The Casebook of Sherlock Holmes* (1924) and Graham Greene's *Brighton Rock* (1938). Aaron Matz notes further examples such as Gaskell's *Mary Barton* (1848) and Maupassant's 'Jadis' (1880) in 'Some Versions of Vitriol (the Novel circa 1890)', *NOVEL: A Forum on Fiction* 42.1 (Spring 2009), pp. 23–39.

experiences.[4] The Italian city would of course be where his sanity began to unravel in the autumn of 1908, and 'Henry Luxulyan' is filled with ominous forebodings. Luxulyan speculates as to whether Venice causes madness or merely affects those already susceptible to it, but what draws him to the city in the first place is unclear. 'I came to Venice for peace,' he says, having made no entries in his journal for almost a year, but any peace or rest is soon disturbed by sinister fancies, 'subtle terrors' and a growing sense that the city is 'turning evil'. Although Luxulyan seems haunted by his past rather than by the phantom afflicting Magnus in Vernon Lee's 'A Wicked Voice' (1890), Symons creates a memorably sinister environment, of shadow, mysterious sounds, and 'the insidious coiling of water about one'. In such a place, it becomes impossible to separate reality from feverish dreams, and though the entry of 27 November suggests that the Baroness has come to Venice, it is by no means certain that she has actually done so. The reader is left only with the confusions of the diarist's apparent convalescence, a state in which his personality has lapsed into abeyance and he drifts like a weed on the current.

* * *

When Henry Luxulyan died in Venice, a few years ago, he left a written request that all his papers should be sent to me under seal. He was a townsman of mine, and that, I think, had been almost the only link between us, though I had known him from childhood, and we used to meet, more or less accidentally, and at long intervals, all through his life. As a boy he had few friends; he did not seek them; and I was never sure that he looked upon me as in any real sense a friend. It was always vaguely supposed that he was very clever, and as he took part in no boyish games, and did not ride, or swim, or even walk much, but seemed to brood, and linger, and be thinking, it was supposed that he had interests of his own, and

---

[4] The first to be published was 'Venice in Easter' (*Harper's Monthly Magazine*, April 1895), followed shortly by the four poems of 'Intermezzo: Venetian Nights' (*London Nights*, June 1895), the impressionistic essay 'Venetian Glamour' (*Saturday Review*, 14 October 1899) and the poem 'Venetian Night' (*Images of Good and Evil*, 1900). His lengthiest account of the city is the chapter on Venice in *Cities* (1903), which began as 'Venice in Easter' and 'The Soul of Venice' (*Saturday Review*, 9 November 1901) and which was further enlarged for *Cities of Italy* (1907). 'Venetian Sensations' appeared in the *Saturday Review* (6 August 1904) following his third visit to Venice, this time in the company of Rhoda. Another article, 'Music in Venice' (*Saturday Review*, 17 October 1908) was written just before his breakdown in the city in September 1908, and Symons later remarked that it was 'a document in which my madness is most evident' (*Confessions*, p. 7). After his breakdown, Symons published numerous, occasionally garbled recollections of the city. These include 'Venice: Minuet' and 'Venice' (*Knave of Hearts*, 1913), 'Venice: On the Giudecca' (*Land and Water*, 15 November 1917), 'A Masque of Kings in Venice' [1894] (*Wanderings,*1931), and 'Venice 1897' (*Amoris Victimia*, 1940).

would one day be or do something remarkable. He was never communicative about anything, but once or twice in later years, he spoke to me of his historical studies, and I gathered that he was making researches (for a book, I supposed) into the life of Attila:[5] a subject remote and gloomy enough, I thought, to be naturally attractive to him. For some years I lost sight of him altogether, and then, to my surprise, met him at the house of a German Baron and his wife, who were settled in London, where they entertained lavishly. It was the last house at which I had ever expected to meet him; though indeed the Baroness was a woman of considerable learning, and very intelligent and sympathetic. I found that he had become her librarian, and was living in the house. He looked ill and restless. Whenever I dined at the house, he was always there. I noticed that the Baroness treated him more like a friend than a librarian; appealing to him on every occasion as if he had the management of the whole household. I never had much private talk with him, but he seemed glad to see me, and referred sometimes, but never very definitely, to his work, which I encouraged him to persevere with. He seemed almost pathetically alone; but I remembered that he had never cared to be otherwise. The nervous restlessness which I had observed in him was more marked every time that I saw him; and it was with no surprise that I heard he had broken down, and was in Venice, trying to recover. But it was in Venice that he took the fever of which he died.

I never knew why he left that strange request that his papers should be sent to me; nor was there any message among them, or the least indication of what he wanted me to do with them. Most of them were concerned with the life of Attila, but there were not three properly finished chapters; and the mass of fragments, quotations, references, tentative notes, mutually destructive and unresolved conjectures, baffled my utmost endeavours, and remained for me, and I fear must always remain, so much lost labour, like an enigma of which the key is missing. But in the midst of these papers, thrust as if hurriedly into one of the bundles, so that the string had cut into the outer leaves of loose manuscripts, there was a thin book bound in parchment, almost filled with Luxulyan's close, uneasy writing. It was a journal, many times begun and relinquished, ending with a date not many days before his death. Between the pages were two letters, in a woman's handwriting. I burnt the letters without reading them; then I read the journal.

What I print here is printed with but few omissions; only I have changed the names, and not left any allusion, as far as I know, to circumstances which it is likely that anyone could easily identify. For the omissions I make myself wholly responsible; as, indeed, for the printing of the journal at all. It seems to me a genuine document; odd, disconcerting, like the man who wrote it; profoundly

---

[5] Attila, often known as 'the Hun', ruled the Huns from 434 until 453 AD. His name became a byword for barbarism and savagery. In 452 he invaded northern Italy. Some of those who fled his advance retreated to the Venetian lagoon, and founded what would become Venice.

disconcerting to me, on reading it, as I discovered the real subterranean being whom I had known, during his lifetime, only by a few, scarcely perceptible outlines on the surface. Such as it is, I give it here, reserving till afterwards something more which I shall have to say by way of comment or epilogue.

* * *

April 5. — I have been talking with the doctor today, and he tells me that my nerves are seriously out of order.[6] There, of course, he is quite right, and he tells me nothing I did not know already. Only, why tell me? That is just what it does me no good to think about. If I am to keep in even so shaky an equilibrium as this, which at least might be worse, it is essential for me to forget there is any danger. What folly, to be a doctor and honest!

For my part, I was quite frank with him. I told him it was terrible, to be alone and to think about death every day of one's life. He put out a soothing hand professionally, and began to say something about 'with care' and 'I see no reason why,' and so forth; 'no reason why, with care, you should not live, well —' 'How long,' I interrupted him, as he hesitated. 'Thirty years, forty years,' he said confidently, 'why not? I tell you there is no reason why you should not die an old man.' And he thought he was comforting me! I only said, 'It is horrible.' 'In heaven's name,' he said, with real amazement, 'what is horrible?' I told him: this dwindling away, this continual losing of all the forces that hold one to life, this inevitable encroachment of the other thing, the darkness; and the uncertainty of it all, except the ending. 'Come now,' he said, as if he were arguing with a child, 'be reasonable; you don't expect to live for ever?' 'That is just it,' I said; and then I put it to him: 'don't you find it horrible to think of?' 'I never think of it,' he said. 'I have to see to it every day. One accustoms oneself to the things one sees every day. You brood over it because it is hidden away from you.'

He said that as if he was saying something fine, courageous, even intelligent.

I shivered as he spoke so lightly of seeing people die every day, and I said, 'You think nothing of it!' 'To me,' he said, more seriously, 'it is the one quite natural thing in the world. One is tired, one lies down, one sleeps. And even if one isn't conscious of being tired, there is nothing so good as sleep.' It struck me that he was quoting from Marcus Aurelius,[7] in a sort of roundabout way, and I let him go on talking; but when he looked at me and said: 'I have never met anyone before

---

[6] See Symons's sonnet, 'Nerves' in the 1897 edition of *London Nights*.

[7] Marcus Aurelius Antoninus Augustus (121–180 AD), Emperor of Rome 161–180. Last of Machiavelli's 'Five Good Emperors', he was a Stoic philosopher whose *Meditations*, written in Greek between 170 and 180, underpin much of the doctor's advice here. They also feature significantly in Pater's *Marius the Epicurean*, a novel which had an enormous influence on Symons.

who worried over the thought that he would have to die when he was seventy, eighty, ninety: how do you know you won't live to be ninety?' the simplicity of the man struck me as being laughable; a child could have reasoned better, and I said: 'If I live to be ninety I shall never have passed a day without thinking about death, and I know that I am logically right in never losing sight of the only thing in the world which is of infinite importance. You call it morbid, but what if only I am wide awake, after all, and you others are walking straight into a pit with your eyes shut?' It was then that he repeated that my nerves were seriously out of order. He told me that I must find distraction. In other words, I must shut my eyes from time to time. Well, there is no doubt about it. That is what I must try to do. But how?

April 6. — I suppose it is only because I am nervous, and because the doctor told me I must not live so much by myself, but I am beginning to think again about Clare, and I had not thought of her for a long time. When one has lived with a woman, in the same house with her, every day and every night for three years: think, there are one thousand and ninety-five days in three years! well, something remains, in the very look and touch of the furniture, in the treacherous blank of the mirrors, which forget nothing, and hide so much, something that will never wholly go; and I must not expect to release my senses, as I have released my mind and my will, from the power of that woman.[8]

Only, the less I think about her the better; and there is no danger of my wanting her back again. That would be singularly inconvenient, if, as I can but suppose, she is perfectly happy with that ordinary person whom she had the curious taste to prefer to me. One must guard against being ridiculous, even when one is alone with oneself, and I am content to seem no hero to this serviceable valet, my journal;[9] but it is partly the incapacity of good taste in them that makes women so intolerable. There are men of whom I have said to myself: Now, if Clare fell in love with this man, or that man, it would seem to me so natural, so legitimate; I could almost despise her for not submitting to a fascination which is insensitive not to feel. But a poseur, a fop, a cad; one of those men whom every man sees through at the first hand-shake; a sleek flatterer, whose compliments are vulgarities; the shopman air of 'inquire within upon everything'; yes, that is the man who takes his choice of women. Is vulgarity a curable thing? and will the vulgarity of women ever be cultured out of them?

---

[8] Compare Symons's poem, 'White Heliotrope' from *London Nights*, which pictures a prostitute in her rooms and 'The mirror that has sucked your face | Into its secret deep of deeps, | And there mysteriously keeps | Forgotten memories of grace'. Whether Clare is an avatar of the lost Lydia can only be conjectural, but it is clear that memories of that relationship continued to torment Symons despite his marriage.

[9] Luxulyan's bookishness is evident from the embedded reminiscences of his reading. Here he recalls the words of the French society hostess Mme Cornuel (1605–94): 'Il n'ya point de héros pour son valet de chambre'. These come from *Lettres de Mlle Aissé à Madame C* (1787) and soon acquired proverbial status.

I once tried to believe that there are women and women; but I have never found that the 'and' meant anything essential.

April 7. — I dined out at night, with my Jew friends, the Kahns, whom I have not cared to see for so long; and the distraction has done me good. They were charming, sympathetic, not obtrusively anxious about me; they welcomed me as if I were really a friend; and there were some pleasant people at the dinner-table. Only, I do not understand how they could ask to dinner a certain Baroness von Eckenstein who was there. One should preserve a certain decency in intercourse; there are things one should be spared! I sat opposite to her, and she talked to me a good deal across the table; she seemed intelligent; she might be all that is admirable. Her figure was firm, ample, almost majestic, and the face had once been not less finely designed, but over the whole left side, from the forehead to the neck, there was a great white scar, shapeless, horribly white, and scored as with deep cuts, which had formed cicatrices of a yet more ghastly white. The bloodless and livid skin, ploughed and wrinkled with these raised cicatrices, was drawn tightly over the cheek-bone. The eyelid, strangely misshapen, was alone the natural colour of flesh, but this eyelid looked as if it were artificially attached to the underpart of the eyebrow, and on the forehead above the eye there was a white scar, as if the flesh had been cut away to form the eyelid. I dared not look at her, and yet, in spite of myself, my eyes kept seeking her face. A death's head would be a more agreeable companion at table. They tell me she is newly come to London, very rich, very hospitable; Mrs Kahn, with her intolerable indulgence, means to make a friend of her; if I go there again I am sure to meet her, and only the thought of that disgrace of nature makes me shiver. Must I cut myself off again from just what had promised to be a real distraction? I will stay at home, work, not think, bury myself in my books.

April 8. — I realise, on thinking it over in a perfectly calm mood, without any sort of nervous excitement, that I have always been afraid of women; and that is one reason, the chief perhaps, why I have always been so lonely, both when Clare was with me, and before and after it. Just as I cannot get out of my head that there is some concealed conspiracy against me, in earthly things, so there seems to be, in the other sex, a kind of hidden anger or treachery, which makes me uneasy. I was never really happy when a woman sat on the other side of the table, at the other corner of the fireplace. Vigny was right:

'Toujours ce compagnon dont le coeur n'est pas sûr.'[10]

---

[10] 'Toujours ce compagnon dont le coeur n'est pas sûr | La femme, enfant malade et douze fois impur' ('Always this companion whose heart is uncertain | Woman, a sick child and a dozen times impure'), *La Colère de Samson* from Alfred de Vigny's *Les Destinées* (1864). Lhombreaud points out that Symons is often reminiscent of De Vigny (1797–1863) in his 'haughtiness' and 'disdain', and notes that De Vigny appears in *A Garden-Party in Vague Space*, a short play he was writing in the asylum in April 1909. Other characters included Baudelaire, Flaubert, Gautier, and George Sand (Lhombreaud, *Arthur Symons*, pp. 189, 264).

I will quote no more: the verse becomes Biblical; and indeed it is of Samson and Delilah. Just what attracts me in a woman revolts me: the 'love strong as death,' which is no more than 'la candeur de l'antique animal,' raised to the power of self-expression.[11] It bewilders, distracts yes, terrifies me. That women are better and worse than we think them, I am certain; and no doubt nature was wise in setting us on our knees before the enigma. To be so mysterious and so contemptible! Merely for us to think that, shuts us away from them, our possible friends, as by a great wall, outside which there can be only enemies. We capitulate, perhaps, but it is the enemy who has conquered.

April 9. — I have been working hard, going nowhere, and I suppose staying indoors too much. I begin to be restless again. The Kahns have written asking me to dine with them on Sunday: will that woman be there? Hans Greger is coming with his old music, and I should like to hear the viols and harpsichord again.[12] I think I must go.

Meanwhile some rumours of war which I read on the newspaper placards have set me puzzling over one of my favourite enigmas. Is it not incredible that there should be people in the world who will kill one another, and even themselves, for any one of a multitude of foolish reasons? As if life was not short enough at the longest, and one's bodily pains troublesome enough without even the added risk of accidents; and yet we must do our best to aid the enemy of us all; we must make ourselves lieutenants of death; and for what? The thing begins in our fantasies of honour, precedence, patriotism, or by whatever name, big or small, we choose to christen the tiny germ of unreason. War reduces to an absurdity, with its pompous mortal emphasis, the whole argument. I have been thinking out a theory of this disease of humanity, to which scientific people should have given a name. It might be studied, in cellars, as they study bacilli.[13]

April 10. — Today has been one of those days in which London becomes intolerable. The dust-carts in the street, the reek of chop-houses, the unwashed bodies in frowsy clothes, stink on the air, and the air is too heavy to drain off this odious foulness, and one breathes it, and seems to sicken. I am sure some loathsome gas is rising up out of the canal under my windows; my head turns if

---

[11] Like Symons, Luxulyan elides the sacred and profane with dangerous ease. Here he splices the *Song of Solomon* (8.6) and the 'animal simplicity' of Baudelaire's 'Sonnet d'Automne' from *Les Fleurs du mal* (1857).

[12] Greger is probably modelled on Arnold Dolmetsch (1858–1940), the early music revivalist and instrument maker during the 1890s. Dolmetsch made viols, recorders and harpsichords in his Surrey workshop; Symons attended his concerts during the 1890s. He dedicated the poem 'On an Air of Rameau' (1897) from *Images of Good and Evil* to him. The same volume's 'Airs for the Lute' (1897–98) is dedicated to Madame Elodie Dolmetsch.

[13] Before his breakdown, Symons was notably apolitical. This changed after his illness. 'Enchanted at hearing that England will go to war,' he told his wife in August 1914. 'One thing forsooth. Let Germany be damned!' (Beckson, *Arthur Symons: A Life*, p. 286).

I lean out and look over; and now it is between two lights, almost too dark to see by daylight and not dark enough to draw the curtains and turn on the electric light. It is the time of day that I hate most; it is the only time of the day when I actively want to be doing something, and when I am acutely miserable because I have nothing to do.

The last half-hour, since I wrote these words, has been as miserable a half-hour as I remember spending in my life. And yet there is nothing to account for it, except this absurd sensitiveness which is growing upon me. Why is it that one clings to life when it bores one in this manner? I am not sure that I have ever felt what people call the joy of living: life has always seemed to me a more or less ridiculous compromise; and yet there is nothing I dread so much as any sort of truth, the truth which might put an end, once and for all, to this compromise. Was there ever any one so illogical? I hate life, and yet I want to go on living for ever. Sometimes, coming back at night, after a concert in which some great music has struck one into a profound seriousness, a strange and terrifying sensation takes hold of me as the cab turns suddenly, out of a tangle of streets, into a broad road between trees and houses: one enters into it as into a long dimly lighted alley, and at the end of the road is the sky, with one star hung like a lantern upon the darkness; and it seems as if the sky is at the end of the road, that if one drove right on one would plunge over the edge of the world.[14] All that is solid on the earth seems to melt about one;[15] it is as if one's eyes had been suddenly opened, and one saw for the first time. And the great dread comes over me: the dread of what may be on the other side of reality. And it seems as if all the years of the longest life, measured out into days and hours, would not be long enough to hold me back from the horror of that plunge.

April 11. — She deceived me: all women deceive. I have no right to condemn her any more than I condemn my doctor for deceiving me when I am ill. He tells me: You will be better tomorrow; knowing that the only way to make me better is to make me think I am going to be so. It would be worse for us if women did not deceive us.

She was vain, selfish, sensual: should I have cared for her if she had not been all three? To almost everybody she seemed gentle and modest: was it really that I knew her better, or did everybody else know something about her which I had never discovered? That is the odd thing which I am beginning to wonder. She

[14] The nocturnal walk described here is strongly reminiscent of a similar episode in Arthur Machen's *The Three Impostors* (1895). See 'The Novel of the Iron Maid' with its image of 'street leading into street, as it seemed to world's end.' *The Three Impostors*, ed. by David Trotter (London: Everyman, 1995), p. 100.
[15] In Karl Marx and Friedrich Engels's *The Communist Manifesto* (1848, English translation 1850), modern industrial society is one in which 'all that is solid melts into air.' *The Communist Manifesto*, trans. by David McLellan (Oxford: World's Classics, 1992), p. 6.

lived with me for three years, and then left me. Whose fault was it that she left me after three years? In this wholly unusual state of humility in which I find myself at present, I cannot say that the fault was not partly mine, and partly that she was a woman. What a thing it is to be a woman, and how perplexing are even their virtues! They are not made, as we are, all of a piece; they are not made to be consistent; they think so little of what we think so much of; even sex is a light, simple, and natural thing to them, to which they attach none of our morbid valuations. It is for all this that, when I am not in this particular mood, I hate and fear them; but today it all seems so natural, and women themselves seem so pardonable. Think of the daily habits of their life: how many times a day they dress and undress themselves, and all it means. With each new gown a woman puts on a new self, made to match it.[16] All day long they are playing the comedian, while we do but sit in the stalls, listen, watch and applaud. At least the play is for our entertainment; we pay them to act it: let us be indulgent if the acting is not always to our taste.[17]

April 13. — I have just come from the Kahns'. Certainly there is no music like this old, tinkling, unwearied music of Greger's for giving one a sort of phantom or ghostly peace, as if the present faded into the distance, and life became a memory, half sad and half happy, and above all not too poignant. I can no longer allow myself to hear Wagner, much less Tschaikowsky:[18] music made to make people suffer.

Of course the Baroness was there. She sat by me at dinner, but on my left, and I could only see the unspoilt half of her face. Every now and then I thought of the other half, and a kind of sickness came over me. Once I turned to my other neighbour, in the middle of a sentence. But, for the most part, I forgot, and then it seemed to me that I was talking with the most accomplished woman I had ever met. She has travelled, knows many languages, many people; she has the feeling, and, I think, some of the knowledge of an artist; we spoke of music, painting, the art of living; and, oddly enough, she has a passion for just my own subject; history

---

[16] A veiled recollection of Baudelaire's remark in 'The Painter of Modern Life':

> Show me the man who, in the street, at the theatre, or in the Bois [de Boulogne], has not enjoyed, in a wholly detached way, the sight of a beautifully composed attire, and has not carried away with him an image inseparable from the woman wearing it, thus making of the two, the woman and the dress, an indivisible whole.

Baudelaire, *Selected Writings on Art and Literature*, trans. by P. E. Charvet, p. 424.

[17] Another example of Symons's fondness for theatrical metaphors when describing 'real life'. Perhaps there is a recollection of Benjamin Disraeli's *Lothair* (1870), in which the hero's remark, 'But the time comes when one can neither dance nor sing,' brings the response, 'Oh! then we become part of the audience,' said Madame Phoebus, 'the people for whose amusement everybody labours' (Chapter 73).

[18] For Wagner, see 'Pachmann and the Piano'. For Tchaikovsky, see 'Christian Trevalga'. During the *fin de siècle*, the music of both composers was often associated with 'unhealthy' or 'morbid' emotions.

is her favourite reading, and when I spoke of one of my own hobbies, of Attila, she quoted Jornandes,[19] and a passage, I remembered, that Thierry has not translated: she must have read it in Latin. How has she found time to do all this? To me she does not seem very young, but I suppose she is very little over forty. She spoke of everything with great frankness; only, never of herself. I have hardly spoken to the husband, to whom I have never seen her speak. He is very tall, very dark, very thin, with an air of politeness so excessive that it seems a kind of irony. She has asked me to come and see her; she promises me the use of her library. Can I, I wonder, ever get the better of that repugnance which rises in me when I see the ragged mask, the mended eyelid?

April 14. — I have been filling these pages with rumours and apprehensions, and now, just when I least expected it, something definite has happened, which seems to make them all very trivial and secondary. The Argonaut Building Society[20], into which I had put nearly all the little money I had, has failed; there has been swindling; I am ruined. What am I to do? I shall have to earn my living, heaven knows how; I shall have to give up my work, sell my books, find some cheaper rooms. This is the one thing I never thought would happen. I have been afraid of most things but poverty, and now it is poverty which has come upon me. Perhaps something will be saved out of the wreck of this false Argonaut. I must wait until I know for certain that there is nothing.

April 15. — I called on the Baroness von Eckenstein. I did not expect to see such a library. It was made by three generations of savants, and continued by herself. There are folios not in the British Museum; one that I had come to think had never existed.[21] If she will really let me sometimes use her library, I can sell my books cheerfully. She has a remarkable intelligence. But for that scar she would have been singularly handsome. What can have caused it, I wonder? It is like the scar which I once saw on the face of a woman over whom her rival had thrown vitriol.[22] I am far from supposing any such vulgar tragedy in the household of the Eckensteins!

---

[19] Roman historian, author of the *De origine actibusque Getarum* (*The Origin and Deeds of the Getae/Goths* (c. 551 AD), the earliest surviving history of the Goths. His name is usually given as Jordanes. Augustin Thierry (1795–1856), French historian.

[20] Sudden ruin of this kind is a familiar, often melodramatic contrivance in Victorian fiction, though here it is used to initiate the next phase of the plot rather than to offer a dramatic conclusion. Symons probably has in mind the collapse of Jabez Balfour's Liberator Building Society and its many related investments in 1892, a disaster which brought ruin to many small investors and was probably responsible for a hundred suicides. Following a lengthy trial in 1895, Balfour was sentenced to 14 years imprisonment. He was released in 1906.

[21] This repository may be inspired by Symons's recollections of Count Waldstein's library in Dux, Bohemia, where he discovered the previously unpublished fourth and fifth chapters of Book Twelve of Casanova's *Memoirs* in 1899.

[22] In 'Bertha at the Fair: A Sketch', an account of a trip to Brussels in the company of Leonard Smithers, Symons tells of his encounter with a woman who 'was scarred on the cheek: a wicked

April 16. — No further news yet from the Argonaut. I can only anticipate the worst. Nothing but rain without, and this intolerable suspense in one's mind. I can neither work nor think.

April 17. — Today the weather has changed, and see how this barometer of my nerves registers the change! I have been walking in Regent's Park[23], the nearest country, and I feel singularly good, wise, and happy. That uninteresting park, uninteresting in itself, has a gift of refreshment, as one turns into it out of the streets. I find myself leaning against the railing to watch a little dark creature with red legs and a red bill, that swims between the swans, and clambers up on the grass, and runs about there stealthily with a shy grace.[24] There is an island, to which all the water-birds go, and it is grown over with trees and bushes and green weeds, down to the edge of the water, and they go there when they want to be alone, as one goes into a deep wood, out of the streets in which people stare. Today I was perfectly happy, merely walking about the park. I sat under a tree for half an hour, and it was only when I realised that a queer sound which had come to me at intervals, a mournful and deep cry, which I had heard in a kind of dream, was the crying of the wild beasts, over yonder, inside their bars, that I got up and came away.

I have gone back to my journal at three o'clock in the morning, because I cannot sleep, and one of my old horrors has taken hold of me again. I am writing in order to give myself almost a sense of companionship: this talking to oneself on paper is so different from the loud emptiness of the night, when one is awake, and one's thoughts cry out. I woke up suddenly, and felt the darkness about me, like a horrible oppression. I felt as I have sometimes felt when the train has been carrying me through a long tunnel. All the blood went to my head, as if I were stifling, and I had a need of daylight. I turned on the electric light, but it made no difference; it was no more than the light in the railway-carriage while the darkness is thundering about one's ears, I had the sensation of a world in which the daylight

---

Baron, she told us, had done that, with vitriol.' This may be in part the inspiration for the Baroness's disfigurement in this story. *The Savoy* 3 (July 1896), p. 88.

[23] Regent's Park, designed by John Nash and championed by George IV, was planned during the Napoleonic Wars and finished in 1828. The Zoological Society of London opened its gardens there the same year, its array of animals soon augmented by the royal menagerie and the collection from the Tower of London. Symons felt that 'it is only the parks that make summer in London almost bearable', but confessed that he had 'never been able to love Regent's Park'. He liked its flowers and waterfowl, but found the 'sounds of roaring, crying, and the voices of imprisoned birds' from the zoo to be 'distressing' (*Cities and Sea-Coasts and Islands*, p. 167). For another evocation, see 'In Regent's Park' (1904) in *Lesbia and Other Poems* (1920).

[24] Neither Luxulyan nor his creator had much interest in ornithology. The speaker of 'A Prelude to Life' cannot distinguish between a blackbird and a thrush: precise labelling tended to be at odds with Symons's impressionist ethos. The bird described here is clearly a Common Moorhen (*Gallinula chloropus*).

had been blotted out, and men stumbled in a perpetual night, which the lamps did but make visible.[25] I felt that I should not be able to go on breathing unless I thrust the thought out of my mind, and I got up and turned on all the lights and walked to and fro in the rooms, and then came in here to quiet myself in the way I have found so good, by writing down all these fears and scruples of mine, as coldly as I can, as if they belonged to somebody else, in whose psychology I am interested. Already the uneasiness has almost left me. And yet who knows if I am only wrapping the blanket round my head once more, in order that I may run through fire and not see it?

April 18. — I have had one of my old headaches today, partly because I slept so little last night and partly because there has been thunder, at intervals, all day long; and now at night, when it is quite cool again, after the rain which washed off the suffocating heat of the day, the sky still gives a nervous twitch now and again, like a face which has lost control of its muscles. Yesterday it seemed as if Spring had come, but today a premature Summer leapt out on the world, in one of those distressing paroxysms of the elements in which I get more than my share of the general discomfort. It is only for the last few hours that I have recognised myself, and already I find it difficult to remember that other self, which lay on the sofa with half-shut eyes and a forehead eaten away by the little sharp teeth of the nerves. How we measure ourselves by time, and time by ourselves! Then, it seemed incredible that I should ever be my usual self again; my focus had been suddenly altered, and nothing was the same. I think we ought to be more grateful for such occasions than we are; for this sort of readjustment is certainly useful. All habits, and not only what we call bad habits, are hurtful; and life is one long habit, which it is good to vary sometimes.[26]

I suppose that my headache is not quite gone yet, and that it is this which makes me write down these obvious reflections. I must stop writing for tonight.

April 20. — I have had a strange, generous, almost incredible letter from the Baroness. She has heard from the Kahns that I have lost all my money, and she offers me the post of librarian; I can live in the house, and I am to have a salary which is much more than I had before the Argonaut went to pieces. I have only to say yes, and I am saved.

Can I accept this charity? It is nothing less. What can I give in return? Nothing. What can have induced her to offer me this immediate kindness? That she is

---

[25] Reminiscent of James Thomson's *The City of Dreadful Night* (1874, 1880), which Symons read during the late 1880s. He included an essay on Thomson in *Studies in Two Literatures* (1897). The passage also recalls these appropriate lines from Milton's *Paradise Lost* (1667): 'A dungeon horrible, on all sides round | As one great furnace flam'd; yet from those flames | No light, but rather darkness visible | Served only to discover sights of woe' (I, ll. 60–63).

[26] An allusion to Walter Pater's claim, 'our failure is to form habits', from the 'Conclusion' of *The Renaissance* (1873).

generous I do not doubt; but to this point? I must revise my opinions about women.

There is charity, certainly, and I shall soon be penniless, and not well able to refuse it. She prizes her library; she wishes it to be put in order, catalogued, kept in order, added to; she saw my interest, she knew that I am perfectly capable to do what she wants to have done. Is there anything unnatural after all in what must after all remain her immense kindness?

One thing remains. Can I accustom myself to see her every day, to sit at table with her, to be constantly at her call? At first it will not be easy, and then afterwards, who knows? but that would be the worst of all, I may come to find a sort of perverse pleasure in looking at her, the pleasure which is part horror, and which comes from affronting and half encouraging disgust.

April 28. — I have written nothing in my journal for the last week; too many things have happened, and I have seemed to go through them almost mechanically. I am already in my new quarters; I have my rooms, near the library in which I work, in the vast house at Queen's Gate; and I am already more than half regretting my old flat over Regent's Canal, where I could be alone from morning to night.[27]

There was no serious question of refusing this most fortunate opportunity; I had no choice: it was this or nothing, for if I recover £100 out of the Argonaut, it will be the utmost I have to hope for. The Baroness is a woman of action; she insisted, she arranged everything, and I found myself here without having done more than consent to let things be done for me. Certainly that is a form of arrangement which suits me, and life here seems to go not less smoothly; I have but to accept it, not without a certain satisfaction. The Baron must be enormously rich; there is something almost ostentatious in the display of gold, silver, and silk. Nothing is simple; the cost of these expensive things seems as if ticketed upon them; and there are coronets everywhere. But I, who never seriously thought about money until the little I had melted away, have never realised what an efficacious oil can be distilled out of gold for making all the wheels of life go smoothly. I am treated as one of the family; I profit hardly less than they from all that I care for in the possession of riches.

And yet, there is something here which weighs upon me; a sort of moral atmosphere which renders me uneasy. I see clearly, what I had guessed before, that there is no affection, that there is even a certain degree of alienation, between

---

[27] Queen's Gate, a street in South West London built in late 1850s and known for its large Italianate houses. Regent's Canal, also known as the North Metropolitan Canal, opened in 1820 and runs from Paddington Basin to the Thames at Limehouse. A stylish photogravure of one of its bridges was included in Alvin Langdon Coburn's *London* (1909). Taken in the winter of 1906–07, the picture was intended to be used in the Coburn and Symons collaboration, *London: A Book of Aspects*, though the book never appeared in its original format.

the Baron and Baroness. Nothing can be more polite, but with a sort of enigmatical politeness, which hides I know not what, than the Baron's manner towards his wife. He is scrupulously, exaggeratedly, polite towards everyone; and his excessive ceremony with me puts a certain restraint upon me. I imagine that he detests me, merely from the extreme care with which he tries to convince me of his amiability. The whole man seems to me false; or, it may be, he has acted a part so long that the part has fastened itself upon him. His eyes and his mouth seem never to say the same thing; both guard, as at two doorways, the thoughts which are at work in his brain.

The attitude of the Baroness towards her husband has a different inflexion of meaning; it is frigidly polite, but with a more evident shade of aversion. If he puts forward an opinion, she contradicts it; while he assents, outwardly, to all her opinions, but with an ironical air which seems itself a negation. He is a great sportsman, and I have never seen him with a book in his hands; she cares passionately for reading, and hates every form of sport. But it is not merely a difference of temperament; there is, I am convinced, something very definite which sets a barrier between them. What is it? Here is a problem, for once outside the eternal, wearing, for the most part inevitable, problem of myself, which I shall do well to study. How gladly I welcome anything which can distract me from my own sensations, in which I have so long lived isolated, alone with myself!

May 5. — The library is even finer than I thought. The labour of cataloguing it will be an amusement. For the present I do none of my own work; I am absorbed in this new occupation. How strange, how fortunate, to be at the same time taken outside myself in my thoughts, and away from what becomes monotonous in my studies! I have found, it would seem, precisely the distraction which the doctor ordered me. Only, the old solitary life seems a thing to regret, now I have left it behind me; and ought I not to regret the self which I left with it?

It is certain that I shall never accustom myself to look at the Baroness without repugnance. From my childhood I have never been able to endure the sight of any human disfigurement. I used to faint at the sight of blood, and I have always looked away when I have seen people crowding about a man or a horse fallen in the street. It is not pity, it is a very sensitive egoism: before an accident I imagine the thing happening to me, or I imagine myself obliged to touch the wound or the broken limb. I never look at the Baroness without a mental shiver at the thought of what that dead, furrowed, and discoloured skin must be like to the touch.

May 9. — I have got no further in my study of these two enigmatical people, who seem to have not one thought, not one feeling, in common, and yet who seem to live so calmly side by side, in this vast house where they need never meet except at meals, or when the presence of strangers isolates them. I am wholly unable to talk with the Baron, who ignores me with the most punctilious deference. He never enters the library, and, in the drawing-room, is never without a newspaper, of which he rarely turns the pages. With the Baroness I can always talk; I can even, what is rare with me, listen. For a woman, her ideas are surprisingly well informed: quotations, of course, but arranged with a personal sense of decoration. She can discuss general questions broadly, with a rare frankness, a kind of eager sincerity. What does the Baron think, I wonder, behind that screen of the newspaper, if, as he sits motionless, he is listening, as I cannot but believe, to every word that is said? I often look at the newspaper, hoping to see it at least quiver, if not drop to the floor, and the man leap out of his ambush. The Baroness interests me a little more every day, and this interest is oddly balanced by my equal difficulty in looking or in not looking at her. When she is talking with me she invariably arranges herself so as to be on my left; often she leans her head on her left hand, as if to shield even what remains unseen. How horribly she must suffer from this living mask, under which she is condemned to exist! How long, I wonder, has she worn it, and shall I ever know the cause? Is she always conscious of its presence, of the eyes that seek to avoid it, and return, despite themselves, stealthily? I can conceive no more exquisite torture. Or yes, there is one. Suppose this woman, in whom I can distinguish a quite unusual force and energy of emotion, were to fall in love again: she is at the age of lasting passions, and what could be more natural in her? That would be a tragedy which I hardly like to think of; the more so, as I can easily conceive how powerful must have been her attraction before the time of this accident. There is something almost magnetic in her nature, and I can see that the Kahns, for instance, are attracted by her to the point of hardly seeing her as she is, of forgetting to look at her with their own eyes.

May 15. — The dinner-parties which women in society condemn themselves to the task of giving become less and less intelligible to me as I see them from so close a point of view. How little pleasure they seem to give to any except very young or very old people! It is a kind of slavery: penal servitude with hard labour. I am sure neither of the Eckensteins gets the slightest personal pleasure out of these big dinners which they are so constantly giving. I am equally sure that the people who accept their invitations would generally rather not come; that they accept them largely because it is difficult to write and say I will not come; partly out of a vague hope, almost invariably deceived, that they will meet some delightful new person; partly out of the mere social necessity of killing time. I have never seen so much before of a London season, and I shall be glad when it is over.

August 10. — They have taken a house for the summer down here in this remote part of my own county, Cornwall; there is fishing for the Baron, and golf not far off, and boating, I suppose. The heat in London was becoming intolerable; my old headaches began to come back; and I was only too glad to say yes when the Baroness asked me, almost hesitatingly, if I would come with them. Here I have nothing to do; we walk on the cliffs, drive across Cornwall and back again, sit under the trees on this lawn, from which one can hear the sea, not quite knowing if it is the sound of the sea or of the trees. In short, one is idle, and in the open air. I am well again already; only, inexpressibly lazy.

The Baroness and I are thrown together so much, by the mere loneliness of the place, and the determined absence of the Baron, that we are getting to know one another better. In driving and walking she invariably keeps on my left; for which I am grateful to her. She is a good walker, and cares for the sea, I think, as much as I do.

Is it chiefly the influence of the place, the weather, the homeliness and familiarity of the old manor-house, where we sit and walk in the garden, as in a grassy opening in the midst of a wood?[28] That, and the stillness and unconfined space on the cliffs, where one can sit silent for so long, until only intimate words come; all that, I am sure, has had its influence on both of us, certainly on me. The Baroness has begun to question me about myself, and I, who hate confidences, find myself telling her what I have told no one.

I have told her about Clare, about my thoughts, my ideas, my sensations, all that I have up to now only confessed to my journal. How is it that she draws my secrets out of me, and how is it that I feel a pleasure in telling them to her?

August 15. — Today we drove to the Lizard,[29] and sat for an hour on that high peak of rocks which goes down into the sea at this last southerly edge of England. The sea was steel-blue, almost motionless except where it made a little circle of foam around each rock, and it seemed to stretch endlessly, as if it flowed over all the rest of the world. Ships were going by, with sails and black smoke, with a great haste to be somewhere. We sat silent for a time, and then she began to tell me about herself; little confidences of no moment, only they seemed to be hesitating on the verge of some fuller confidence. At first I thought she was going to tell me all; but the wind began to get chill, and the sun faded out behind clouds, and her mood changed, and she got up, and we went back to the carriage.

August 20. — At last I know the whole story, or as much of it as I am likely to know. Last night, after dinner, we were sitting alone in the garden, in a corner where the trees darken the grass; she sat with her hand half covering her face, in that attitude which is habitual with her, though only the right side of her face was visible, and the long silence became more and more intimate until at last she spoke. She began to tell me of herself, and first of her childhood among the Bohemian woods, her escapes from the army of governesses and tutors, her dreams in the depths of the forest, the 'Buch der Lieder' read by moonlight and

---

[28] A familiar question in Symons's travel essays. It is addressed explicitly at the opening of 'An Autumn City'.

[29] The Lizard is a peninsula in south Cornwall which takes its name from the Cornish 'An Lysardh' ('the high court'). It has a notoriously hazardous coast, and a lighthouse was built at Lizard Point in 1752.

thrust under the pillow as she fell asleep: in short, a very pretty, very German, sentimental education.[30] Then the young English tutor, with his tragic beauty, his Byronic sighs; she pities, admires, falls in love with him; their meetings, declarations; they plot a romantic elopement, but the coachman turns traitor; the Byronic gentleman is dismissed, and the girl sent to her cousins in Vienna, where she begins to see the world, and to dream more worldly dreams. The Baron presents himself, with his title, his money, his serious reputation; the parents implore her to accept him, and she accepts him, in order that she may accomplish a social duty. By this time she has made innumerable friends, Vienna is the world to her, she cannot exist without people, excitement, admiration; and when the Baron, who hunts during half the year, takes her away to his castle, and leaves her there, from morning to night, day after day for months together, she lives the life of a prisoner, alone with her books and her more and more discontented thoughts. Time passes, and the husband whom she has never loved becomes a polite stranger, then an unwelcome guest. He sees indifference passing into aversion, and makes no attempt to arrest the course of things. It is enough if she is submissive, and his pride does not so much as dream of a revolt.

Meanwhile there are neighbours, hunting friends who come to the castle, and among them is a young Frenchman. She told me simply, quietly, as if she were telling me the story of someone else, how this man had gradually attracted her, how delicately and perseveringly he had made love to her, and how his presence rendered the tedium of her life less insupportable. She loved him, she believed that he loved her, and a new happiness came into her life. One day the husband, who had appeared to suspect nothing, came back unexpectedly. She had been playing the piano, her lover was seated just behind her, and as she rose from the piano and flung herself passionately into his arms, she saw, over his shoulder, the reflection of her husband's face in the mirror. He had opened the door while she was playing, and stood motionless, holding the door half open, with his eyes fixed upon them. Before she could make a movement the door had closed silently. It did not open again. The lover left the castle hastily, meeting no one on the way. Hours passed, and she sat watching the door, quiet with terror. At last she could bear it no longer, and she went straight to her husband's apartments. The painters had been at work, and their tools, paints, brushes, and bottles were still lying about. Her husband was seated at his writing-table. As she entered the room he put down the pen, turned to her calmly and said: 'I am writing to ask Xavier to dinner, but you will have to fix the date. I have a little surprise for him.' He rose, took three steps towards her, with a look of inexpressibly sarcastic malignity, and,

---

[30] *Buch der Lieder* ['Book of Songs'] (1800) by Heinrich Heine (1797–1856), a central work of the German romantic canon. See 'An Episode in the Life of Jenny Lane'.

stooping rapidly, picked up a bottle from the floor, and flung the contents in her face. She shrieked in agony as the vitriol burnt into her like liquid fire, and she rolled over at his feet, shrieking.

When, after months of suffering, the bandages were at last taken off, and she could resume her place at the table, she found, on coming downstairs to dinner, one guest awaiting her with her husband. It was her lover. She had not seen him, no word from him had reached her, since the accident. During dinner the Baron was cheerful, almost gay; he related amusing stories, turning from one to the other with an air of cordiality, and affecting not to notice that neither spoke more than a few words. Soon after dinner, the guest excused himself. A few days afterwards it was reported that he had left the neighbourhood.

August 21. — I lay awake last night for several hours, unable to get this horrible story out of my head. I thought these were things that no longer happened, or only in Russia, perhaps; I thought we were at least so far civilised. It is the meanness of the revenge that horrifies me most in its atrocity. And that these two people, after that moment's revelation of the one to the other, should have gone on living together, under the same roof: it is incredible. There, I suppose, is civilisation, the hypocrisy of our conventions, which, if they cannot suppress the brute in the human animal, are prompt to cloak the thing once done, to pretend that it never was done, never could have been done.

Now, when I sit at table between that man and woman, I scarcely know whether I am judge, witness, or accuser. What had been instinctive in my distrust of the man has become a mental revulsion not less intense than the physical revulsion which I must always feel towards the woman. Only, towards her, I have a new feeling, a kind of sympathetic confidence, mingled with pity; and it pleases me that she has confidence in me. It would give me pleasure if I could aid her, in some way that I cannot even conjecture, to avenge herself on that diabolical tyrant, her husband.

September 25. — As I look back over these pages it seems to me that I have lost the habit of writing down my thoughts about general questions, which my once wholly personal preoccupations brought constantly before me. How a journal changes with one's life, if it is really, as mine is, the confidant of one's moods, the secret witness of one's growth or decay! I suppose it is that, as I accustom myself to look for my interest outside the circle of my own brain, I become less personal, less sick with myself. My old terrors, my old preoccupations, have loosened their hold on me, I think; my brain is getting more quiescent, more conventional. If only the nerves do not break out again, as I find it so easy to realise their doing; if I can avoid excitement, that is, keep myself as I am now, an interested spectator of other people's lives, with no too eager interests of my own: that will at last set me wholly to rights. And, certainly, this divine Cornish air, half salt, half honey, will have done something for me, in helping to cure me of a too narrow, London philosophy.

August 3. — It is almost exactly a year since I have written anything in my journal, which I find where I left it, forgotten in the corner of a drawer in the Cornish manor-house, to which we have gone back again this summer. I am glad to be here again, but, all the same, it is not quite as it was last year. The Baroness and I are better friends than ever. I am more accustomed to her, she is kindness itself. Ah yes, that is it. Her kindness begins to become fatiguing; I would prefer a little liberty. Why is it that good people forge chains with their kindness, adding link to link with the best intentions in the world, until one is tripped up and weighed down and held by the fetters of innumerable favours?[31] To break so much as a link is held to be ingratitude. But one's liberty, then, is there anything comparable in the price one pays, and in the utmost one can receive in place of it?

Is it that a woman is unable to conceive of the fatigue of kindness? How incomprehensible to them must be that marvellous sentence in *Adolphe*: 'Je me reposais, pour ainsi dire, dans l'indifférence des autres, de la fatigue de son amour.'[32] And, even if it is not love, the heaviest of all burdens when it comes unasked, there is still a fatiguing weight in that affectionate vigilance which is one long appeal for gratitude, in that sleepless solicitude which 'prevents,' in both senses of the word, all one's goings. I am beginning to find this with the Baroness, who would replace Providence for me, but with a more continual intervention.

August 18. — O this intolerable demand on one's gratitude, this assumed right of all the world to receive back favour for favour, to be paid for giving! Must there be a market for kindness, and balances to weigh charity by the pound weight? I am not sure that the conventional estimation of gratitude as one of the main virtues, of gratitude in all circumstances and for all favours received, has not a profoundly bourgeois origin. I have never been able clearly to recognise the necessity, or even the possibility, of gratitude towards any one for whom I have not a feeling of personal affection, quite apart from any exchange of benefits. The

---

[31] 'We forge our own chains in a moment of softness,' wrote George Egerton in 'A Cross-Line' (*Keynotes*, 1893). The image of the loving chain was often used by sexual radicals of the 1890s. Its ur-text is Shelley's 'Epipsychidion' (1823) with its image of 'With one chained friend, perhaps a jealous foe, | The dreariest, and the longest journey go', the lines which supplied the title of E. M. Forster's *The Longest Journey* (1907). Symons was not involved with the type of radical sexual politics associated with critics of marriage, but he was deeply sceptical about the self-sacrifice and duty which marriage demands.

[32] Benjamin Constant (1767–1830), *Adolphe* (1816). The plot concerns Adolphe, an alienated, highly self-conscious young man, who falls in love with an older woman, Ellénore, the Polish mistress of the Comte de P***. The novel foregrounds detailed accounts of feelings and psychology rather than dwelling on exterior detail, and Luxulyan, with his tendency to see life imitating art, is obviously aware of the similarities between it and his own situation. The quotation translates as 'I was resting, so to speak, in the indifference of others, from the burden of his love.' As Luxulyan becomes more emotionally involved with the Baroness, his writing becomes increasingly personal and literary allusions, perhaps a distancing mechanism, largely disappear.

conferring of what is called a favour, materially, and the prompt return of a delicate sentiment, gratitude, seems to me a kind of commercialism of the mind, a mere business transaction, in which an honest exchange is not always either possible or needful. The demand for gratitude in return for a gift comes largely from the respect which most people have for money; from the idea that money is the most 'serious' thing in the world, the symbol of a physical necessity, but a thing having no real existence in itself, no real importance to the mind which refuses to realise its existence. Only the miser really possesses it in itself, in any significant way; for the miser is an idealist, the poet of gold. To all others it is a kind of mathematics, and a synonym for being 'respected.' You may say it is necessary, almost as necessary as breathing, and I will not deny it. Only I will deny that anyone can be actively grateful for the power of breathing. He cannot conceive of himself without that power. To conceive of oneself without money, that is to say, without the means of going on living, is at once to conceive of the right, the mere human right, to assistance. And when, instead of money, it is some unasked, necessary or unnecessary, gift which is laid before us, to be taken whether we choose or not, what more have we to do than to take it, silently, without thanks, without complaint, as we would pick up an apple that has dropped to us over an orchard hedge? I say all that to myself, and believe it, and yet some irrational obligation weighs upon me, whenever I think of breaking away from this woman and her affection.

October 25. — Can it be possible, or am I falling into the most absurd of misapprehensions? What has happened, that I should seem today to be conscious of what I had not even dreamt of yesterday? Nothing has happened; she, her husband, and I have sat in our usual places at the table and in the garden; not a word different from our usual words has passed between us; and yet … Why is it that no man can ever be friends with any woman? It is the woman, usually, who puts the question. And she, I am certain that she never wanted to be anything but my friend. Then she wanted to be my only friend; she wanted to make my mind her possession. I see it step by step, now that I think back. Then what we call nature came in to trouble the balance. She is a healthy, normal woman; she has all the natural affections. Why is it that tenderness in women must always take the fever? For there is no doubt about it, none. Once you have seen a certain look in a woman's eyes, once a certain thrill has come into her fingers, there is no mistaking. I have seen that look in her eyes, I can still feel the thrill of her fingers, as her hand touched mine, and seemed to forget to let go.

October 26. — I awoke this morning in a cold sweat. I had been dreaming of Clare, I heard her footstep coming along the corridor, the door opened, I knew it was she, but she was veiled, and when she called my name her voice sounded far away, as if the veil muffled it; and I put up my hand to lift her veil, and she prayed me not to lift it, but I would not listen to her, and when I saw her face it was Clare, but with the cheek and eyelid of the Baroness. One of us shrieked, and I awoke trembling.

It is still early morning, but I have no mind to sleep again, and perhaps dream. I must try to put these ugly thoughts out of my head, and here is a morning which should help me, if anything in nature could. Is it that some sense, which other people have is lacking in me? I have never found that peace in nature of which I have heard so often, and which, on such a morning as this, when the light begins to glow softly over the world, and the wind comes in salt from the sea, and the leaves rustle as if at an imperceptible caress, should come to me as simple as to trees. There is a physical delight in it, certainly; but it goes no deeper than the skin of my forehead.

I remember, when I first met the Baroness, thinking how cruel, how ironical, it would be, if she were to fall in love again. I remember also, when I first knew her story, wishing that I could help her: yes, here it is written down, last August: 'if I could aid her, in some way that I cannot even conjecture, to avenge herself on that diabolical tyrant, her husband.' I certainly saw no connection between the two things, nor any relation of myself to either of them. And yet, see how both have come together, and how strangely I stand between them, touching both.

The notion seems to me, at present, incredible; and yet, why? Yet more improbable things have happened, and who am I, or who is she, after all, that, in the malice of nature, no such idea should enter into a woman's head?

I wrote here, not so long ago, 'I am more accustomed to her.' Shall I ever be able to say more than that? And it is terrible to be able to say no more than that.

I suppose, if I loved her, I should notice nothing. Is it that pity would come in to take up all the room? But I have never had any gift for pity; and then, all conjecture is idle, for I certainly do not love her.

October 28. — Is it possible that I could have been mistaken, or is she conscious that she has betrayed her secret, and now hides it away again? Today she has seemed really, not affectedly indifferent. Do I altogether wish that it were so? Have I not got used to being looked after not quite as a stranger, to a kindness on which it has seemed to me that I could always rely? Is there not something I should find myself missing, if it were taken away from me?

October 29. — We are to go back to London in a day or two. It rains every day, and almost all day long. Every one stays indoors, and we seem always to find ourselves in different rooms. After dinner the Baron looks up sometimes from his newspaper; the talk is quite formal, because he joins in it. Can she have shown him some sign of encouragement, or is it he? And is she keeping back something, or am I wrong in all that I have conjectured? Nothing is as it was. I shall be glad when we are back in London.

November 2. — We are back in London. I hardly see her now. For nearly a week she has avoided me, and I am astonished to find myself, I can hardly say piqued, and yet there is a little pique in it too. It is so evident to me that she is playing a part, but the part is well played, and I feel oddly disquieted. I hate change, uncertainty, that kind of uneasiness which women used to cause me, but which I have so long given up feeling. I miss the old freedom of her talk, her confidences to me, her faculty for taking an interest in one's ideas, one's personal sensations. How odd that this should have come to mean so much more to me than I knew! And there is something else that I miss, in her new reserve, now that it comes suddenly up between us as a barrier. I used to wish for just such a barrier. And now it annoys me to find it there. It is only restlessness on my part, I know, but it surprises me to find that I am capable of so near an approach to, after all, some kind of feeling. I thought I had buried all that quite securely, years ago.

November 5. — Today I have heard news of Clare for the first time during all these years since she went away. And it is not as I fancied; she is not happy, not even well off; she has been seen in poor lodgings at the seaside, and alone. Has the man, the turgid fop and brute, whom I criticised her and all her sex for caring about, left her, then? It looks like it. Could one imagine, on his part, anything else? I knew him so much better than she did! But I am horribly sorry; I do not want to see her again, but I should like, if I could, to help her. I wonder if she will write to me. I shall take it as a compliment if she writes.

November 7. — She has written, and the letter has reached me here, after a little delay. She must think I am not going to write. She wants to see me, and it will perhaps be better for me to see her. She is in London; it would be kinder if I called; and heaven knows there is no danger. Her letter is full of dignity; she knows me and there are no tears in it; the regrets are duly temperate; she does not even ask to be forgiven. 'I am in trouble: you once cared for me: I have not forgotten that you can be kind: will you help me?' That is the substance of her letter. I will write to her to-night, and say that I will come and see her.

1 A.M. — Shall I never understand women? will nothing ever teach me wisdom? I was foolish enough to think that the Baroness would help me, that I could be open with her, as I have been till now. I had no secrets from her in regard to Clare, and she knows how much all that is in the past. I showed her the letter. She read it in silence, with her hand over her eyes. Then, not raising her head, she said, in a voice that seemed her ordinary voice: 'You will go and see her?' 'I think it would be best,' I said. She lifted her head suddenly, clenched the paper in her hand, and flung it on the carpet at my feet. For a moment I was too startled even to move. Her face was convulsed with rage; her face was terrible, more terrible than I have ever seen it. The scar seemed to whiten, the blood rushed to her other cheek and made her forehead purple; her eyes glowed. I stooped to pick up the letter, and began to smooth it out on my knee. I fixed my eyes on it, so as not to see her; and she knew why I did not look at her. She seemed to make a great effort to recover her self-control, and I saw her fingers clutch a fold of her skirt and clench tightly upon it. 'You want to see her?' she said, still in a low voice; and I said, what was quite the truth: 'No, I do not want to see her, I only want to help her, and I think

it would be kinder, as well as more satisfactory, to go than to write.' 'I understand,' she said coldly; 'you want to see her again. I understand your feeling.' I was annoyed at her misinterpretation, and said nothing. 'You still care for her,' she said, 'I can see it, it is useless for you to deny it; you want to go back to her. Well, she is free now: go back to her.' I was going to protest, but she rose, and held up her hand to silence me. Tears were in her eyes, the anger was gone, she could hardly speak. 'Yes,' she said, 'go and see her; I will not keep you from her; if you still love her, there is nothing else to be done. I understand, I understand.' And she sank back in the chair again, with her hands over her face, weeping big tears.

When I saw her suffering, I was sorry, and I knelt down beside her and took away one of her hands from before her face, and kissed the hand still wet with tears. I assured her that Clare was nothing to me now, and I convinced her of my sincerity. She dried her eyes, smiled sadly, and said, 'Then you promise me you will not go and see her.' 'But no, I said, 'I have told you that it is best to go and see her; but you know the whole reason why I mean to do so.' She turned rigid in an instant, and I should have had to go through the whole scene over again, if I had not had the cowardice to say, 'I promise that I will not see her.' She begged me to show her the letter that I wrote. Why should I refuse?

After today there can be no further disguise between us. On her side everything has been said, and on mine everything has been understood. By what I have done today I have put myself into her hands, I have given her the right to arrange my life as she pleases; I have shown her my weakness, I have let her see her own strength. Does it matter how one gives way, or how a woman overcomes? Today I honestly wanted to do the right thing, to be kind to a woman I had once cared for, and I am powerless to do it. These agitations, these restrictions, this sentimental ceremony, are too much for me. How is it that I did not sooner realise the way things were tending, and set a barrier, not only against this passionate foe without, but against this weakness, this kindness, that turn traitors within, and run so readily to the closed gates to open them?

November 8. — The letter I wrote was cold; it was as if one were giving charity. Clare replies gratefully, as if to a benevolent stranger. I have spoilt the idea which she still had of me. I am sorry for it; the more so as I have no desire to see her; but I should like to have behaved at least instinctively. It is for another woman, always, that one is unjust to a woman. And why is it? Is it because I pity this woman so much, that I have been unjust to the other? I did not know till yesterday how much she cared for me. What is going to happen? I ask myself, not liking, or not daring, to wait for an answer. How one evades coming to a conclusion, precisely when too much depends on that conclusion! I have never understood myself, and just now the brain in me seems to sit aside and reserve judgment, while all manner of feelings, instincts, sensations, chatter among themselves. No, I will confess nothing to these pages, and chiefly because it would take a casuist to prepare my confession.

November 9. — She loves me cruelly, with a dull passion that does not come till after youth and the years one calls the years of love are long past. I have had a terrible scene with her; terrible because, for the first time, a woman's love seems to me a wholly serious thing, and one's own feeling to matter less. My own feeling: what is it here? Shall I understand one woman, at last, when the desire to do so is over? Passions, then, are real things in women, and, if no one is responsible, at least one cannot always hold aloof from them, or go by on the other side. She loves me, and she can conceal it no longer; and she is ashamed that I should see her as she is, and she exults in her shame, and is reckless and timorous, and is at my mercy, and does not know that it is just this that holds me, and that I cannot, if I would, turn away from one now helpless, and a beggar. Something in her helplessness takes hold of me like a great force, breaks down my indifference; because, I think, it convinces me, to the roots of my mind, as no woman ever before convinced me, that what one calls love may be life itself, carrying away all the props of the world in its overflow. I am afraid of this horrible reality; but I cannot escape it.

November 10. — I try to persuade myself that I have become her lover wholly out of pity; but the more intimate self which listens is not to be persuaded. Certainly I do not love her, but is it only because she loves me, and because she is the most unfortunate of women, that ... No, there is something else, some animal attraction, which comes to me in spite of my repugnance; a gross, unmistakable desire, which I would not admit even to myself if the consciousness of it were not forced upon me. What I should not have believed in another, I experience, beyond denial, in myself.

Shall a man never know what it is in him that responds, without love, to a woman's gesture? Is it a kind of animal vanity? Is it that love creates, not love, but a flattered readiness to be loved?[33] Did I not think how terrible it would be if she fell in love again, and did I not mean, for the main part, because she could expect no return? And I was wrong. Something has taken hold of me, an appeal, a partly honest and partly perverse attraction; and I say to myself that it is pity, but though pity is part of it, it is not all pity; and I find myself, as I have always found myself, doing the exact opposite of what seems most natural and desirable. Why?

---

[33] In the chapter on Verlaine in *The Symbolist Movement in Literature*, Symons writes: 'All love is an attempt to break through the loneliness of individuality, to fuse oneself with something not oneself, to give and to receive, in all the warmth of natural desire, that inmost element which remains, so cold and so invincible, in the midst of the soul. It is a desire of the infinite in humanity, and as humanity has its limits, it can but return sadly upon itself when that limit is reached. Thus human love is not only an ecstasy but a despair, and the more profound a despair the more ardently it is returned.' *The Symbolist Movement in Literature*, p. 51.

November 20. — I have made a mistake, but it was inevitable. I have put back my shoulders under the yoke, and all the peace is over. I have had just time enough to rest, and to get ready for the old labour, and now I am troubled with all a woman's ingenuity of trouble: her nerves, her cares, her affections, her solicitudes, her whole minute and never-ceasing possession. How am I to explain myself? There was no choice; it is useless to regret what could but have been accepted. She has a calm will to love, she is like some force of nature against which it is useless to struggle.

November 22. — I do not know why it is, but all my old nervous uneasiness is coming back on me again, against all sense or reason. I have that curious feeling that something is going to happen; I find myself listening to noises, unable to sit quiet, watching my own brain. All the restlessness has come back, and some of the fear. I am afraid of this woman's love. I could not leave her, but I am afraid of what will happen to me.

December 3. — No, I shall never get accustomed to it; the same physical horror will always be there; it has been there when the attraction was strongest; it has never been out of my mind, or away from the eyes of my senses. She is aware of it, and suffers; and I am helpless before her suffering. And it is this, nothing but this, which turns my thoughts morbid, whenever I think over a situation which might otherwise have had nothing unusual in it. The husband studies me with a kind of curious and mocking interest, which he allows to remain on his face when he sees us together. Does he suspect, know, approve, or disapprove? Do I seem to him ... But in any case all that is beside the question: I once thought that it would be a generous revenge to make him suffer; now I am conscious how idle the thought was. Is it not all idle, is not everything more or less beside the question?

I am tired of writing in my journal, always the same things. I will shut the book, and perhaps not open it again.

January 5. — I have not written anything in my journal for years (how many years is it?), and I do not know what impulse or what accident has led me to open it again, and to turn over some of the pages on which the dust has settled, and to begin to write there as I am doing, half mechanically. What is it that seems strange as I read what I have written here? I suppose that I should have considered, discussed, questioned the very things which are now as if they had always been. I do not dream of changing them, any more than I dream of changing the course of life itself, on its inevitable way. But a rage in me never quite dies out: against this woman who has taken me from myself, and against life that is wasting me daily. I have no happiness if I look either forward or backward. I have always succumbed to what I have most dreaded, and every reluctance has turned in me to an irresistible force of attraction. And now I am softly, stealthily entangled, held by loving hands, imprisoned in comfort; I do some good at last, for certainly I help to make a wronged and pitiable woman happy; I have no will to break any bond, and yet I am more desolately alone than I have ever been, more fretted by the old self, by apprehensions and memories, by the passing of time and the lack of hope or desire. I would welcome any change, though it brought worse things, if I could but end this monotony in which there is no rest; end it somehow, and rest a little, and be alone.

October 12. — I have been ill, I am better, I am in Venice. Surely one gets well of every trouble in Venice, where, if anywhere in the world, there should be peace, the oblivion of water, of silence, the unreal life of sails? I have come to an old house on the Giudecca, where one is islanded even from the island life of Venice: I look across and see land, the square white Dogana, the Salute, like a mosque, the whole Riva, with the Doges' Palace. There lies all that is most beautiful in the world, and I have only to look out of my windows to see it. Palladio[34] built the house, and the rooms are vast; the beams overhead are so high that I feel shrunk as I look at them, as if lost in all this space; which, however, delights my humour.

October 14.—The art in life is to sit still, and to let things come towards you, not to go after them, or even to think that they are in flight.[35] How often I have chased some divine shadow, through a whole day till evening, when, going home tired, I have found the visitor just turning away from my closed door.

To sit still, in Venice, is to be at home to every delight. I love St. Mark's, the Piazza, the marble benches under the colonnade of the Doges' Palace, the end of land beyond the Dogana, the steps of the Redentore; above all, my own windows. Sitting at any one of these stations one gathers as many floating strays of life as a post in the sea gathers weeds. And it is all a sort of immense rest, literally a dream, for there is sleep all over Venice. I have been sitting for a long time in St Mark's, thinking of nothing. The voices of the priests chanting hummed and buzzed like echoes in an iron bell. They troubled me a little, but without breaking the enchantment, as importunate insects trouble a summer afternoon. Very old men in purple sat sunk into the stalls of the choir, loth to move, almost overcome with sleep; waiting, with an accustomed patience, till the task was over.

Here (infinite relief!) I can think of nothing. She writes to me, and I put aside the letters, and I forget quite easily that some day she will come for me, and the old life must begin over again. I do not dread it, because I do not remember it. I am still weak, and I must not excite myself; I must sink into this delicious Venice, where forgetfulness is easier than anywhere in the world. The autumn is like a gentler summer; no such autumn has been known, even in Venice, for many years; and I am to be happy here, I think.

---

34 Andrea Palladio (1508–80), Venetian architect revered for his Roman-influenced 'Palladian' style.

35 Luxulyan's credo is much like Roserra's 'sympathetic submissiveness to things' in 'An Autumn City', and to the artistic opinions of Peter Waydelin. The view is, of course, Symons's own.

October 25. — I have been roaming about the strange house, upstairs, in these vast garrets paved with stone, with old carved chimneys, into which they have put modern stoves, and beams, the actual roof-trees overhead; nearly all unoccupied space, out of which a room is walled up or boarded off here and there. Some of the windows look right over the court, the two stone angels on the gateway, and the broad green and brown orto, the fruit garden which stretches to the lagoon, its vine trellises invisible among the close leaves of the trees. Beyond the brown and green, there is a little strip of pale water, and then mud flats, where the tide has ebbed, the palest brown, and then more pale water, and the walls and windows of the madhouse, San Servolo,[36] coming up squarely out of the lagoon.

October 26. — Does the too exciting exquisiteness of Venice drive people mad? Two madhouses in the water! It is like a menace.

I went out in the gondola yesterday on the lagoon on the other side of the island. It was an afternoon of faint, exquisite sunshine, and the water lay like a mirror, bright and motionless, reflecting nothing but a small stake, or the hull, hoisted nets, and stooping back of a fisher and his boat. I looked along the level, polished surface to where sails rose up against the sky, between the black, compact bulk of the forts. The water lapped around the oar as it dipped and lifted, and trickled with a purring sound from the prow. I lay and felt perfectly happy, not thinking of anything, hardly conscious of myself.[37] I had closed my eyes, and when I opened them again we were drifting close to a small island, on which there was a many-windowed building, most of the windows grated over, and a church with closed doors; the building almost filled the island; it had a walled garden with trees. A kind of moaning sound came from inside the walls, rising and falling, confused and broken. 'It is San Clemente,' said the gondolier over my shoulder; 'they keep mad people there, mad women.'[38]

November 1.—She writes affectionate letters to me, without a respite; she will not let me alone to get well. For I am sure I could get well here if I were quite left to myself. And now even Venice is turning evil. Is it in the place, in myself, is it my disease returning to take hold of me? Is it the power of the woman coming back across land and water to take hold of me? I am getting afraid to go about this strange house at night; the wind comes in from the sea, and tears at the old walls and the roof; I scarcely know if it is the wind I hear when I wake up in the night.

---

[36] An island in the Venetian lagoon that has been a monastery, a nunnery, a military hospital, and, from the late 1700s, an asylum. The latter was closed by the Italian government in 1978.

[37] Here and elsewhere in the story, Symons draws on his essay, 'Venetian Sensations' from the *Saturday Review* (6 August 1904), composed shortly before 'Henry Luxulyan'.

[38] The island of San Clemente was home to Europe's first women-only asylum, which opened in 1844. By the end of the century it was also admitting male patients, and had been substantially developed. It remained an asylum until 1992. Ironically, it later became a luxury hotel.

November 3. — There is something unnatural in standing between water and water and hearing the shriek of a steam-engine. I am hardly too far, I suppose, from the railway-station, to have actually heard it. But the idea seems a foolish joke, unworthy of the place.

November 6. — Every day I find myself growing more uneasy. If I look out of the windows at dawn, when land and water seem to awaken like a flower, some poison comes to me out of this perhaps too perfect beauty. I dread the day, which seems to follow me and drag me back, after I have escaped another night; I never felt anything like this insidious coiling of water about one.

I came to Venice for peace, and I find a subtle terror growing up out of its waters, with a more ghostly insistence than anything solid on the earth has ever given me. Daylight seems to mask some gulf, which, with the early dark and the first lamps, begins to grow visible. As I look across at Venice from this island, I see darkness, and lights growing like trees and flowers out of the creeping water, and, white and immense, with its black windows and one lighted lamp, the Doges' Palace. Nothing else is real, and the beauty of this one white thing, the one thing whose form the eye can fasten upon, is the beauty of witchcraft. I expect to see it gone in the morning.

And the noises here are mysterious. I hear a creak outside my window, and it comes nearer, and a great orange sail passes across the window like a curtain drawn over it. Bells break out, and ring wildly, as if out of the water. Steamers hoot, with that unearthly sound to which one can never get accustomed. The barking of a dog comes from somewhere across the water, a voice cries out suddenly, and then the shriek of steam from a vessel, and again, from some new quarter, a volley of bells.

November 9. — The wind woke me from sleep, rattling the wooden shutter against the panes of the windows, and I could hear it lifting the water up the steps of the landing-place, where there is always a chafing and gurgling whenever the wind is not quite still. I looked out, and, pressing my face close against the glass, I could just distinguish the black bundle of stakes in the dim water, which I could see throbbing under a very faint light, where the gas-lamp, hung from the next house, shone upon it. Beyond, there was nothing but darkness, and the level row of lights on the Riva, and the white walls, cut into stone lacework, of the Doges' Palace. The wind seemed to pass down the canal, as if on its way from the sea to the sea. I felt it go by, like a living thing, not turning to threaten me.

November 13. — I am beginning almost to wish that she were here. She writes that she is coming, and I scarcely know whether to be glad or sorry. I fear her more than anything in the world, but there is something here which is hardly of the world, a vague, persistent image of death, impalpable, unintelligible, not to be shaken off; and I know not what I am dreading, not the mere fear of water, though I have always had that, but some terrible expectancy, which keeps me now from getting any rest by day or by night.

November 22. — At last something has happened, nothing indeed to my hurt, but it has broken the strain a little. The last days have been windless, warm, and, till yesterday afternoon, cloudless. Suddenly, as I sat in the Piazza, the daylight seemed to be put out by a great blackness which came up rapidly out of the north, and hung over half the sky. A wind swept suddenly in from the lagoon, and blew sharply across the open space and along the arcades. In hardly more than a moment the Piazza was empty. I went down to the Riva, and called to my gondolier, who swung to and fro in his moored boat. The water was blackening, and had begun to race past. He called to me that we must wait, and I saw one or two gondolas hurrying up the Grand Canal, carried along by the tide, the men rowing hard. As the rain began I went into the Grand Hotel, and sat looking out on the water, which blackened and whitened and flung itself forward in actual waves, and splashed right up the steps and over the balcony. The rain came down steadily, and the lightning flickered across the sky behind the Salute, and lit up the domes, the windows, the steps, and a few people huddled there. Every now and then the water turned white; I saw every outline as it shouldered forward like a sea and broke on the marble steps; and the water was empty, not a gondola, not even a steamer; and then a steamer which had turned home drifted past without a passenger. I went out, and felt the rain on my face, and the water splashing on the steps; not far off I could see the gondolas tossing on their moorings. I seemed to be on the shore of some horrible island, and I had to cross the sea, which there was no crossing. I was afraid the gondola would come for me; but nothing, I thought, should tempt me upon that tossing water: I saw the black hull whirled sideways, and the man reeling over on his oar. No gondola came, and I slept that night in the Grand Hotel, which seemed to me, as I heard the water splashing under my windows, impregnably safe.

November 27. — She is here, she has become kind to me now, only kind and gentle; I am no longer afraid of her love. I have been ill again, and she has taken care of me, she has taken me away from this horrible Giudecca. I look out on a great garden, in which I can forget there is any water in Venice; I am near the land and I see nothing but trees. The house is full of pictures, beautiful old Venetian things; it is like living in another century, yet in the midst of a comfort which rests me. I am no longer afraid of her love; I seem to have become a child, and her love is maternal. When I look at her I can see her face as it was, as it is, without a scar; I see that she is beautiful. If I get well again I will never leave her.

December 12. — There is a phrase of Balzac which turns over and over in my head. It is in the story called 'Sur Catherine de Médicis,' and he is speaking of the Calvinist martyr, who is recovering after being tortured. 'On ne saurait croire' says Balzac, 'à quel point un homme, seul dans son lit et malade, devient personnel.'[39]

---

[39] 'One never thinks at what point a man, alone and ill in bed, becomes individual' is a sentiment that occurs in *Sur Catherine de Médicis*, a historical novel in four parts (1830–42)

Since I have been lying in bed, in this queer fever which keeps me shaking and hot (some Venetian chill which has got into my very bones), I have had so singularly little feeling of personality, I seem to have become so suddenly impersonal, that I wonder if Balzac was right. The world, ideas, sensations, all are fluid, and I flow through them, like a gondola carried along by the current; no, like a weed adrift on it.[40]

* * *

The journal ends there, and the writing of the last page is faint and unsteady.

Here I might leave the matter, but I am impelled to mention a circumstance which I always associate in my mind with the tragical situation revealed in poor Luxulyan's journal. A year after it had come into my hands, and while I was still hesitating whether or not to have it printed, I happened to be passing through Rome, where the Eckensteins had gone to live; and a sort of curiosity, I suppose, more than any friendly feeling I had for them, suggested to me that I should call upon them in the palace which they had taken in the Via Giulia.[41] The concierge was not in his loge, and I went up the first flight of broad low marble stairs and rang at the door. It was opened by a servant in livery. 'Is the Baroness von Eckenstein at home?' I asked; and as the man remained silent, I added, 'Will you send in my card?' He still stared at me without replying, and I repeated my question. At last he said: 'Madame la Baronne died the day before yesterday. She was buried this morning.'

I can hardly say that I was profoundly grieved, but the suddenness of the announcement struck me with a kind of astonishment. I inquired for the Baron;

---

by Honoré de Balzac (1799–1850), revised and included in his 'La Comédie humaine', his vast panoramic treatment of French life, in 1846. Symons expanded the quotation in a later essay:

> When a man gets into bed, almost all of his friends have a secret desire of seeing him die; some, to assure themselves that his existence matters more to himself, than theirs does to them; others in the disinterested hope of studying his agony.

'Aspects of Cornwall' (1922) in *Wanderings*, p. 268. Despite his associations with realist art, Balzac was much admired by Symons, not least because of his fascination with 'perverse' subject matter. His essay, 'Balzac', first appeared in the *Fortnightly Review* 65 in May 1899 (pp. 745–47) and was later reprinted in *Studies in Prose and Verse* (1905). After his breakdown, Symons added this essay to *The Symbolist Movement in Literature* (1919 edition) even though Balzac hardly meets the criteria for inclusion.
[40] Edwin F. Block, Jr. suggests this is an echo of Byron's 'I am as a Weed, | Flung from the rock, on Ocean's foam to sail | Where'er the surge may sweep, or tempest's breath prevail' (*Childe Harold's Pilgrimage*, Canto III, ll. 14–16) adding that the 'passage unites the Romantic ideal of passive experience with the Paterian perception of the world as flux'. *Rituals of Dis-Integration: Romance and Madness in the Victorian Psychomythic Tale* (New York: Garland, 1993), p. 189.
[41] The address at which Symons first met the Comtesse de la Tour in February 1897.

he was in, and I was taken through one after another of the vast marble rooms which, in Roman palaces, lead to the reception-room. Every room was crowded with pictures, statues, rare Eastern vases, tables and cases of bibelots, exotic plants, a profusion of showy things brought together from the ends of the world. The Baron received me with almost more than his usual ceremony. His face wore an expression of correct melancholy, he spoke in a subdued and slightly mournful voice. He told me that his beloved wife had succumbed to a protracted illness, that she had suffered greatly, but, at the end, through the skilful aid of the best surgeons in Europe, she had passed into a state of somnolency, so that her death had been almost unconscious. He raised his eyes with an air of pious resignation, and said that he thanked God for having taken to himself so admirable, so perfect a being, whose loss, indeed, must leave him inconsolable for the rest of his life on earth. He spoke in measured syllables, and always in the same precise and mournful tone. I found myself unconsciously echoing his voice and reflecting his manner, and it seemed to me as if we were both playing in a comedy, and repeating words which we had learnt by heart. I went through my part mechanically, and left him. When I found myself in the street I dismissed the cab which was waiting to take me to the Vatican. I wanted to walk. I do not know why I felt a cold shiver run through me, for the sky was cloudless, and it was the month of June.

MHRA Critical Texts

Jewelled Tortoise

The 'Jewelled Tortoise', named after J. K. Huysmans's iconic image of Decadent taste in *A Rebours* (1884), is a series dedicated to Aesthetic and Decadent literature. Its scholarly editions, complete with critical introductions and accompanying materials, aim to make available to students and scholars alike works of literature and criticism which embody the intellectual daring, formal innovation, and cultural diversity of the British and European *fin de siècle*. The 'Jewelled Tortoise' is under the joint general editorship of Stefano Evangelista and Catherine Maxwell.

For a full listing of titles available in the series and details of how to order please visit our website at www.tortoise.mhra.org.uk

Lightning Source UK Ltd.
Milton Keynes UK
UKOW05n1325270417

300033UK00005B/53/P